Hand
Morningstar

ADVent

Advent
Copyright © 2007 by Lamp Post, Inc.

Requests for information should be addressed to:
Zondervan, *Grand Rapids, Michigan* 49530

Library of Congress Cataloging-in-Publication Data

Burner, Brett A., 1969–
    Advent / by Brett A. Burner and Mike S. Miller.
        p. cm. -- (Hand of the morningstar; v. #1)
     ISBN-13: 978-0-310-71369-2 (pbk.)
     ISBN-10: 0-310-71369-2 (pbk.)
     1. Graphic novels. I. Miller, Mike S. II. Title.
     PN6727.B865A39 2007
     741.5'973--dc22

                                                                        2007003146

This book published in conjunction with Lamp Post, Inc.; 8367 Lemon Avenue, La Mesa, CA 91941

Series Editor: Bud Rogers
Managing Editor: Bruce Nuffer
Managing Art Director: Sarah Molegraaf

Printed in the United States of America

---

07 08 09 10 11 12 • 8 7 6 5 4 3 2 1

HAND OF THE MORNINGSTAR
ADVENT

HE WILL BRING TO LIGHT WHAT IS HIDDEN IN
THE DARKNESS AND WILL EXPOSE THE
MOTIVES OF MEN'S HEARTS.
—1 CORINTHIANS 4:5

SERIES EDITOR: BUD ROGERS
STORY BY BRETT BURNER AND MIKE MILLER
ART BY MIKE MILLER

ZONDERVAN®

ZONDERVAN.com/
AUTHORTRACKER
follow your favorite authors

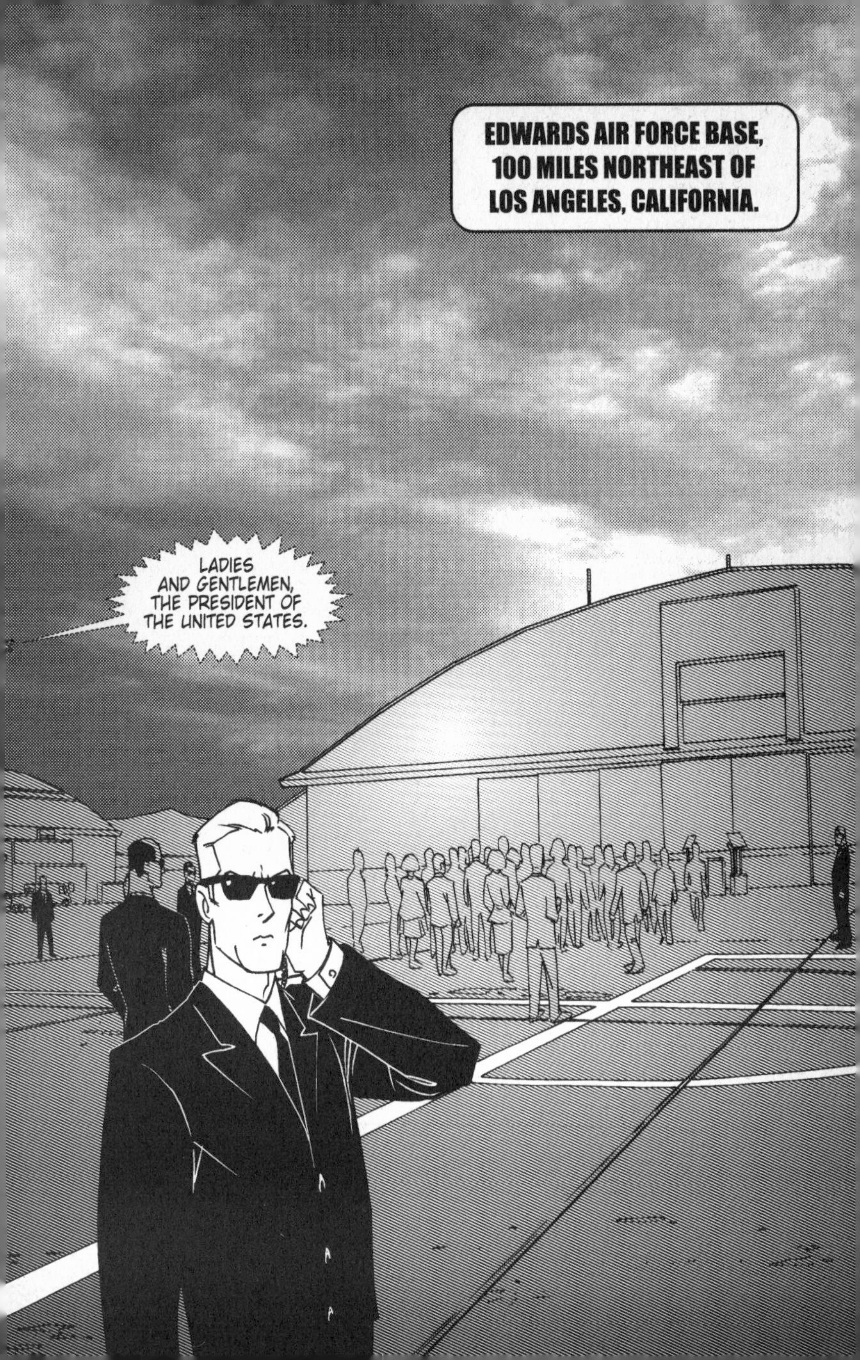
EDWARDS AIR FORCE BASE, 100 MILES NORTHEAST OF LOS ANGELES, CALIFORNIA.
LADIES AND GENTLEMEN, THE PRESIDENT OF THE UNITED STATES.

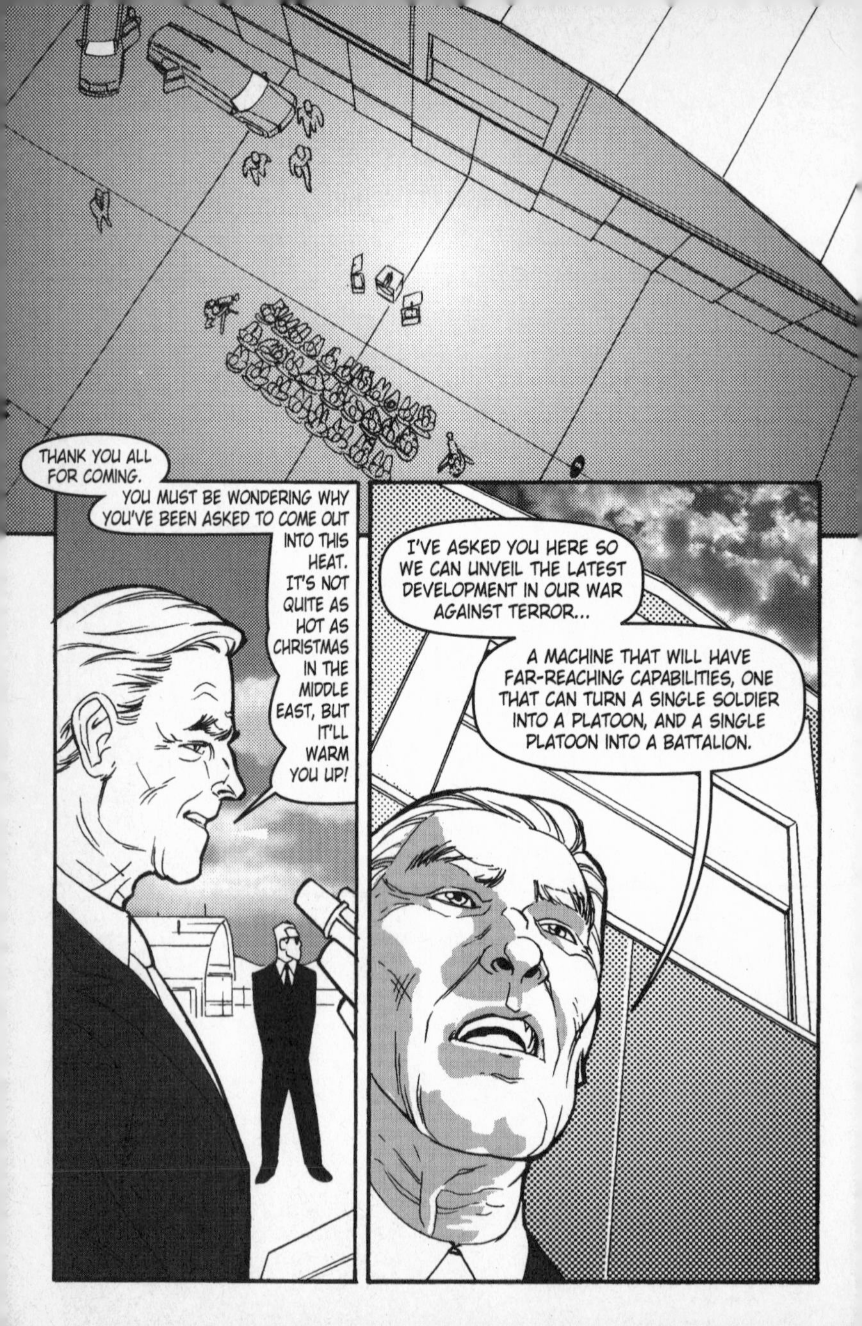
THANK YOU ALL FOR COMING.
YOU MUST BE WONDERING WHY YOU'VE BEEN ASKED TO COME OUT INTO THIS HEAT. IT'S NOT QUITE AS HOT AS CHRISTMAS IN THE MIDDLE EAST, BUT IT'LL WARM YOU UP!
I'VE ASKED YOU HERE SO WE CAN UNVEIL THE LATEST DEVELOPMENT IN OUR WAR AGAINST TERROR...
A MACHINE THAT WILL HAVE FAR-REACHING CAPABILITIES, ONE THAT CAN TURN A SINGLE SOLDIER INTO A PLATOON, AND A SINGLE PLATOON INTO A BATTALION.

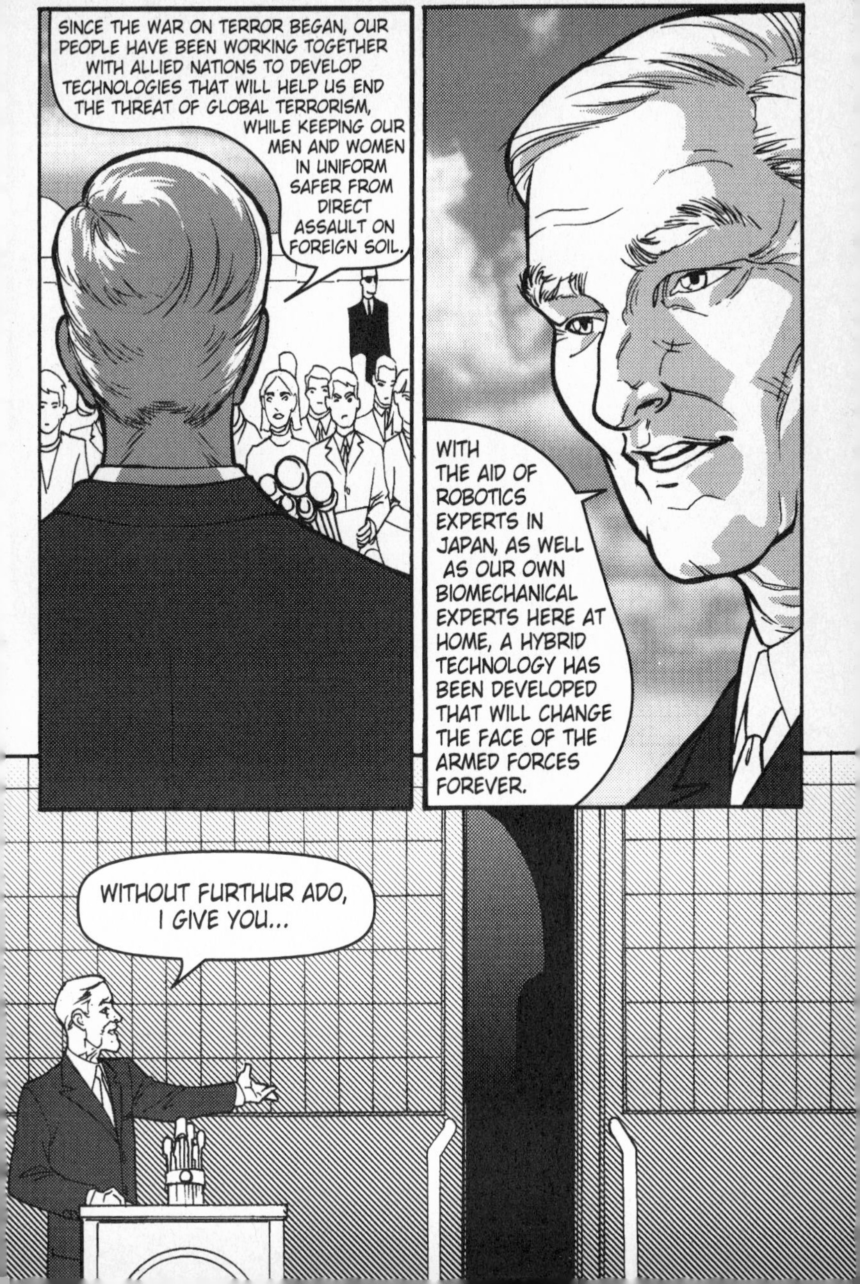
SINCE THE WAR ON TERROR BEGAN, OUR PEOPLE HAVE BEEN WORKING TOGETHER WITH ALLIED NATIONS TO DEVELOP TECHNOLOGIES THAT WILL HELP US END THE THREAT OF GLOBAL TERRORISM,
WHILE KEEPING OUR MEN AND WOMEN IN UNIFORM SAFER FROM DIRECT ASSAULT ON FOREIGN SOIL.
WITH THE AID OF ROBOTICS EXPERTS IN JAPAN, AS WELL AS OUR OWN BIOMECHANICAL EXPERTS HERE AT HOME, A HYBRID TECHNOLOGY HAS BEEN DEVELOPED THAT WILL CHANGE THE FACE OF THE ARMED FORCES FOREVER.
WITHOUT FURTHUR ADO, I GIVE YOU...

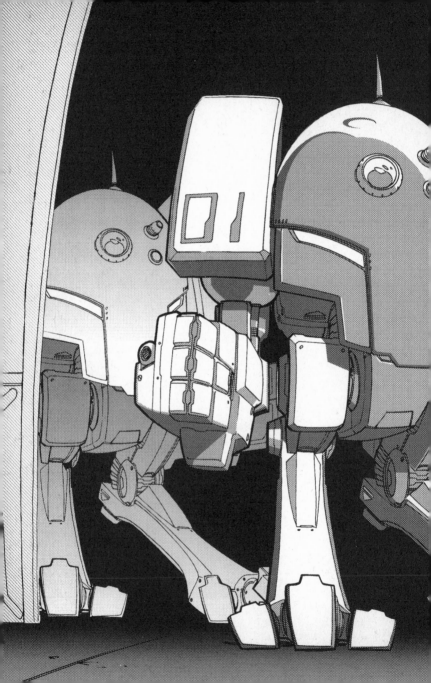

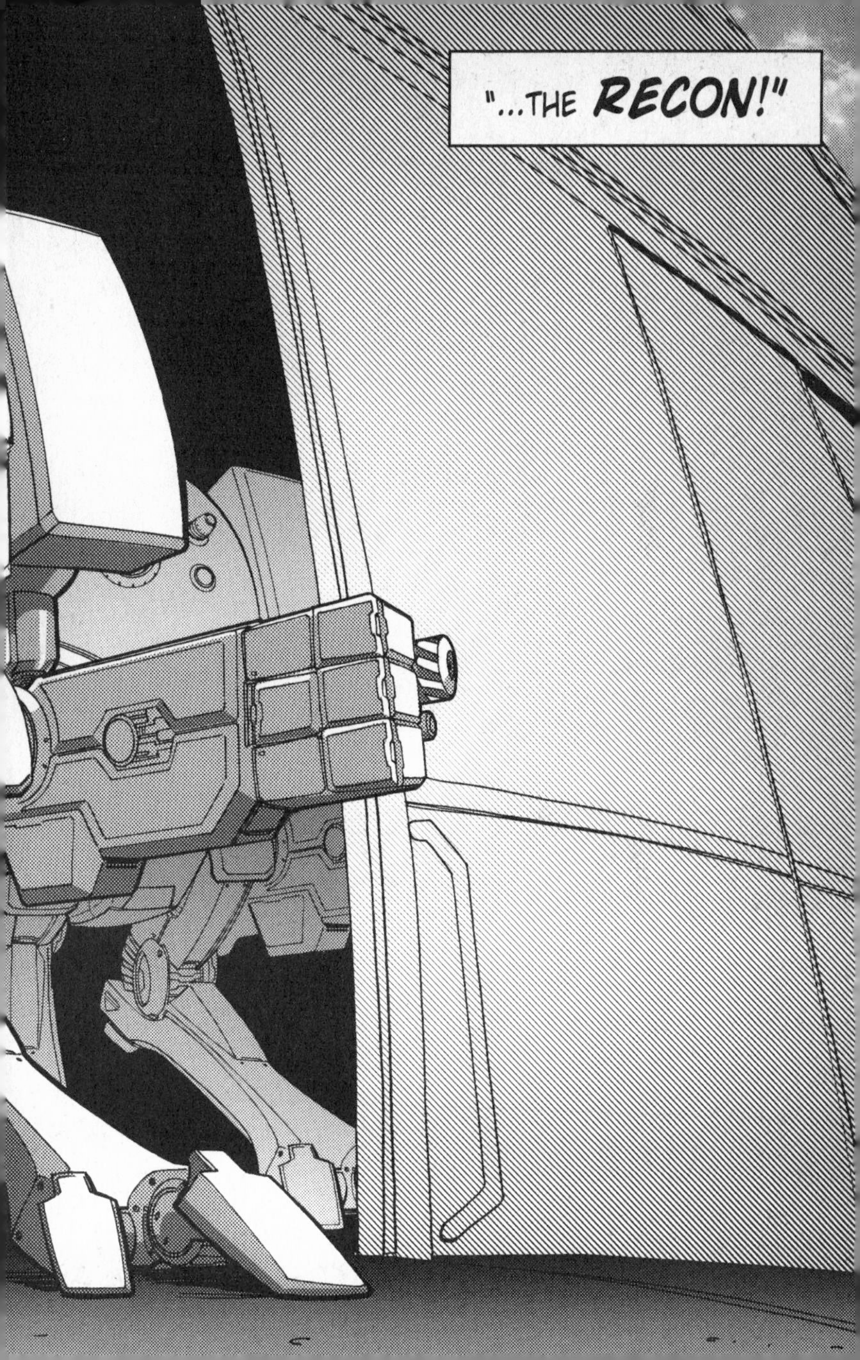
"...THE RECON!"

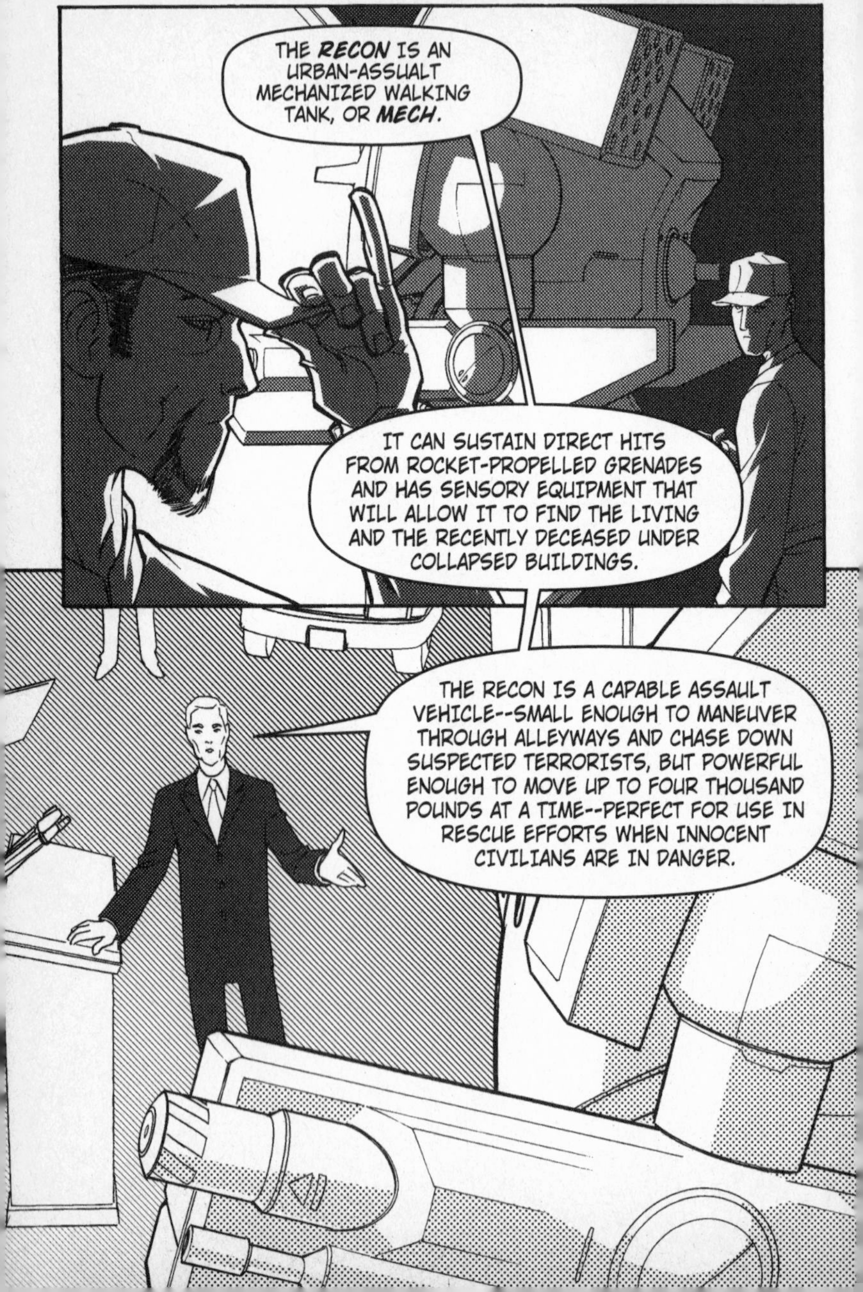
THE ***RECON*** IS AN URBAN-ASSUALT MECHANIZED WALKING TANK, OR ***MECH***.
IT CAN SUSTAIN DIRECT HITS FROM ROCKET-PROPELLED GRENADES AND HAS SENSORY EQUIPMENT THAT WILL ALLOW IT TO FIND THE LIVING AND THE RECENTLY DECEASED UNDER COLLAPSED BUILDINGS.
THE RECON IS A CAPABLE ASSAULT VEHICLE--SMALL ENOUGH TO MANEUVER THROUGH ALLEYWAYS AND CHASE DOWN SUSPECTED TERRORISTS, BUT POWERFUL ENOUGH TO MOVE UP TO FOUR THOUSAND POUNDS AT A TIME--PERFECT FOR USE IN RESCUE EFFORTS WHEN INNOCENT CIVILIANS ARE IN DANGER.

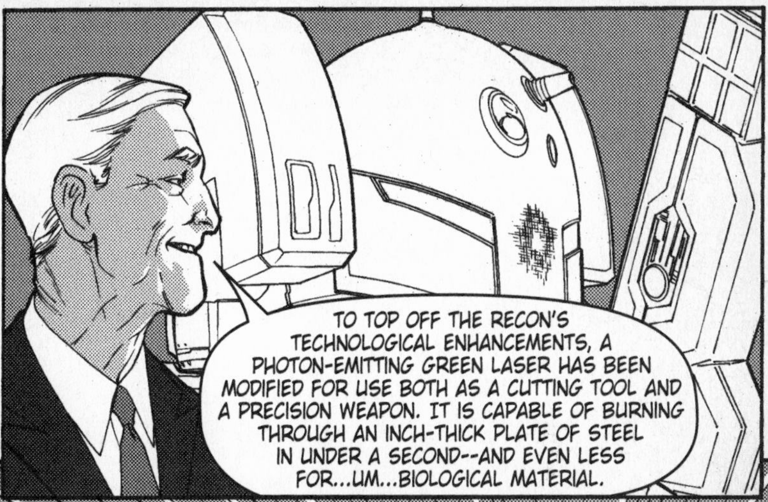
TO TOP OFF THE RECON'S TECHNOLOGICAL ENHANCEMENTS, A PHOTON-EMITTING GREEN LASER HAS BEEN MODIFIED FOR USE BOTH AS A CUTTING TOOL AND A PRECISION WEAPON. IT IS CAPABLE OF BURNING THROUGH AN INCH-THICK PLATE OF STEEL IN UNDER A SECOND--AND EVEN LESS FOR...UM...BIOLOGICAL MATERIAL.

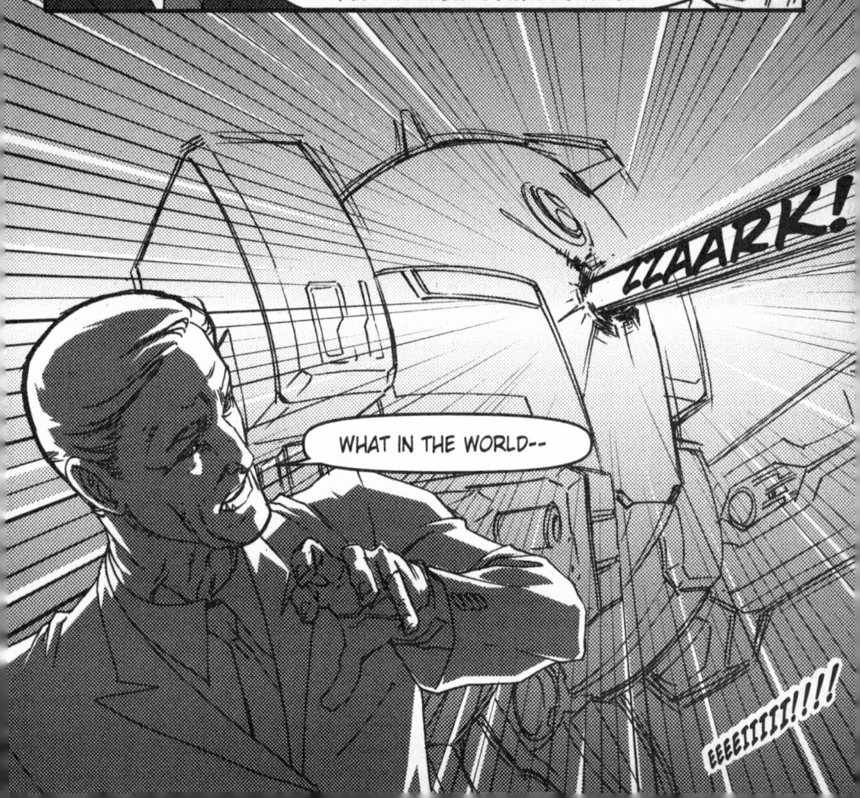
ZZAARK!
WHAT IN THE WORLD--
EEEEIIIII!!!!

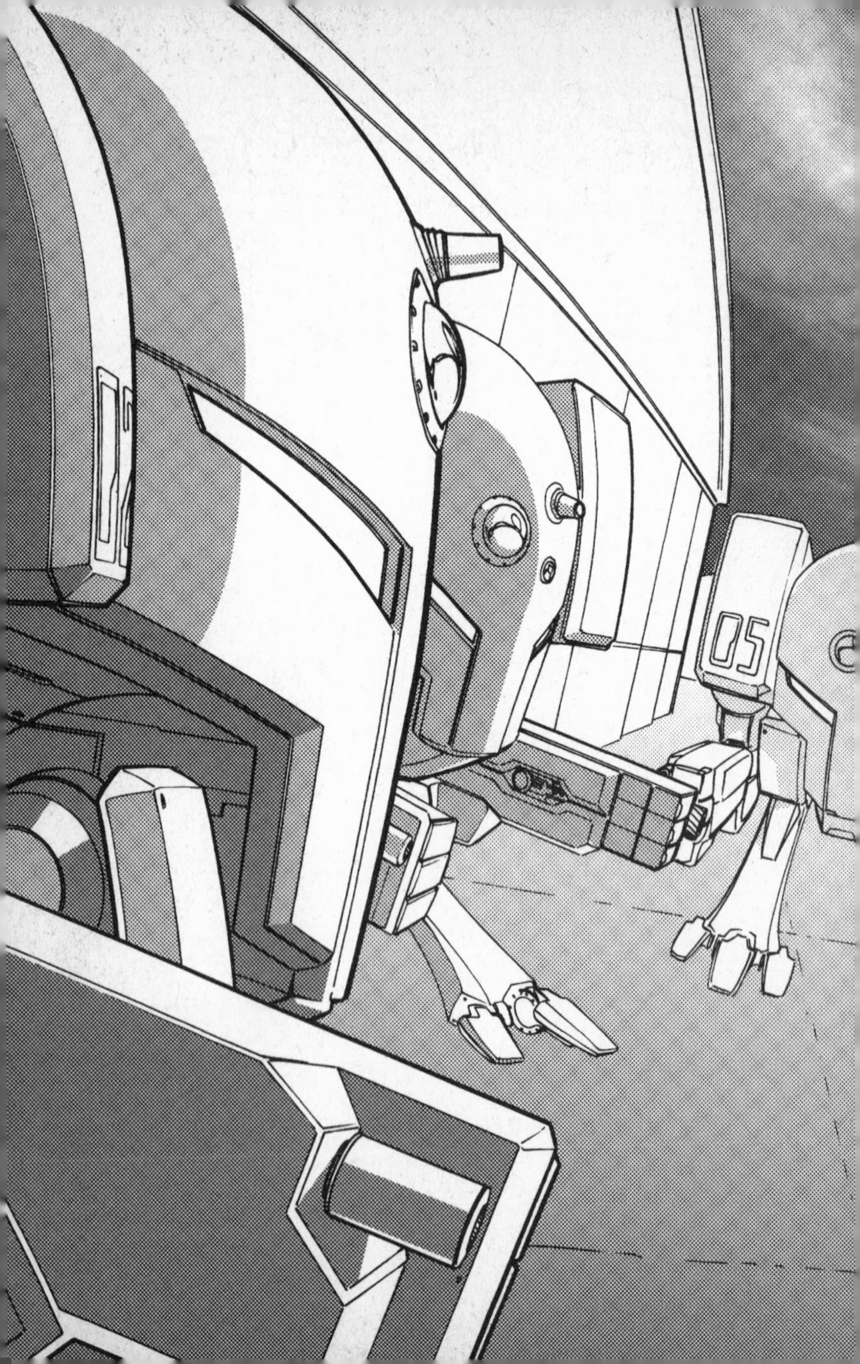
05

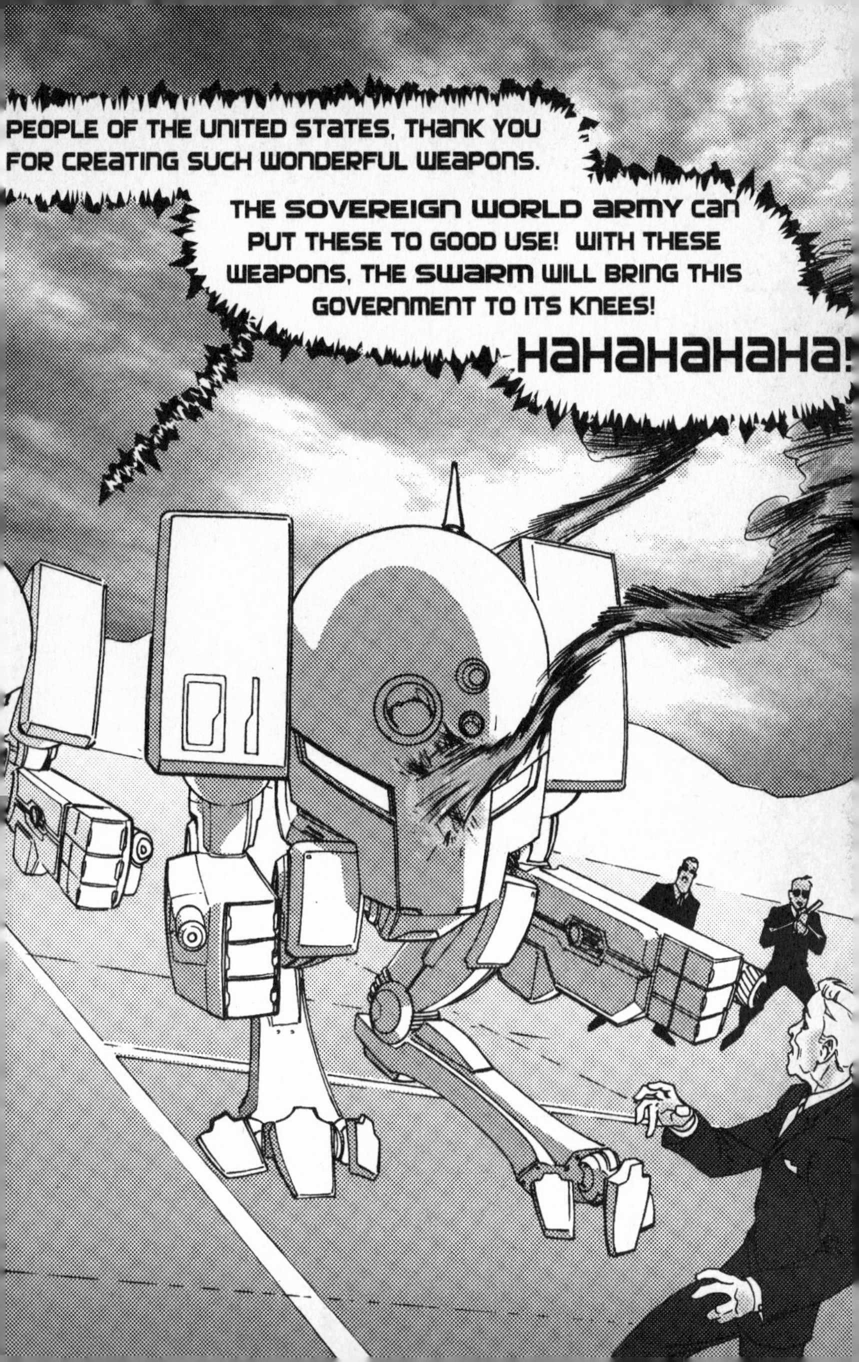
PEOPLE OF THE UNITED STATES, THANK YOU FOR CREATING SUCH WONDERFUL WEAPONS.
THE SOVEREIGN WORLD ARMY CAN PUT THESE TO GOOD USE! WITH THESE WEAPONS, THE SWARM WILL BRING THIS GOVERNMENT TO ITS KNEES!
HAHAHAHAHAHA!

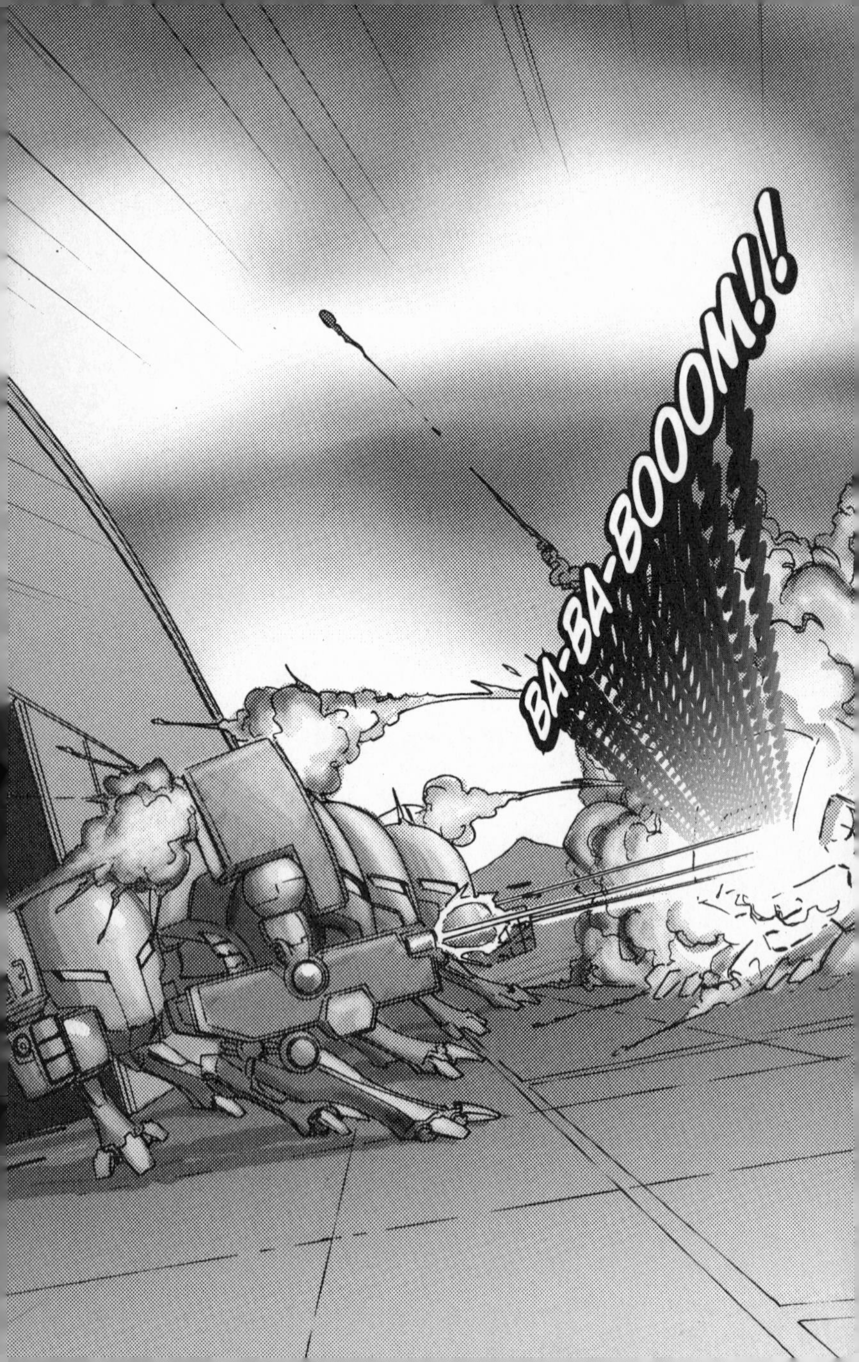
BA-BA-BOOOM!!!

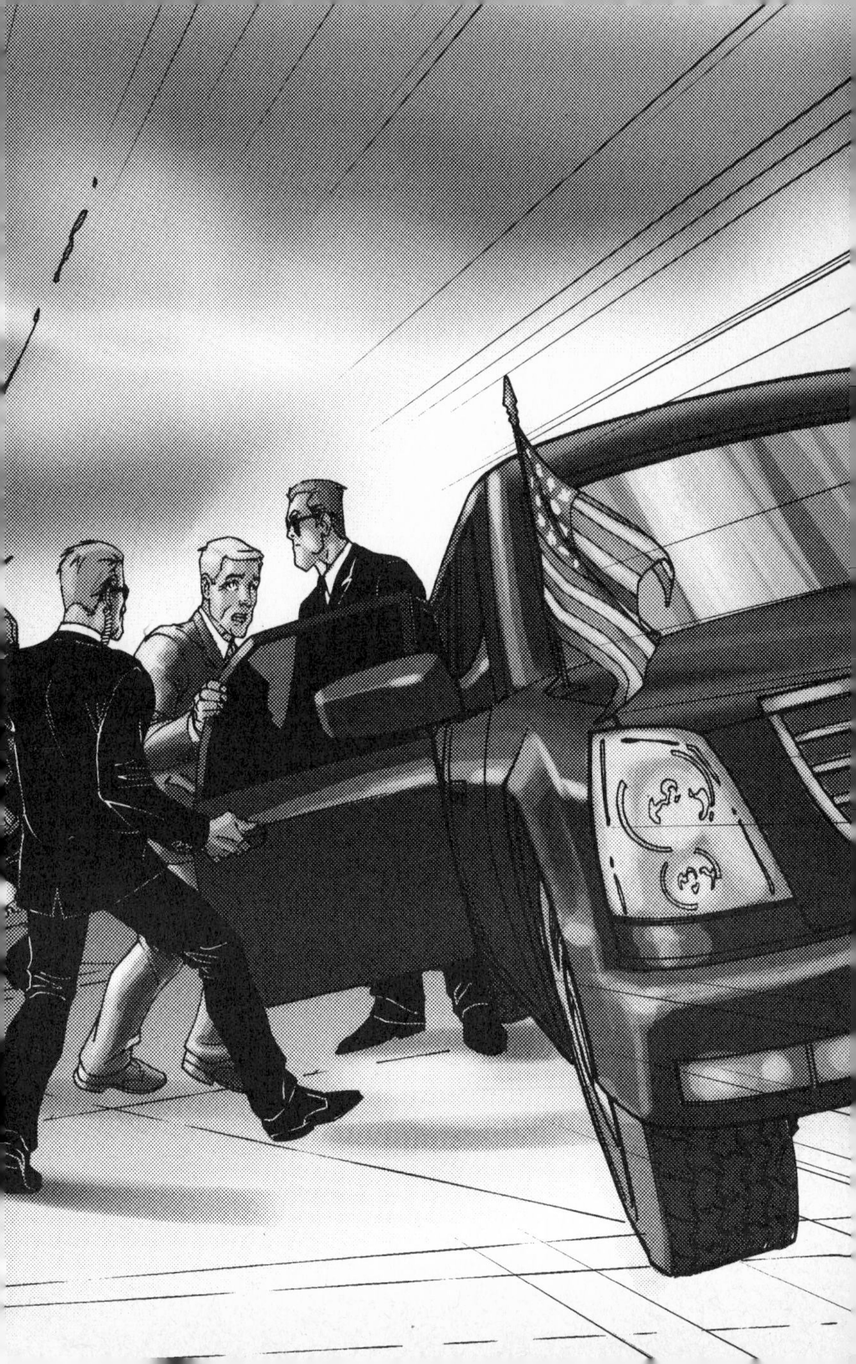

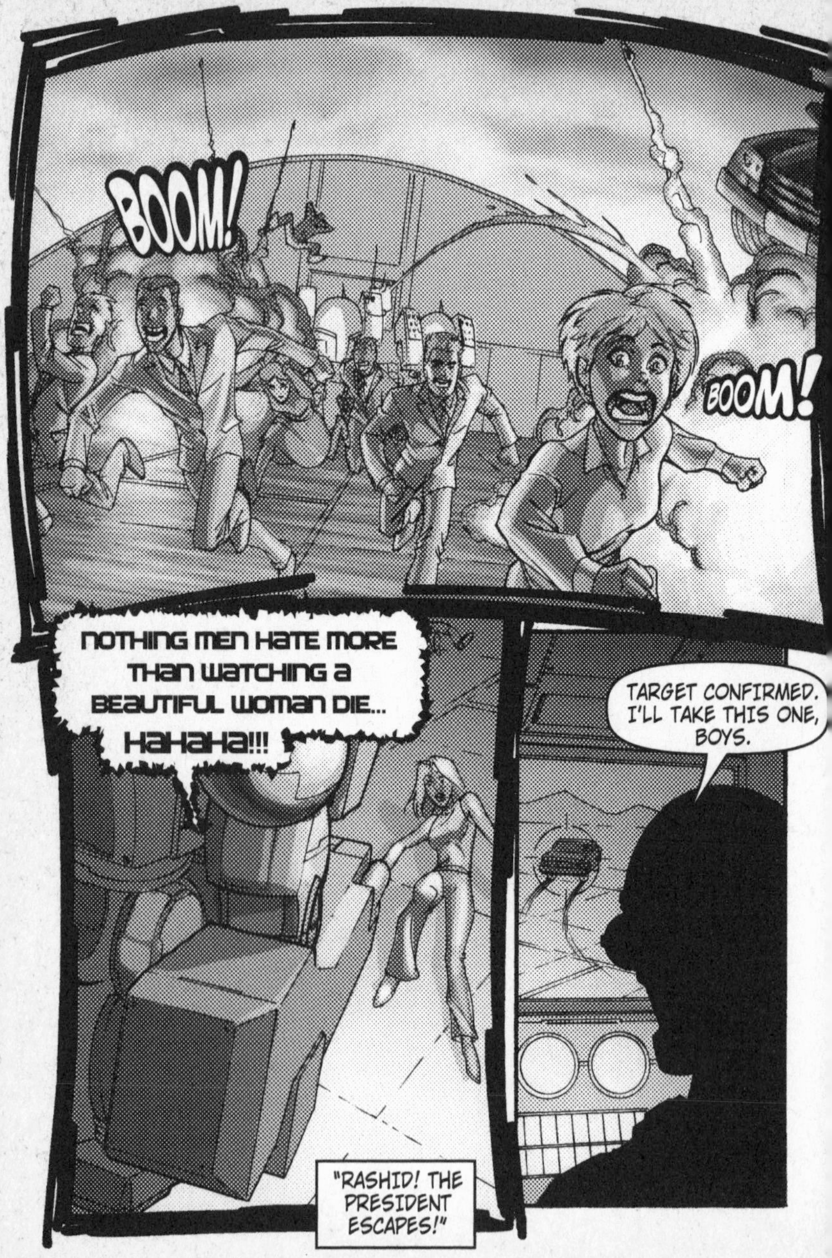
BOOM!
BOOM!
NOTHING MEN HATE MORE THAN WATCHING A BEAUTIFUL WOMAN DIE... HAHAHA!!!
"RASHID! THE PRESIDENT ESCAPES!"
TARGET CONFIRMED. I'LL TAKE THIS ONE, BOYS.

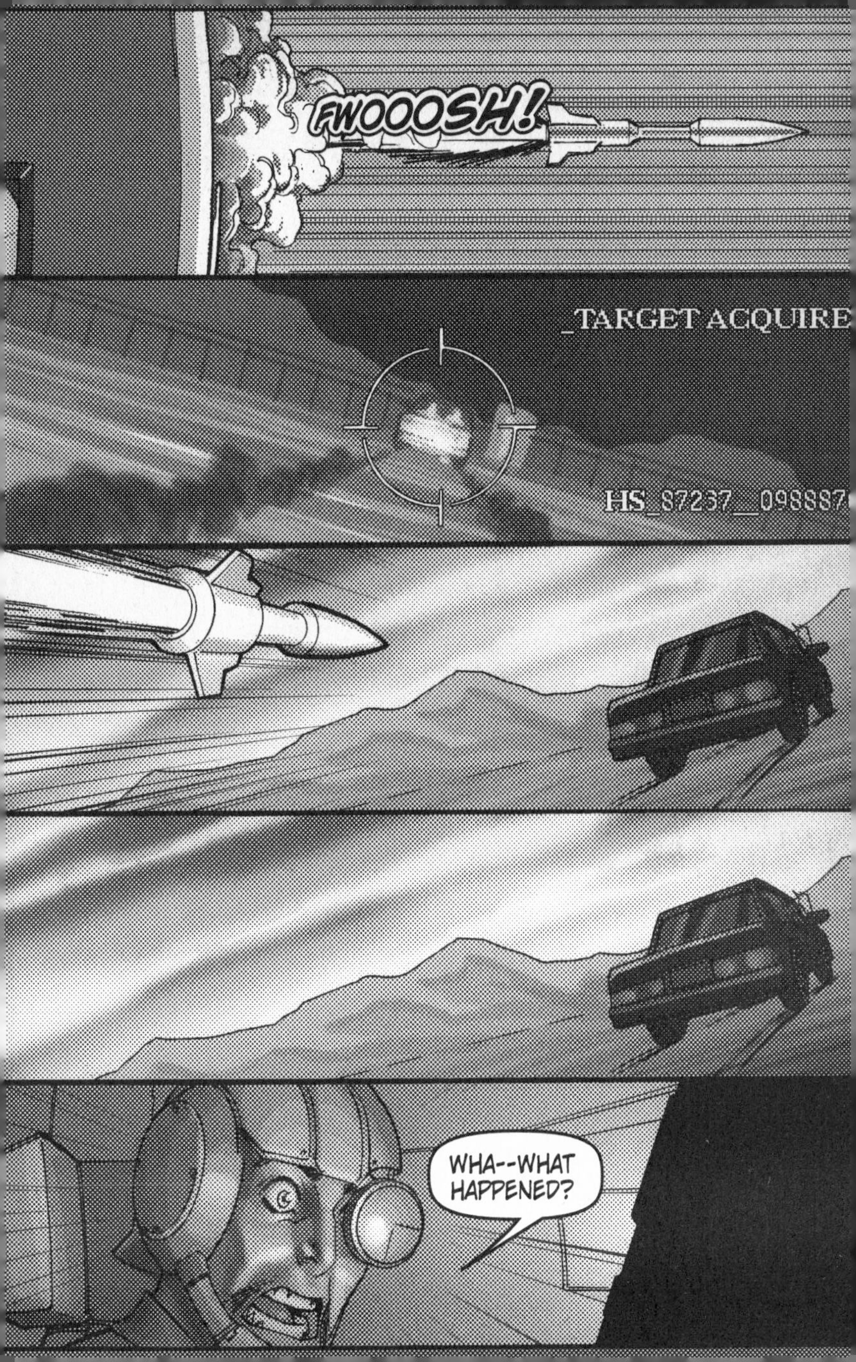
FWOOOSH!
_TARGET ACQUIRE
HS_87237_098887
WHA--WHAT HAPPENED?

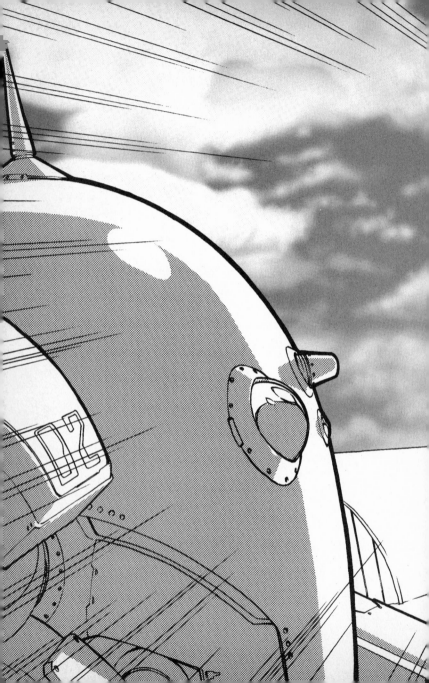

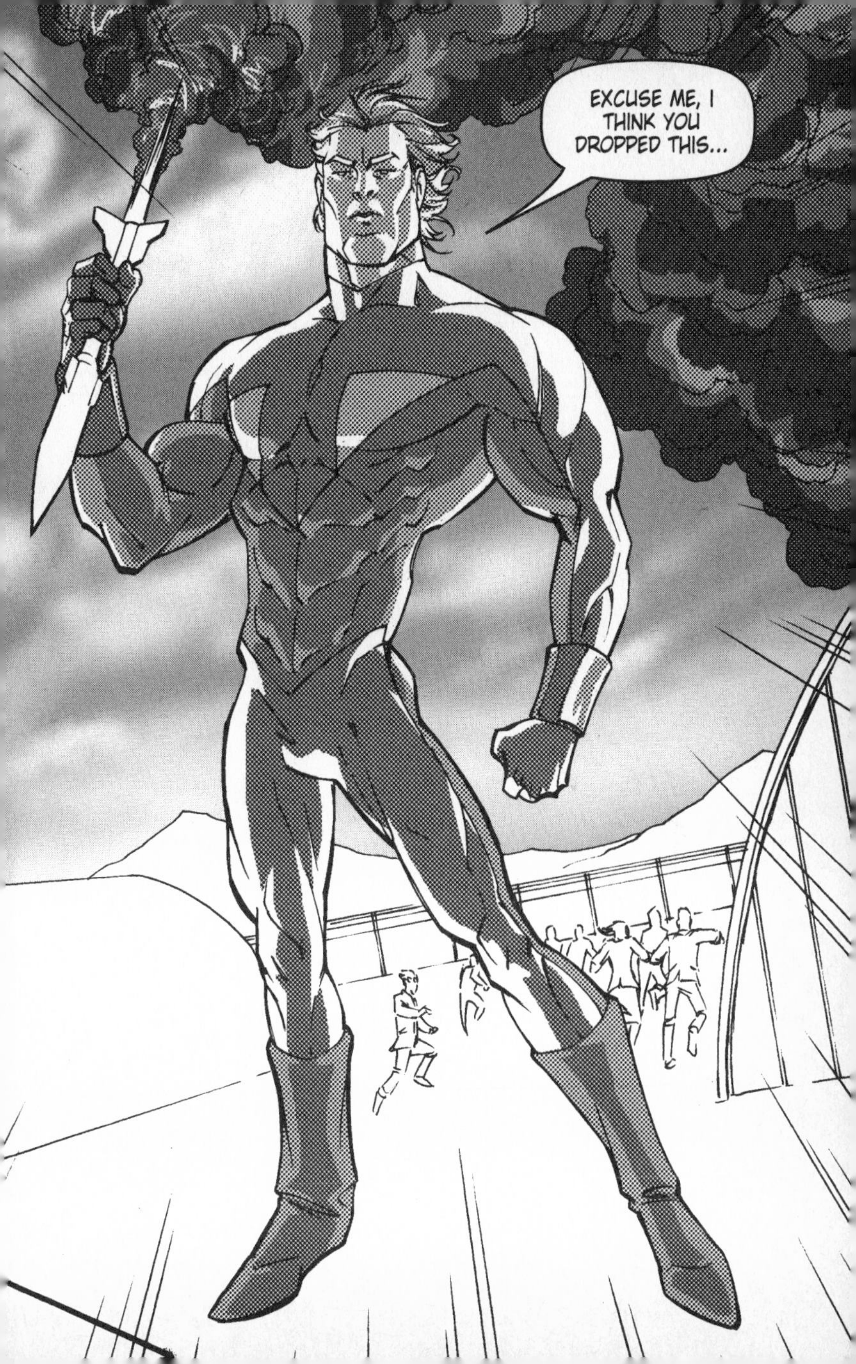
EXCUSE ME, I THINK YOU DROPPED THIS...

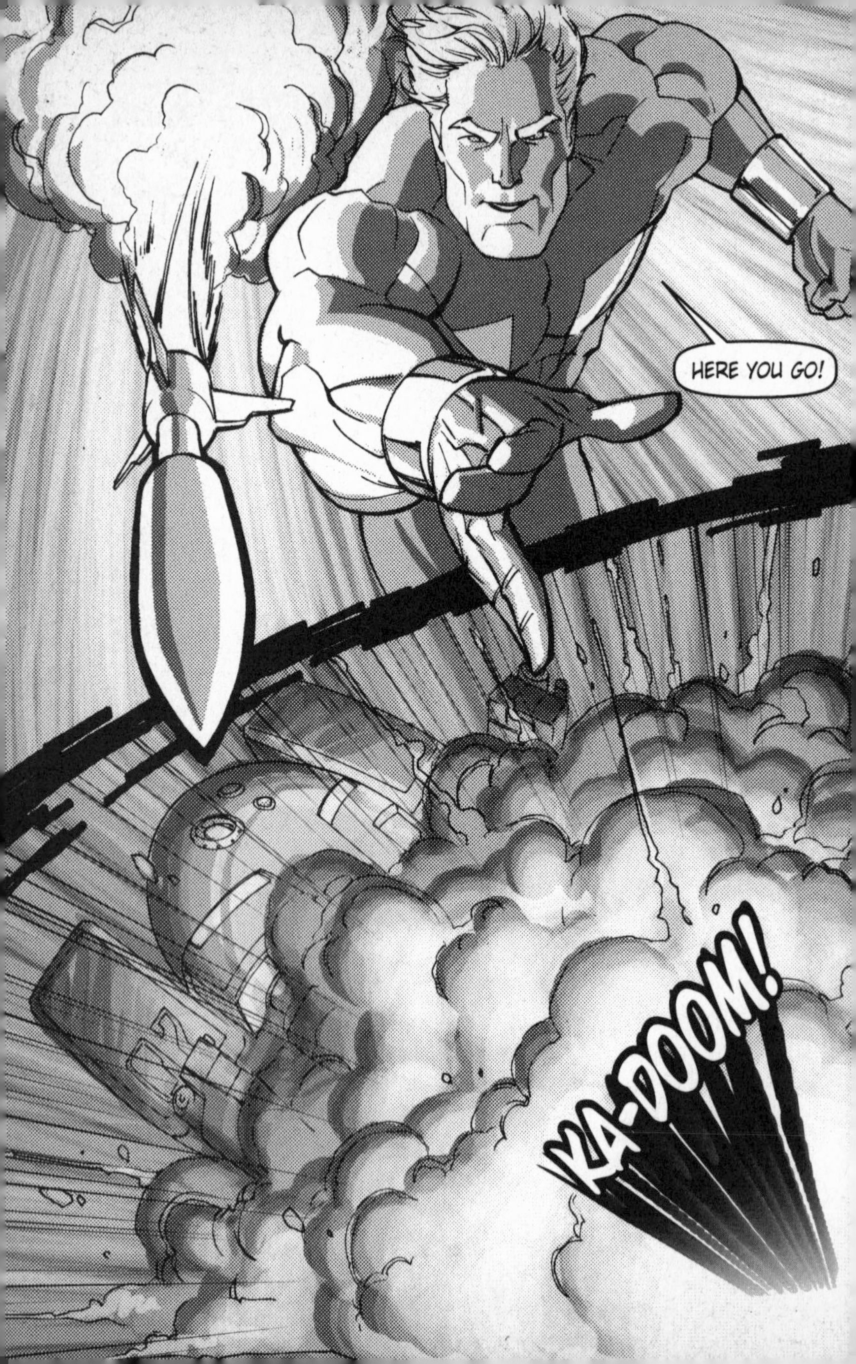
HERE YOU GO!
KA-DOOM!

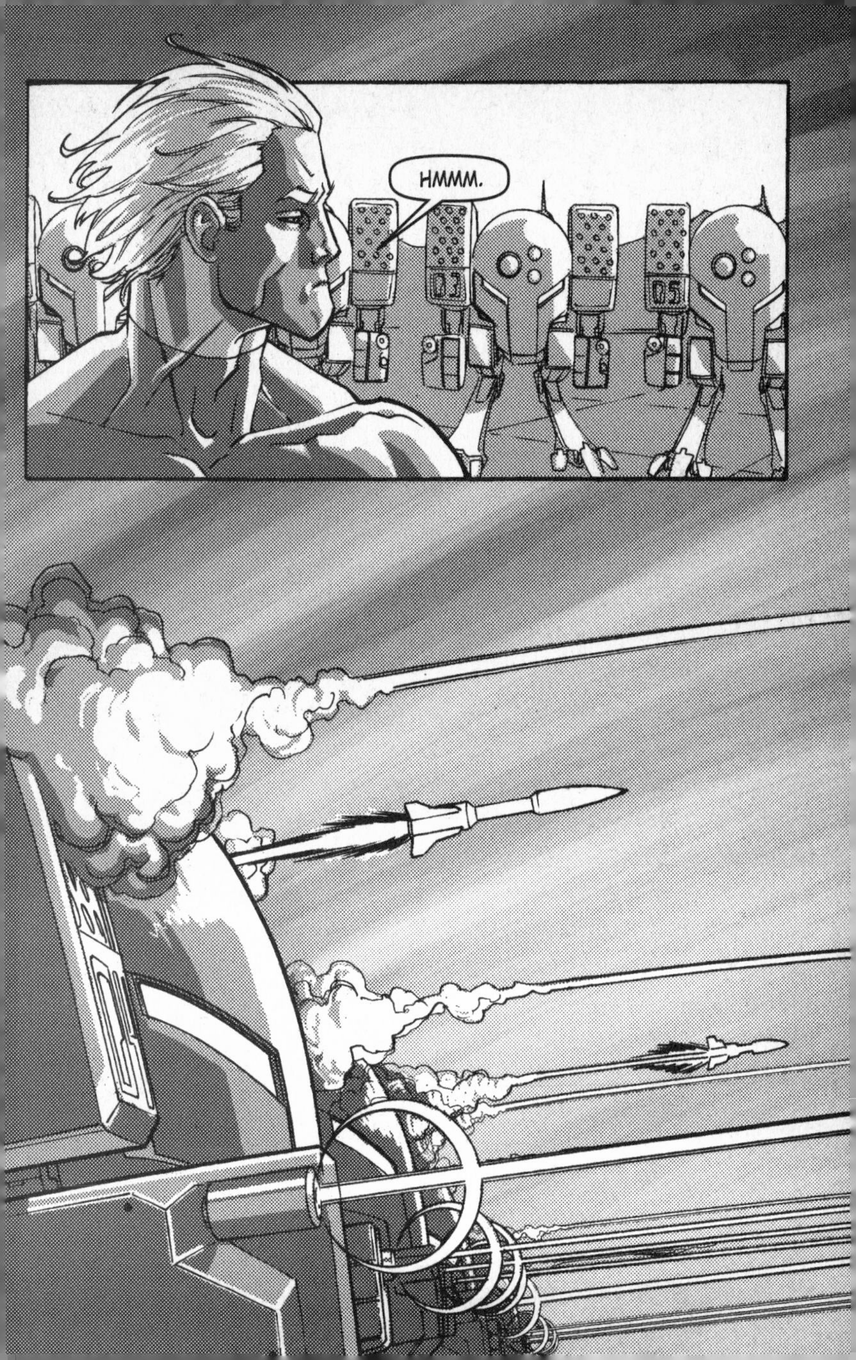
HMMM.
03
05

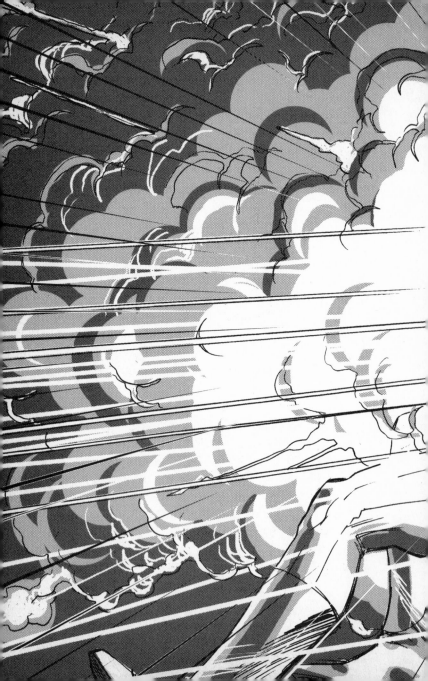

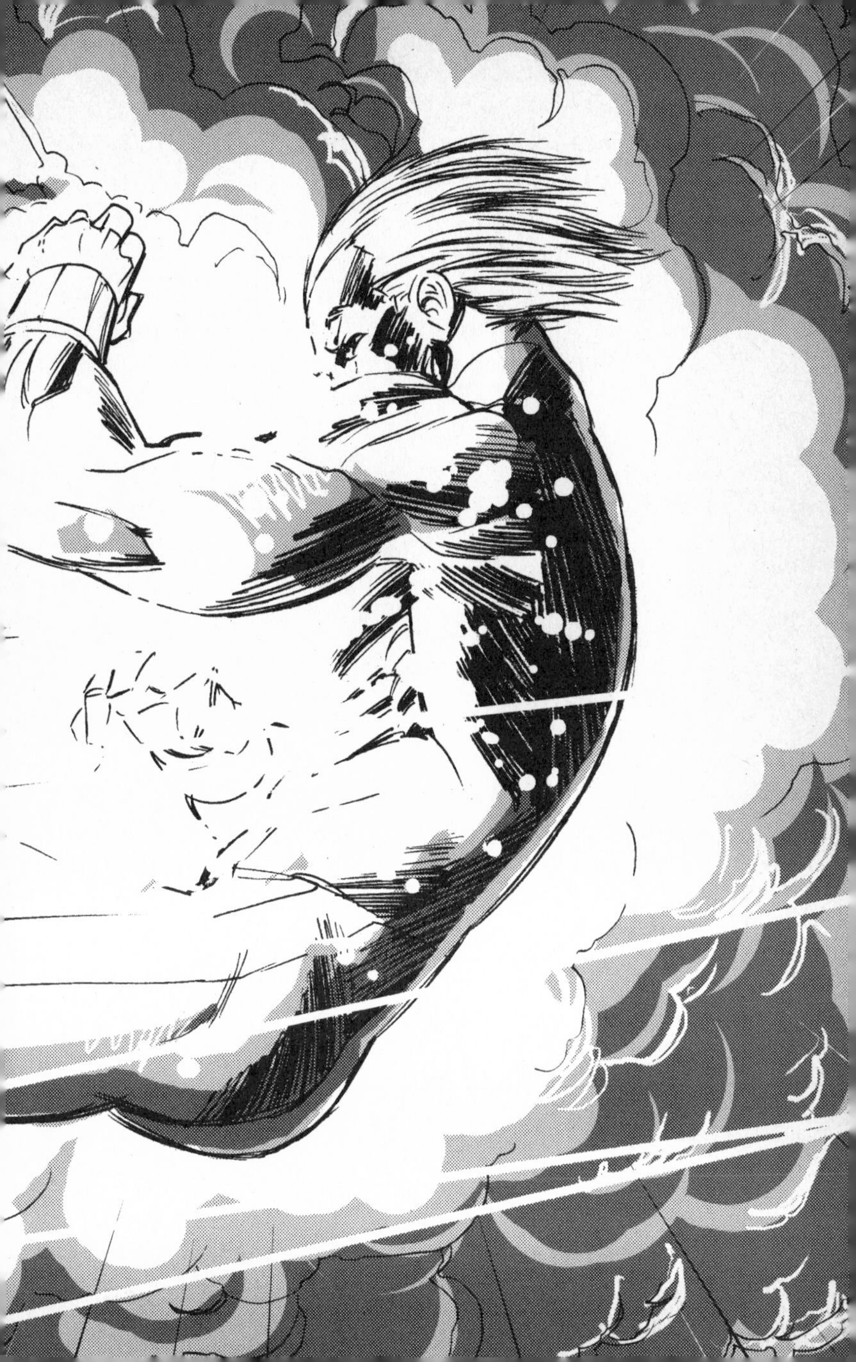

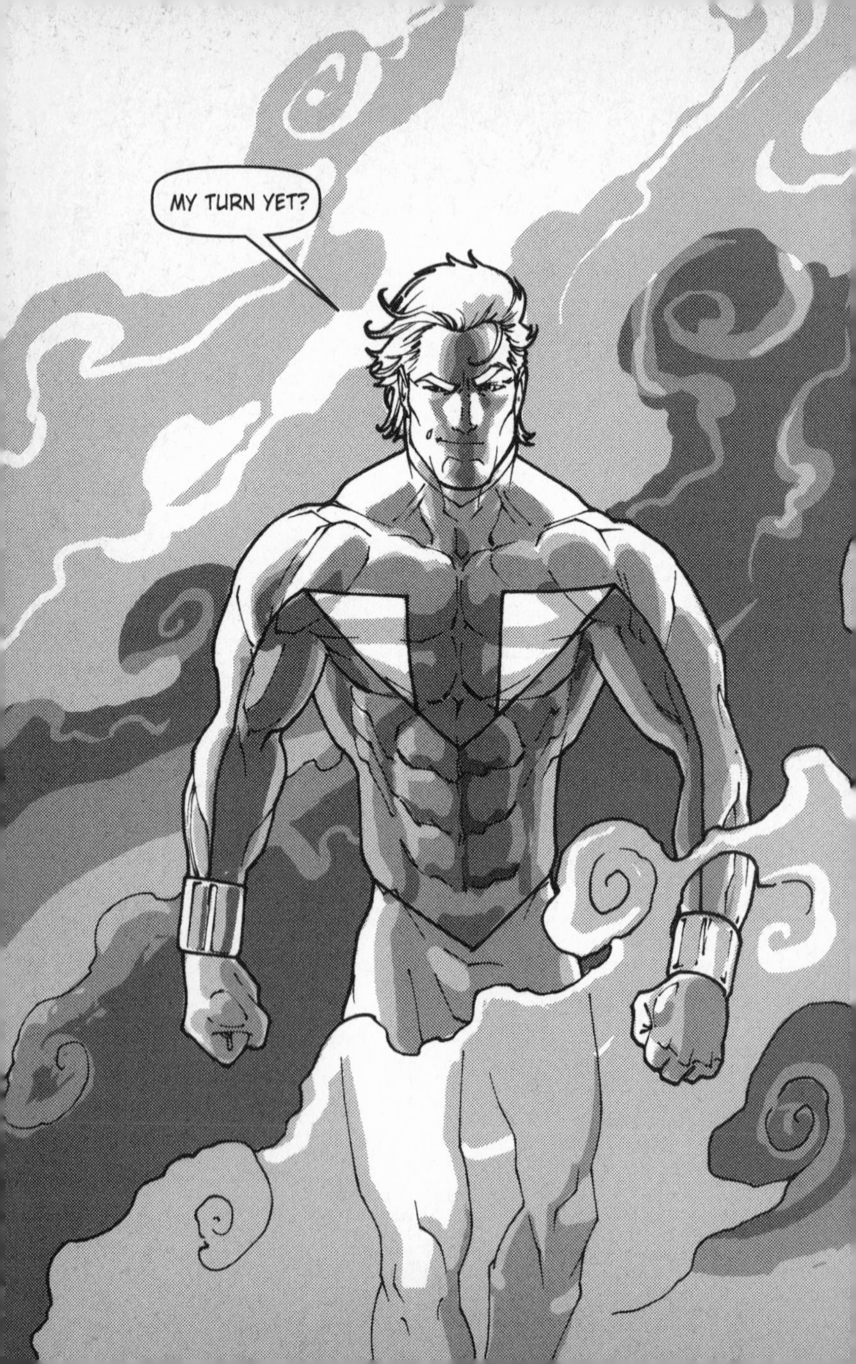
MY TURN YET?

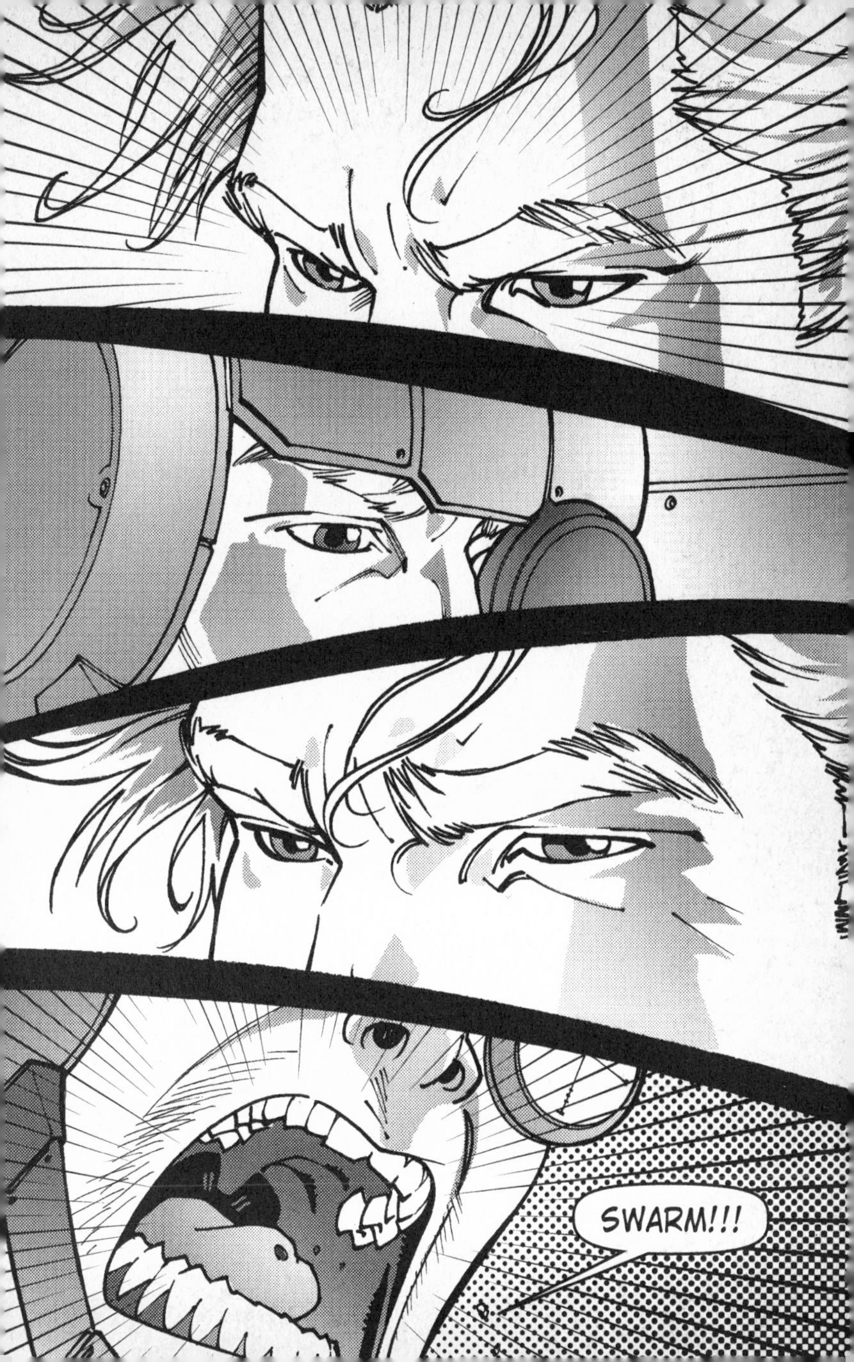
SWARM!!!

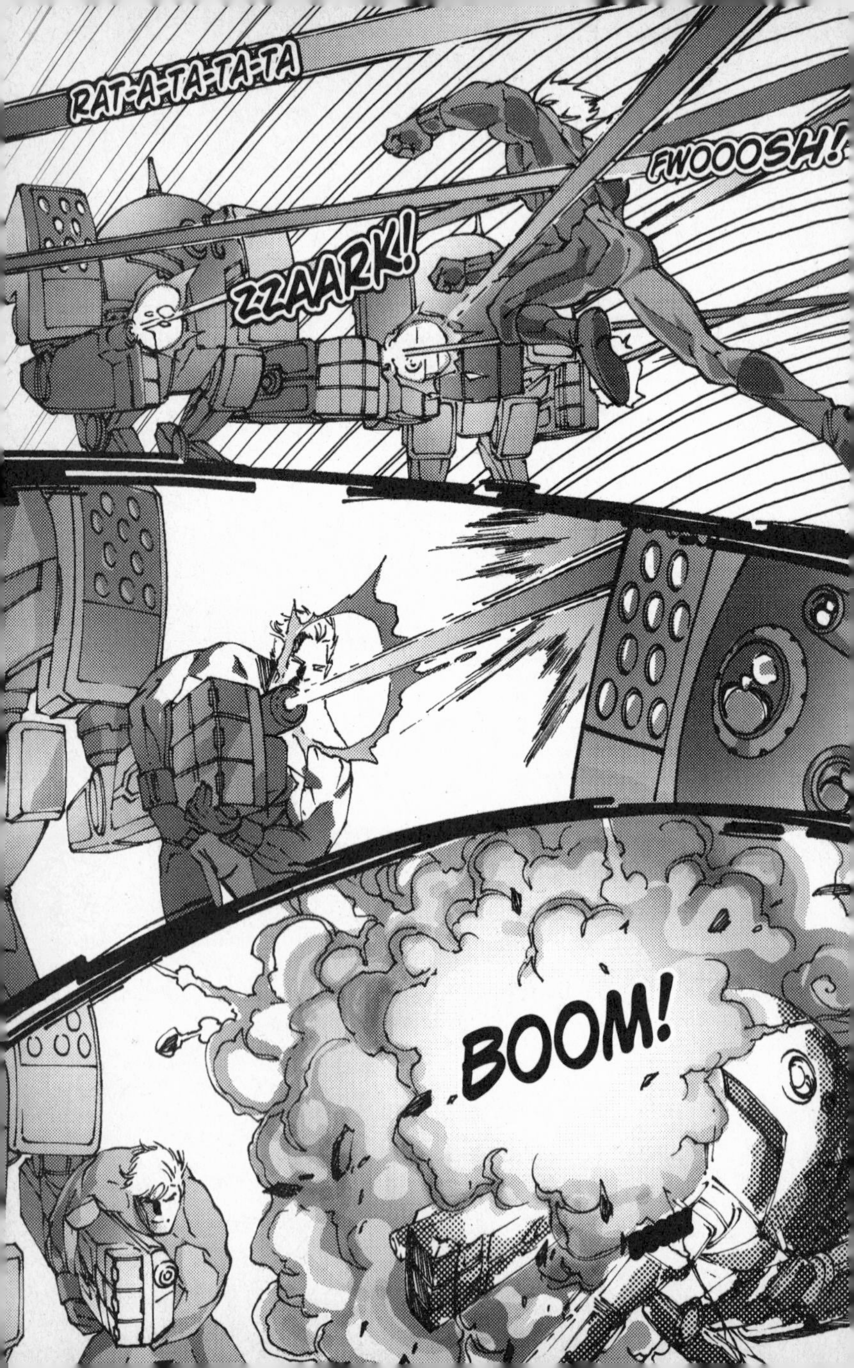
RAT-A-TA-TA-TA
FWOOOSH!
ZZAARK!
BOOM!

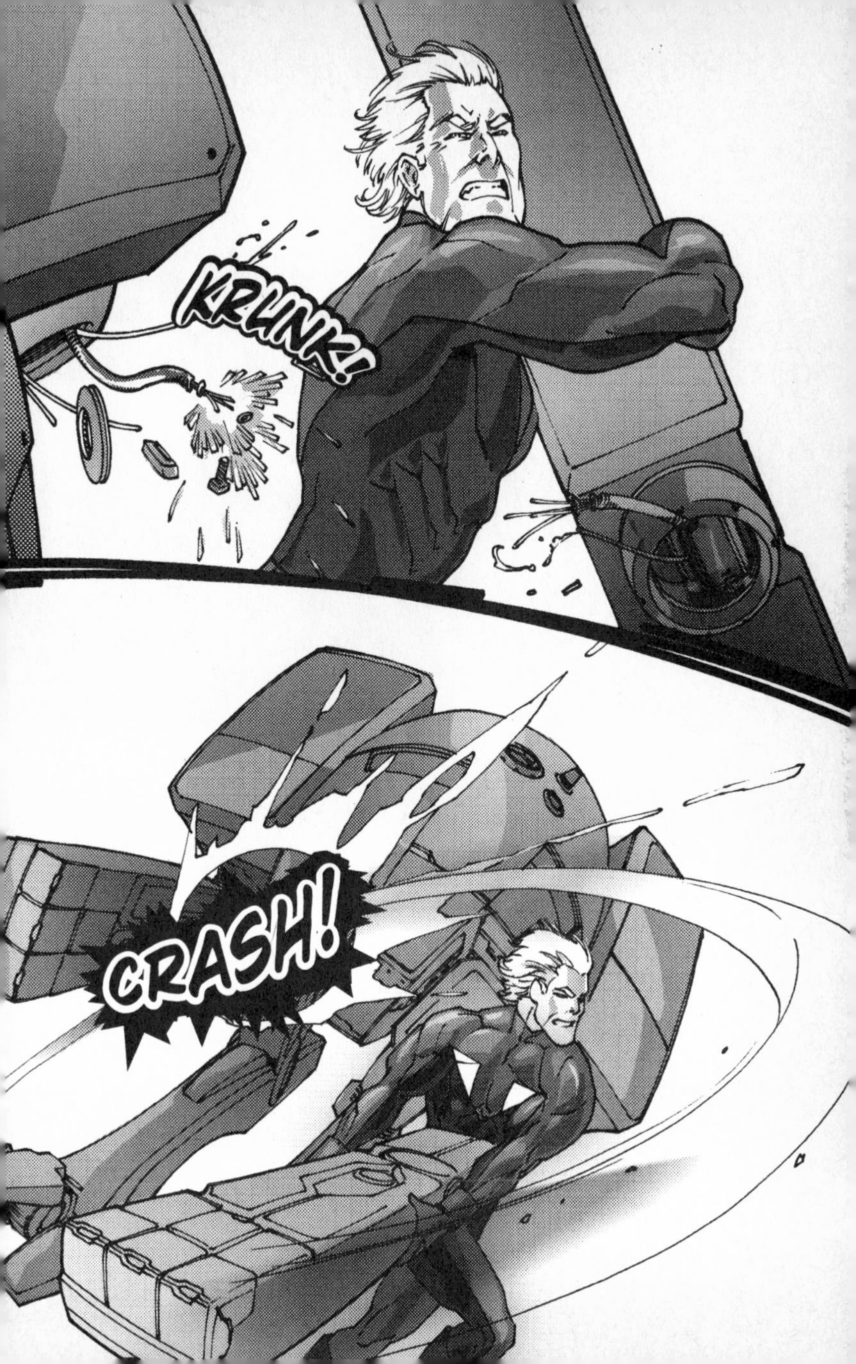
KRUNK!
CRASH!

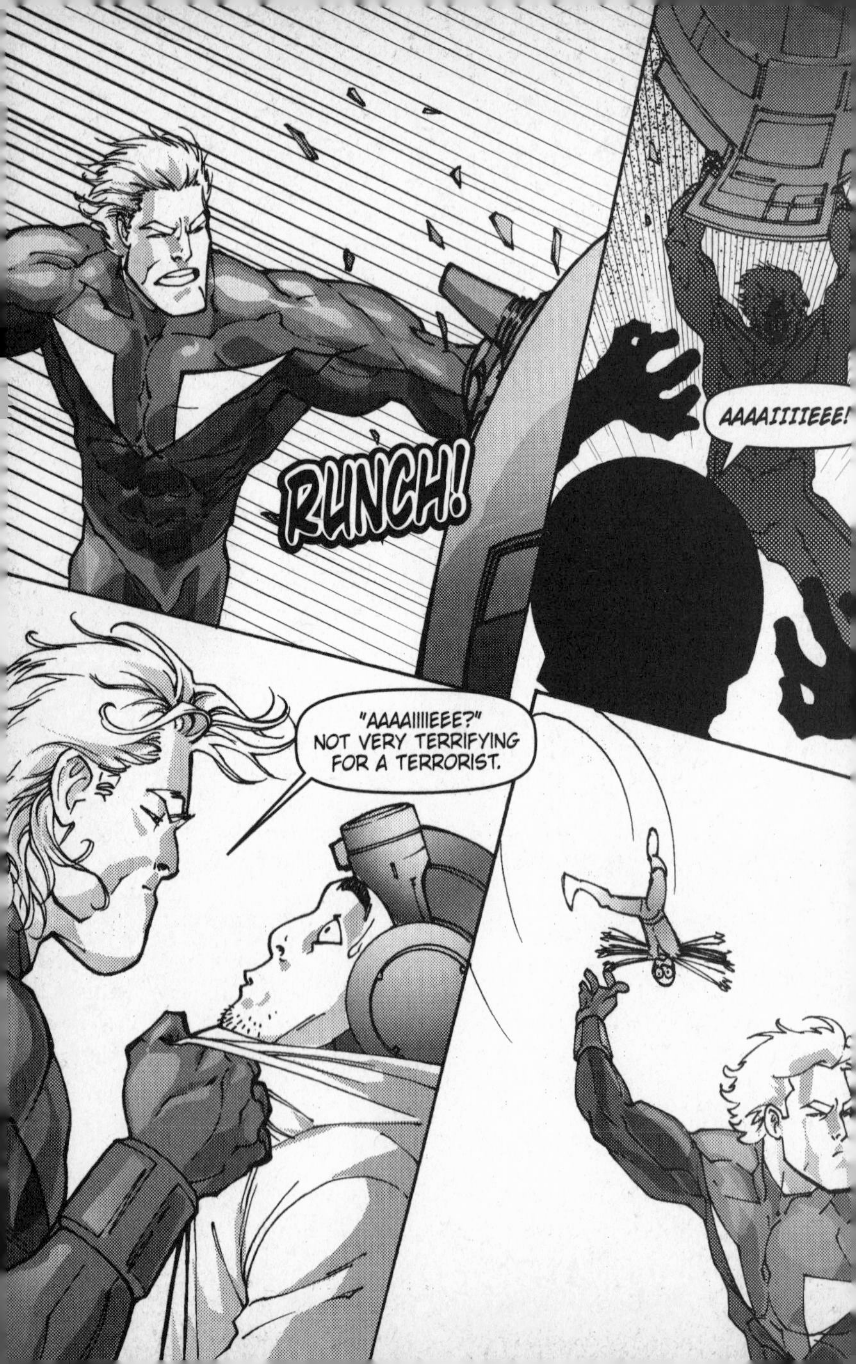
RUNCH!
AAAAIIIIEEE!
"AAAAIIIIEEE?" NOT VERY TERRIFYING FOR A TERRORIST.

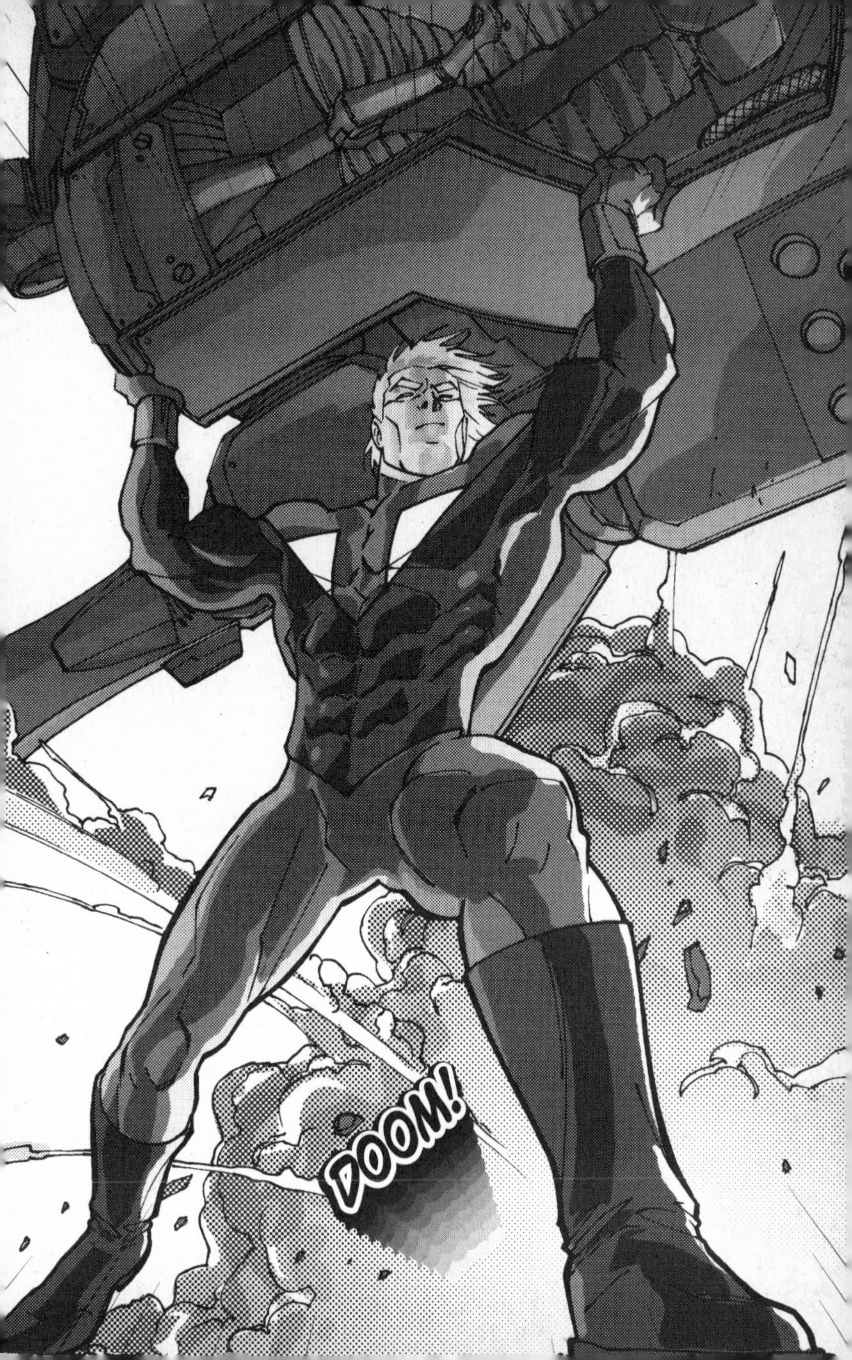
DOOM!

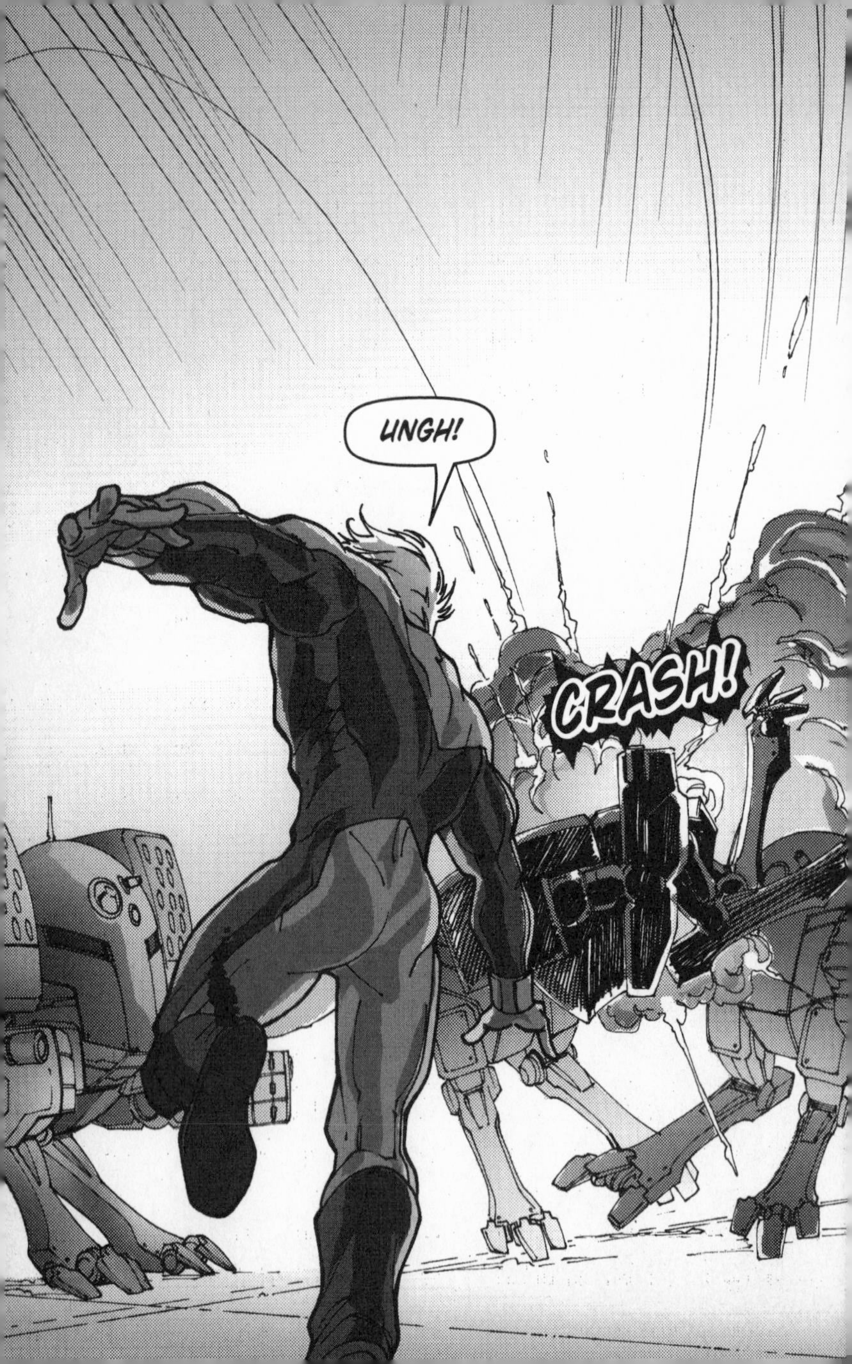
UNGH!
CRASH!

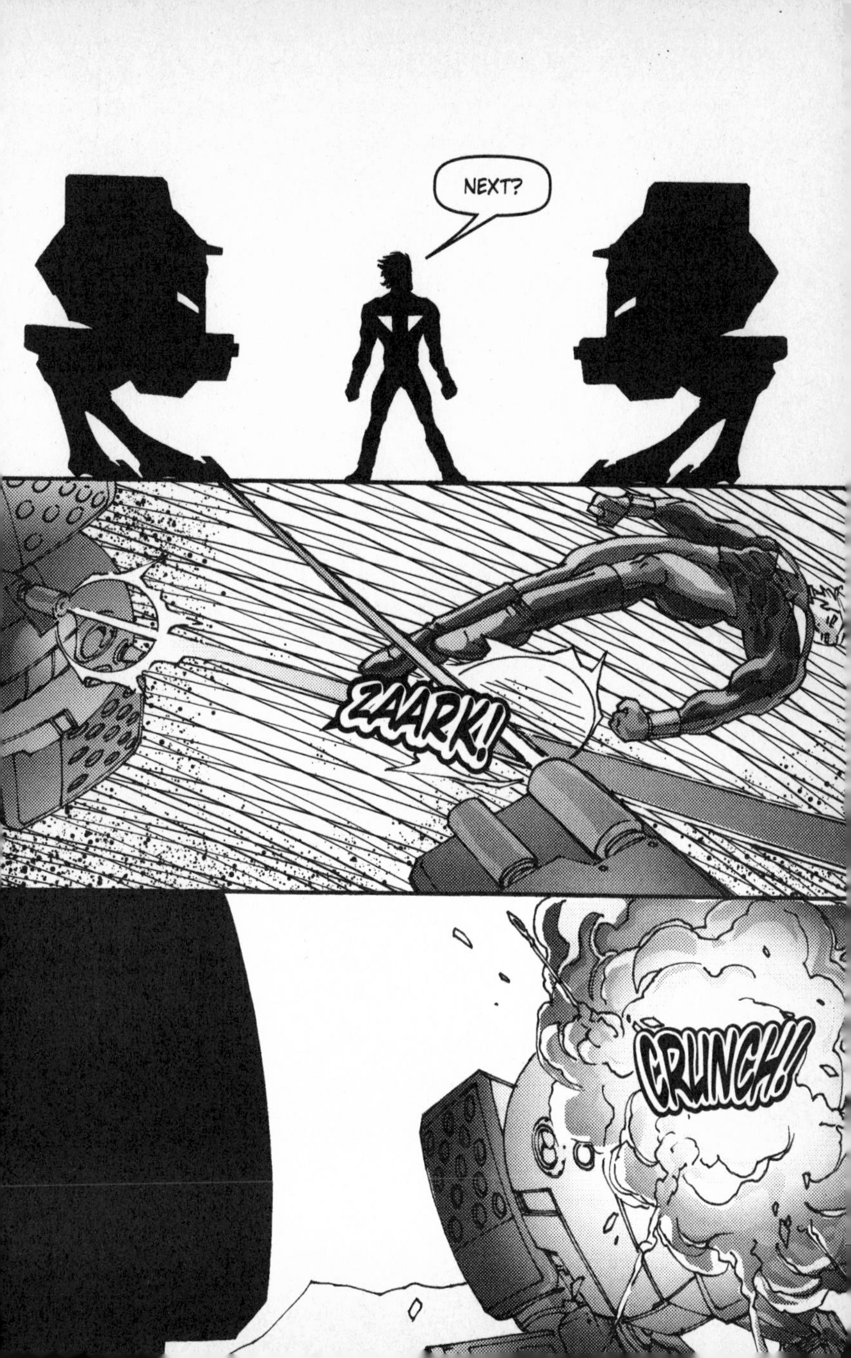
NEXT?
ZAARK!
CRUNCH!

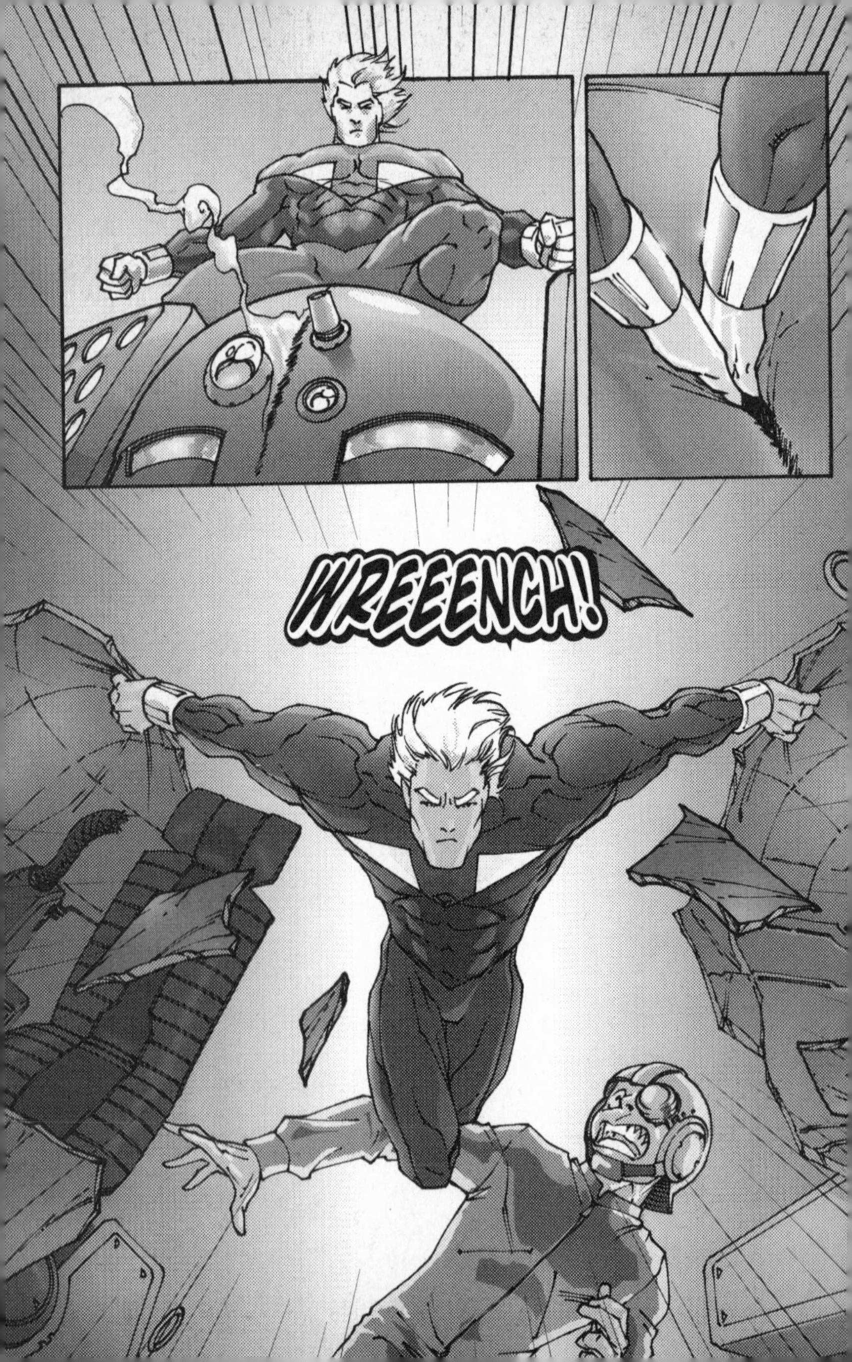
WREEENCH!

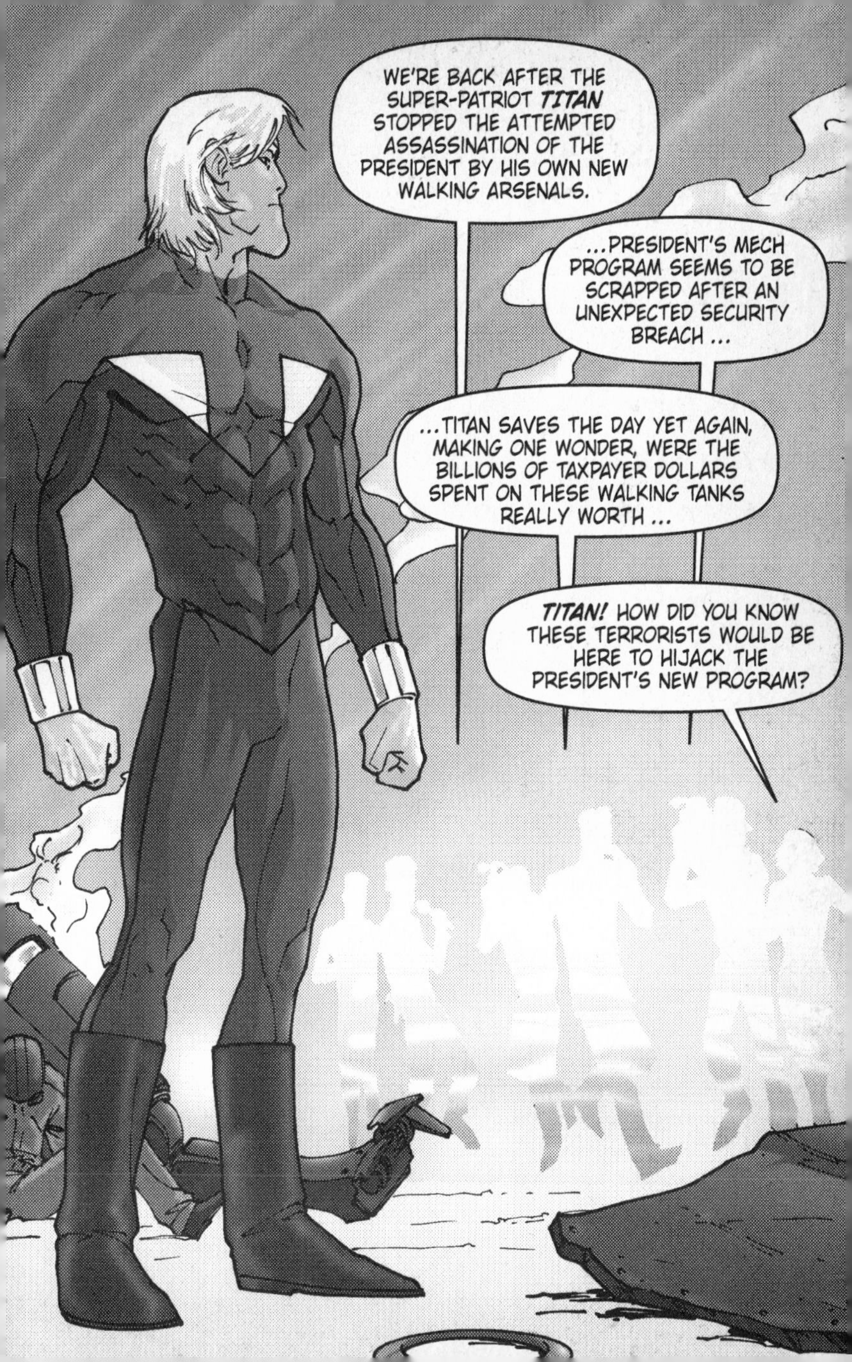
WE'RE BACK AFTER THE SUPER-PATRIOT TITAN STOPPED THE ATTEMPTED ASSASSINATION OF THE PRESIDENT BY HIS OWN NEW WALKING ARSENALS.
...PRESIDENT'S MECH PROGRAM SEEMS TO BE SCRAPPED AFTER AN UNEXPECTED SECURITY BREACH ...
...TITAN SAVES THE DAY YET AGAIN, MAKING ONE WONDER, WERE THE BILLIONS OF TAXPAYER DOLLARS SPENT ON THESE WALKING TANKS REALLY WORTH ...
TITAN! HOW DID YOU KNOW THESE TERRORISTS WOULD BE HERE TO HIJACK THE PRESIDENT'S NEW PROGRAM?

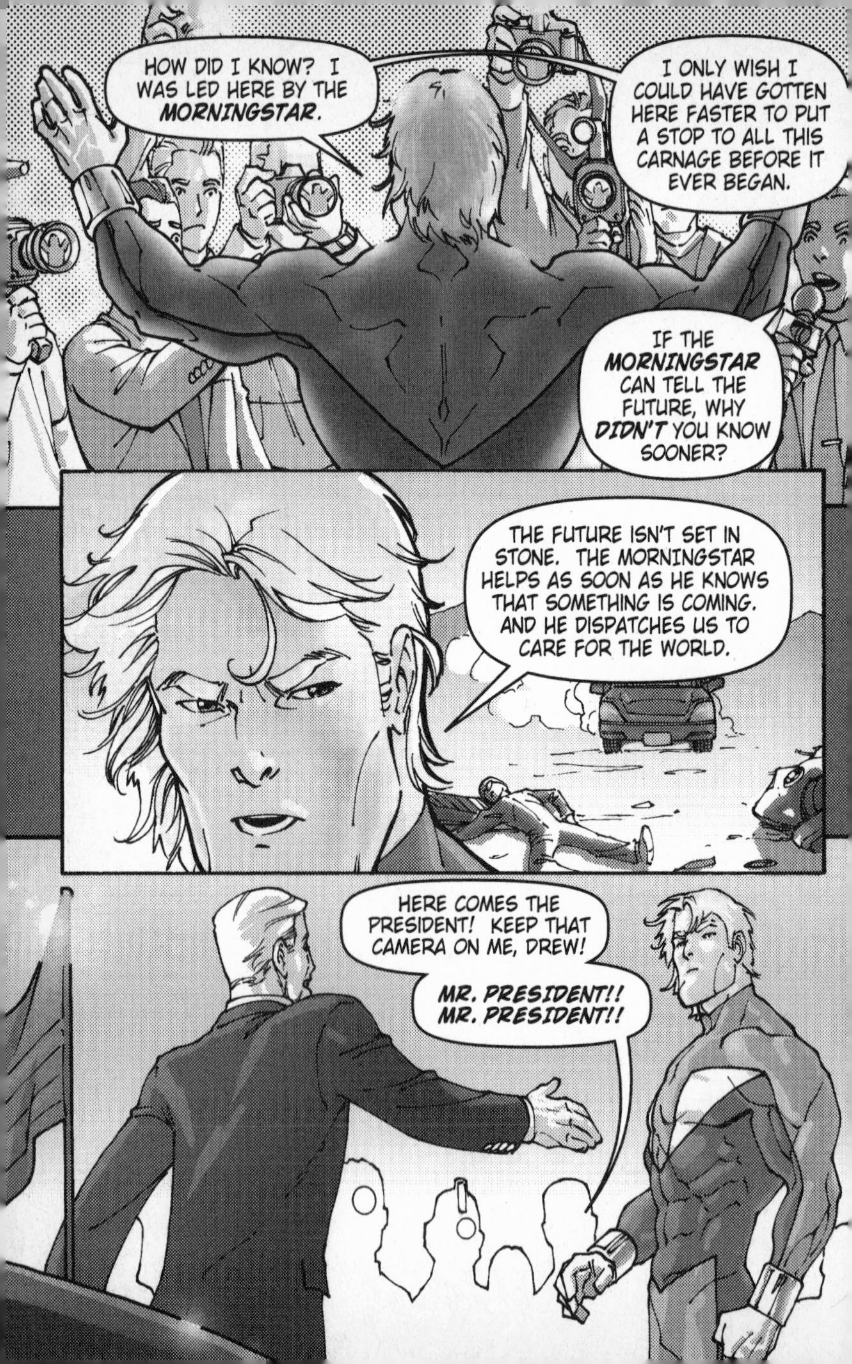
HOW DID I KNOW? I WAS LED HERE BY THE MORNINGSTAR.
I ONLY WISH I COULD HAVE GOTTEN HERE FASTER TO PUT A STOP TO ALL THIS CARNAGE BEFORE IT EVER BEGAN.
IF THE MORNINGSTAR CAN TELL THE FUTURE, WHY DIDN'T YOU KNOW SOONER?
THE FUTURE ISN'T SET IN STONE. THE MORNINGSTAR HELPS AS SOON AS HE KNOWS THAT SOMETHING IS COMING. AND HE DISPATCHES US TO CARE FOR THE WORLD.
HERE COMES THE PRESIDENT! KEEP THAT CAMERA ON ME, DREW!
MR. PRESIDENT!! MR. PRESIDENT!!

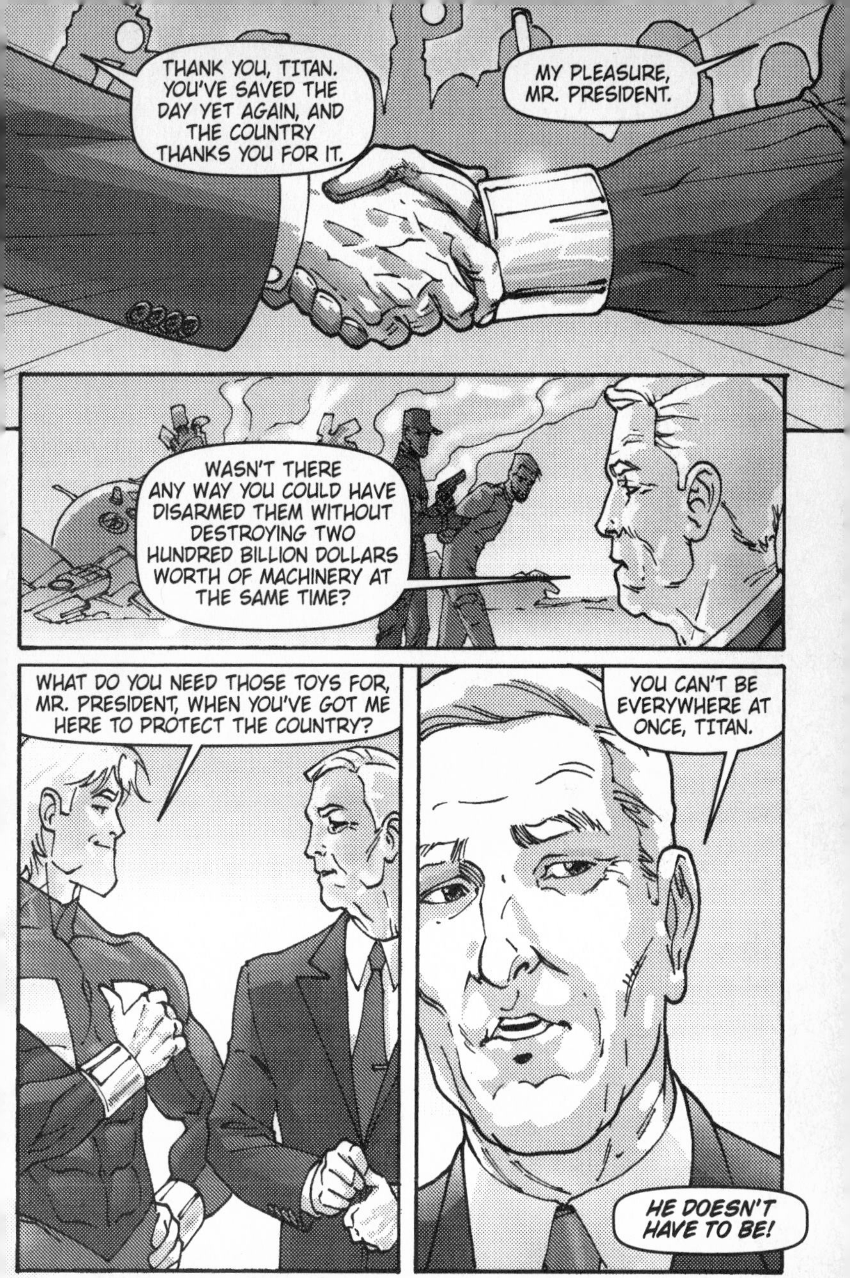
THANK YOU, TITAN. YOU'VE SAVED THE DAY YET AGAIN, AND THE COUNTRY THANKS YOU FOR IT.
MY PLEASURE, MR. PRESIDENT.
WASN'T THERE ANY WAY YOU COULD HAVE DISARMED THEM WITHOUT DESTROYING TWO HUNDRED BILLION DOLLARS WORTH OF MACHINERY AT THE SAME TIME?
WHAT DO YOU NEED THOSE TOYS FOR, MR. PRESIDENT, WHEN YOU'VE GOT ME HERE TO PROTECT THE COUNTRY?
YOU CAN'T BE EVERYWHERE AT ONCE, TITAN.
HE DOESN'T HAVE TO BE!

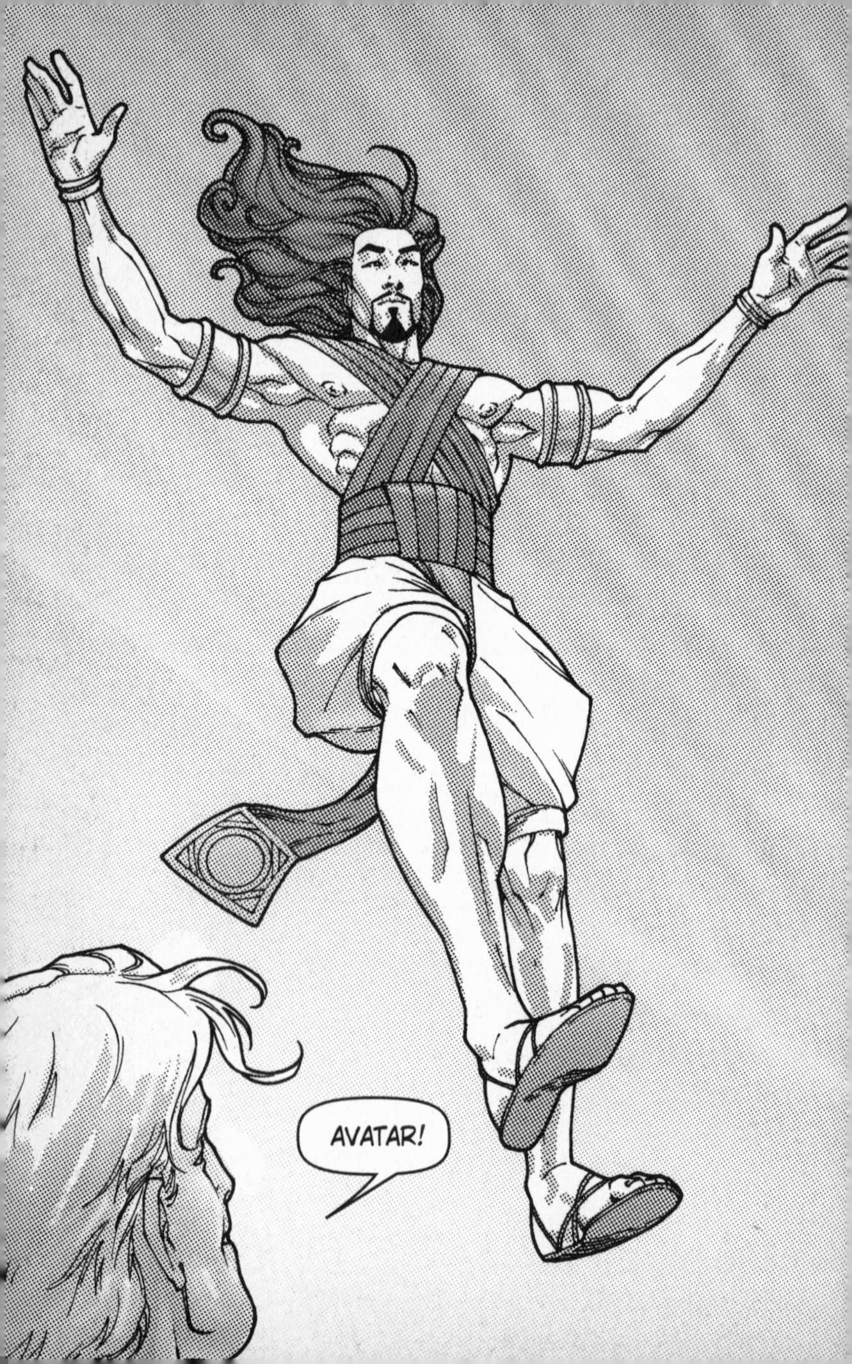
AVATAR!

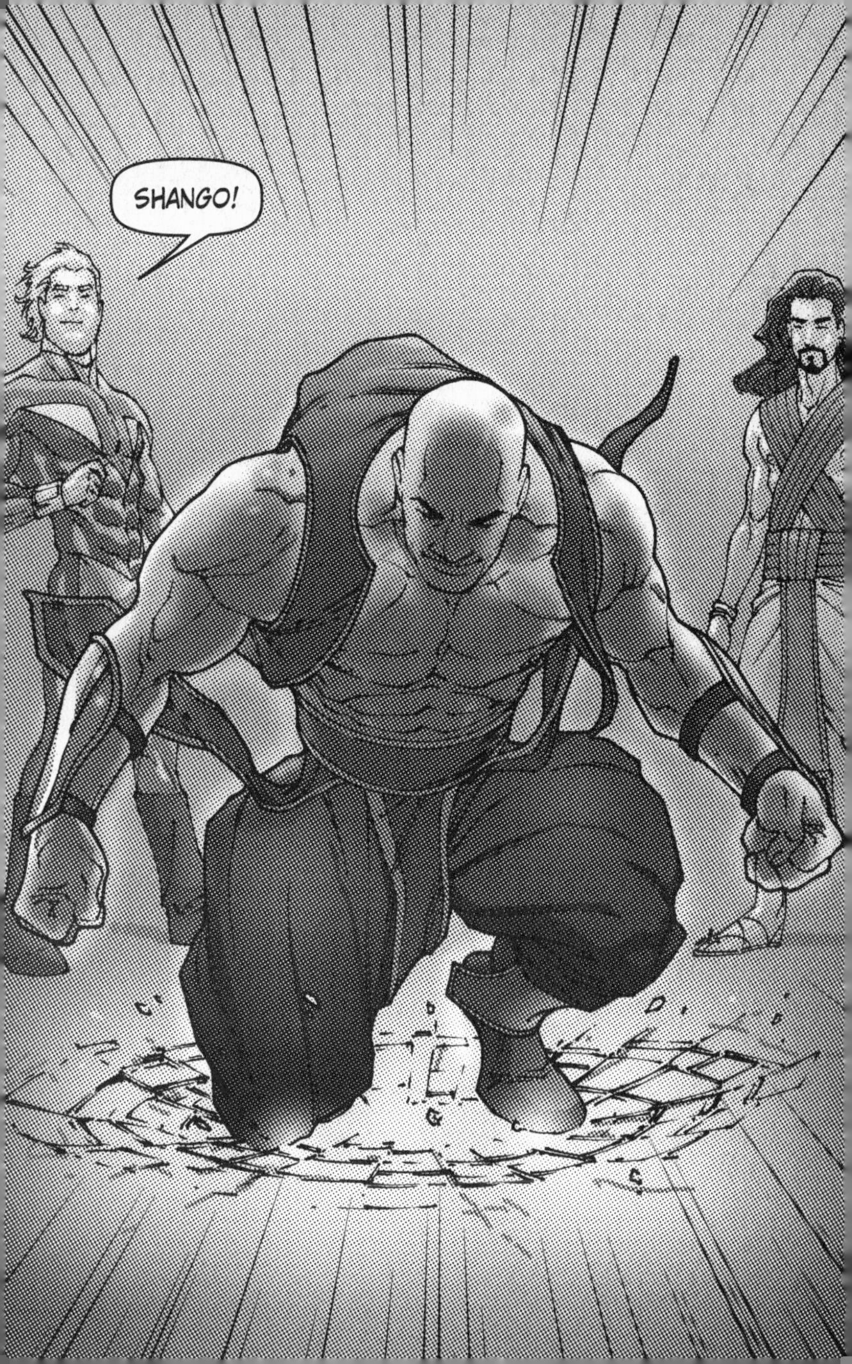
SHANGO!

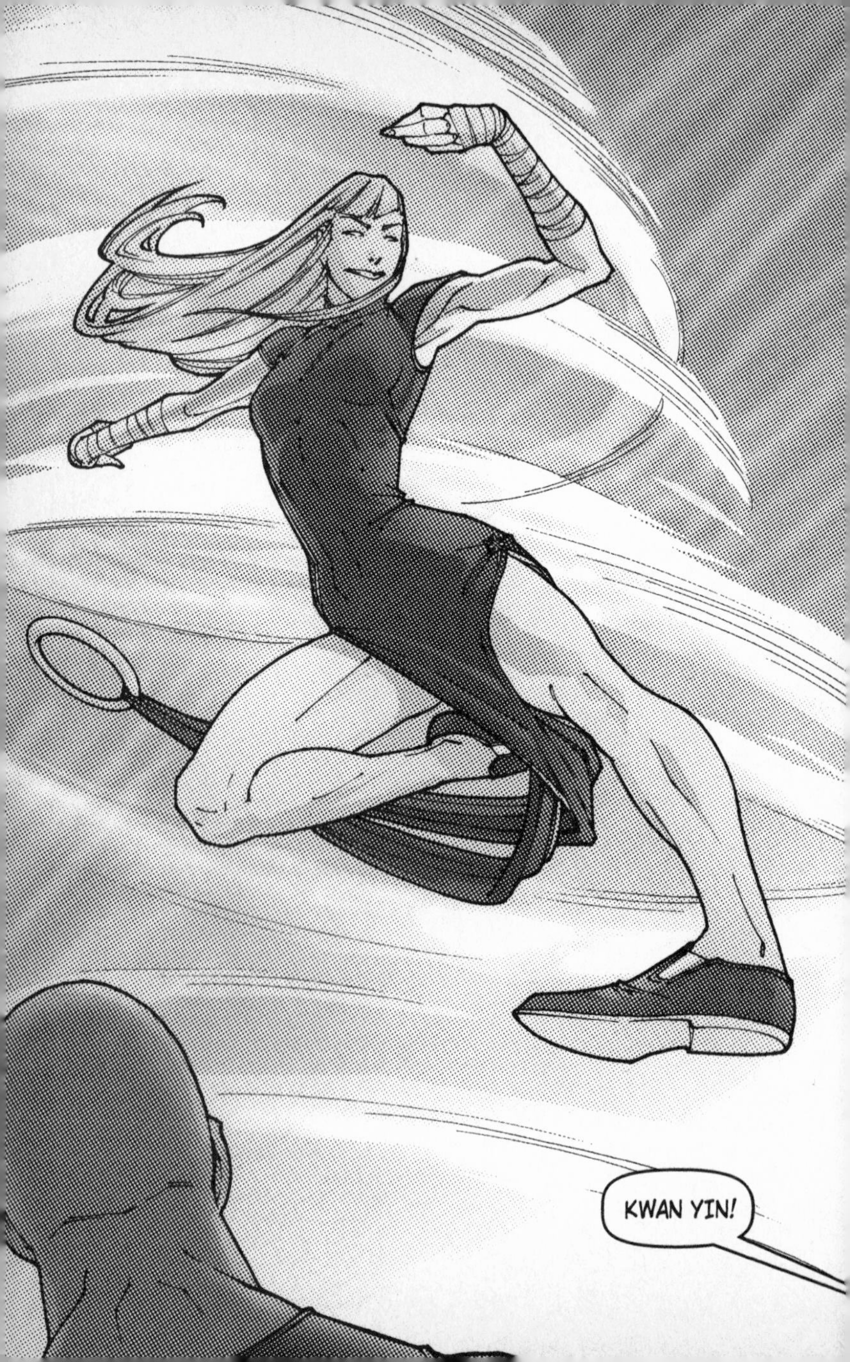
KWAN YIN!

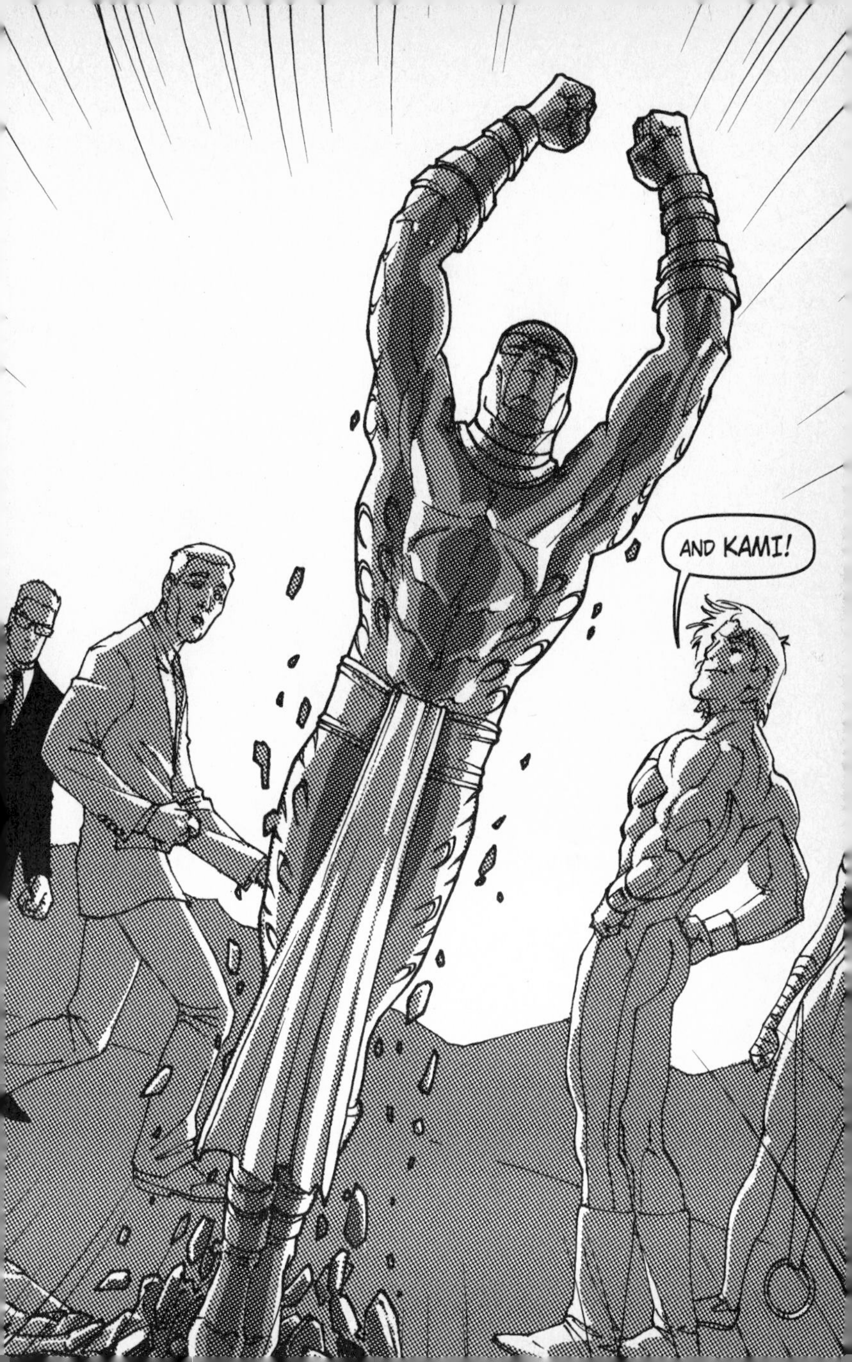
AND KAMI!

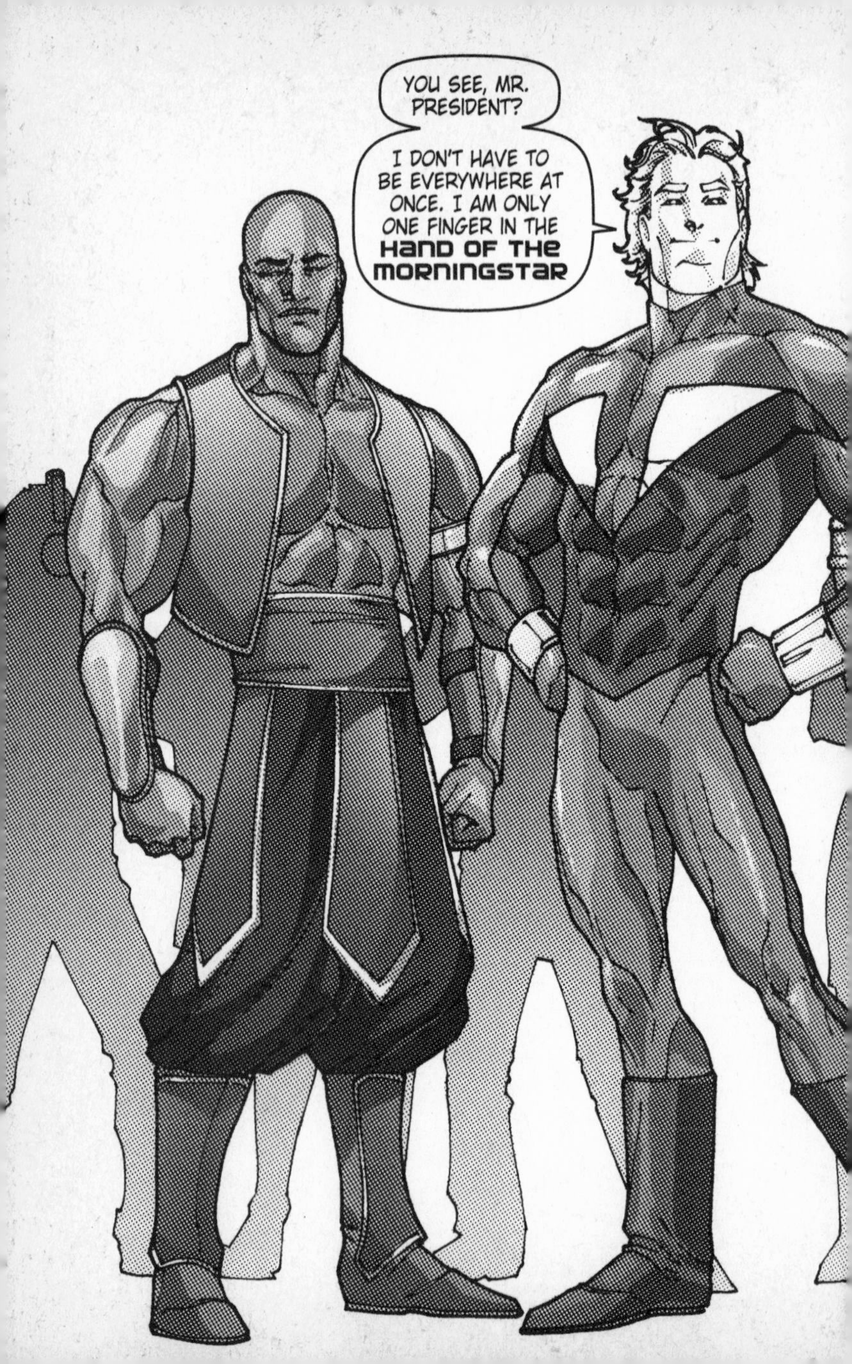
YOU SEE, MR. PRESIDENT?
I DON'T HAVE TO BE EVERYWHERE AT ONCE. I AM ONLY ONE FINGER IN THE HAND OF THE MORNINGSTAR

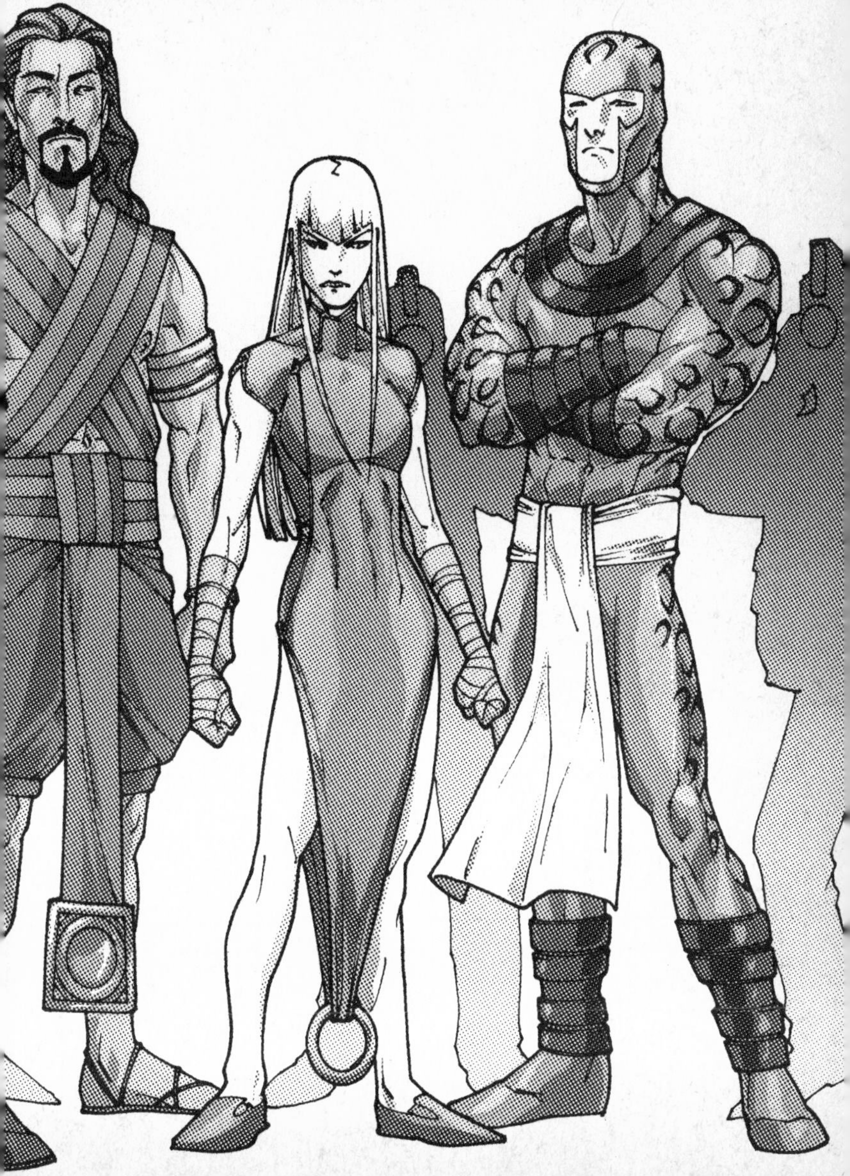

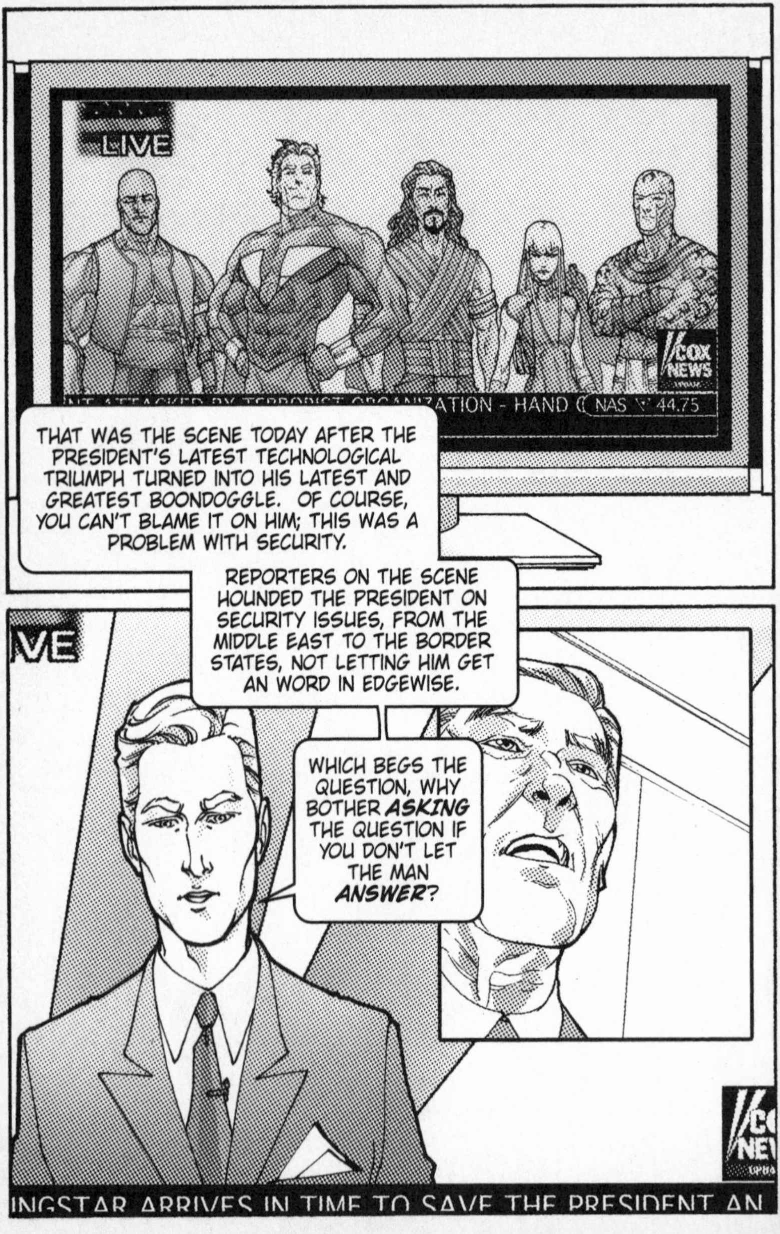

LIVE
NT ATTACKED BY TERRORIST ORGANIZATION - HAND C NAS 44.75
THAT WAS THE SCENE TODAY AFTER THE PRESIDENT'S LATEST TECHNOLOGICAL TRIUMPH TURNED INTO HIS LATEST AND GREATEST BOONDOGGLE. OF COURSE, YOU CAN'T BLAME IT ON HIM; THIS WAS A PROBLEM WITH SECURITY.
REPORTERS ON THE SCENE HOUNDED THE PRESIDENT ON SECURITY ISSUES, FROM THE MIDDLE EAST TO THE BORDER STATES, NOT LETTING HIM GET AN WORD IN EDGEWISE.
VE
WHICH BEGS THE QUESTION, WHY BOTHER ASKING THE QUESTION IF YOU DON'T LET THE MAN ANSWER?
INGSTAR ARRIVES IN TIME TO SAVE THE PRESIDENT AN

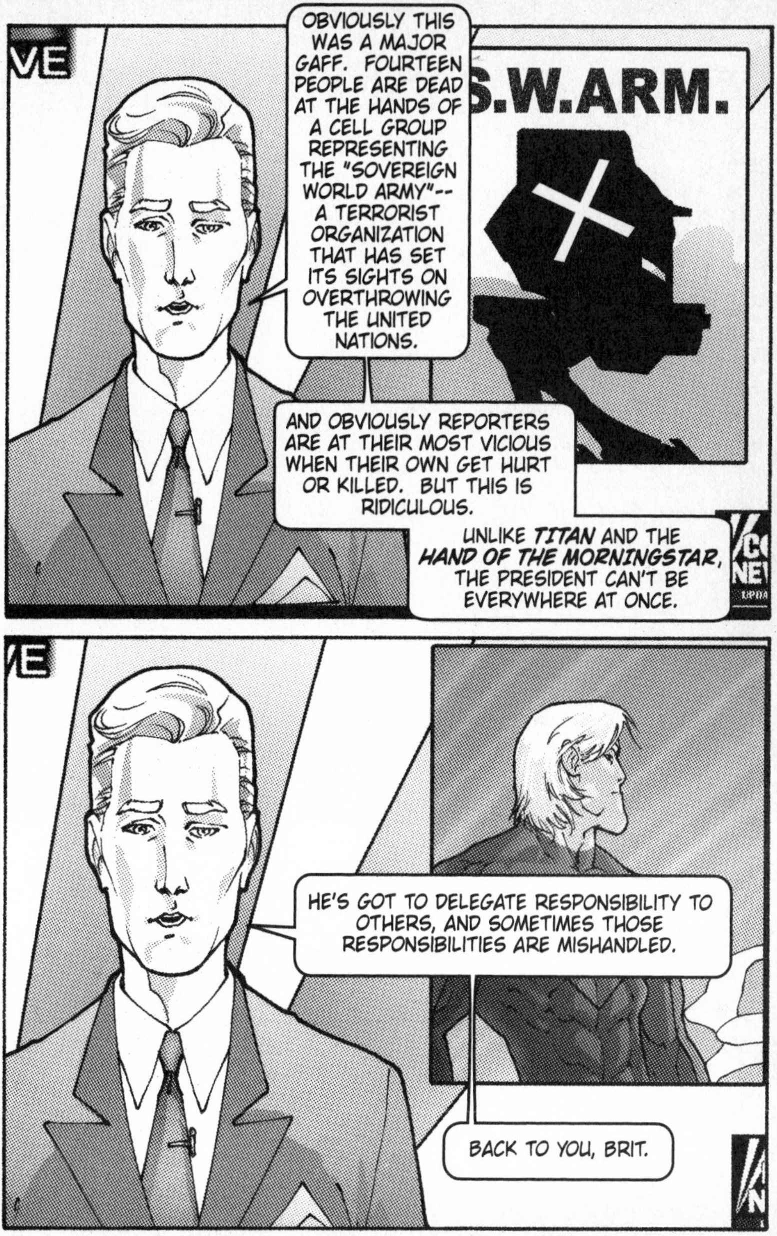
VE
S.W.ARM.
OBVIOUSLY THIS WAS A MAJOR GAFF. FOURTEEN PEOPLE ARE DEAD AT THE HANDS OF A CELL GROUP REPRESENTING THE "SOVEREIGN WORLD ARMY"-- A TERRORIST ORGANIZATION THAT HAS SET ITS SIGHTS ON OVERTHROWING THE UNITED NATIONS.
AND OBVIOUSLY REPORTERS ARE AT THEIR MOST VICIOUS WHEN THEIR OWN GET HURT OR KILLED. BUT THIS IS RIDICULOUS.
UNLIKE ***TITAN*** AND THE ***HAND OF THE MORNINGSTAR***, THE PRESIDENT CAN'T BE EVERYWHERE AT ONCE.
HE'S GOT TO DELEGATE RESPONSIBILITY TO OTHERS, AND SOMETIMES THOSE RESPONSIBILITIES ARE MISHANDLED.
BACK TO YOU, BRIT.

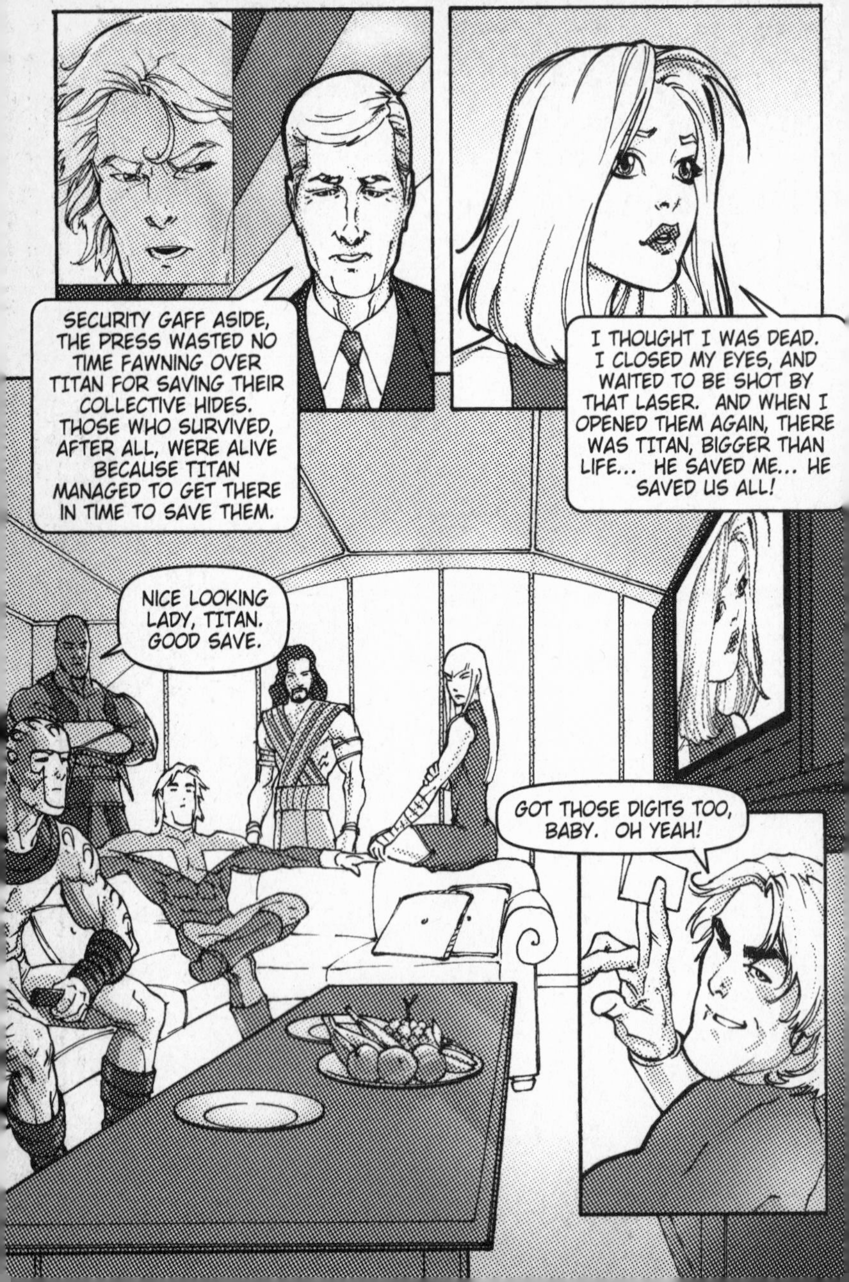
SECURITY GAFF ASIDE, THE PRESS WASTED NO TIME FAWNING OVER TITAN FOR SAVING THEIR COLLECTIVE HIDES. THOSE WHO SURVIVED, AFTER ALL, WERE ALIVE BECAUSE TITAN MANAGED TO GET THERE IN TIME TO SAVE THEM.
I THOUGHT I WAS DEAD. I CLOSED MY EYES, AND WAITED TO BE SHOT BY THAT LASER. AND WHEN I OPENED THEM AGAIN, THERE WAS TITAN, BIGGER THAN LIFE... HE SAVED ME... HE SAVED US ALL!
NICE LOOKING LADY, TITAN. GOOD SAVE.
GOT THOSE DIGITS TOO, BABY. OH YEAH!

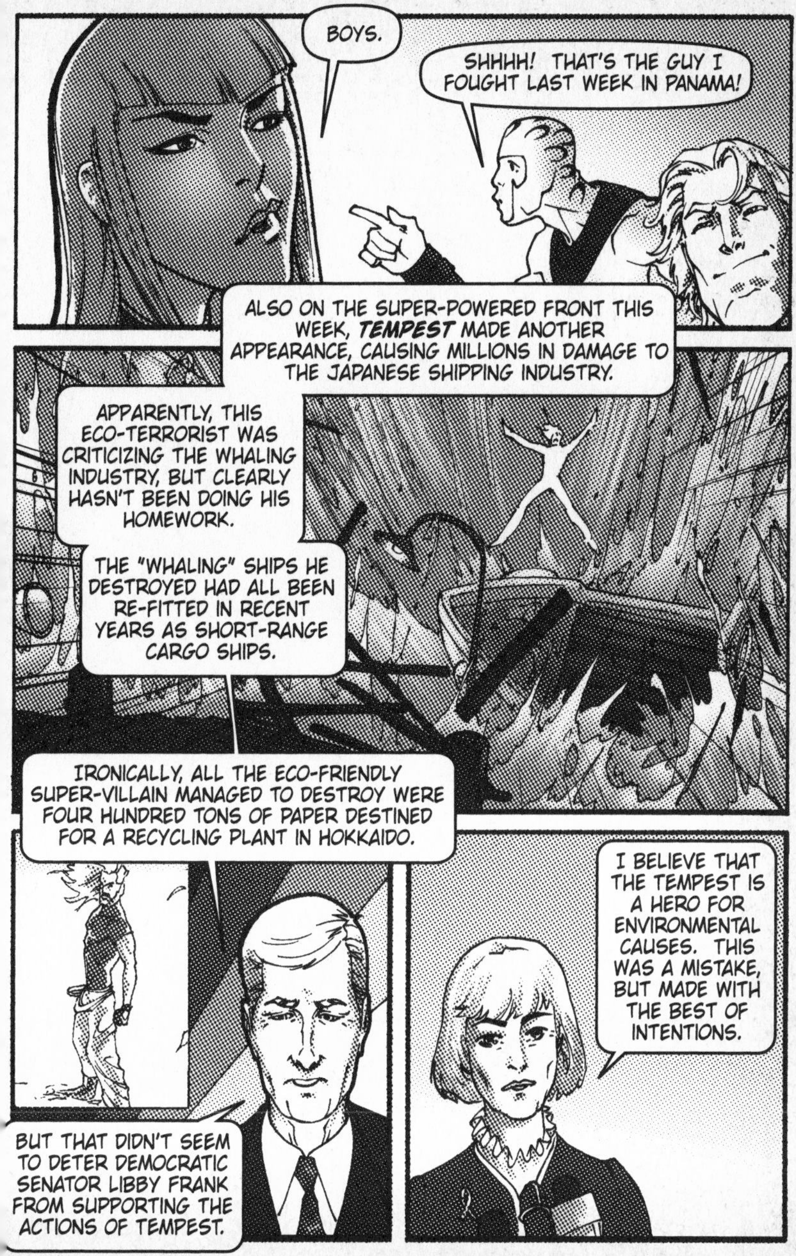
BOYS.
SHHHH! THAT'S THE GUY I FOUGHT LAST WEEK IN PANAMA!
ALSO ON THE SUPER-POWERED FRONT THIS WEEK, *TEMPEST* MADE ANOTHER APPEARANCE, CAUSING MILLIONS IN DAMAGE TO THE JAPANESE SHIPPING INDUSTRY.
APPARENTLY, THIS ECO-TERRORIST WAS CRITICIZING THE WHALING INDUSTRY, BUT CLEARLY HASN'T BEEN DOING HIS HOMEWORK.
THE "WHALING" SHIPS HE DESTROYED HAD ALL BEEN RE-FITTED IN RECENT YEARS AS SHORT-RANGE CARGO SHIPS.
IRONICALLY, ALL THE ECO-FRIENDLY SUPER-VILLAIN MANAGED TO DESTROY WERE FOUR HUNDRED TONS OF PAPER DESTINED FOR A RECYCLING PLANT IN HOKKAIDO.
BUT THAT DIDN'T SEEM TO DETER DEMOCRATIC SENATOR LIBBY FRANK FROM SUPPORTING THE ACTIONS OF TEMPEST.
I BELIEVE THAT THE TEMPEST IS A HERO FOR ENVIRONMENTAL CAUSES. THIS WAS A MISTAKE, BUT MADE WITH THE BEST OF INTENTIONS.

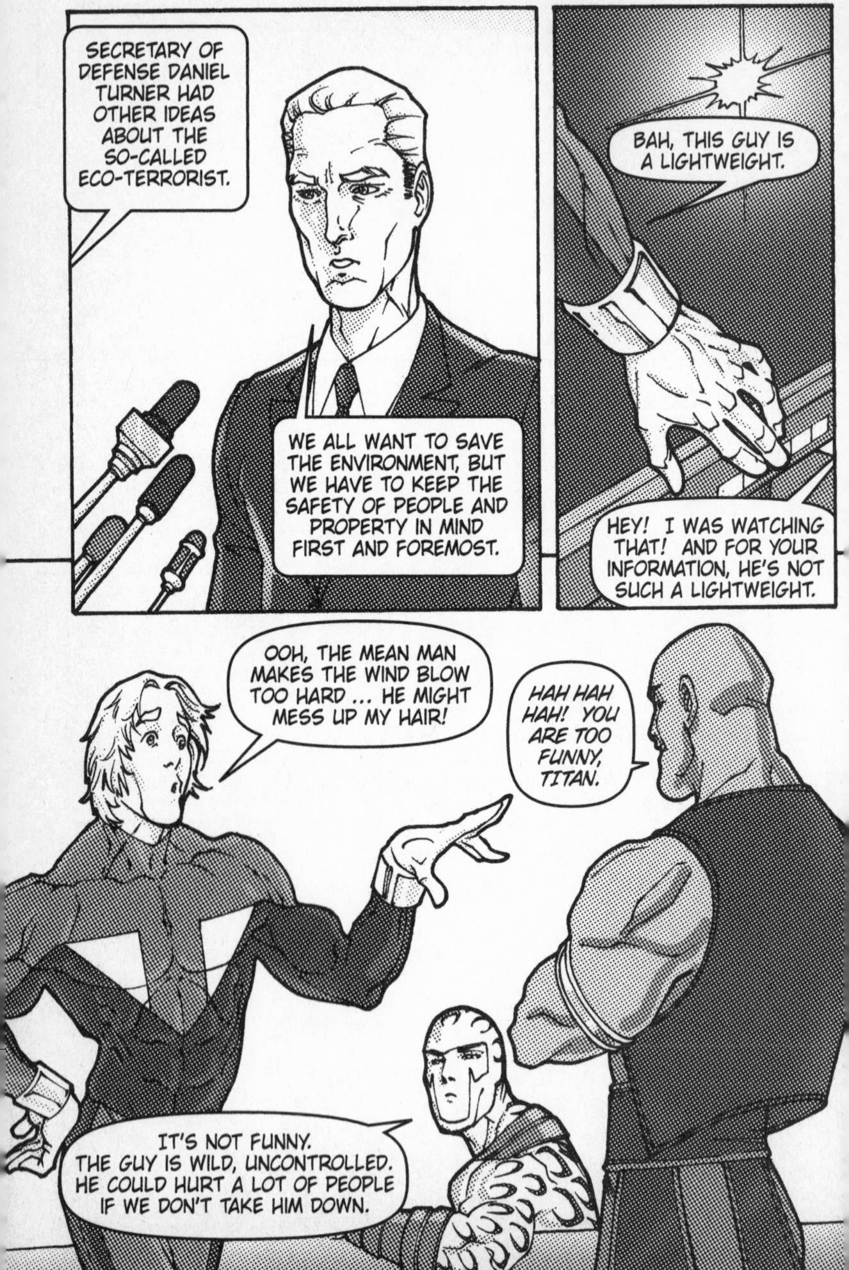
SECRETARY OF DEFENSE DANIEL TURNER HAD OTHER IDEAS ABOUT THE SO-CALLED ECO-TERRORIST.
WE ALL WANT TO SAVE THE ENVIRONMENT, BUT WE HAVE TO KEEP THE SAFETY OF PEOPLE AND PROPERTY IN MIND FIRST AND FOREMOST.
BAH, THIS GUY IS A LIGHTWEIGHT.
HEY! I WAS WATCHING THAT! AND FOR YOUR INFORMATION, HE'S NOT SUCH A LIGHTWEIGHT.
OOH, THE MEAN MAN MAKES THE WIND BLOW TOO HARD ... HE MIGHT MESS UP MY HAIR!
HAH HAH HAH! YOU ARE TOO FUNNY, TITAN.
IT'S NOT FUNNY. THE GUY IS WILD, UNCONTROLLED. HE COULD HURT A LOT OF PEOPLE IF WE DON'T TAKE HIM DOWN.

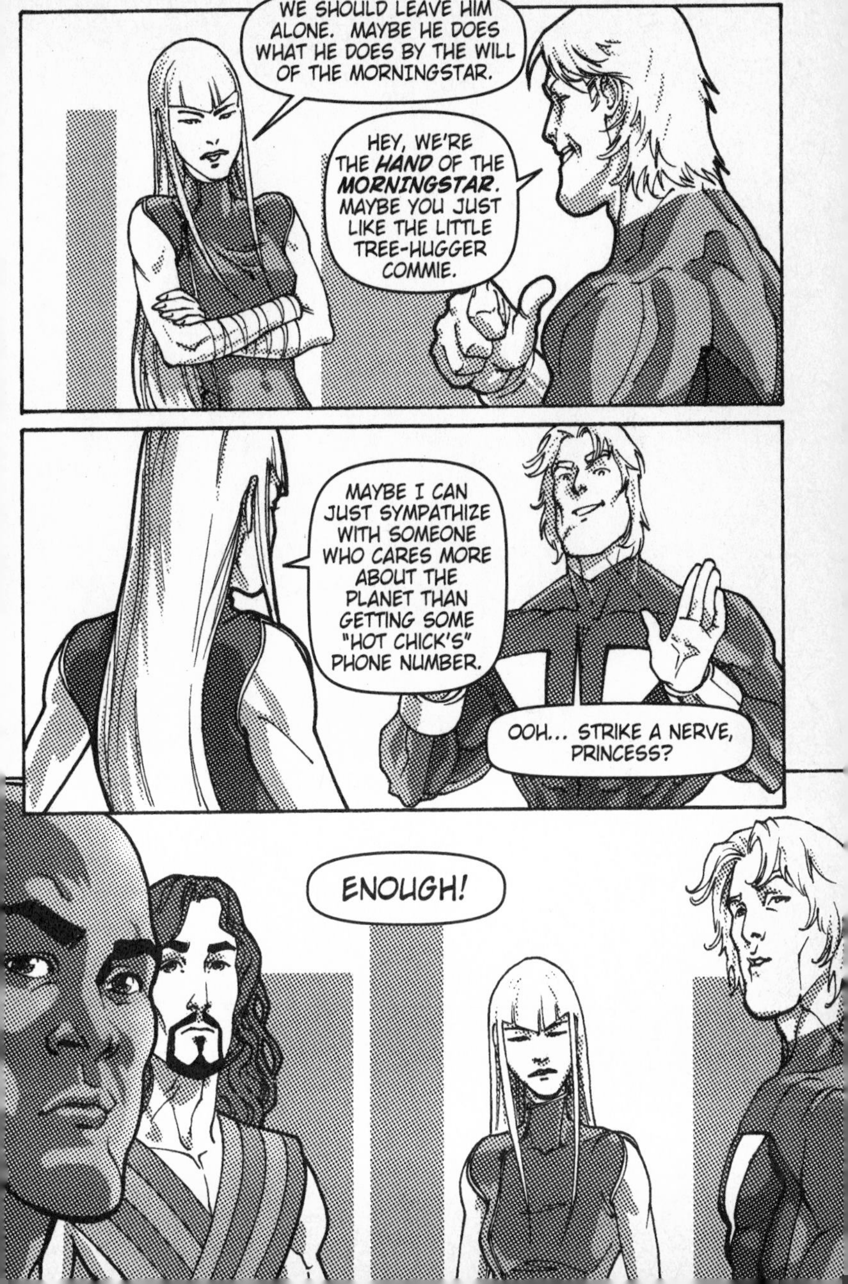
WE SHOULD LEAVE HIM ALONE. MAYBE HE DOES WHAT HE DOES BY THE WILL OF THE MORNINGSTAR.
HEY, WE'RE THE *HAND* OF THE ***MORNINGSTAR***. MAYBE YOU JUST LIKE THE LITTLE TREE-HUGGER COMMIE.
MAYBE I CAN JUST SYMPATHIZE WITH SOMEONE WHO CARES MORE ABOUT THE PLANET THAN GETTING SOME "HOT CHICK'S" PHONE NUMBER.
OOH... STRIKE A NERVE, PRINCESS?
ENOUGH!

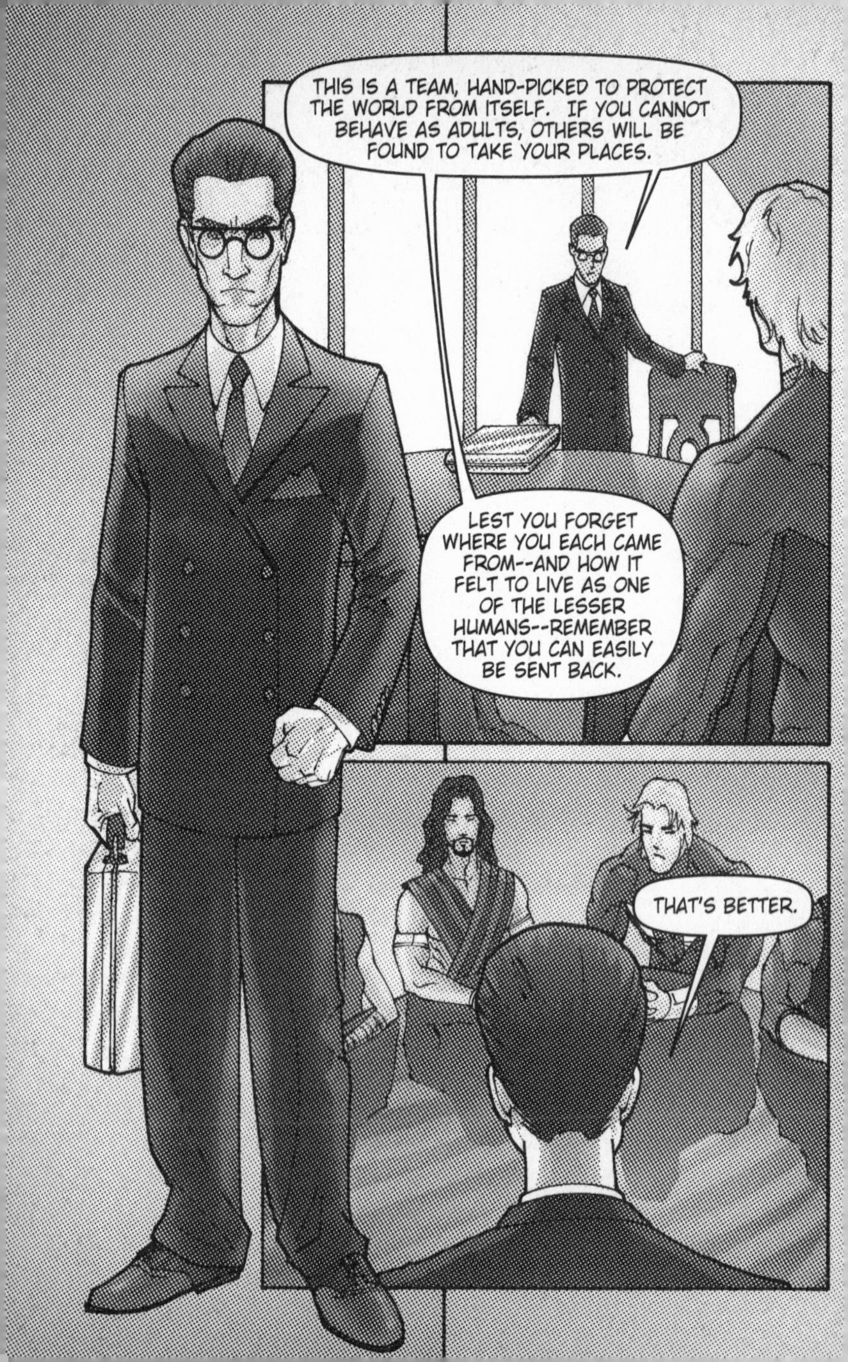
THIS IS A TEAM, HAND-PICKED TO PROTECT THE WORLD FROM ITSELF. IF YOU CANNOT BEHAVE AS ADULTS, OTHERS WILL BE FOUND TO TAKE YOUR PLACES.
LEST YOU FORGET WHERE YOU EACH CAME FROM--AND HOW IT FELT TO LIVE AS ONE OF THE LESSER HUMANS--REMEMBER THAT YOU CAN EASILY BE SENT BACK.
THAT'S BETTER.

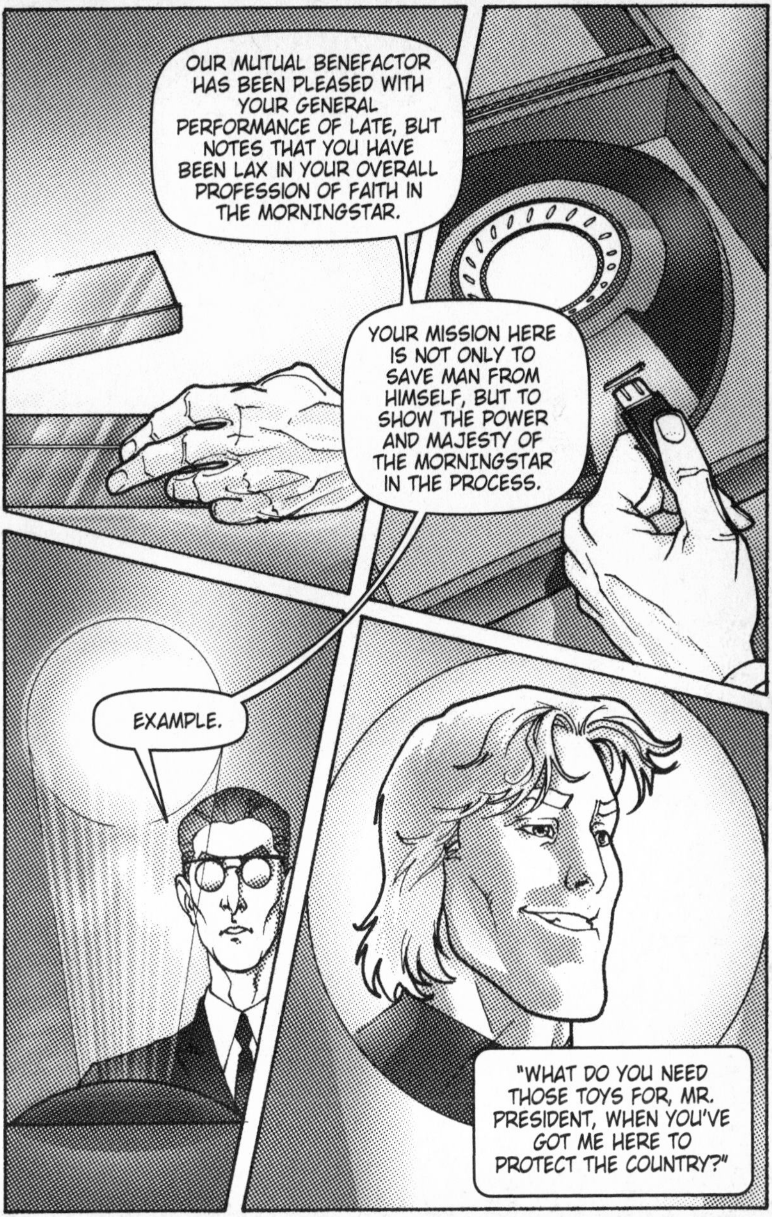
OUR MUTUAL BENEFACTOR HAS BEEN PLEASED WITH YOUR GENERAL PERFORMANCE OF LATE, BUT NOTES THAT YOU HAVE BEEN LAX IN YOUR OVERALL PROFESSION OF FAITH IN THE MORNINGSTAR.
YOUR MISSION HERE IS NOT ONLY TO SAVE MAN FROM HIMSELF, BUT TO SHOW THE POWER AND MAJESTY OF THE MORNINGSTAR IN THE PROCESS.
EXAMPLE.
"WHAT DO YOU NEED THOSE TOYS FOR, MR. PRESIDENT, WHEN YOU'VE GOT ME HERE TO PROTECT THE COUNTRY?"

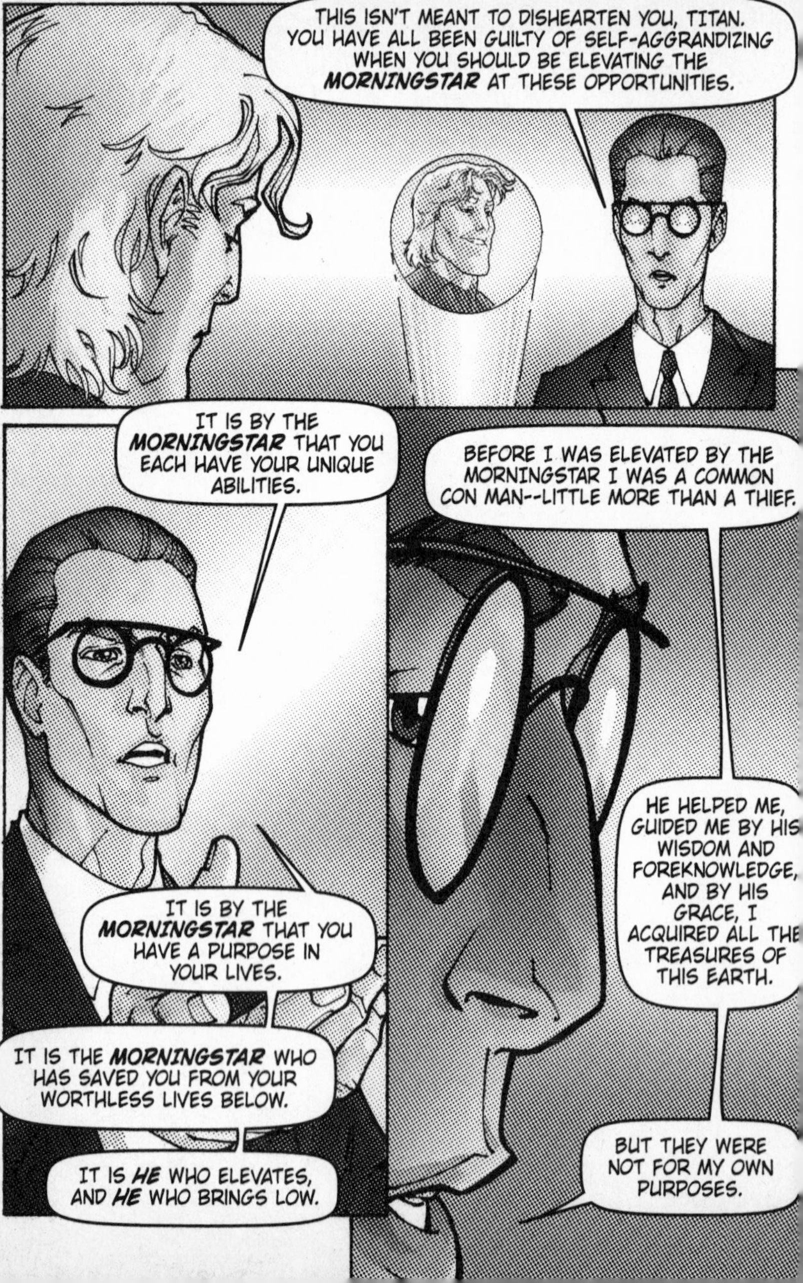
THIS ISN'T MEANT TO DISHEARTEN YOU, TITAN. YOU HAVE ALL BEEN GUILTY OF SELF-AGGRANDIZING WHEN YOU SHOULD BE ELEVATING THE MORNINGSTAR AT THESE OPPORTUNITIES.
IT IS BY THE MORNINGSTAR THAT YOU EACH HAVE YOUR UNIQUE ABILITIES.
IT IS BY THE MORNINGSTAR THAT YOU HAVE A PURPOSE IN YOUR LIVES.
IT IS THE MORNINGSTAR WHO HAS SAVED YOU FROM YOUR WORTHLESS LIVES BELOW.
IT IS HE WHO ELEVATES, AND HE WHO BRINGS LOW.
BEFORE I WAS ELEVATED BY THE MORNINGSTAR I WAS A COMMON CON MAN--LITTLE MORE THAN A THIEF.
HE HELPED ME, GUIDED ME BY HIS WISDOM AND FOREKNOWLEDGE, AND BY HIS GRACE, I ACQUIRED ALL THE TREASURES OF THIS EARTH.
BUT THEY WERE NOT FOR MY OWN PURPOSES.

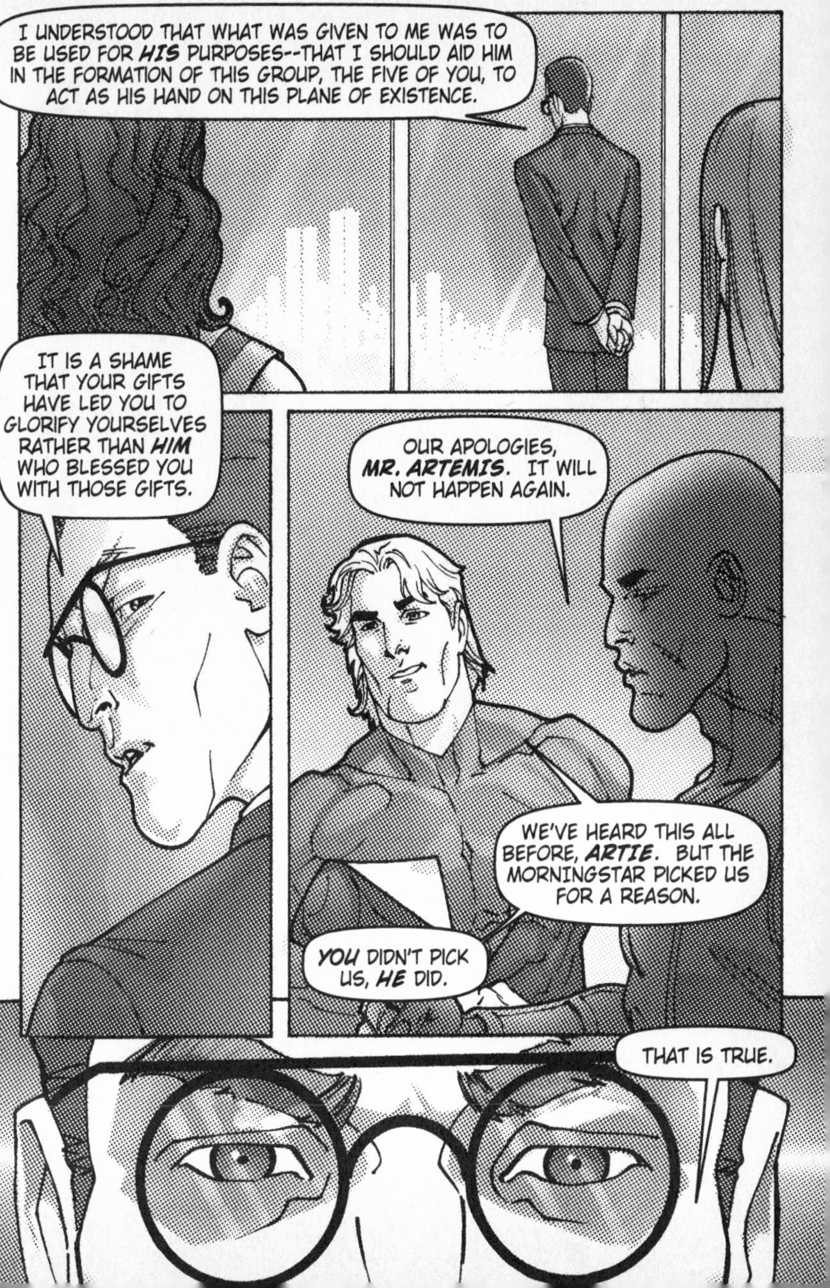
I UNDERSTOOD THAT WHAT WAS GIVEN TO ME WAS TO BE USED FOR *HIS* PURPOSES--THAT I SHOULD AID HIM IN THE FORMATION OF THIS GROUP, THE FIVE OF YOU, TO ACT AS HIS HAND ON THIS PLANE OF EXISTENCE.
IT IS A SHAME THAT YOUR GIFTS HAVE LED YOU TO GLORIFY YOURSELVES RATHER THAN *HIM* WHO BLESSED YOU WITH THOSE GIFTS.
OUR APOLOGIES, *MR. ARTEMIS*. IT WILL NOT HAPPEN AGAIN.
WE'VE HEARD THIS ALL BEFORE, *ARTIE*. BUT THE MORNINGSTAR PICKED US FOR A REASON.
YOU DIDN'T PICK US, *HE* DID.
THAT IS TRUE.

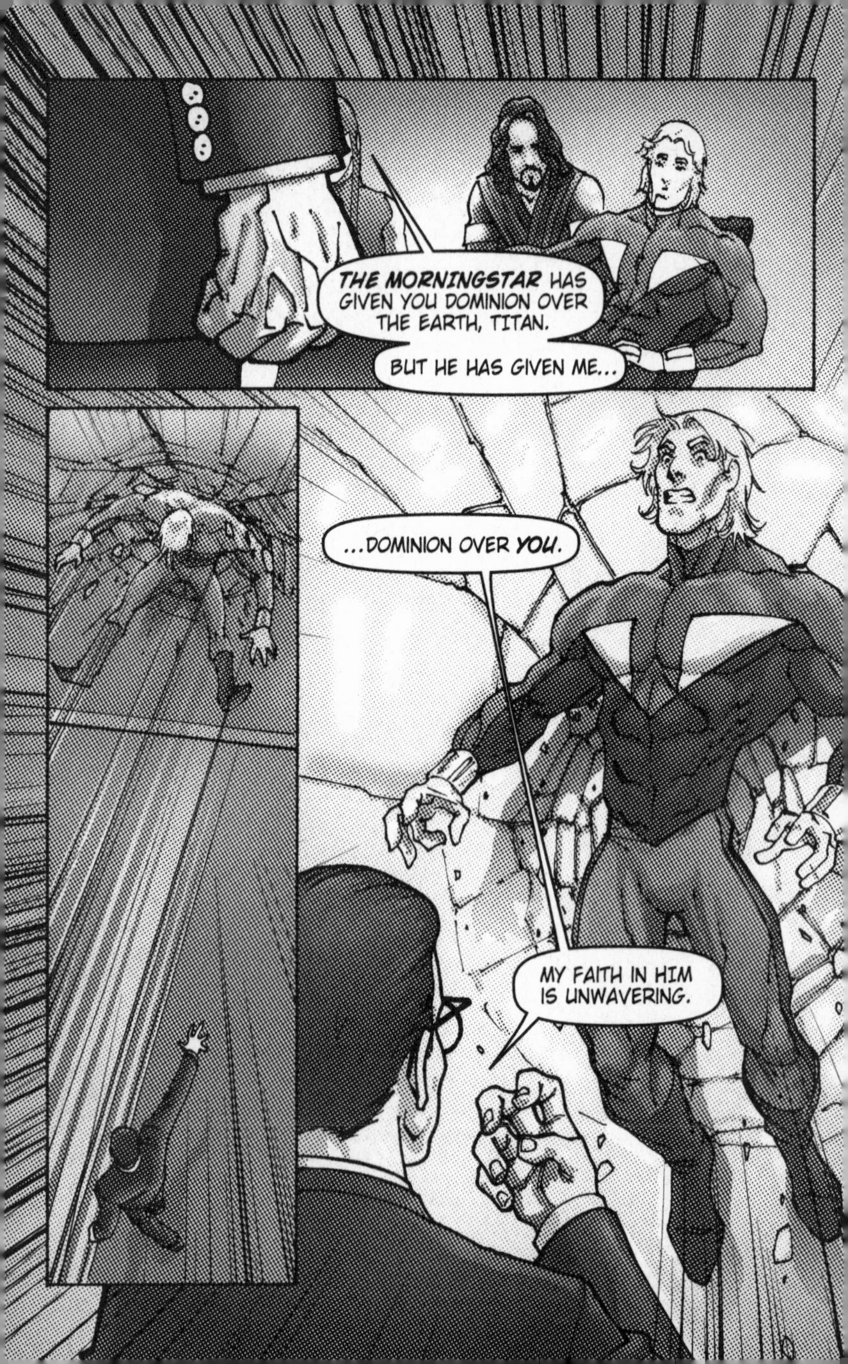
THE MORNINGSTAR HAS GIVEN YOU DOMINION OVER THE EARTH, TITAN.
BUT HE HAS GIVEN ME...
...DOMINION OVER YOU.
MY FAITH IN HIM IS UNWAVERING.

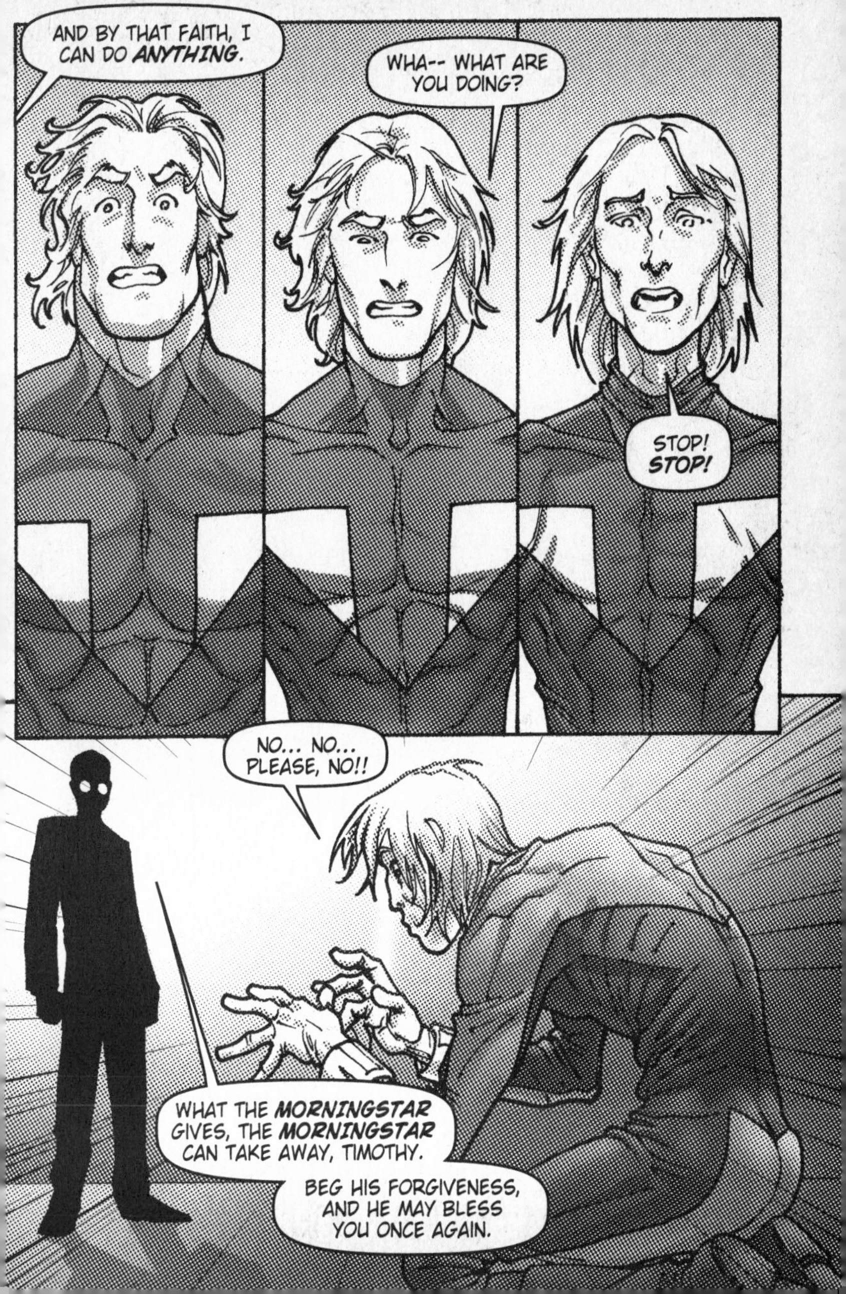
AND BY THAT FAITH, I CAN DO ANYTHING.
WHA-- WHAT ARE YOU DOING?
STOP! STOP!
NO... NO... PLEASE, NO!!
WHAT THE MORNINGSTAR GIVES, THE MORNINGSTAR CAN TAKE AWAY, TIMOTHY.
BEG HIS FORGIVENESS, AND HE MAY BLESS YOU ONCE AGAIN.

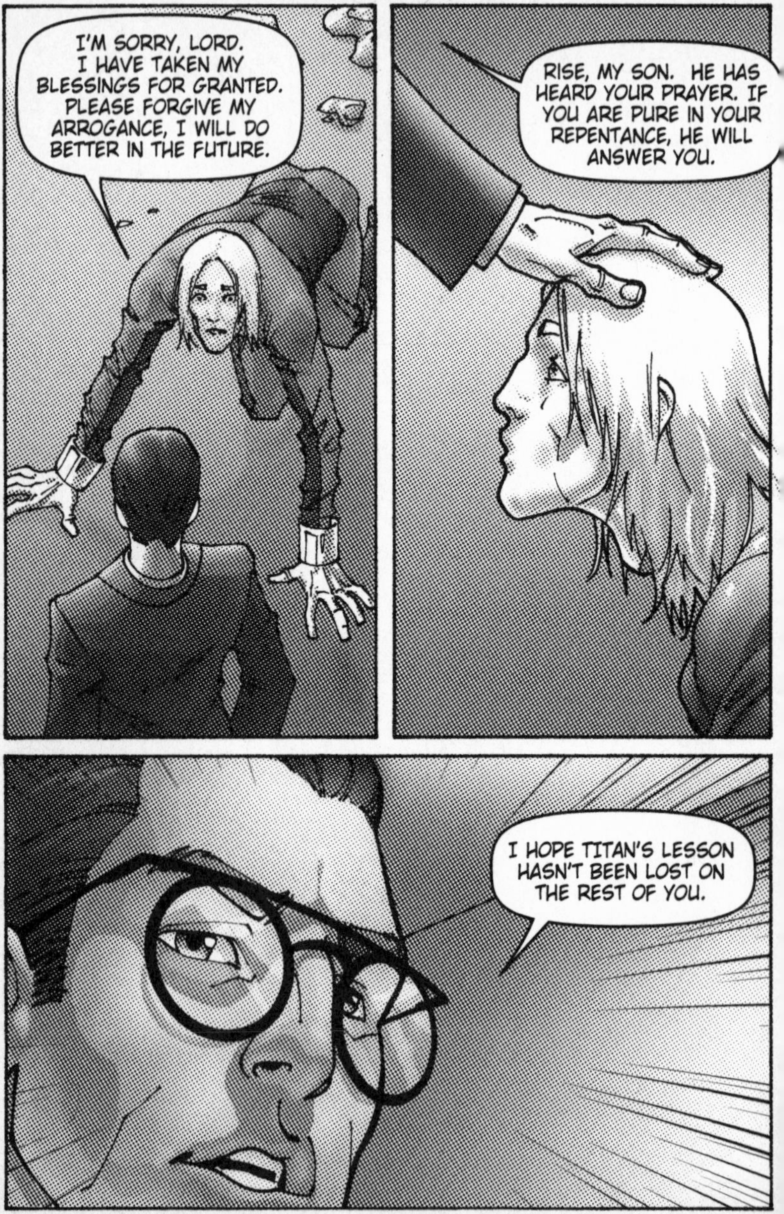
I'M SORRY, LORD. I HAVE TAKEN MY BLESSINGS FOR GRANTED. PLEASE FORGIVE MY ARROGANCE, I WILL DO BETTER IN THE FUTURE.
RISE, MY SON. HE HAS HEARD YOUR PRAYER. IF YOU ARE PURE IN YOUR REPENTANCE, HE WILL ANSWER YOU.
I HOPE TITAN'S LESSON HASN'T BEEN LOST ON THE REST OF YOU.

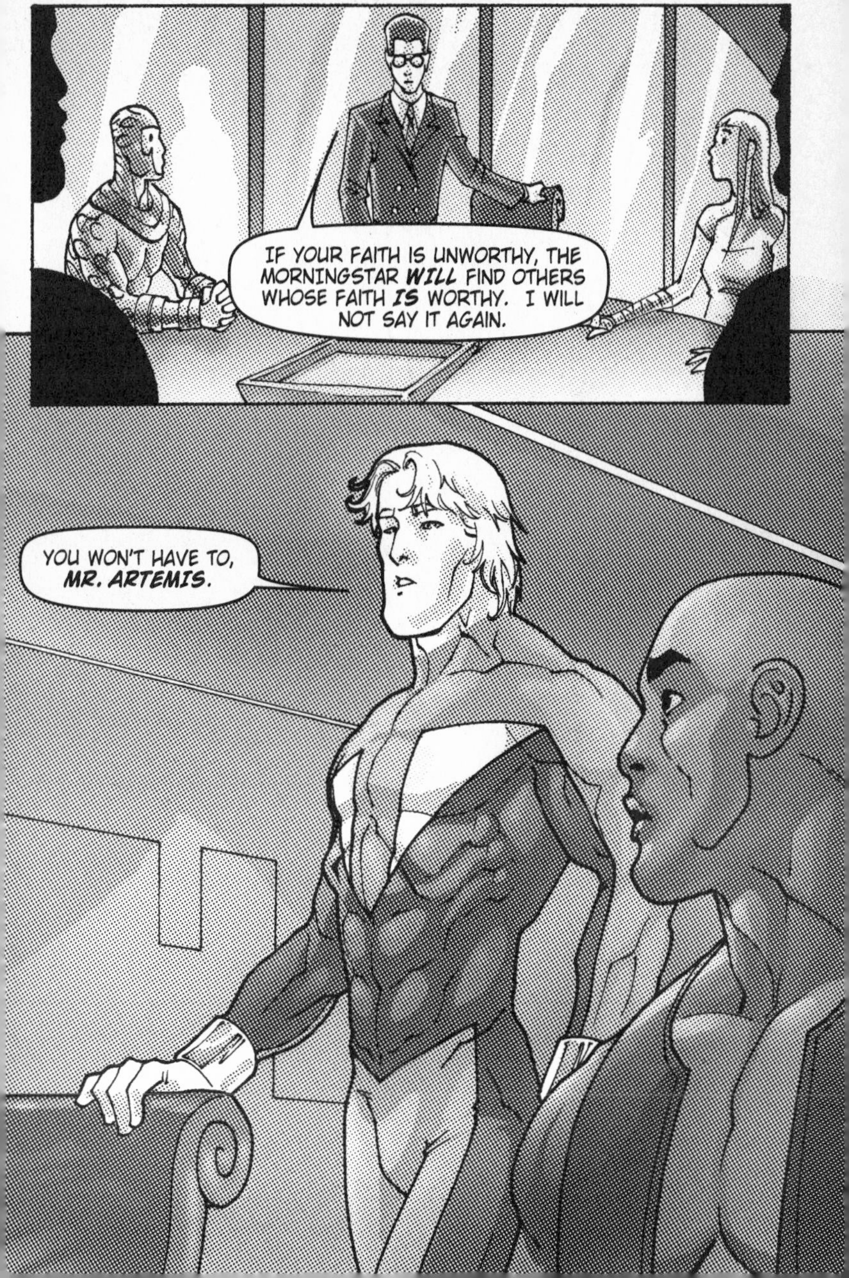
IF YOUR FAITH IS UNWORTHY, THE MORNINGSTAR **WILL** FIND OTHERS WHOSE FAITH **IS** WORTHY. I WILL NOT SAY IT AGAIN.
YOU WON'T HAVE TO, **MR. ARTEMIS**.

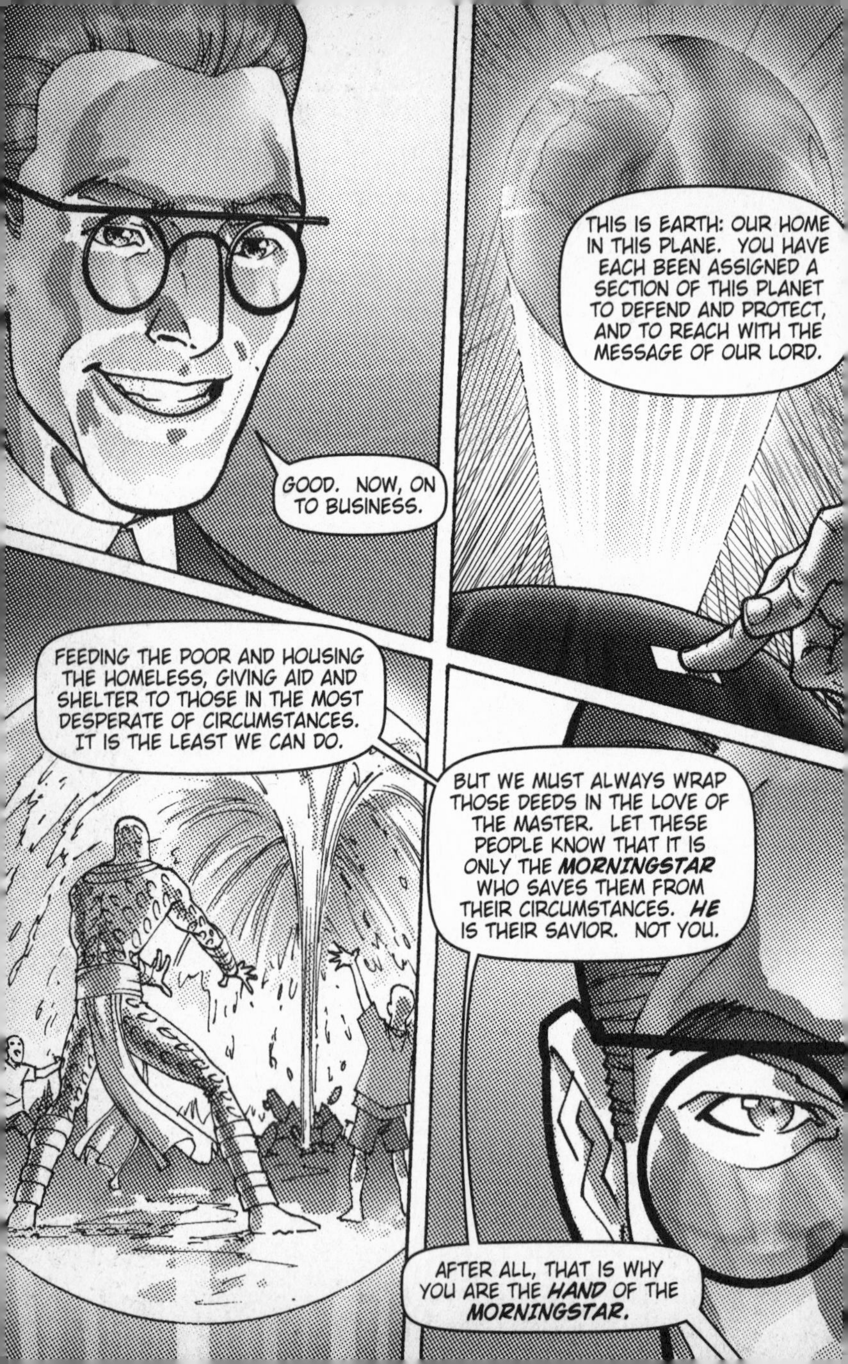
GOOD. NOW, ON TO BUSINESS.
THIS IS EARTH: OUR HOME IN THIS PLANE. YOU HAVE EACH BEEN ASSIGNED A SECTION OF THIS PLANET TO DEFEND AND PROTECT, AND TO REACH WITH THE MESSAGE OF OUR LORD.
FEEDING THE POOR AND HOUSING THE HOMELESS, GIVING AID AND SHELTER TO THOSE IN THE MOST DESPERATE OF CIRCUMSTANCES. IT IS THE LEAST WE CAN DO.
BUT WE MUST ALWAYS WRAP THOSE DEEDS IN THE LOVE OF THE MASTER. LET THESE PEOPLE KNOW THAT IT IS ONLY THE *MORNINGSTAR* WHO SAVES THEM FROM THEIR CIRCUMSTANCES. *HE* IS THEIR SAVIOR. NOT YOU.
AFTER ALL, THAT IS WHY YOU ARE THE *HAND* OF THE *MORNINGSTAR.*

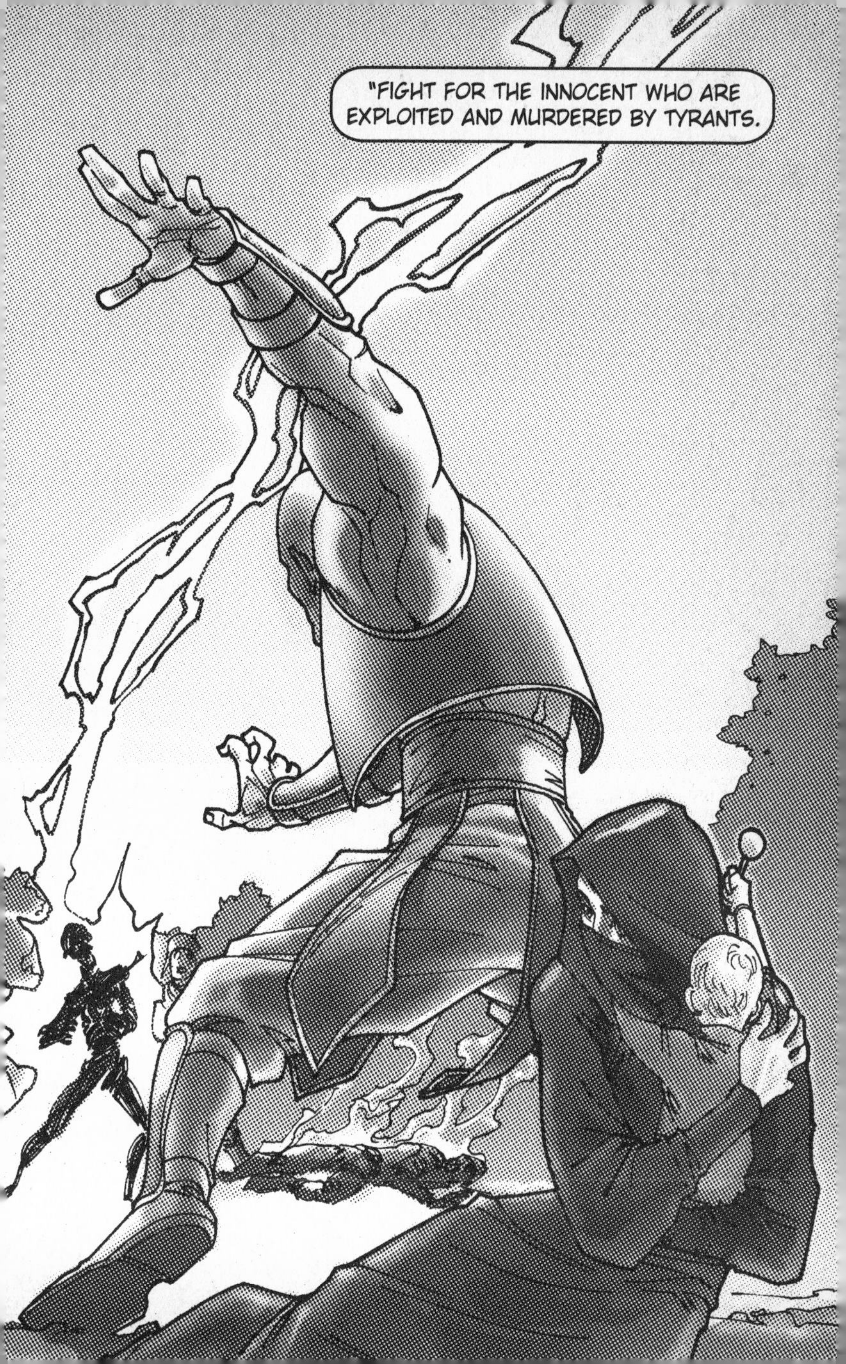
"FIGHT FOR THE INNOCENT WHO ARE EXPLOITED AND MURDERED BY TYRANTS.

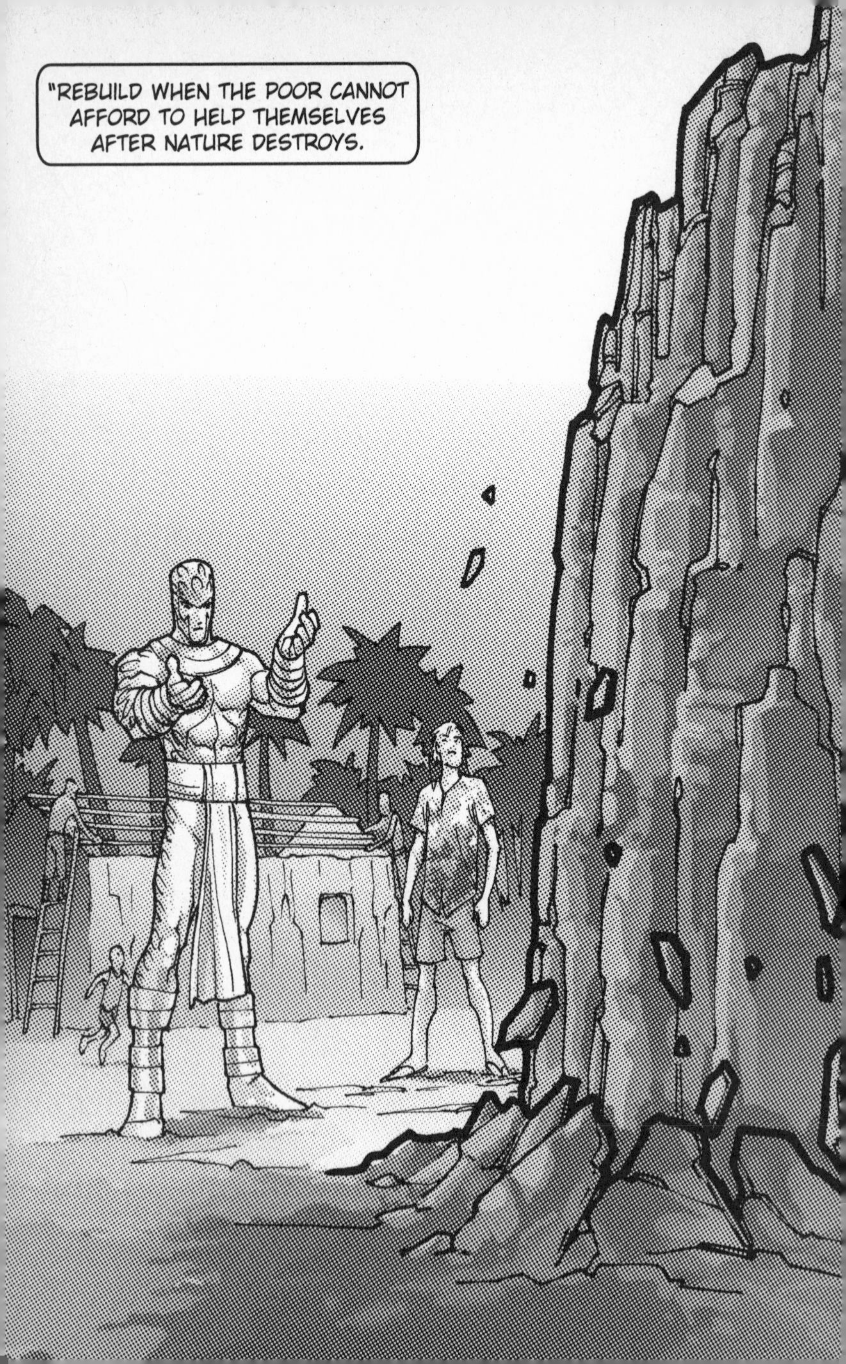
"REBUILD WHEN THE POOR CANNOT AFFORD TO HELP THEMSELVES AFTER NATURE DESTROYS.

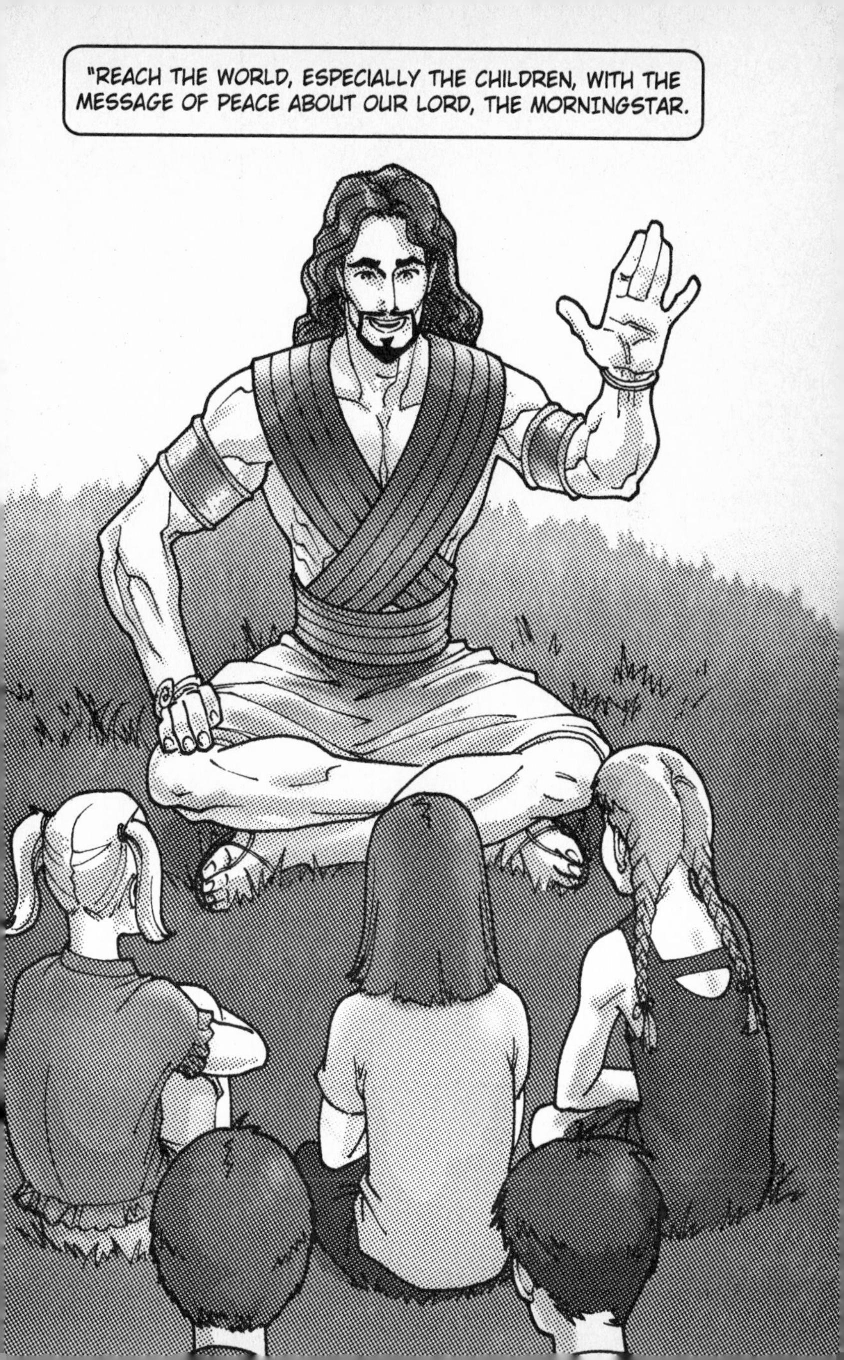
"REACH THE WORLD, ESPECIALLY THE CHILDREN, WITH THE MESSAGE OF PEACE ABOUT OUR LORD, THE MORNINGSTAR.

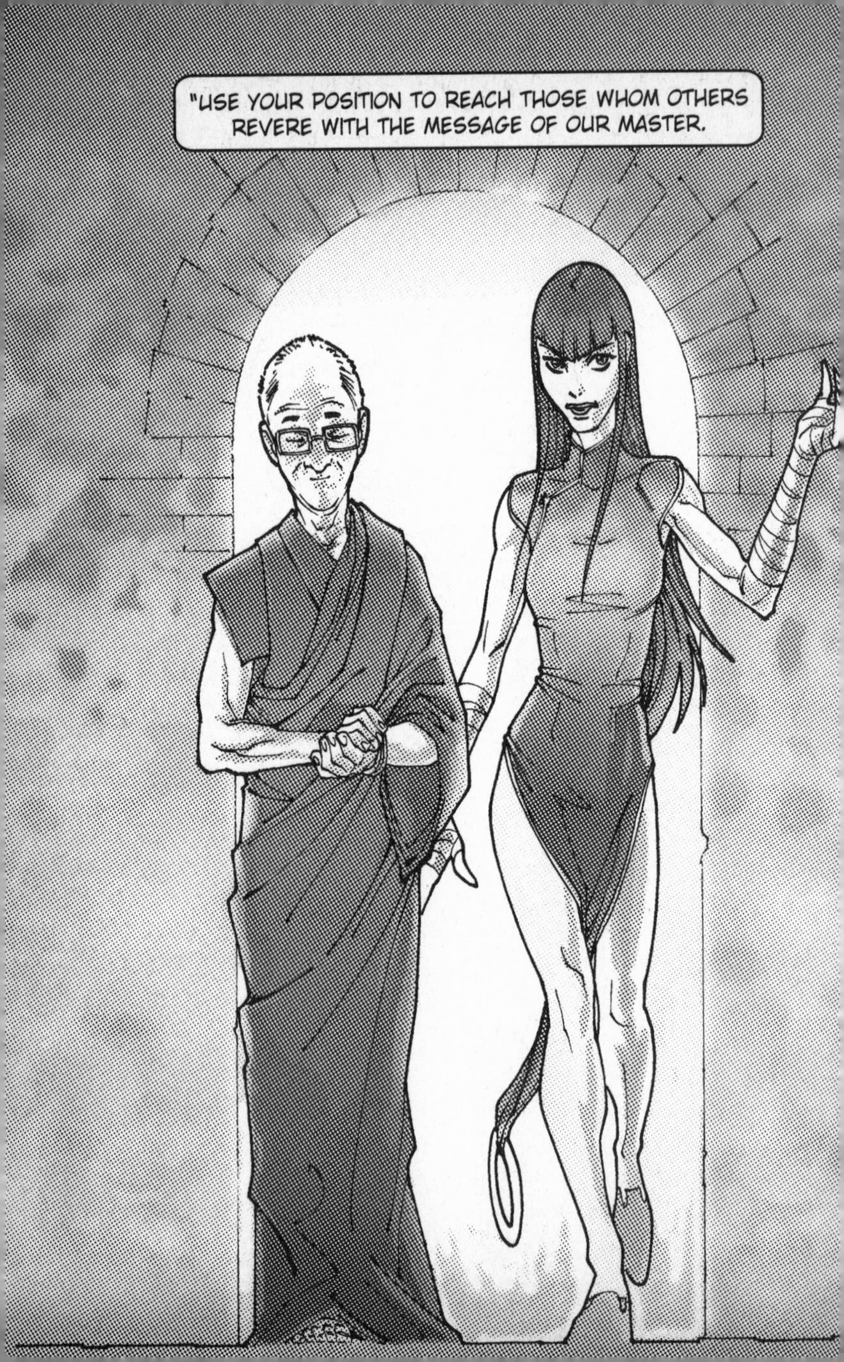
"USE YOUR POSITION TO REACH THOSE WHOM OTHERS REVERE WITH THE MESSAGE OF OUR MASTER.

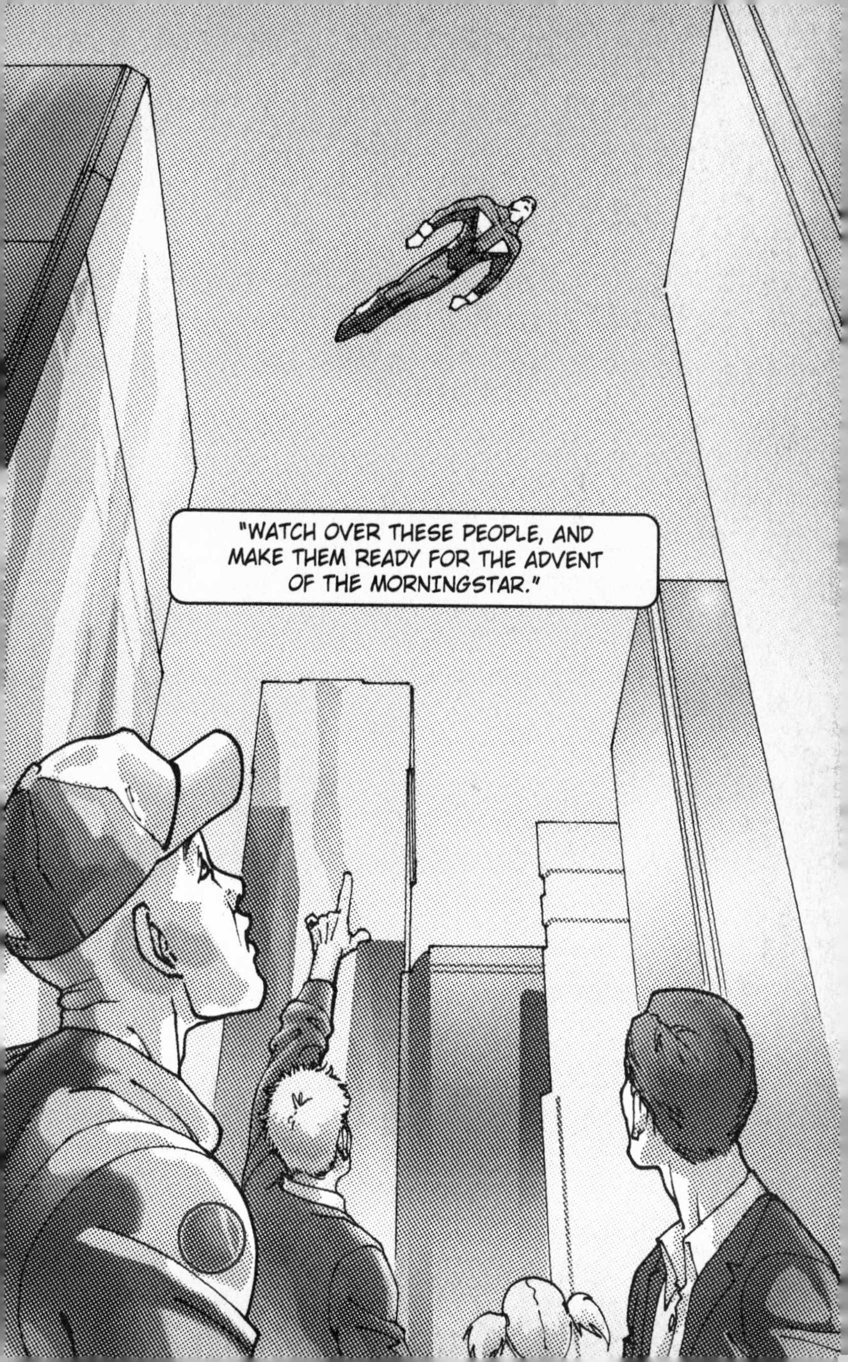
"WATCH OVER THESE PEOPLE, AND MAKE THEM READY FOR THE ADVENT OF THE MORNINGSTAR."

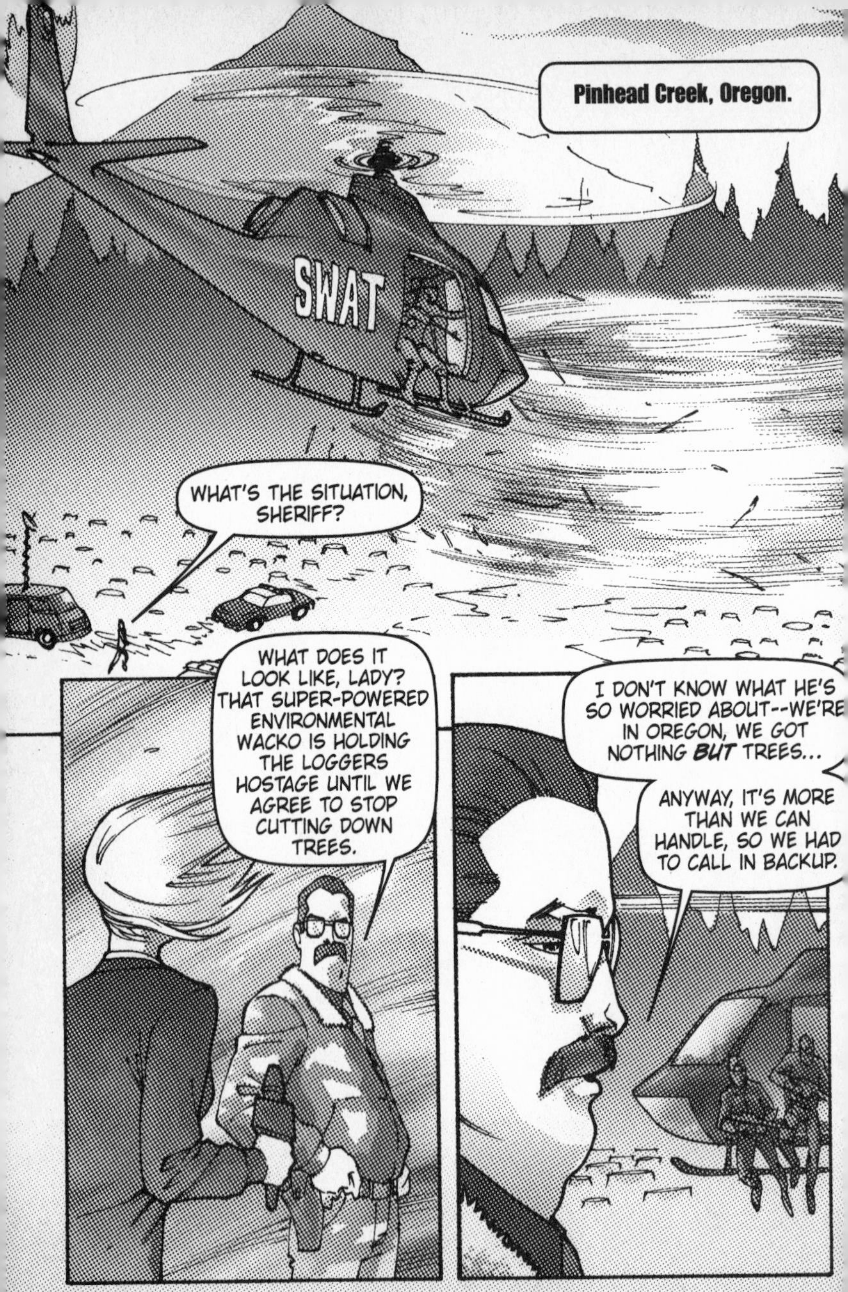
Pinhead Creek, Oregon.
SWAT
WHAT'S THE SITUATION, SHERIFF?
WHAT DOES IT LOOK LIKE, LADY? THAT SUPER-POWERED ENVIRONMENTAL WACKO IS HOLDING THE LOGGERS HOSTAGE UNTIL WE AGREE TO STOP CUTTING DOWN TREES.
I DON'T KNOW WHAT HE'S SO WORRIED ABOUT--WE'RE IN OREGON, WE GOT NOTHING *BUT* TREES...
ANYWAY, IT'S MORE THAN WE CAN HANDLE, SO WE HAD TO CALL IN BACKUP.

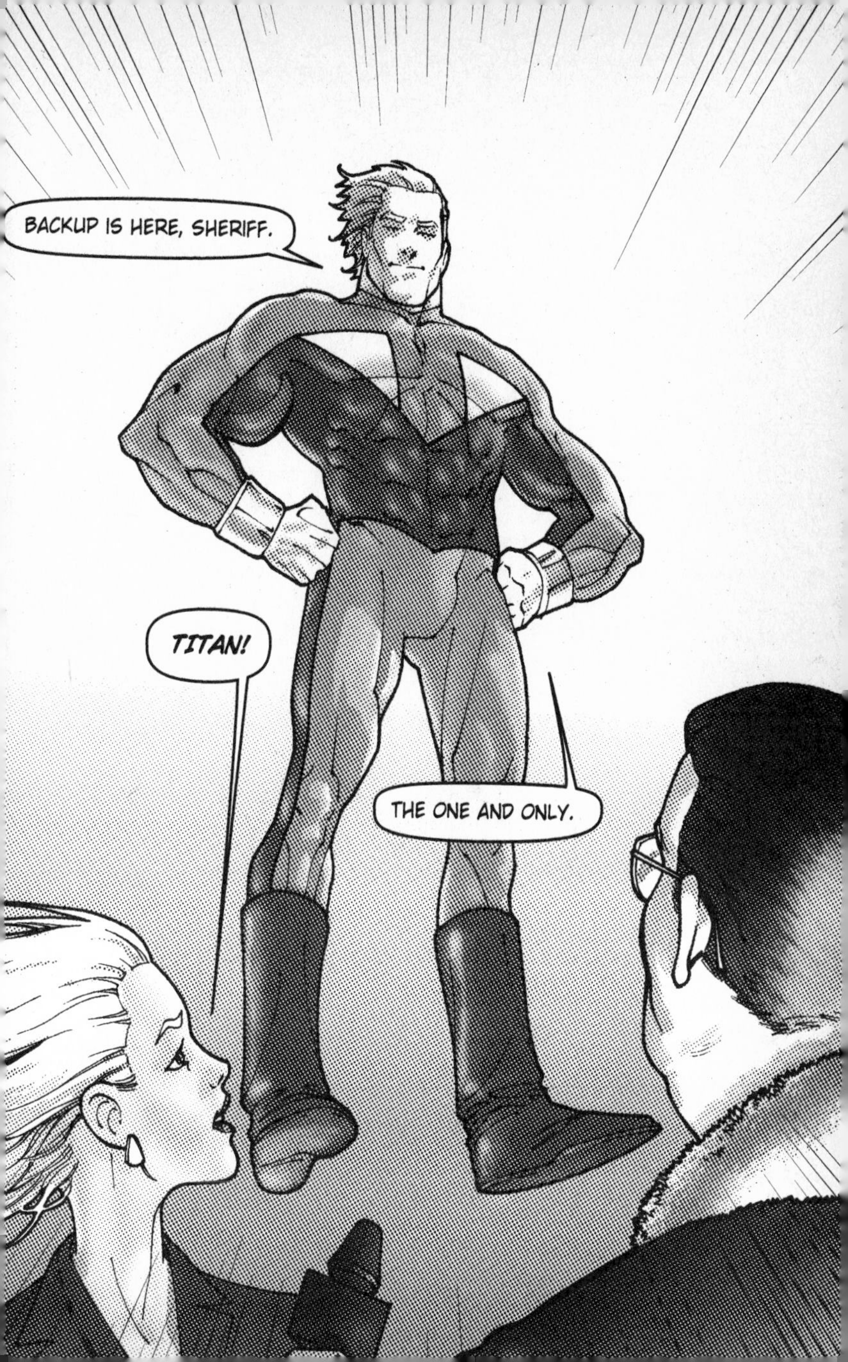
BACKUP IS HERE, SHERIFF.
TITAN!
THE ONE AND ONLY.

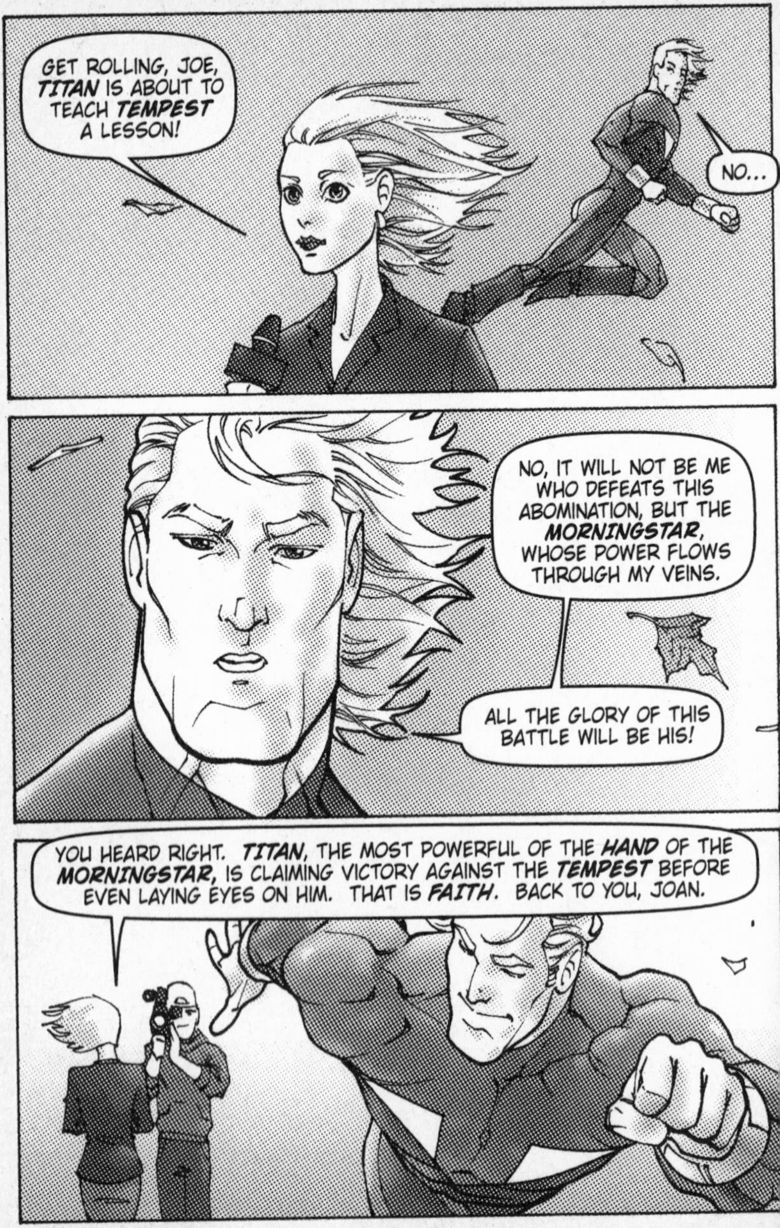
GET ROLLING, JOE, TITAN IS ABOUT TO TEACH TEMPEST A LESSON!
NO...
NO, IT WILL NOT BE ME WHO DEFEATS THIS ABOMINATION, BUT THE MORNINGSTAR, WHOSE POWER FLOWS THROUGH MY VEINS.
ALL THE GLORY OF THIS BATTLE WILL BE HIS!
YOU HEARD RIGHT. TITAN, THE MOST POWERFUL OF THE HAND OF THE MORNINGSTAR, IS CLAIMING VICTORY AGAINST THE TEMPEST BEFORE EVEN LAYING EYES ON HIM. THAT IS FAITH. BACK TO YOU, JOAN.

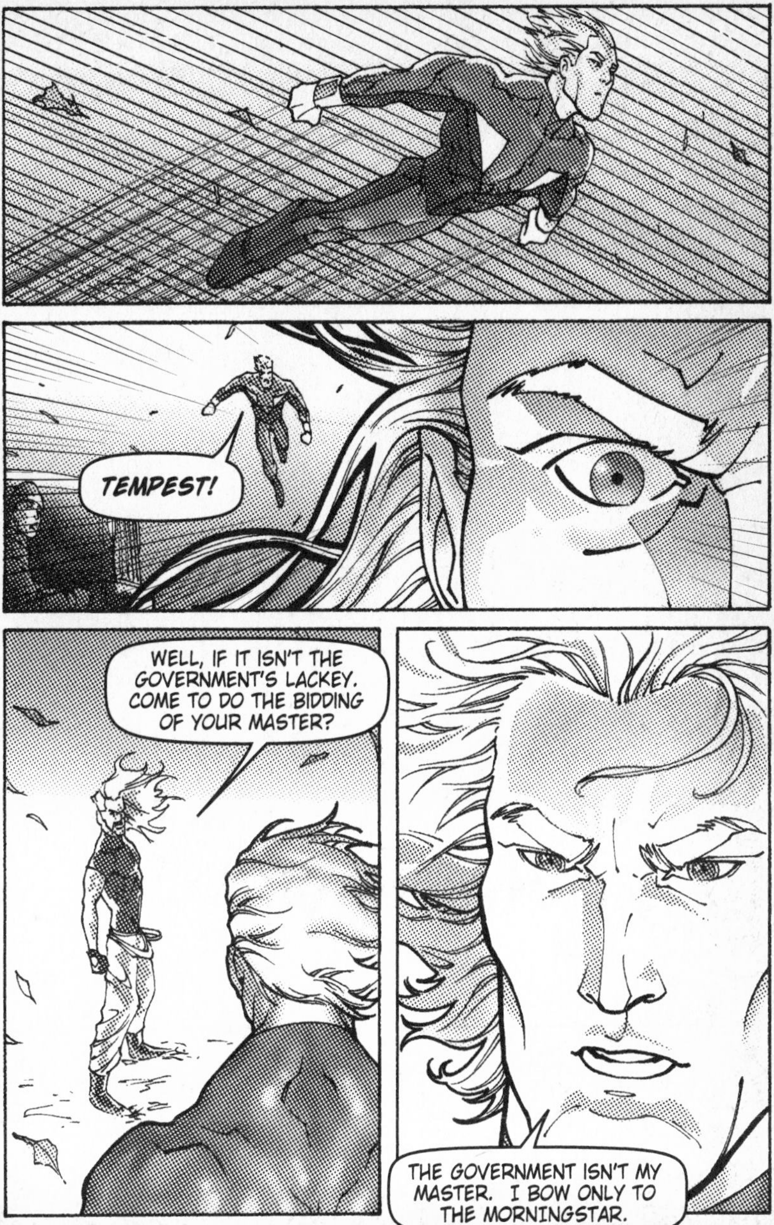
TEMPEST!
WELL, IF IT ISN'T THE GOVERNMENT'S LACKEY. COME TO DO THE BIDDING OF YOUR MASTER?
THE GOVERNMENT ISN'T MY MASTER. I BOW ONLY TO THE MORNINGSTAR.

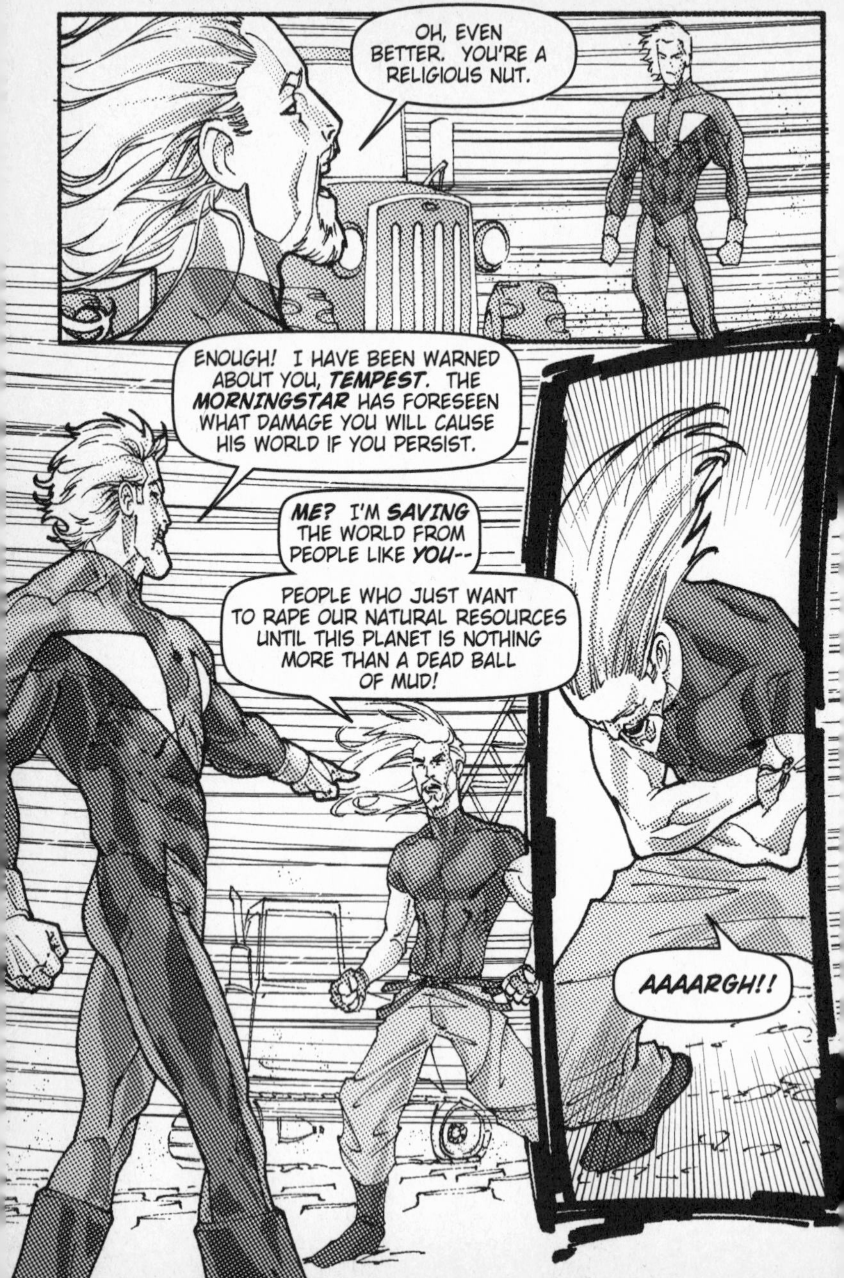
OH, EVEN BETTER. YOU'RE A RELIGIOUS NUT.
ENOUGH! I HAVE BEEN WARNED ABOUT YOU, *TEMPEST*. THE *MORNINGSTAR* HAS FORESEEN WHAT DAMAGE YOU WILL CAUSE HIS WORLD IF YOU PERSIST.
ME? I'M *SAVING* THE WORLD FROM PEOPLE LIKE *YOU*--
PEOPLE WHO JUST WANT TO RAPE OUR NATURAL RESOURCES UNTIL THIS PLANET IS NOTHING MORE THAN A DEAD BALL OF MUD!
AAAARGH!!

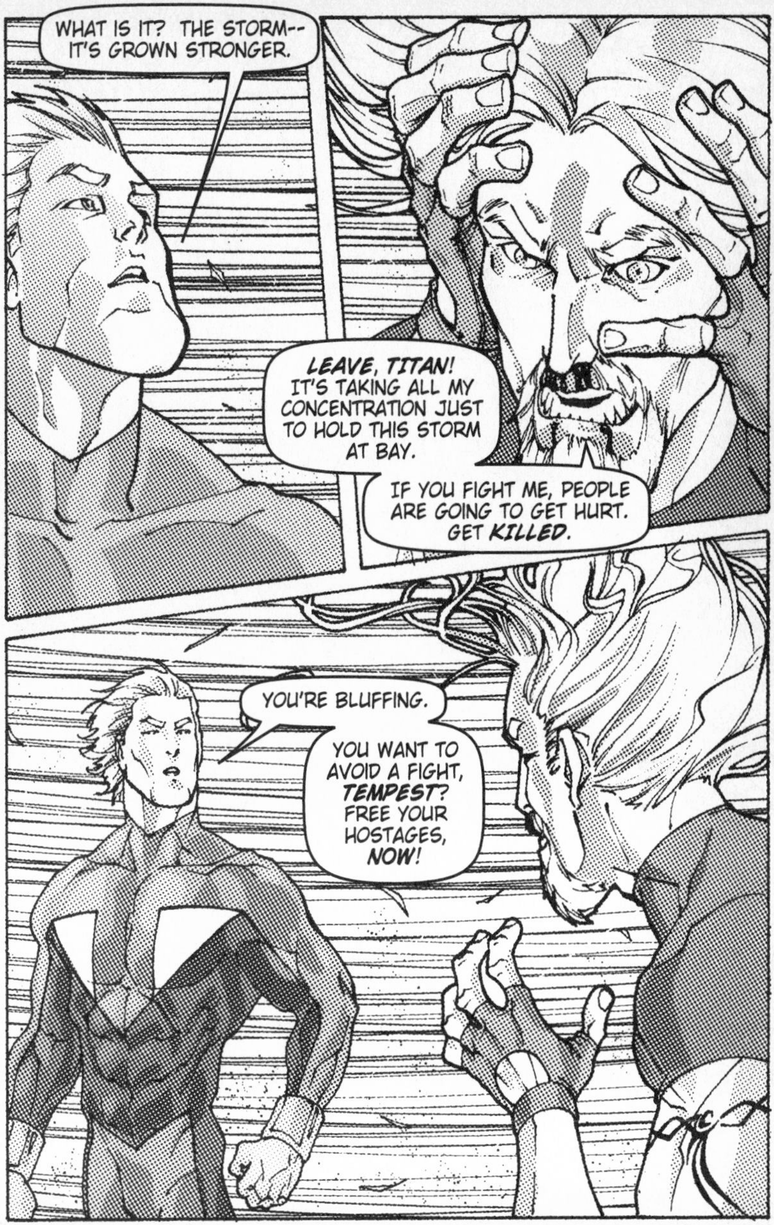

WHAT IS IT? THE STORM-- IT'S GROWN STRONGER.
LEAVE, TITAN! IT'S TAKING ALL MY CONCENTRATION JUST TO HOLD THIS STORM AT BAY.
IF YOU FIGHT ME, PEOPLE ARE GOING TO GET HURT. GET KILLED.
YOU'RE BLUFFING.
YOU WANT TO AVOID A FIGHT, TEMPEST? FREE YOUR HOSTAGES, NOW!

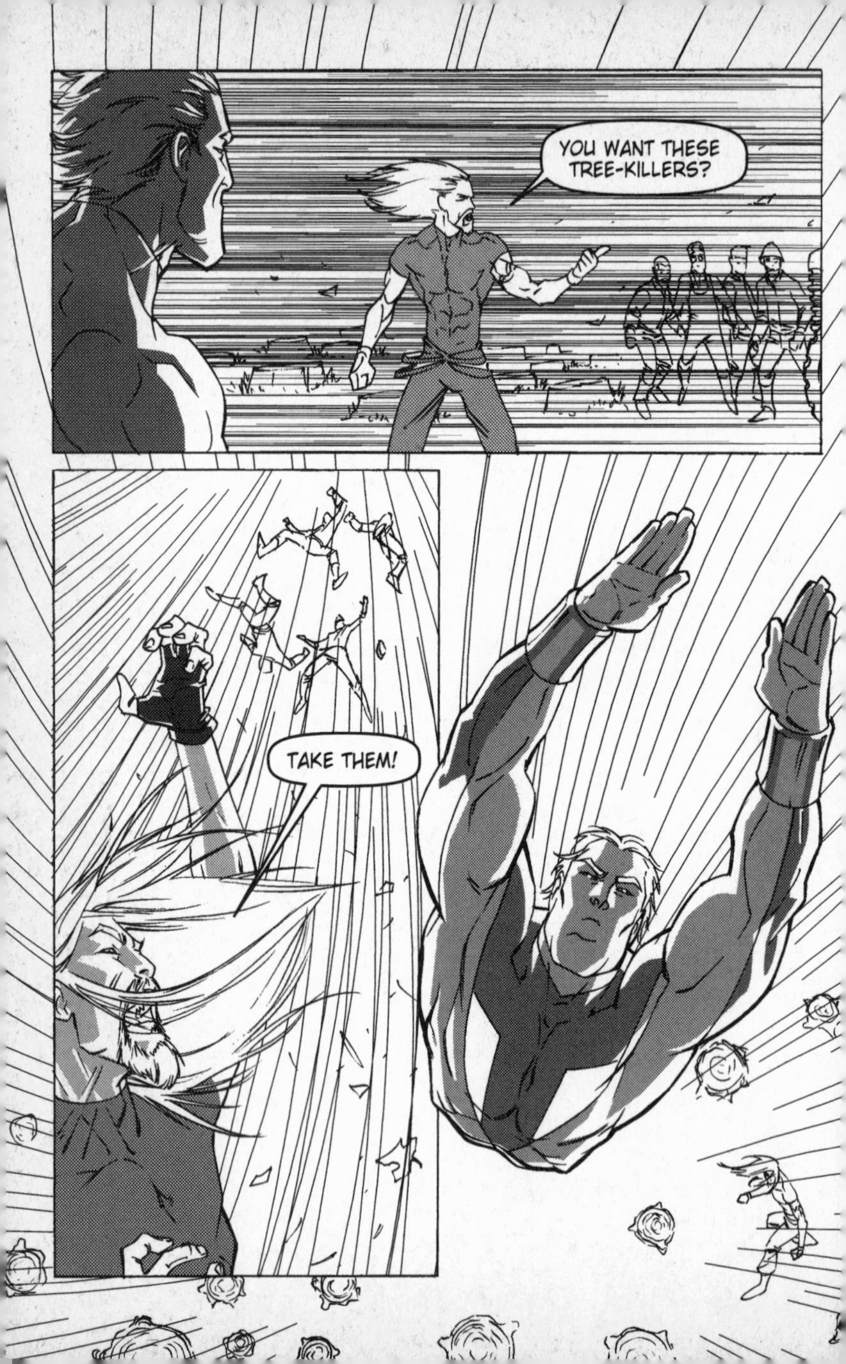
YOU WANT THESE TREE-KILLERS?
TAKE THEM!

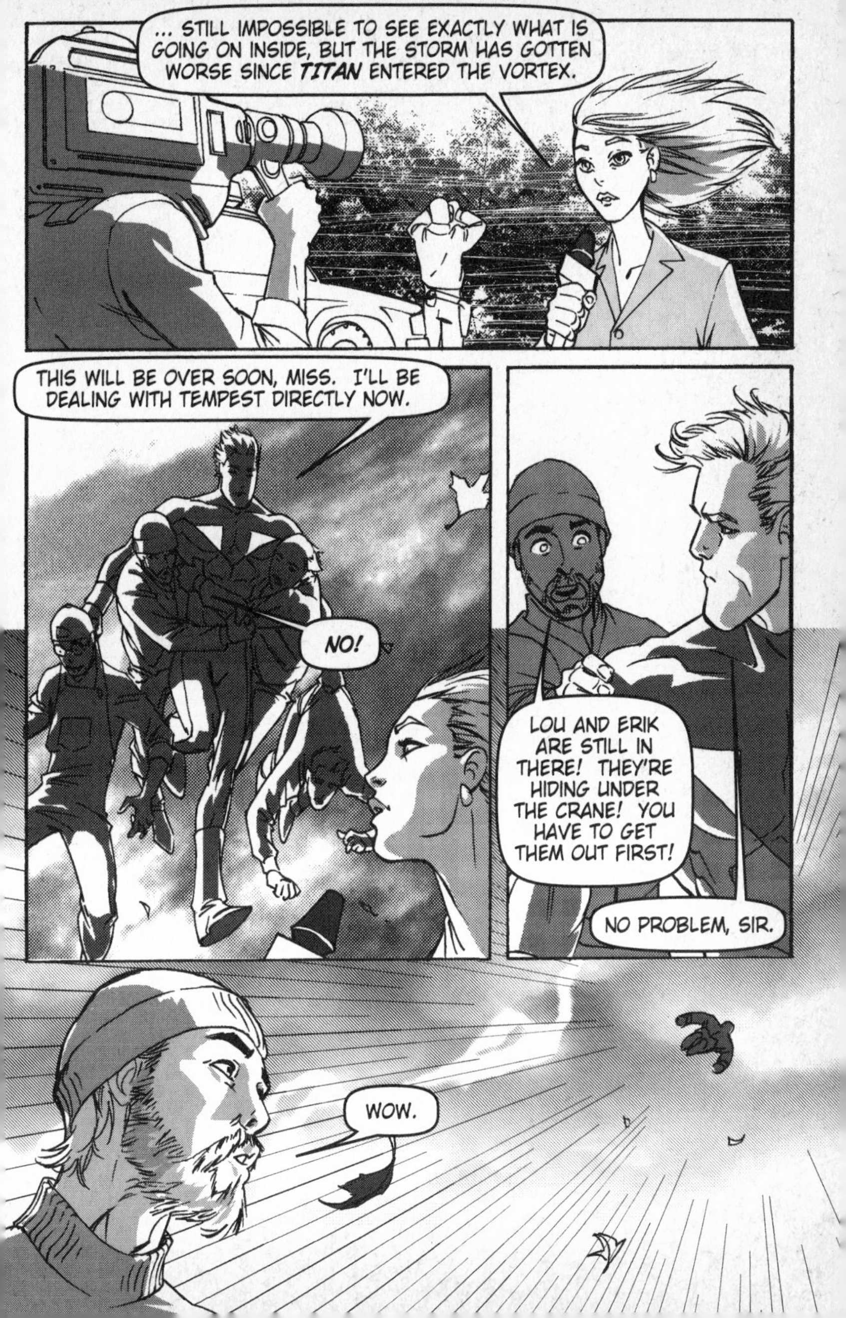
... STILL IMPOSSIBLE TO SEE EXACTLY WHAT IS GOING ON INSIDE, BUT THE STORM HAS GOTTEN WORSE SINCE *TITAN* ENTERED THE VORTEX.
THIS WILL BE OVER SOON, MISS. I'LL BE DEALING WITH TEMPEST DIRECTLY NOW.
NO!
LOU AND ERIK ARE STILL IN THERE! THEY'RE HIDING UNDER THE CRANE! YOU HAVE TO GET THEM OUT FIRST!
NO PROBLEM, SIR.
WOW.

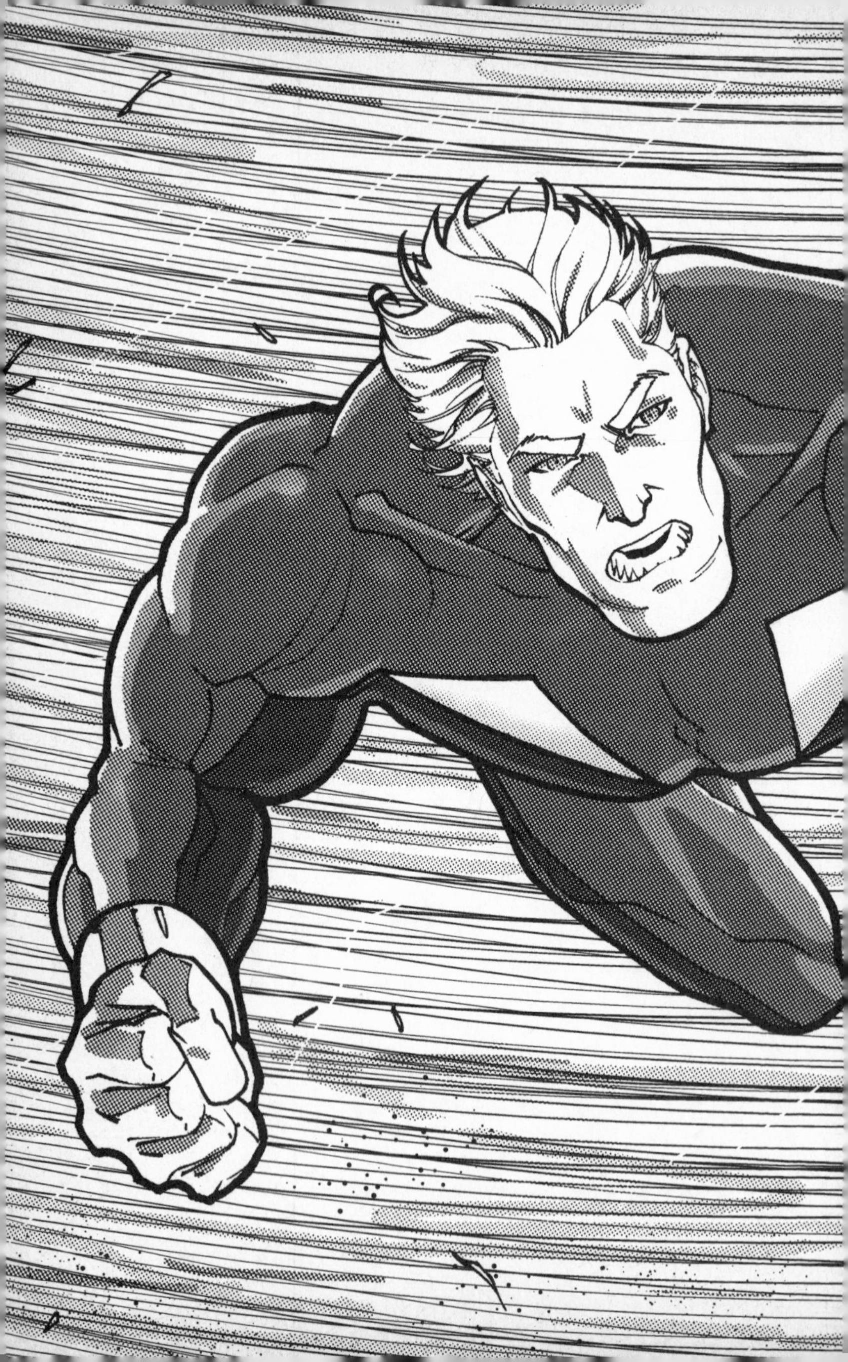

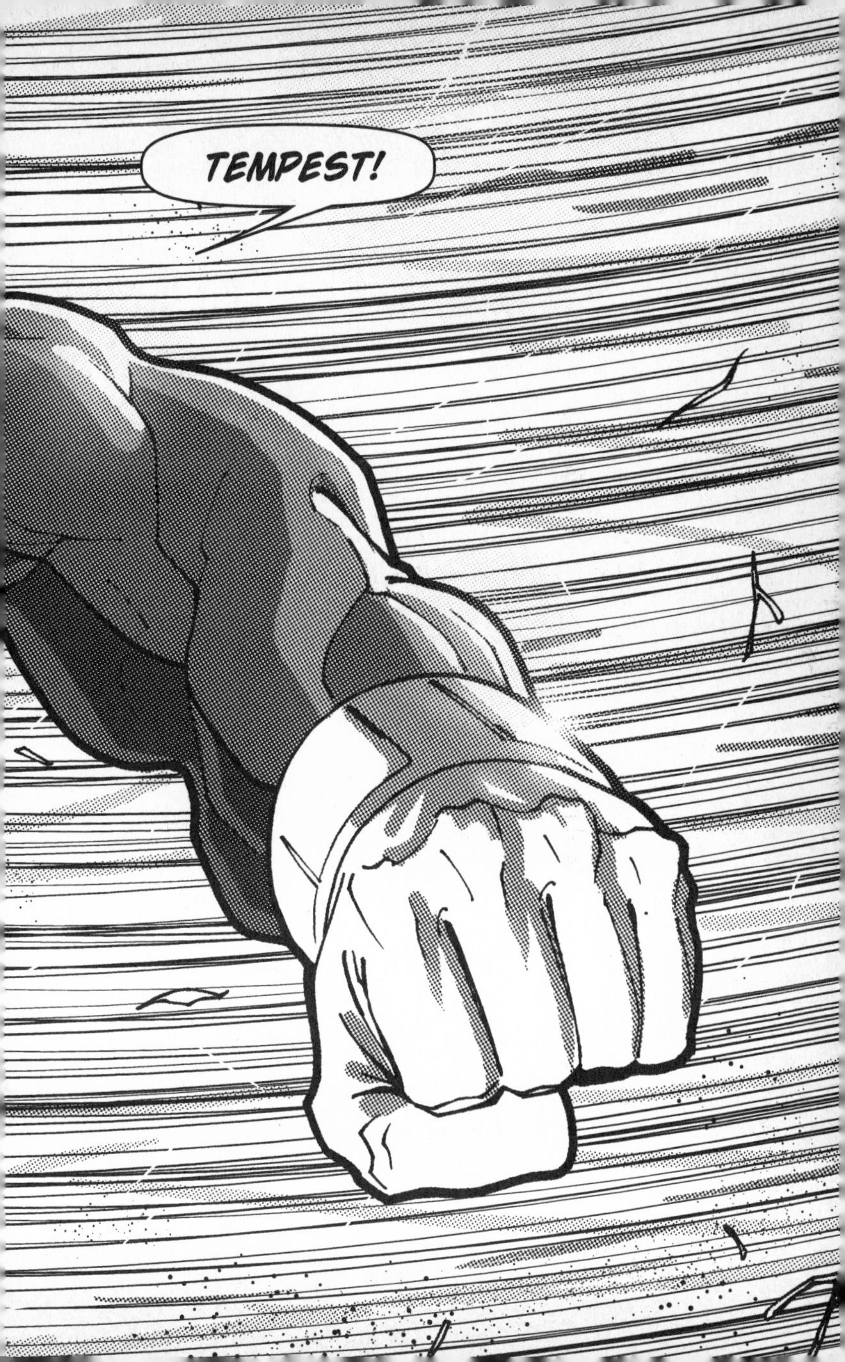
TEMPEST!

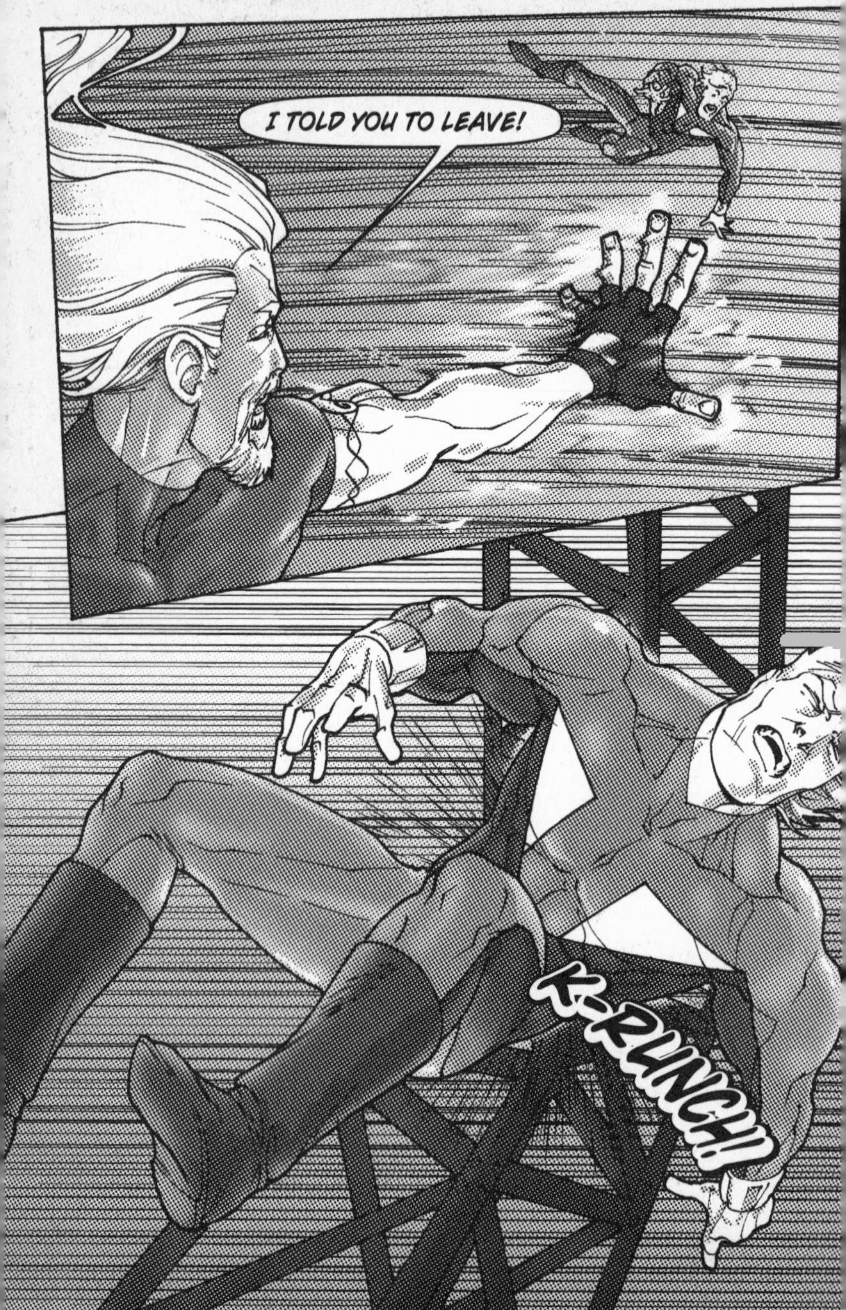
I TOLD YOU TO LEAVE!
K-RUNCH!

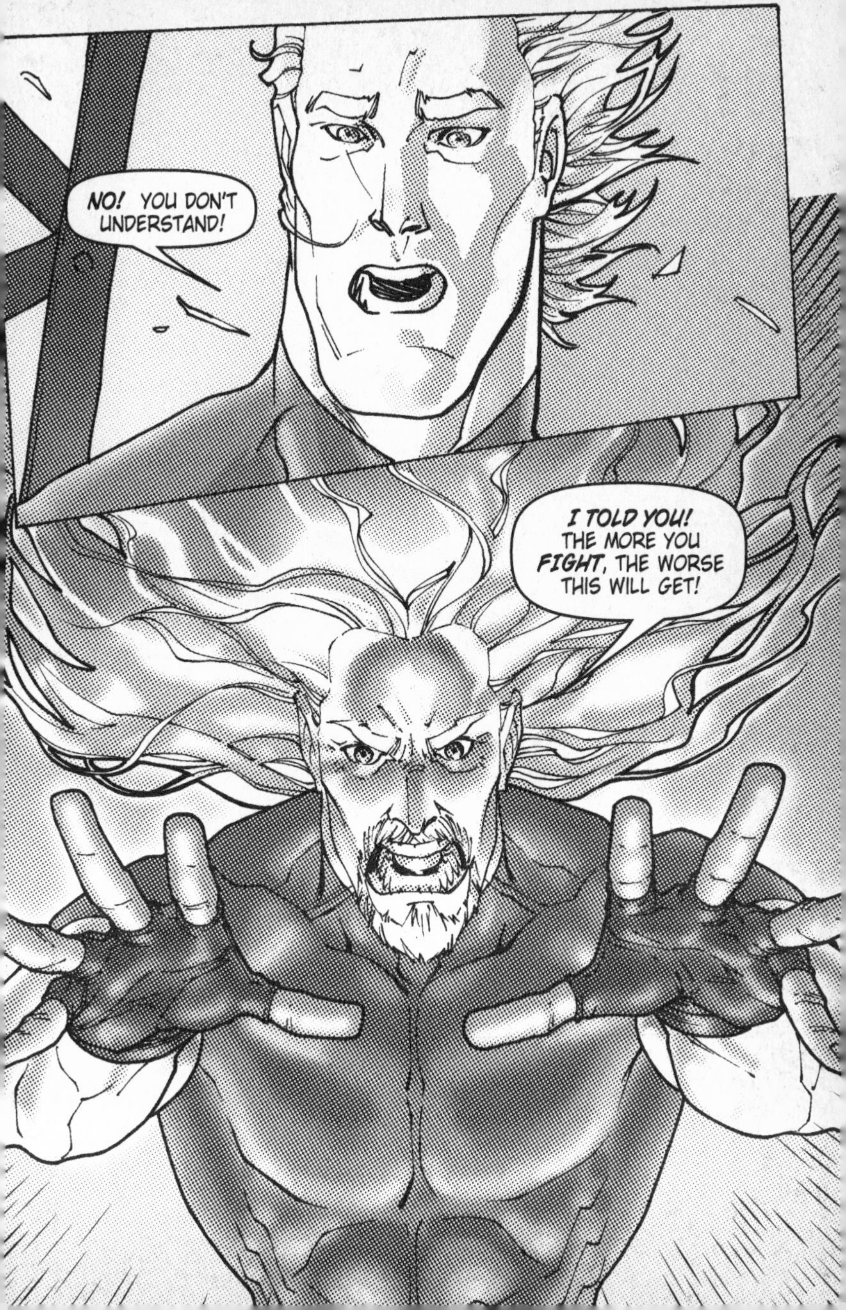
NO! YOU DON'T UNDERSTAND!
I TOLD YOU! THE MORE YOU FIGHT, THE WORSE THIS WILL GET!

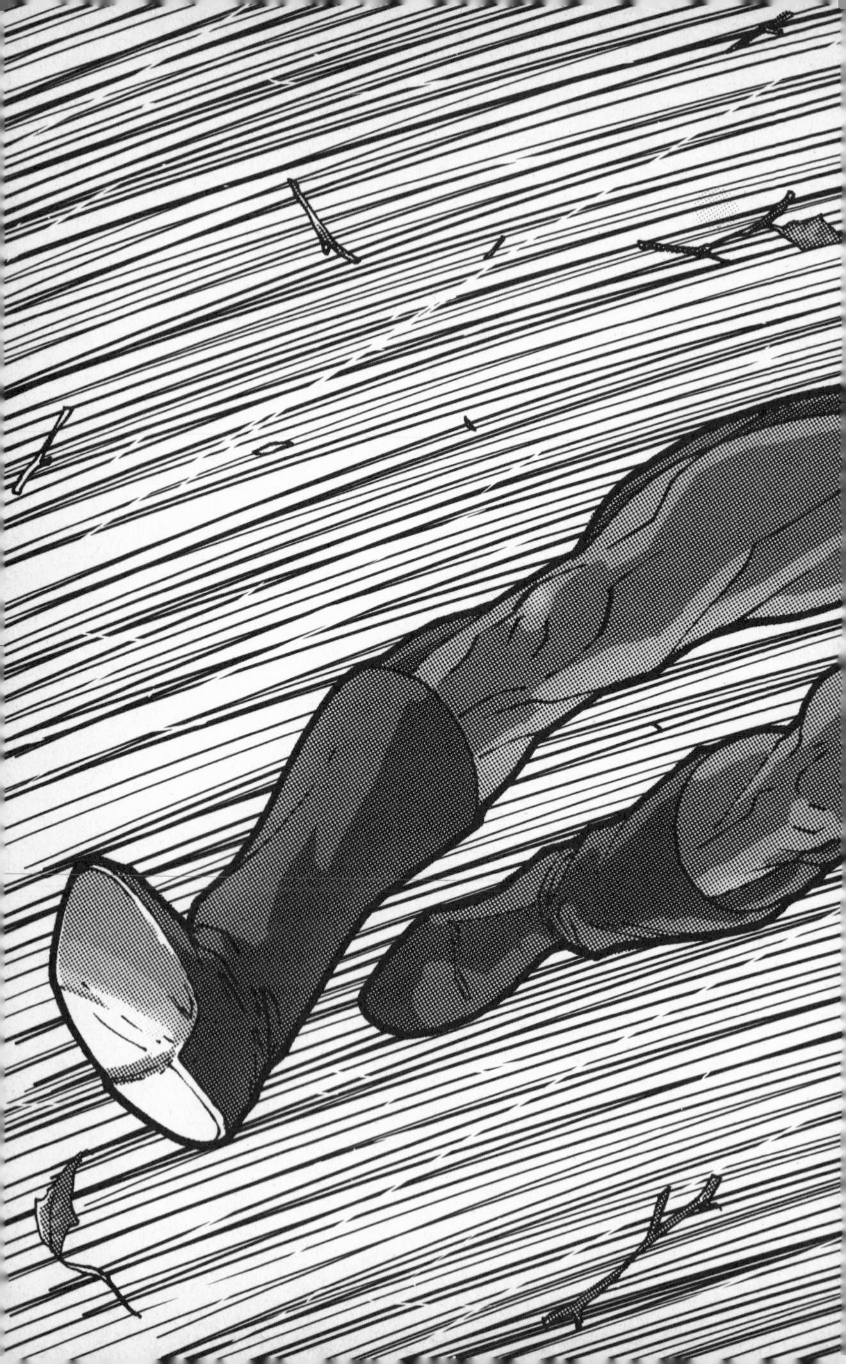

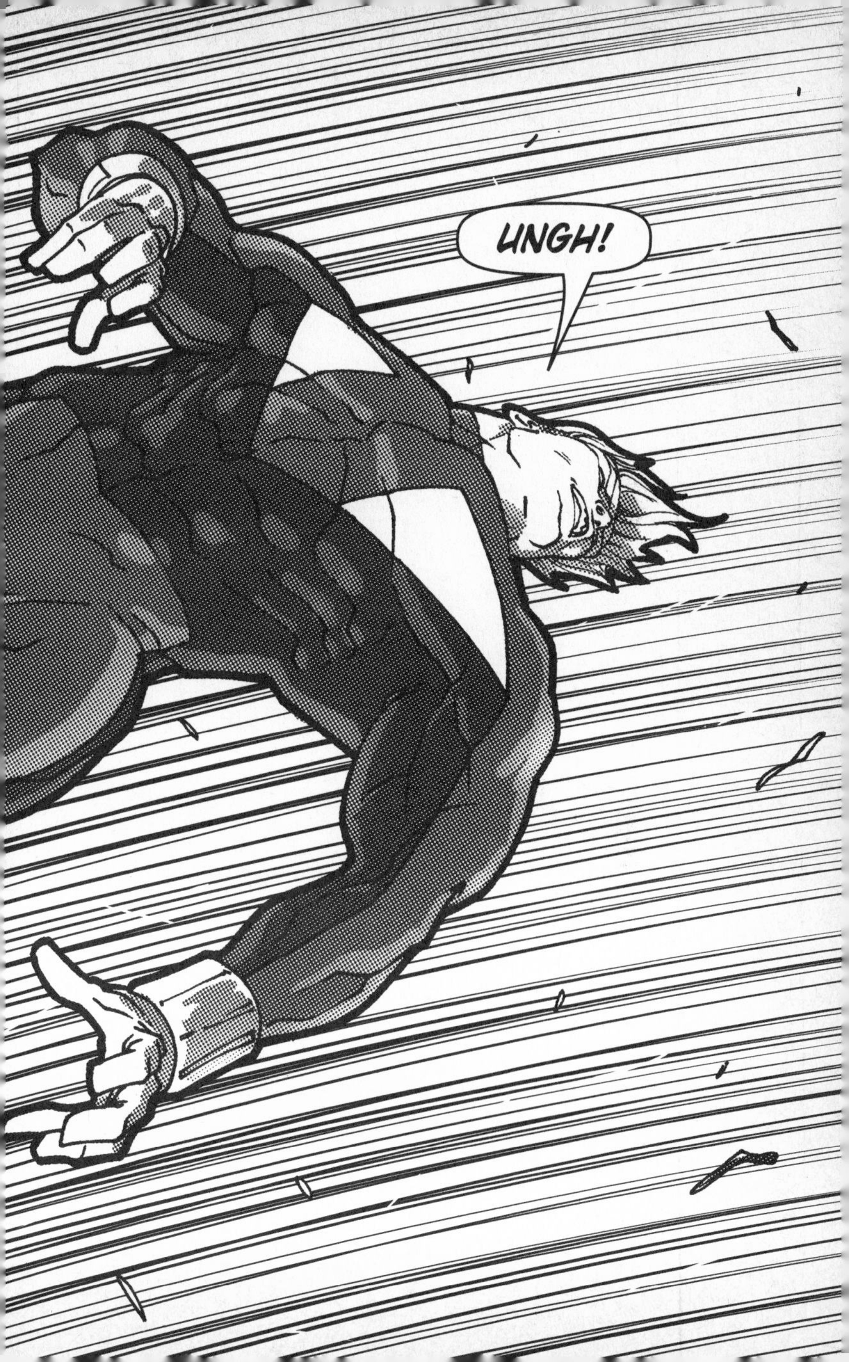
UNGH!

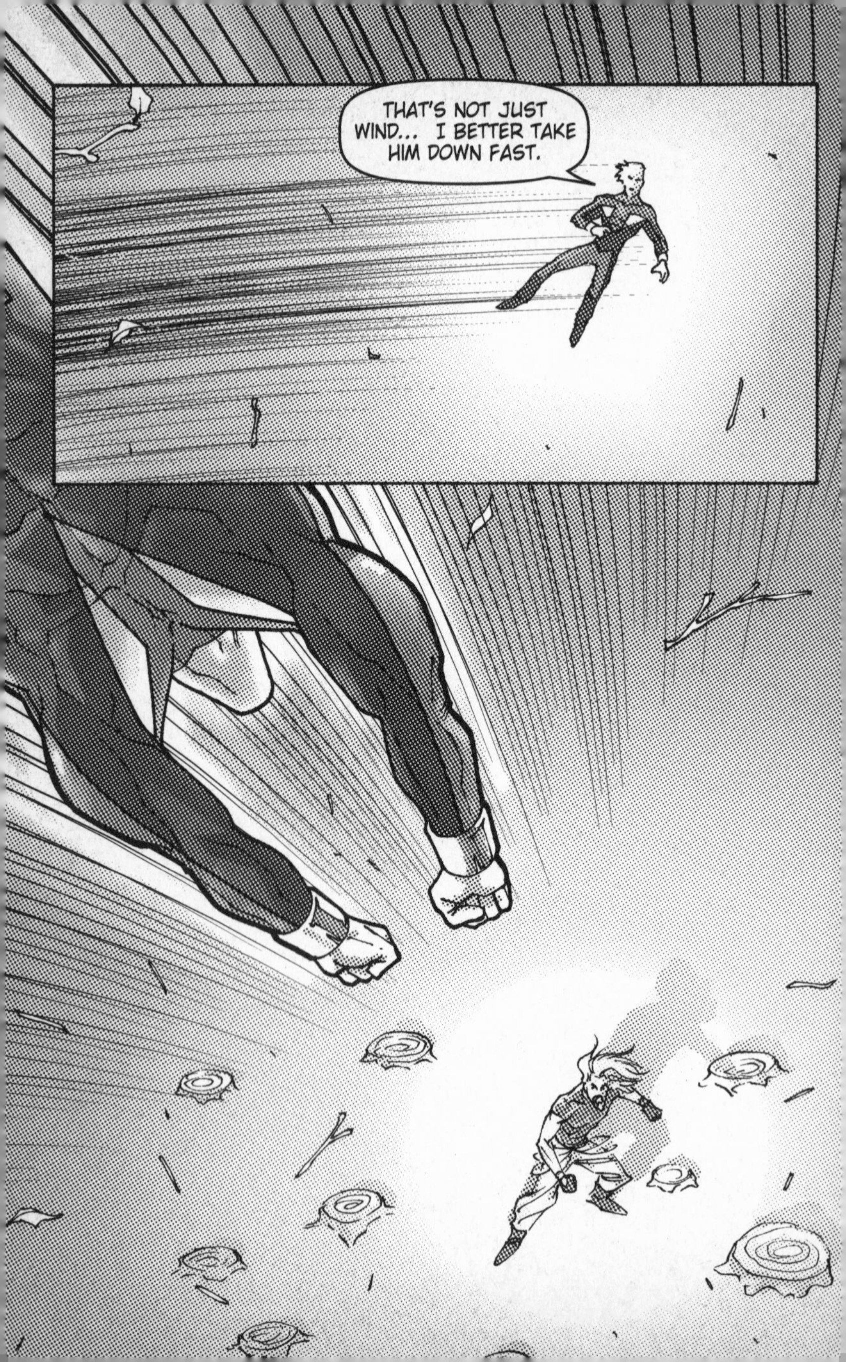
THAT'S NOT JUST WIND... I BETTER TAKE HIM DOWN FAST.

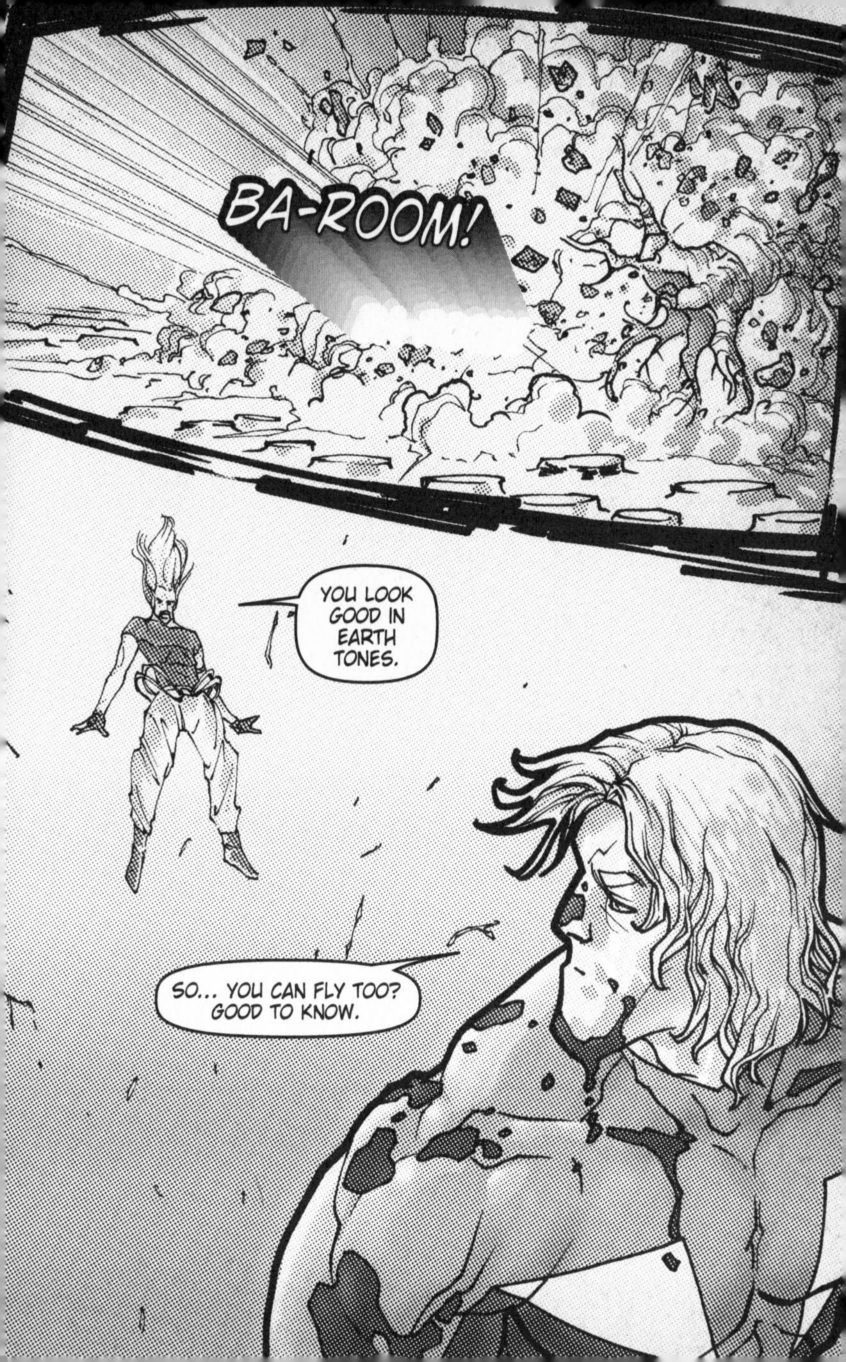
BA-ROOM!
YOU LOOK GOOD IN EARTH TONES.
SO... YOU CAN FLY TOO? GOOD TO KNOW.

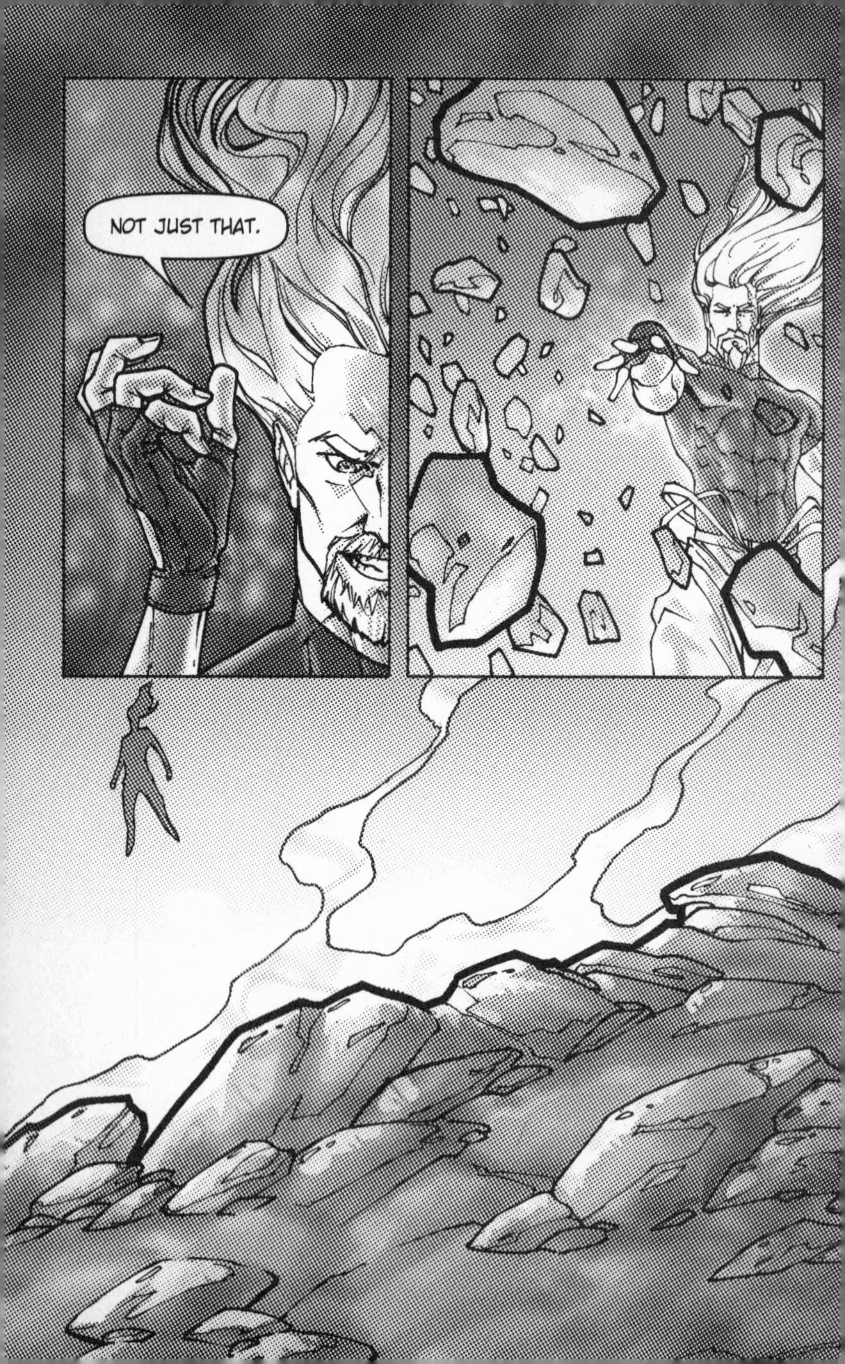
NOT JUST THAT.

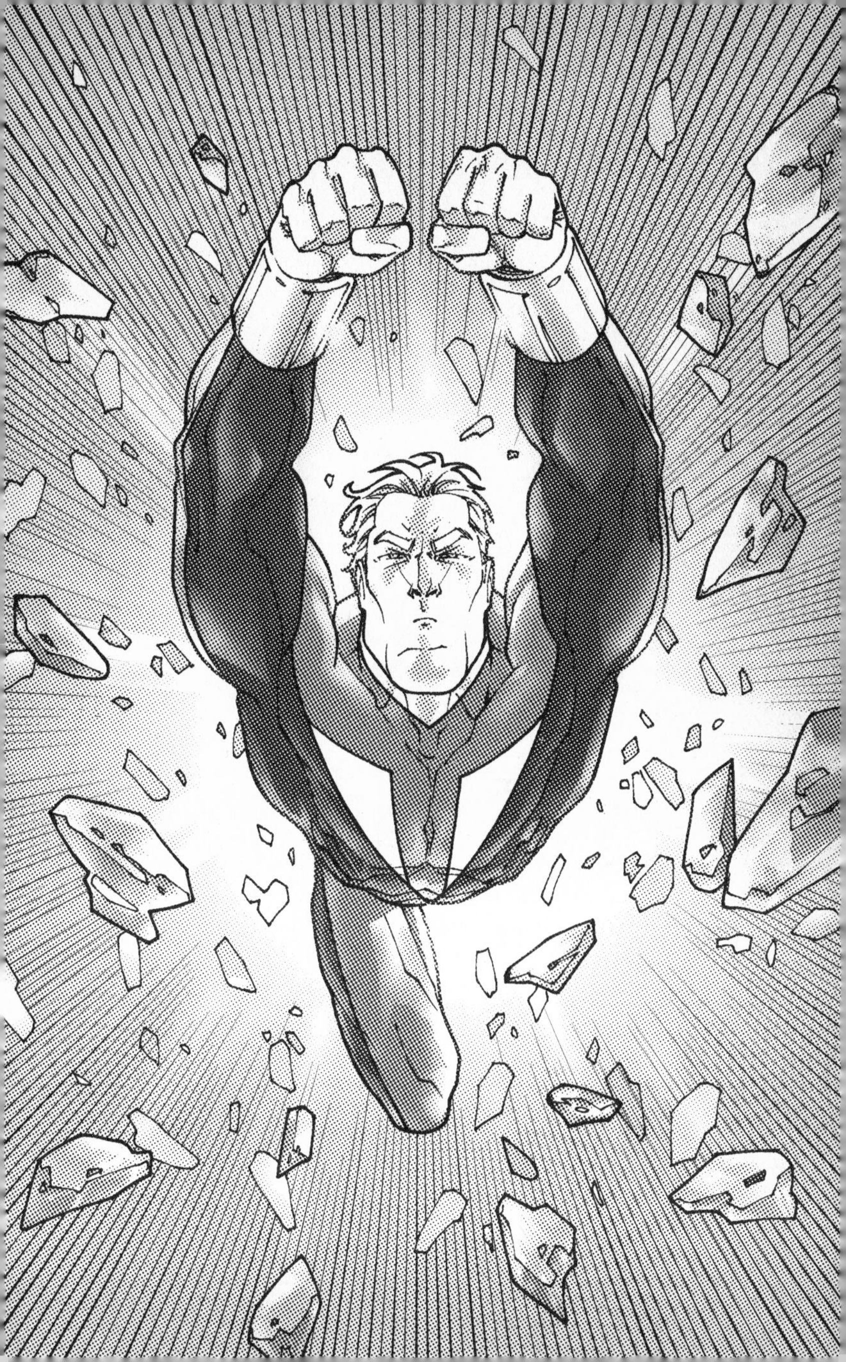

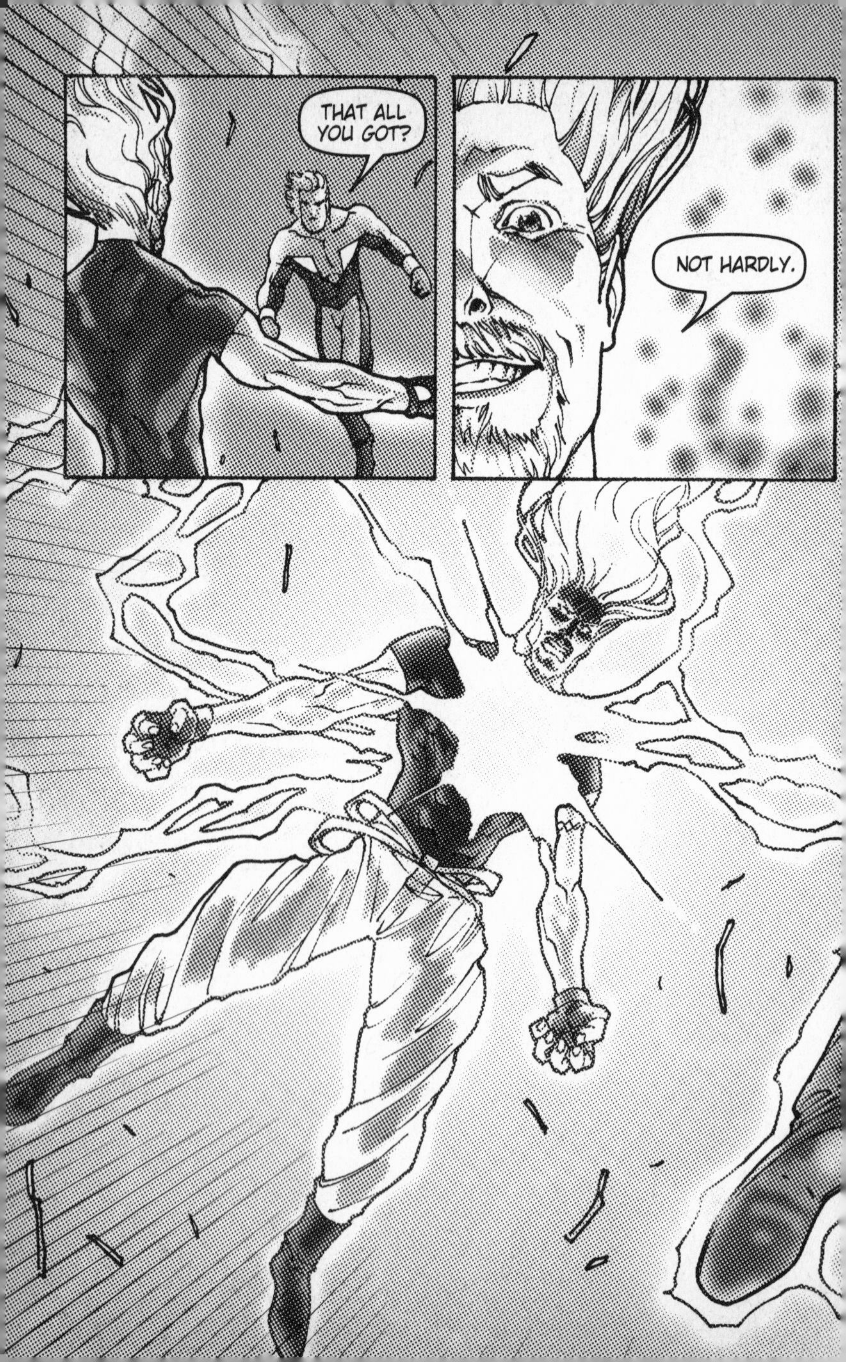
THAT ALL YOU GOT?
NOT HARDLY.

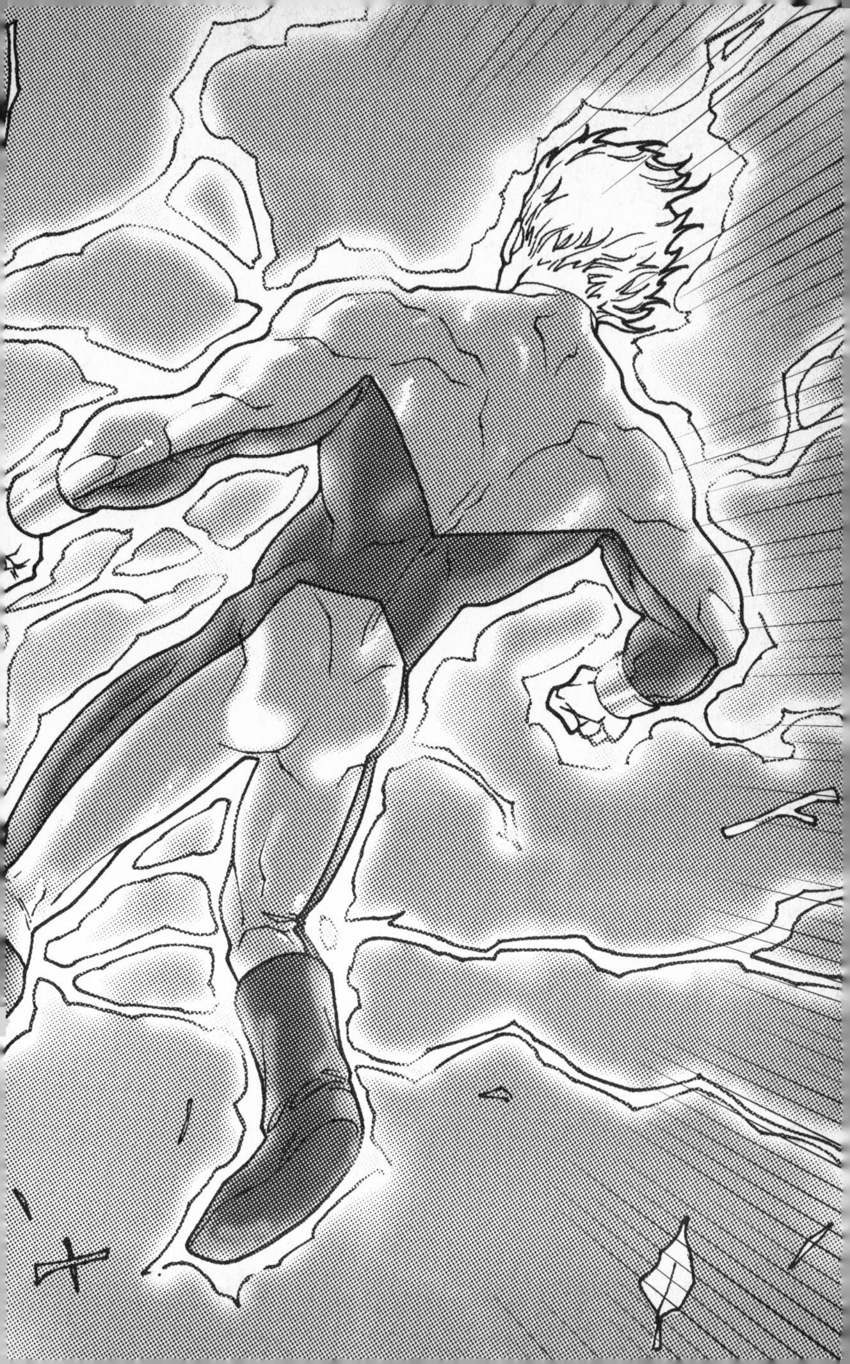

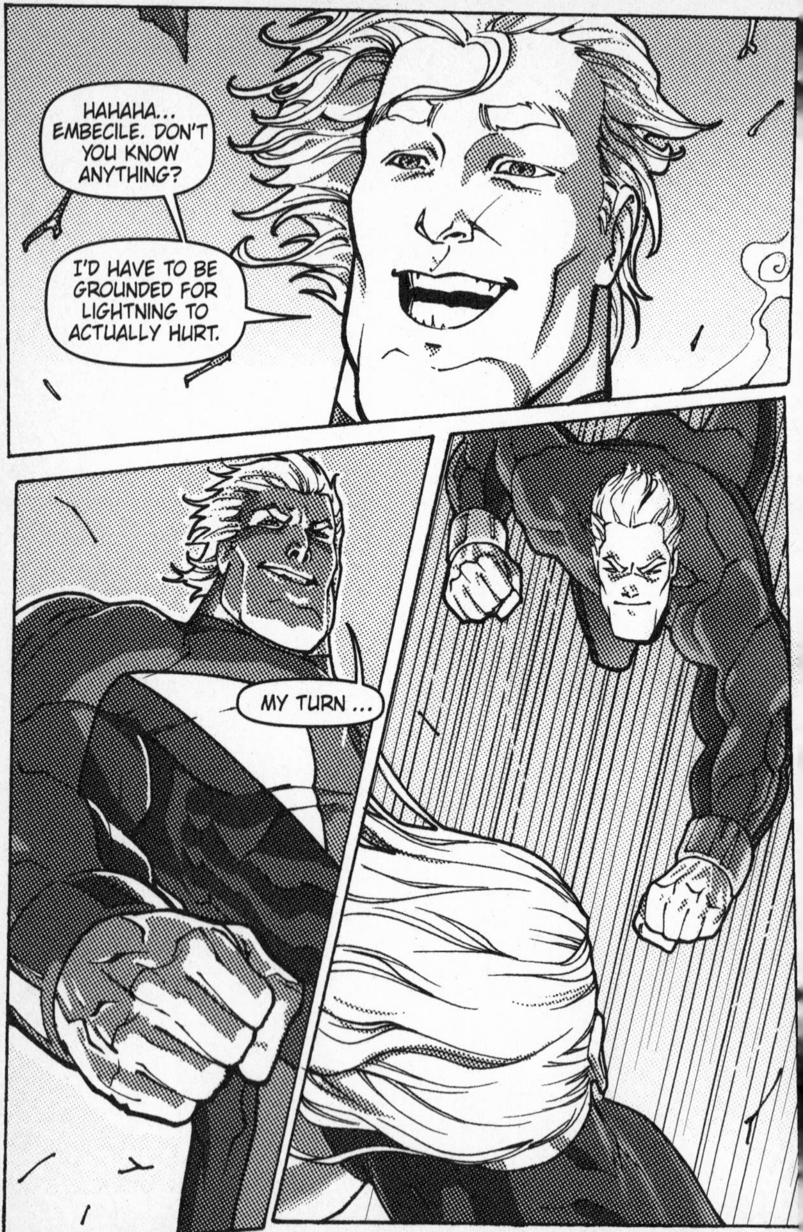
HAHAHA... EMBECILE. DON'T YOU KNOW ANYTHING?
I'D HAVE TO BE GROUNDED FOR LIGHTNING TO ACTUALLY HURT.
MY TURN ...

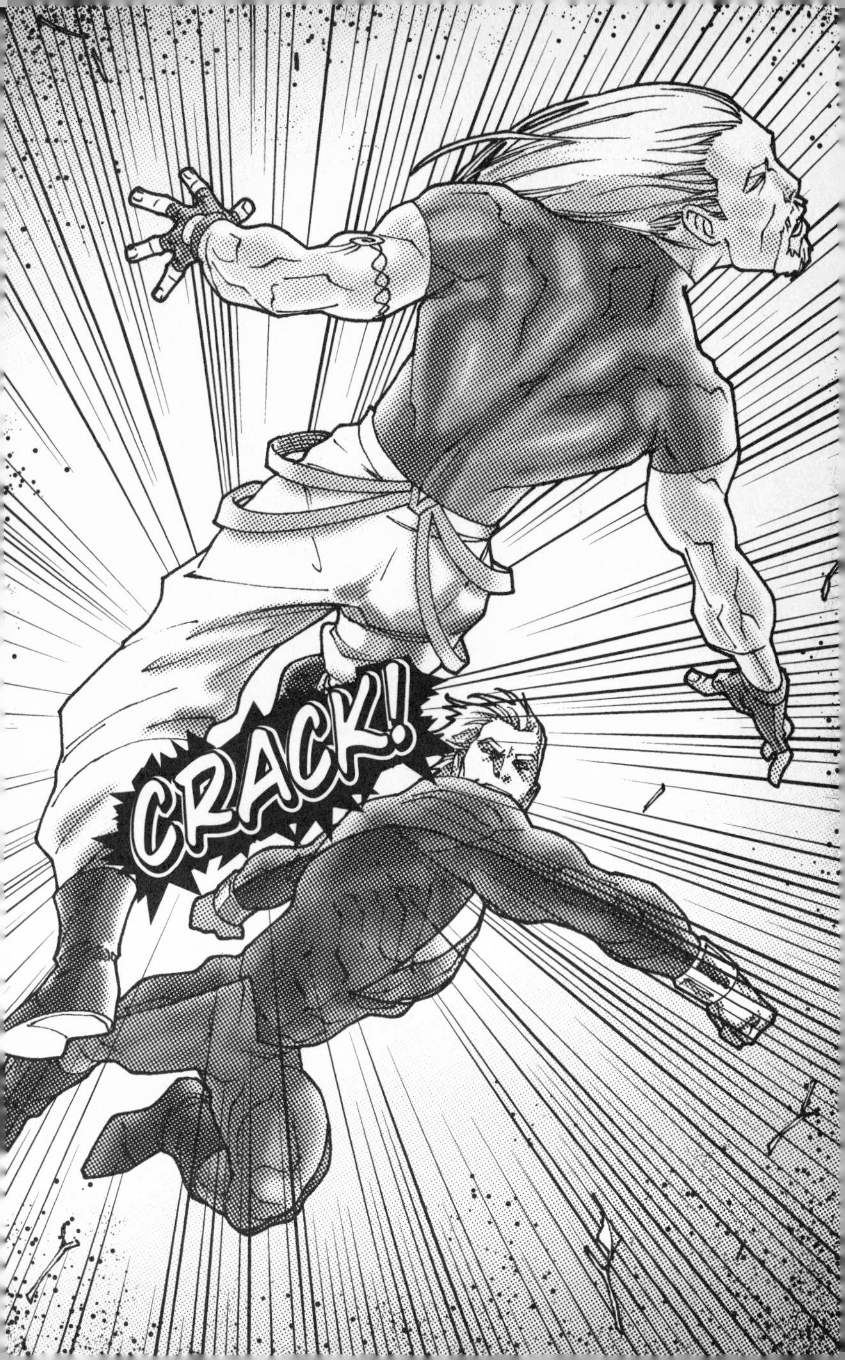
CRACK!

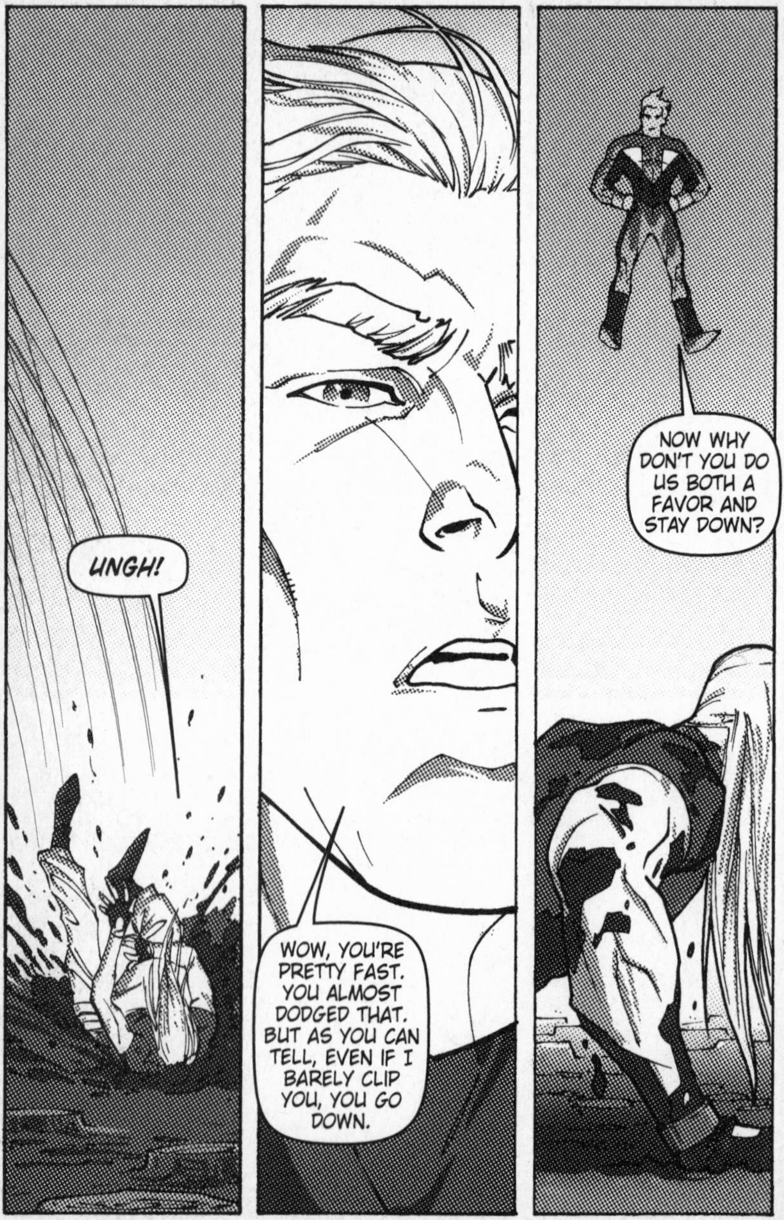
UNGH!
WOW, YOU'RE PRETTY FAST. YOU ALMOST DODGED THAT. BUT AS YOU CAN TELL, EVEN IF I BARELY CLIP YOU, YOU GO DOWN.
NOW WHY DON'T YOU DO US BOTH A FAVOR AND STAY DOWN?

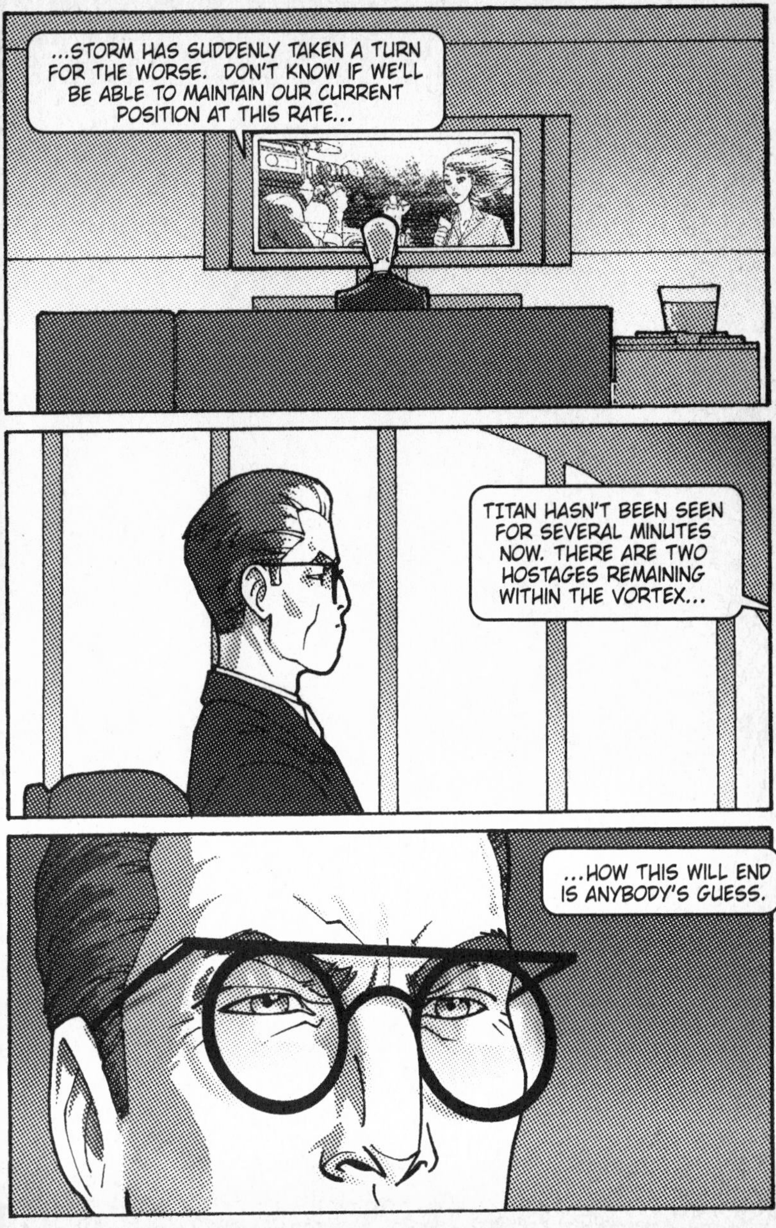
...STORM HAS SUDDENLY TAKEN A TURN FOR THE WORSE. DON'T KNOW IF WE'LL BE ABLE TO MAINTAIN OUR CURRENT POSITION AT THIS RATE...
TITAN HASN'T BEEN SEEN FOR SEVERAL MINUTES NOW. THERE ARE TWO HOSTAGES REMAINING WITHIN THE VORTEX...
...HOW THIS WILL END IS ANYBODY'S GUESS.

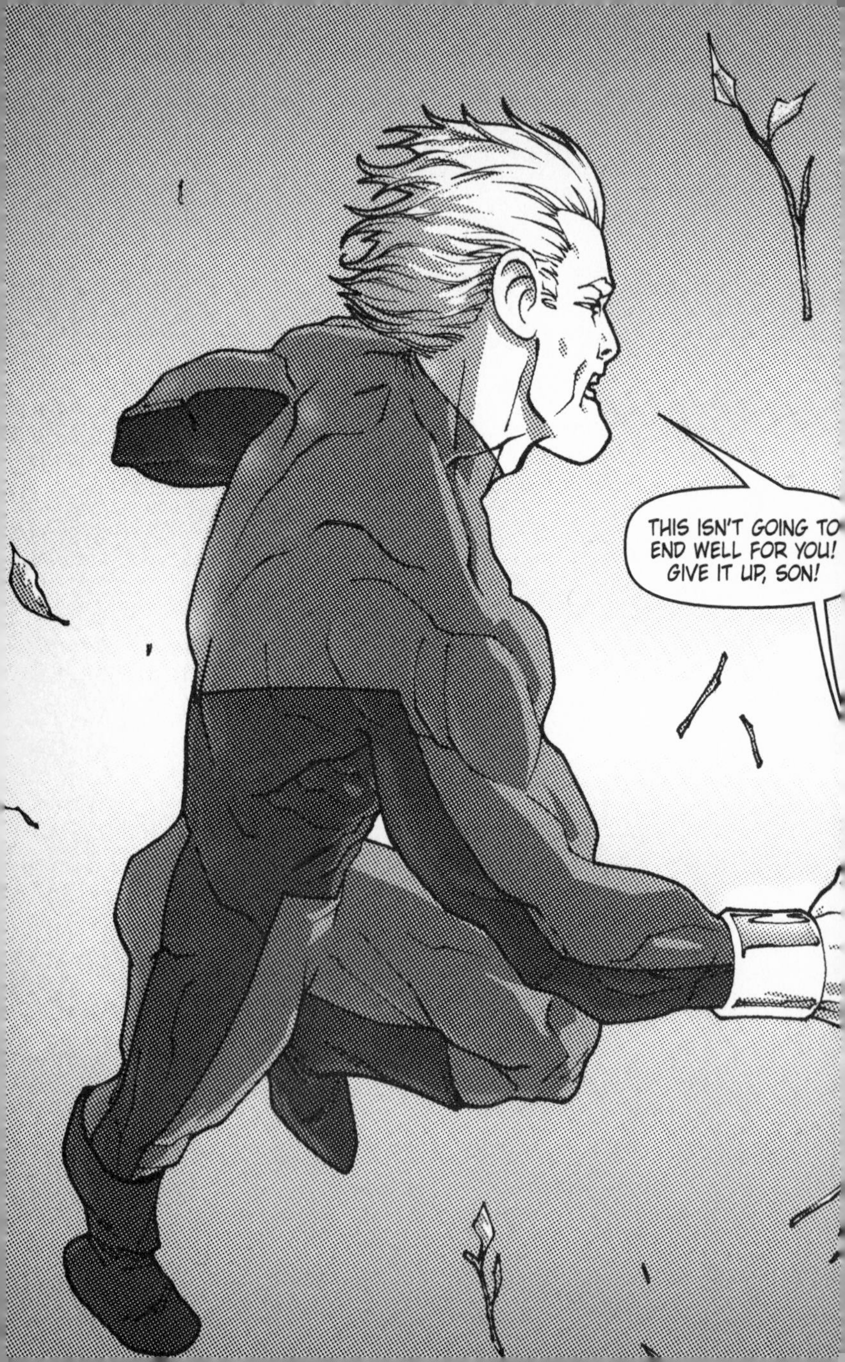
THIS ISN'T GOING TO END WELL FOR YOU! GIVE IT UP, SON!

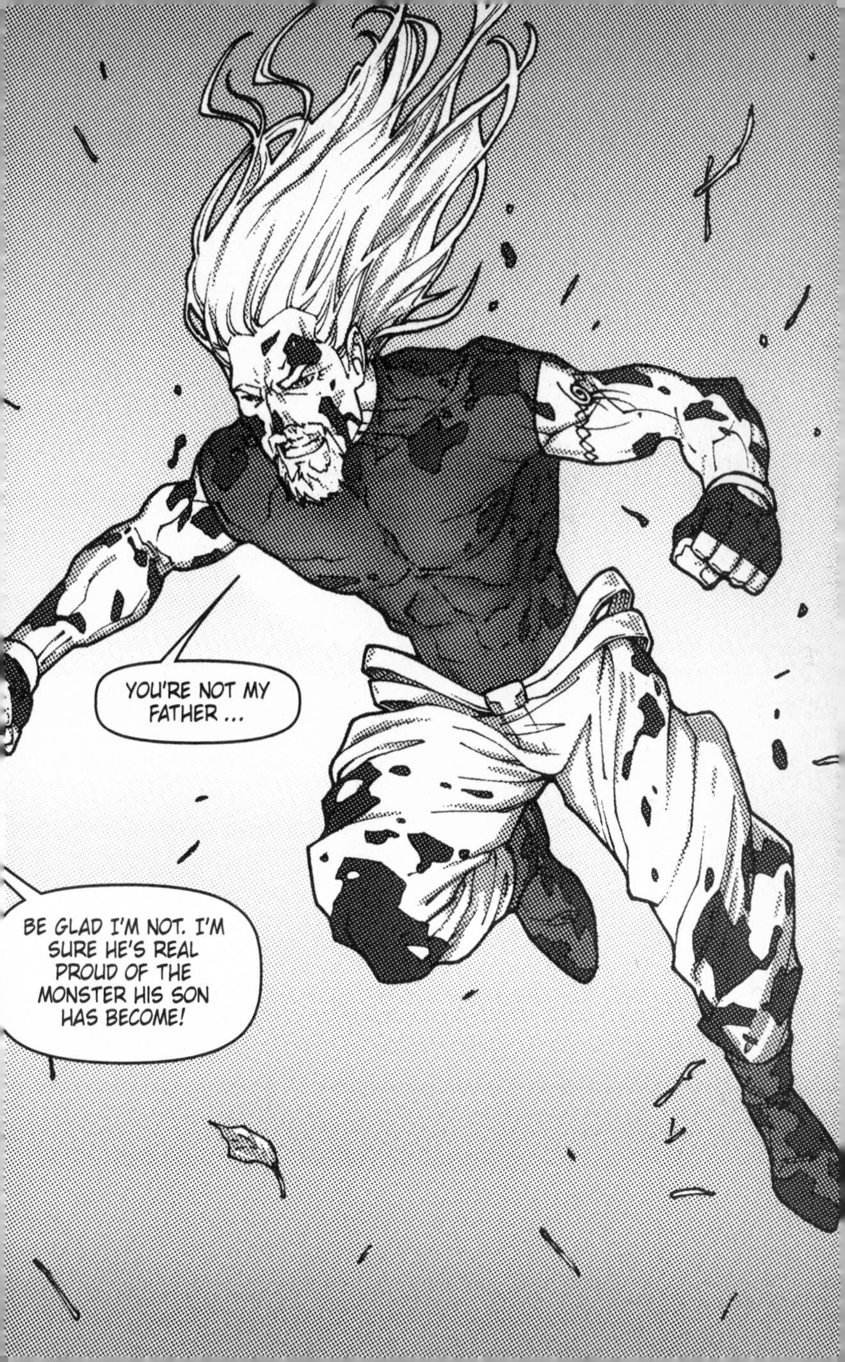
YOU'RE NOT MY FATHER ...
BE GLAD I'M NOT. I'M SURE HE'S REAL PROUD OF THE MONSTER HIS SON HAS BECOME!

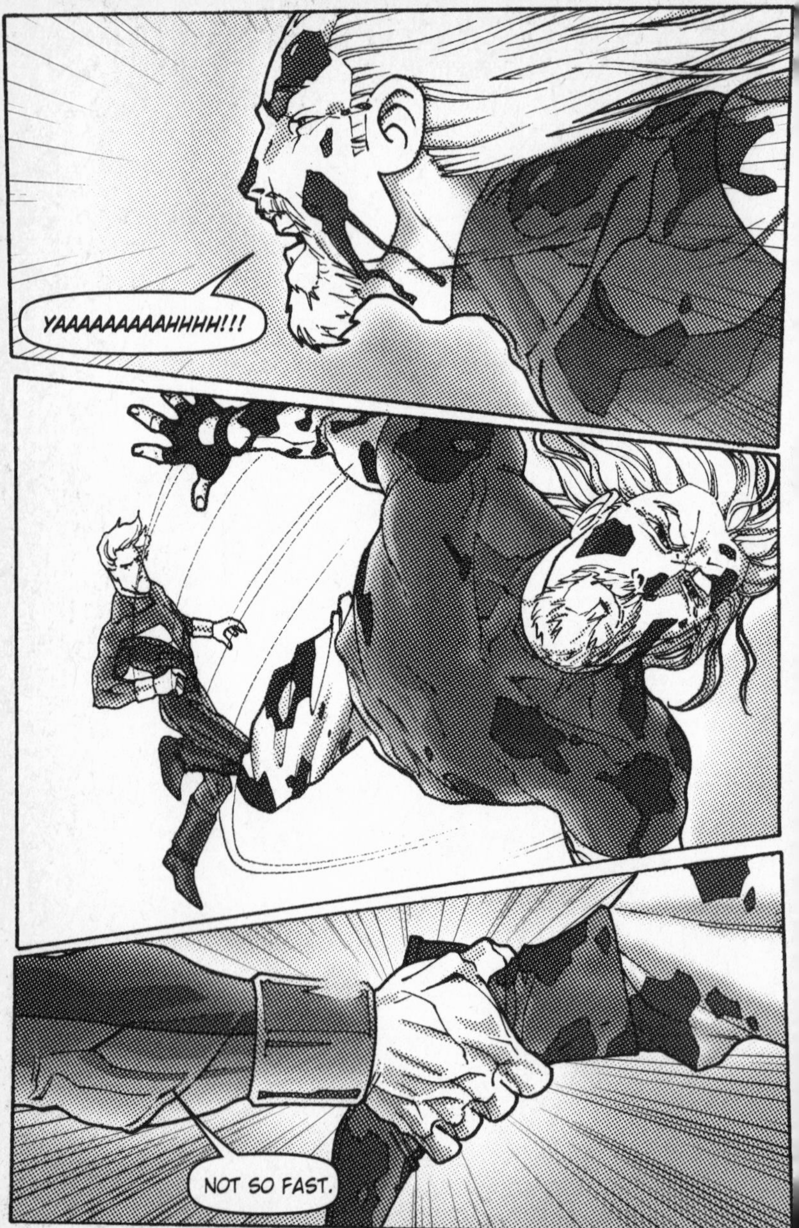
YAAAAAAAAAHHHH!!!
NOT SO FAST.

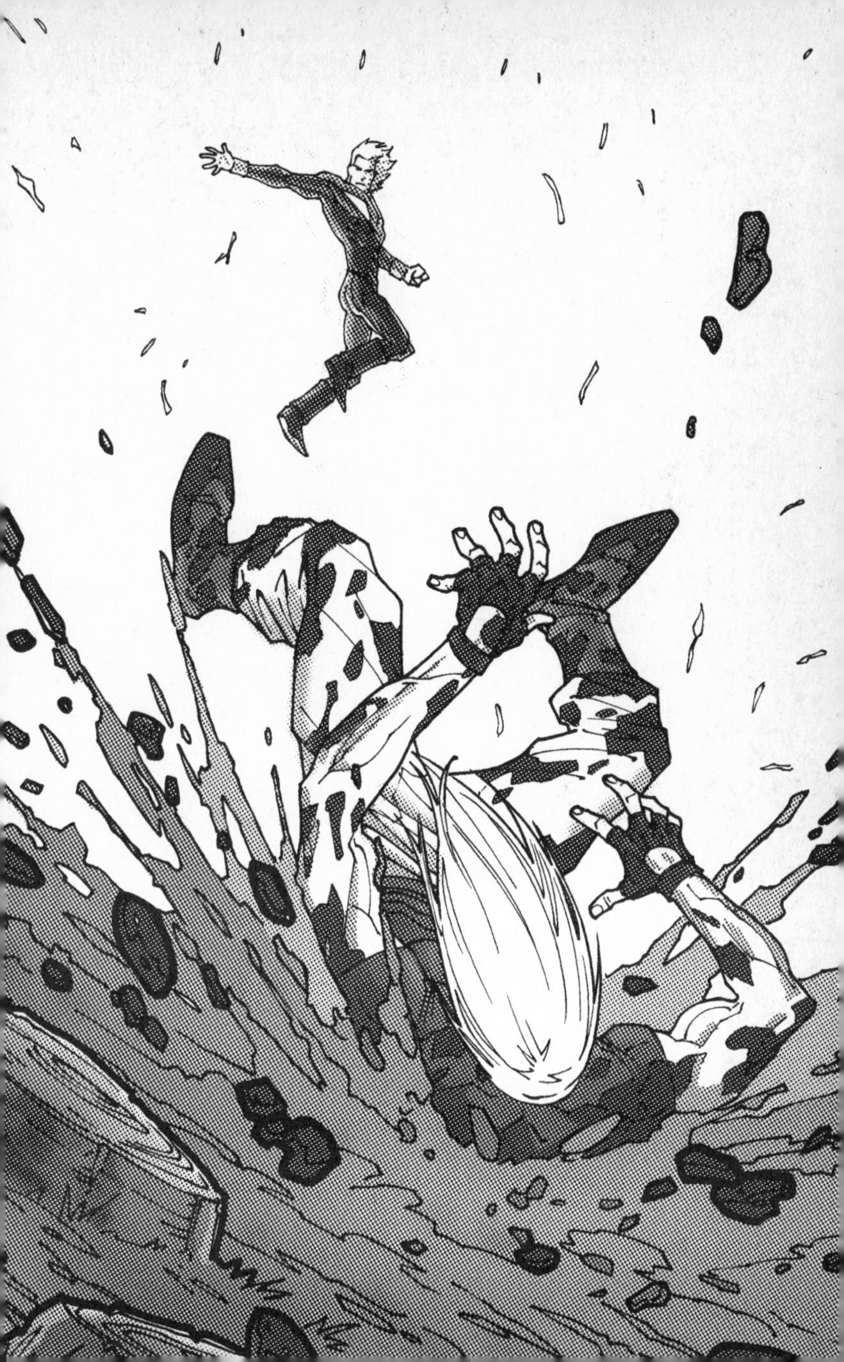

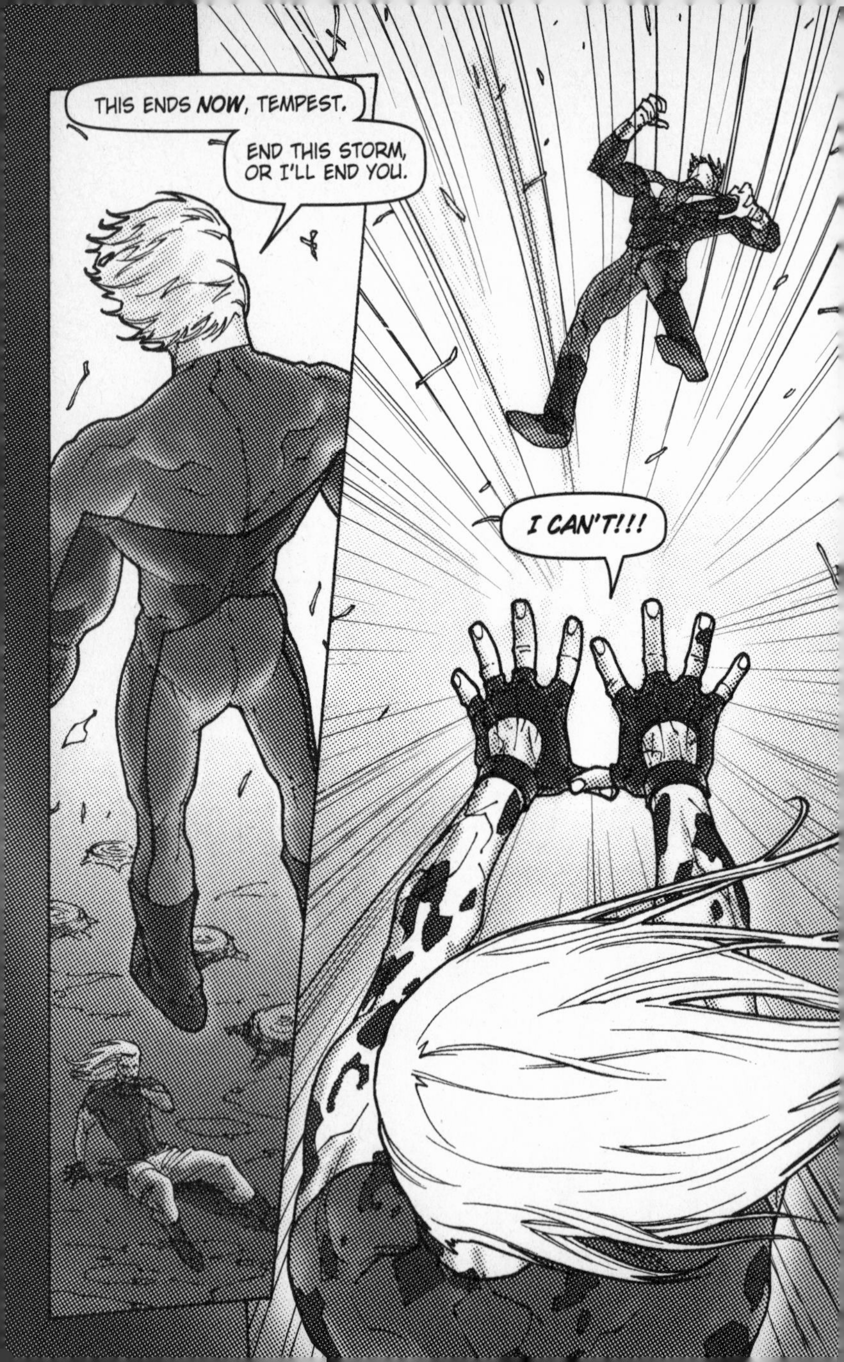
THIS ENDS NOW, TEMPEST.
END THIS STORM, OR I'LL END YOU.
I CAN'T!!!

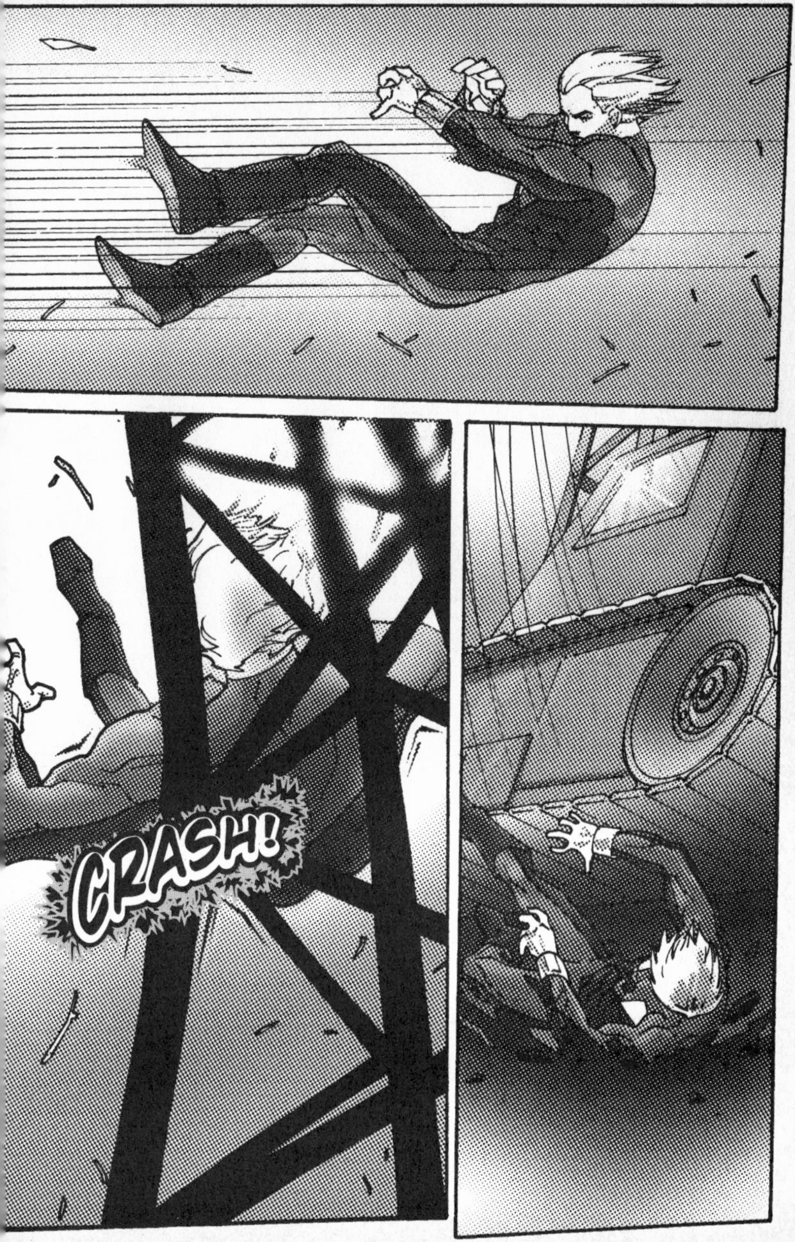
CRASH!

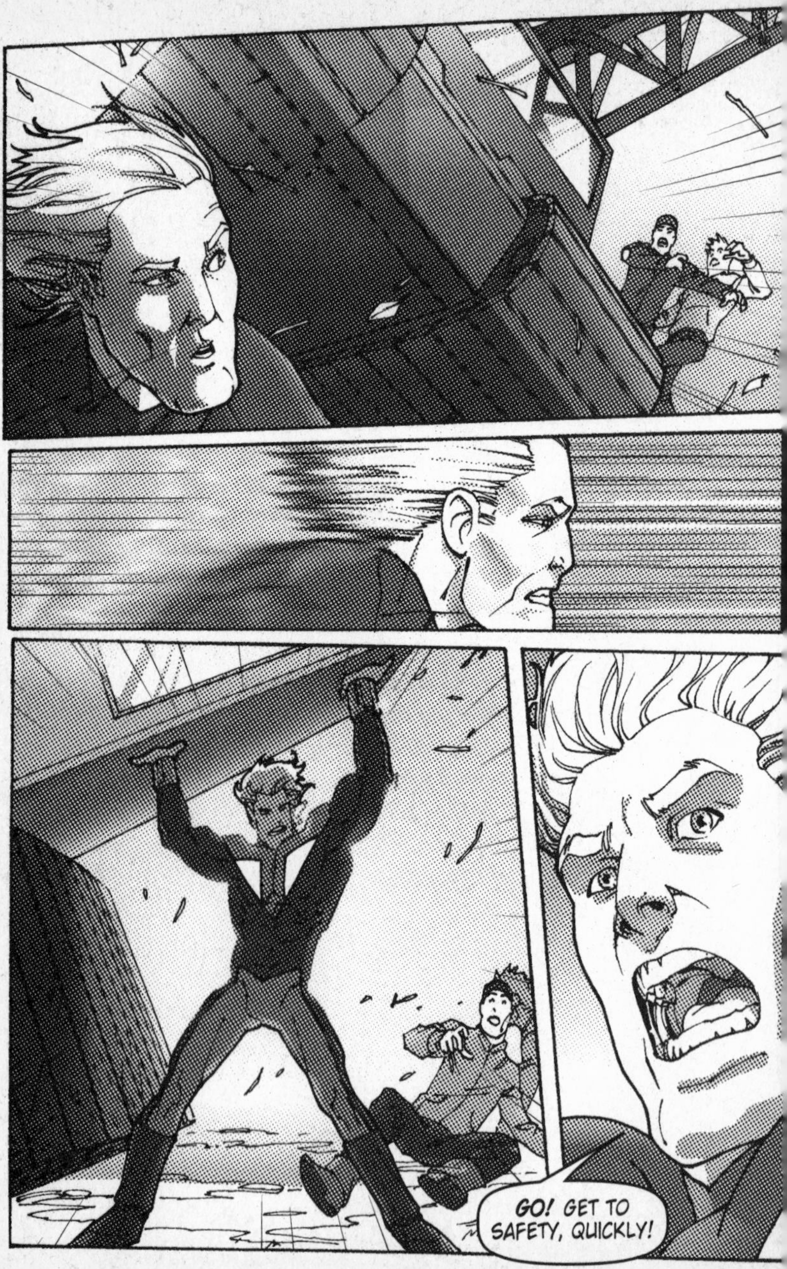
GO! GET TO SAFETY, QUICKLY!

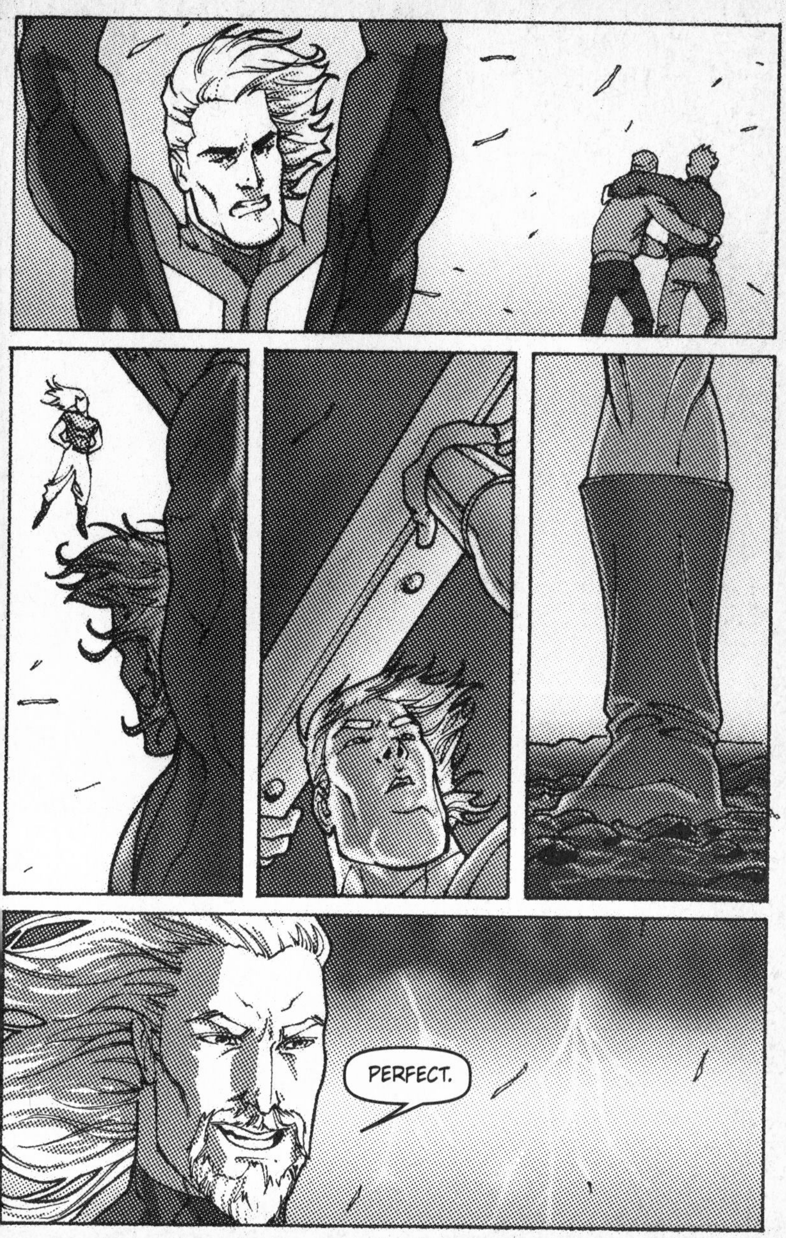
PERFECT.

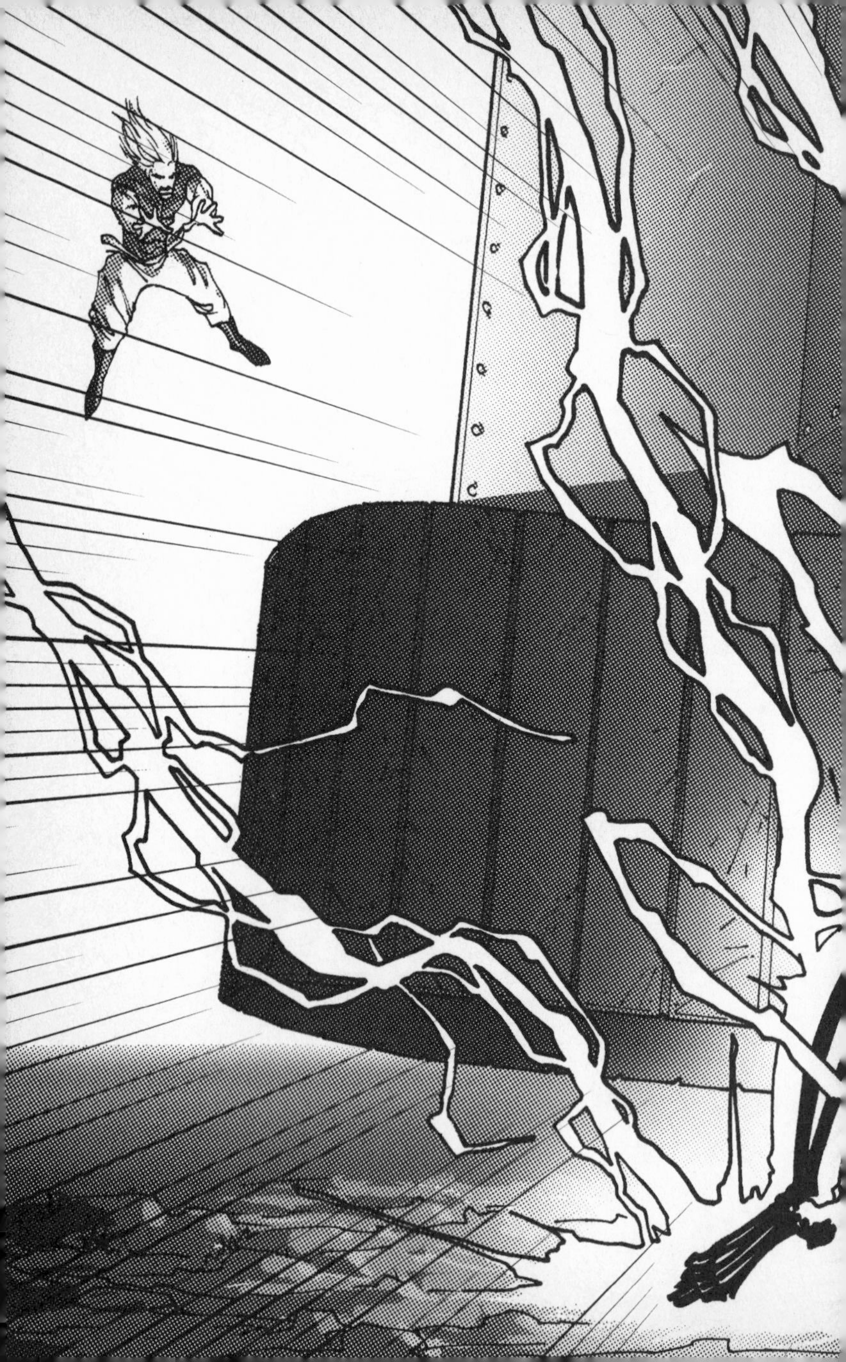

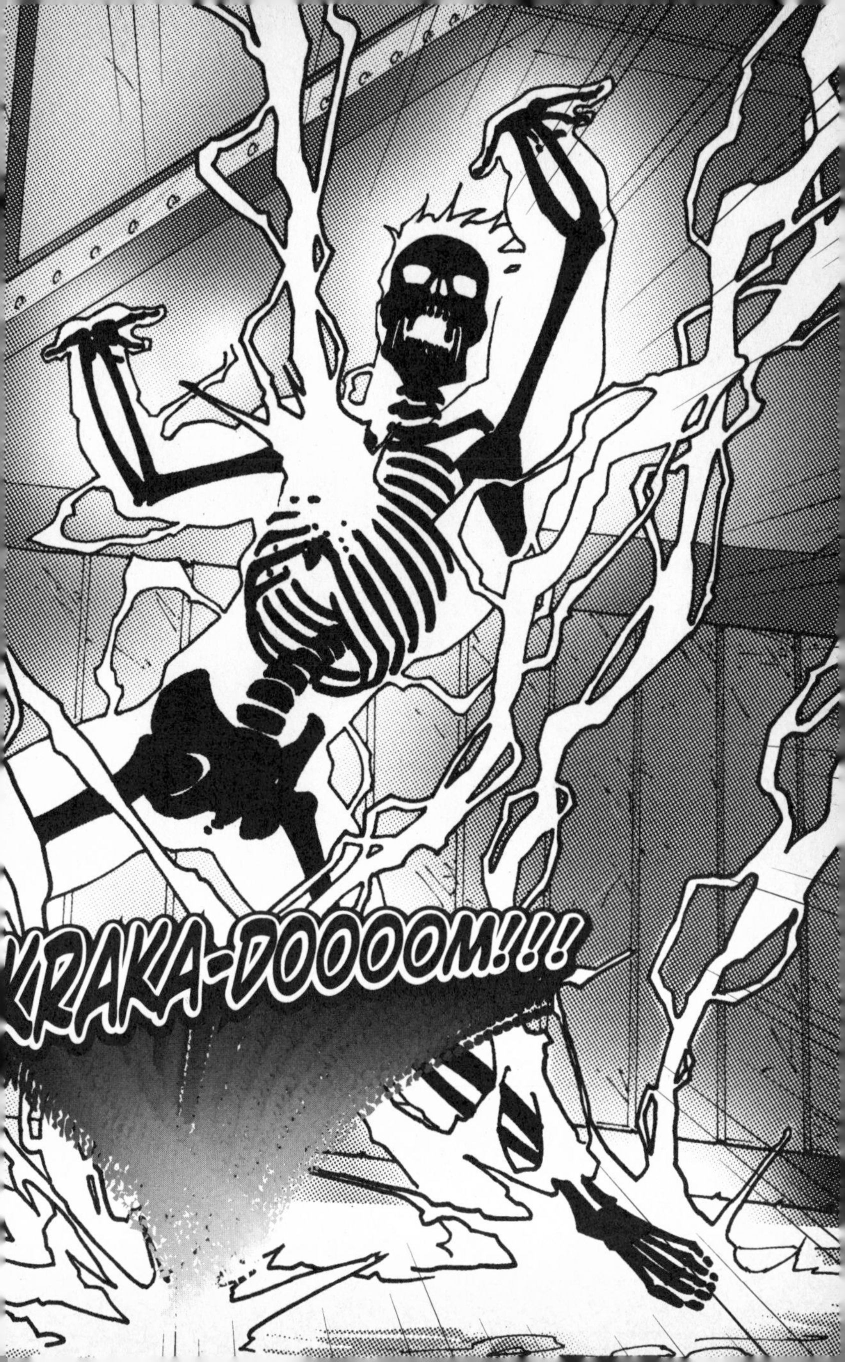
KRAKA-DOOOOOM!!!

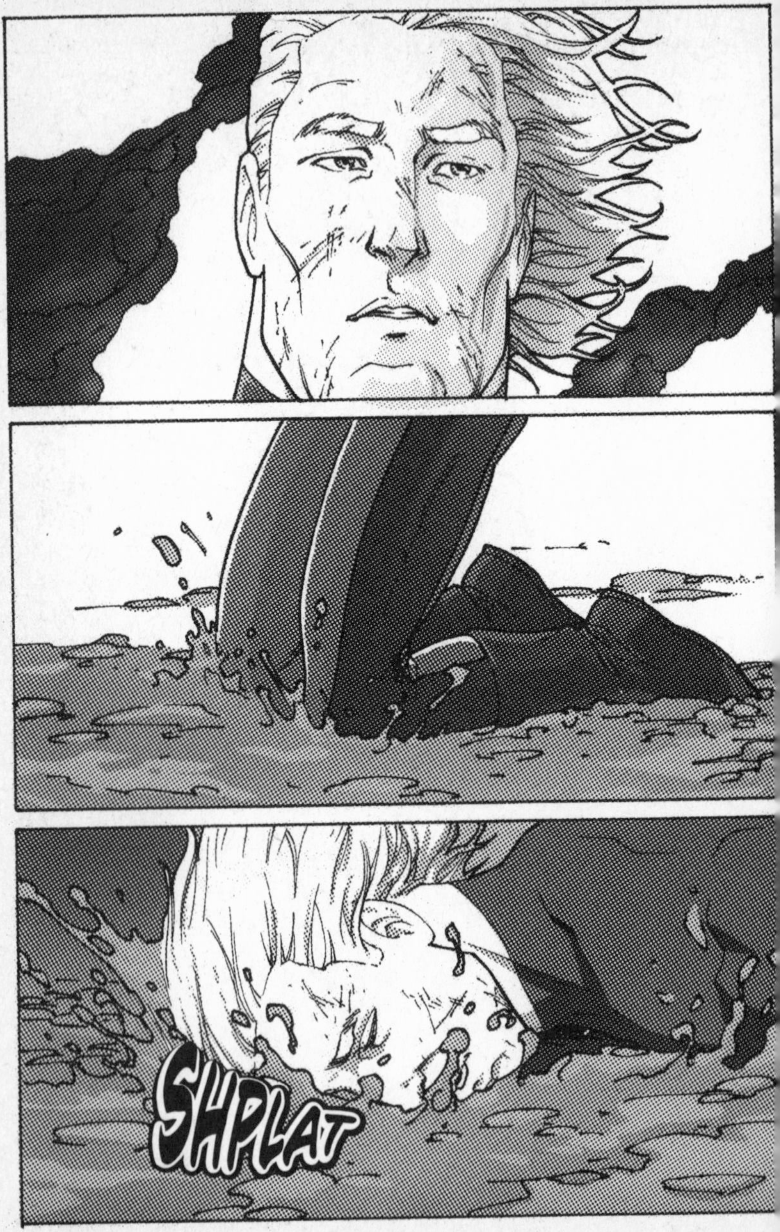
SHPLAT

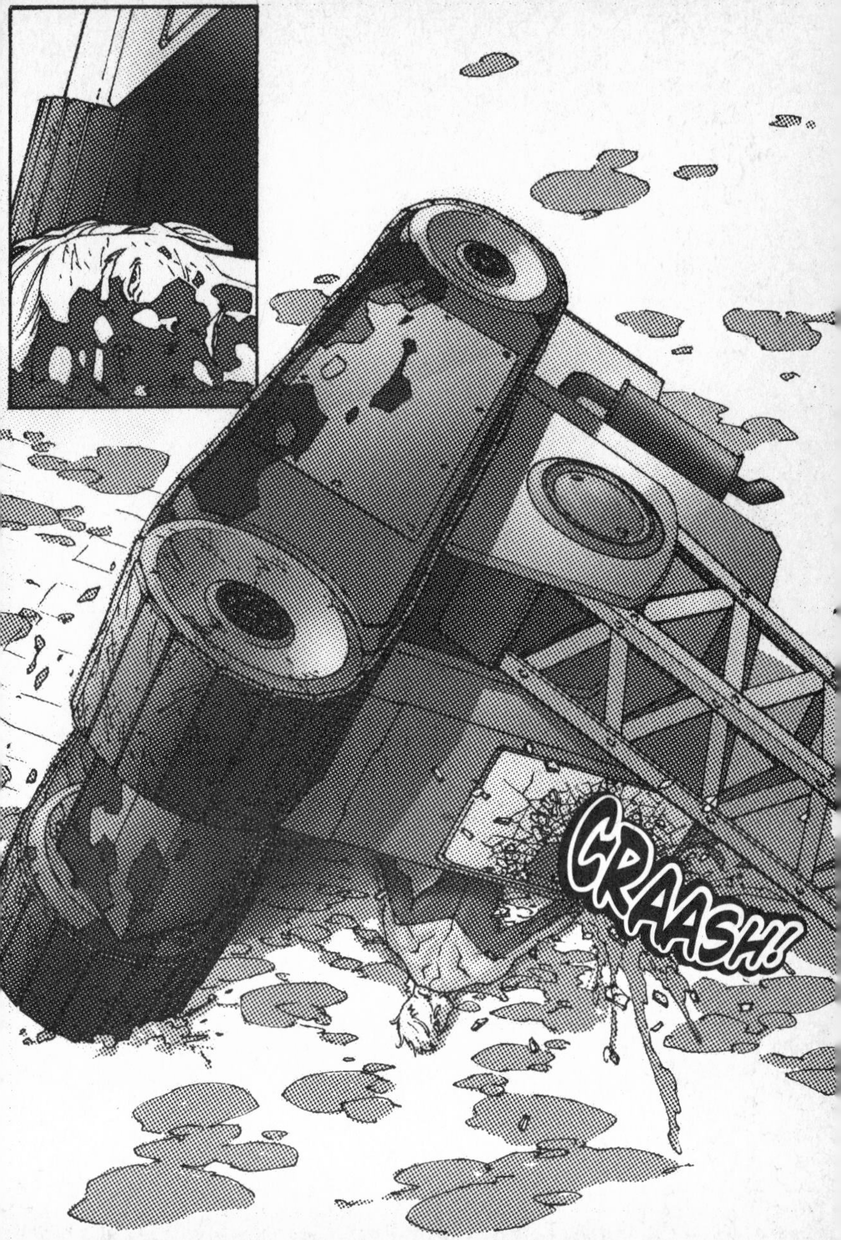
GRAASH!

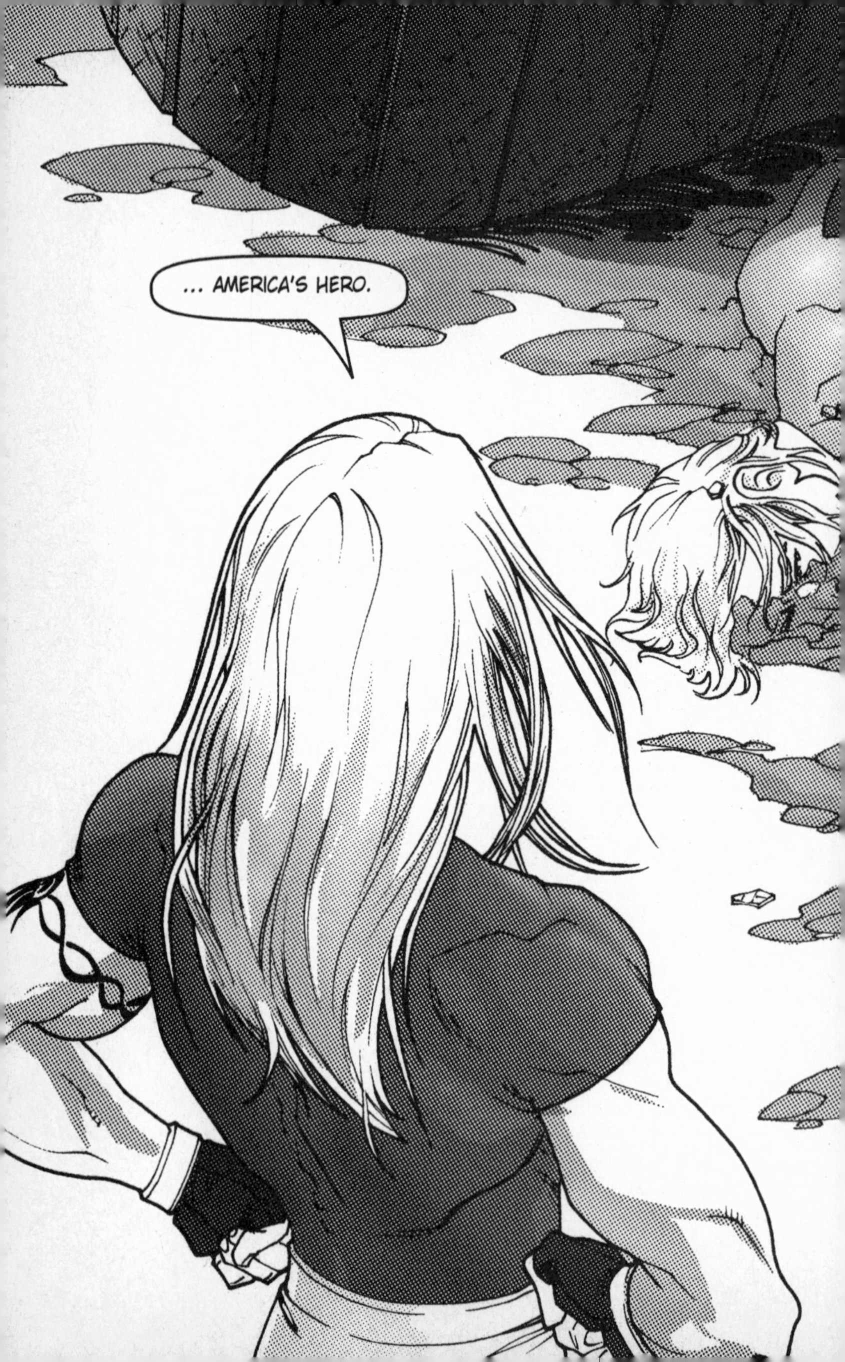
... AMERICA'S HERO.

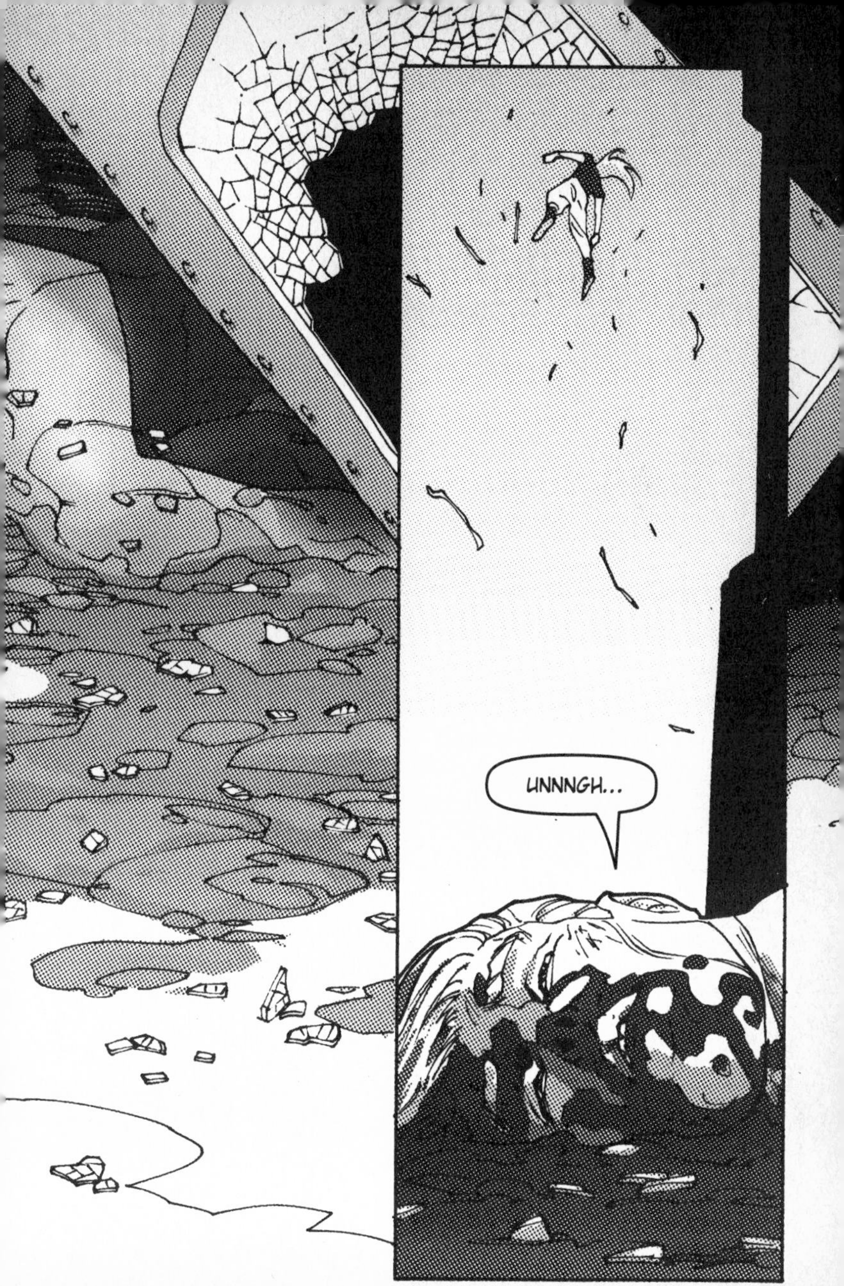
UNNNGH...

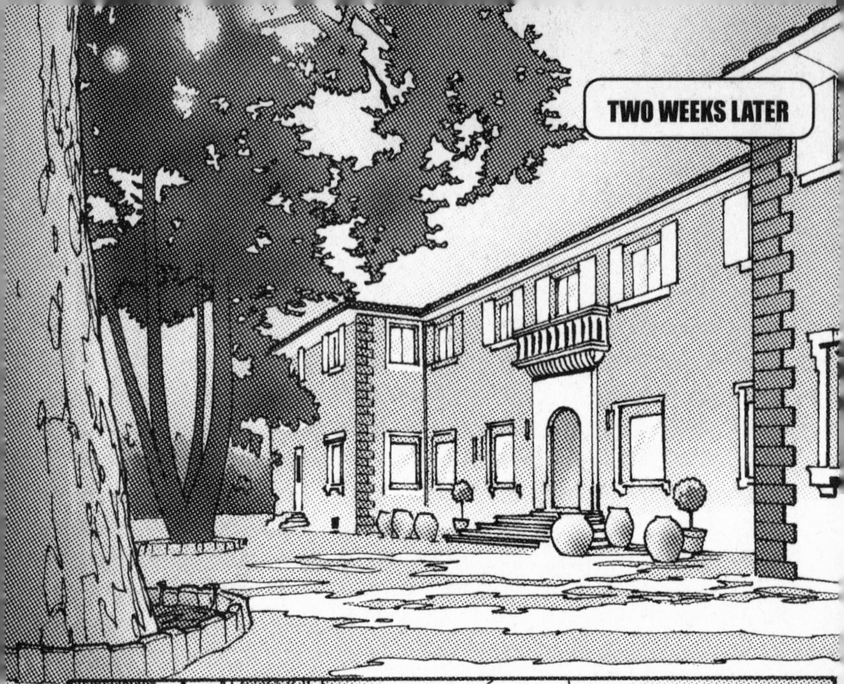
TWO WEEKS LATER

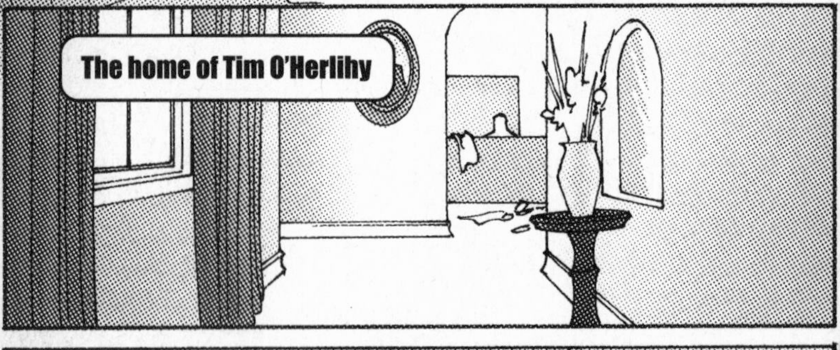
The home of Tim O'Herlihy

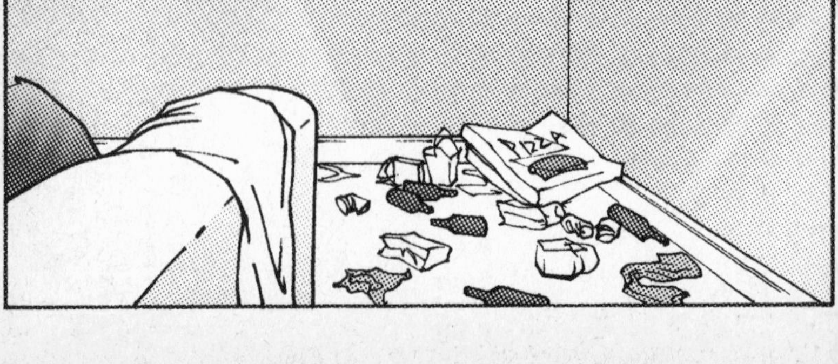
PIZZA

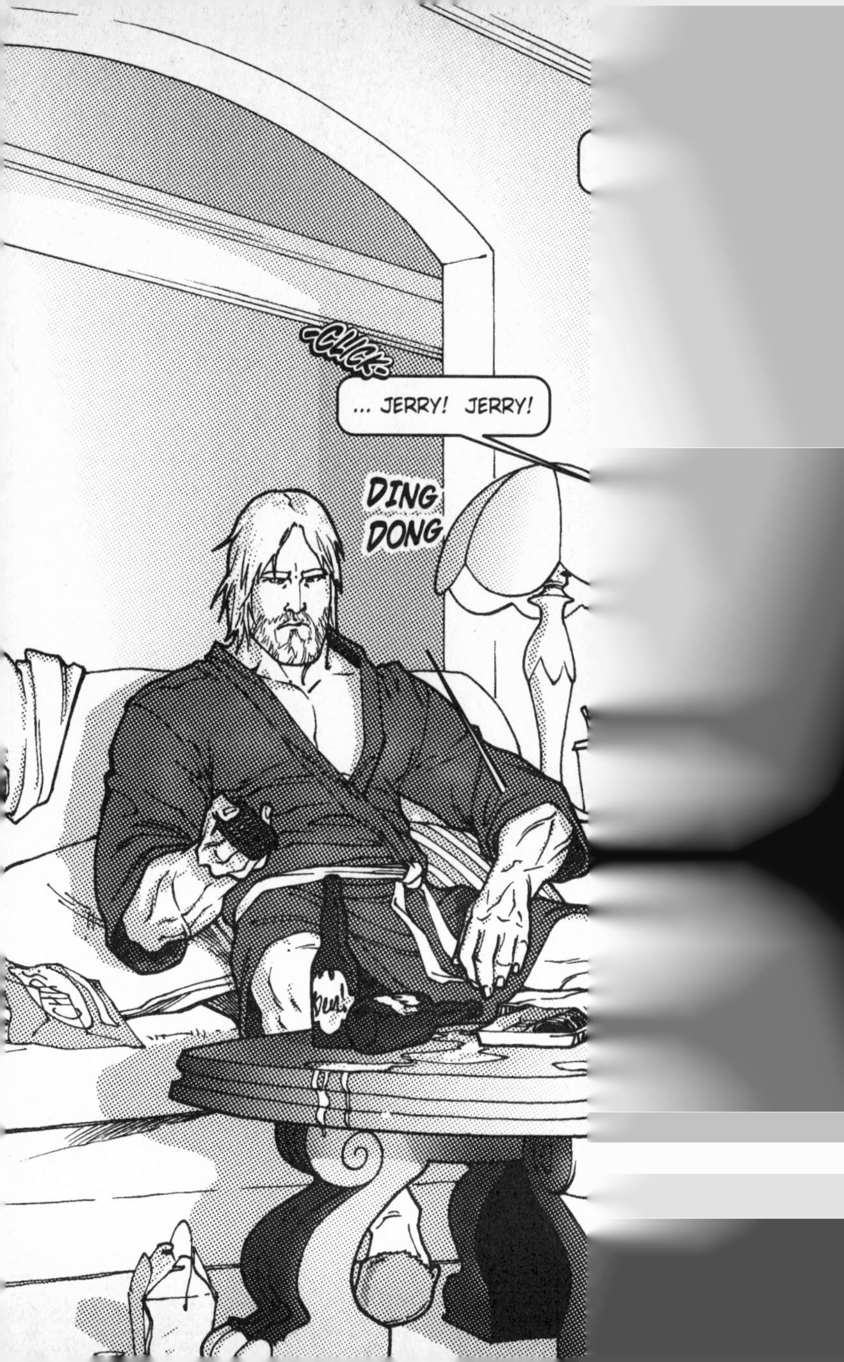
-CLICK-
... JERRY! JERRY!
DING DONG

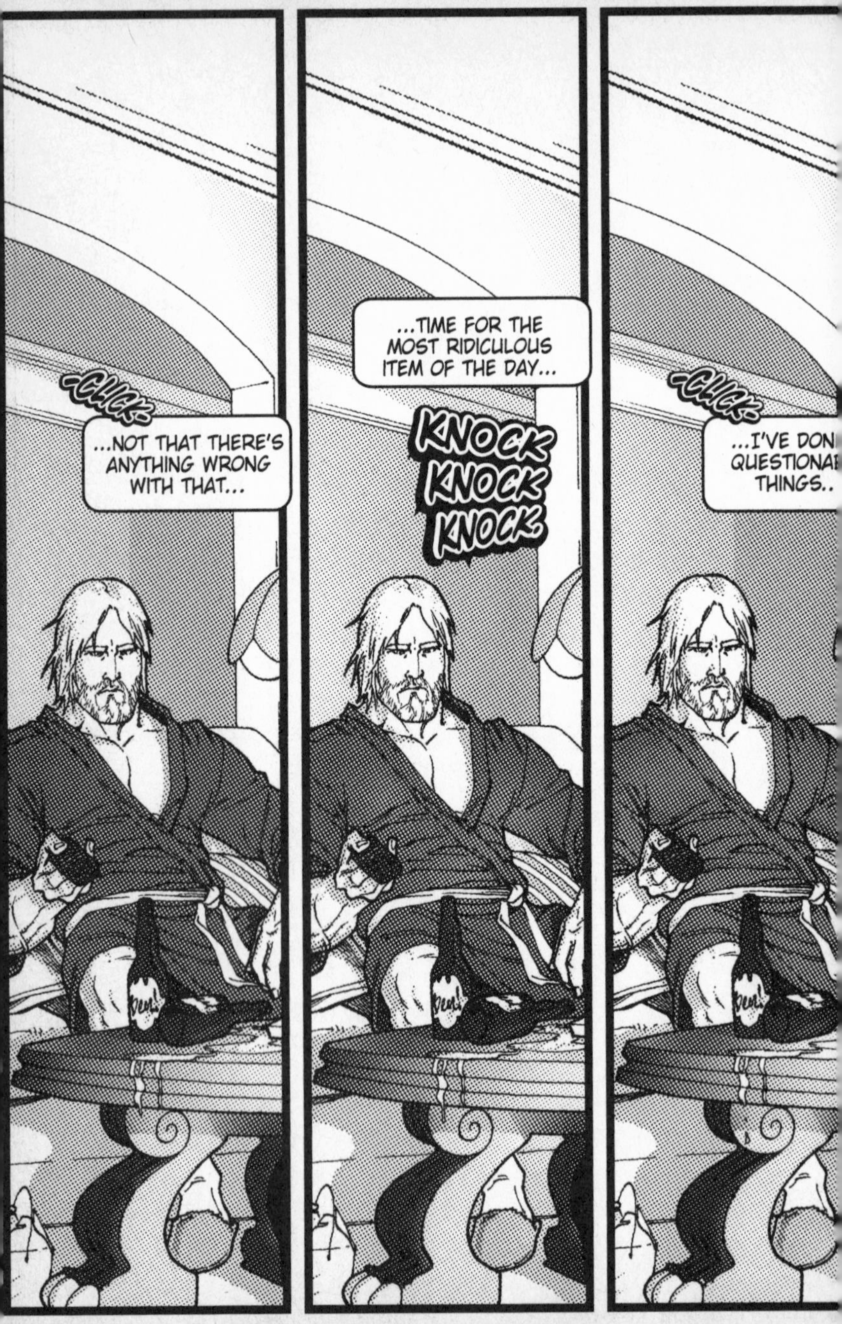
-CLICK-
...NOT THAT THERE'S ANYTHING WRONG WITH THAT...
...TIME FOR THE MOST RIDICULOUS ITEM OF THE DAY...
KNOCK KNOCK KNOCK
-CLICK-
...I'VE DON
QUESTIONA
THINGS..

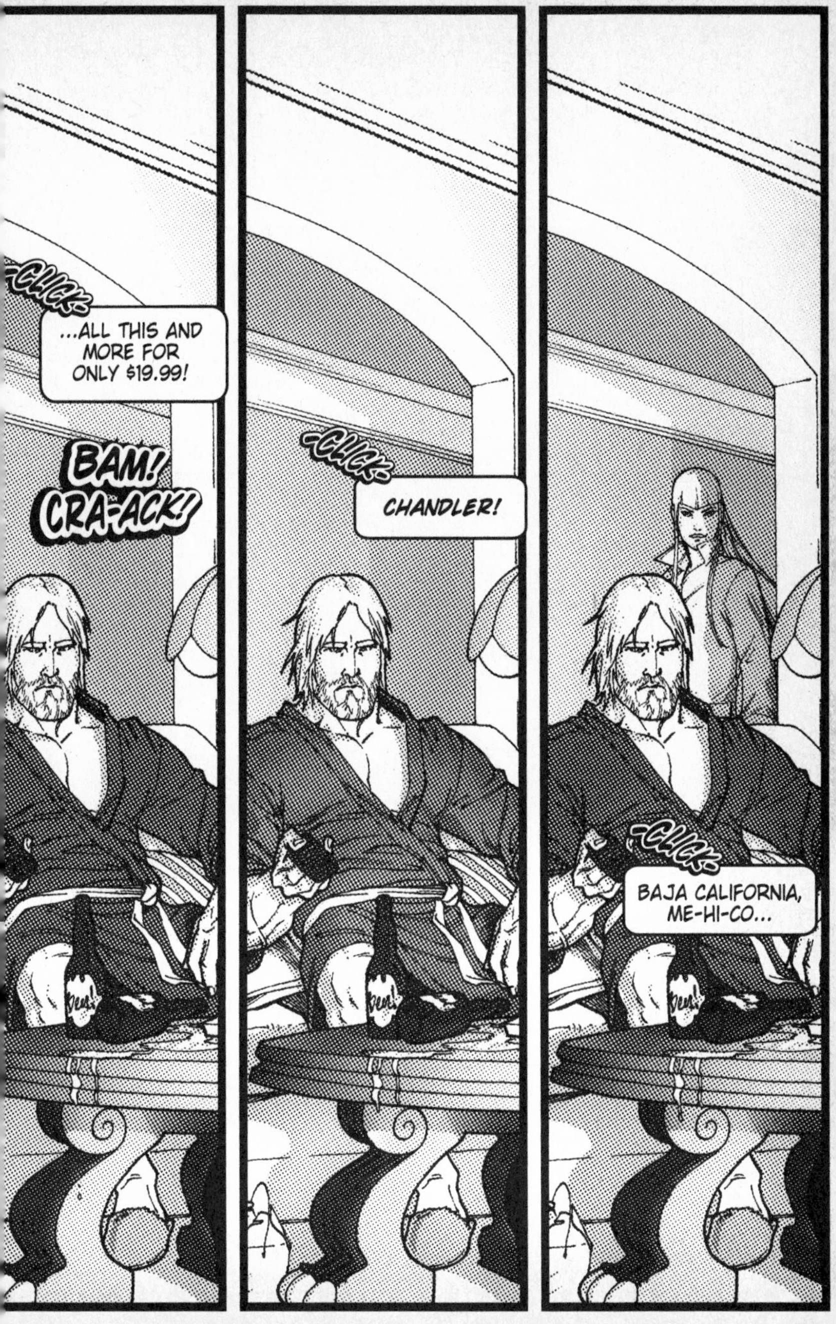
-CLICK-
...ALL THIS AND MORE FOR ONLY $19.99!
BAM! CRA-ACK!
-CLICK-
CHANDLER!
-CLICK-
BAJA CALIFORNIA, ME-HI-CO...

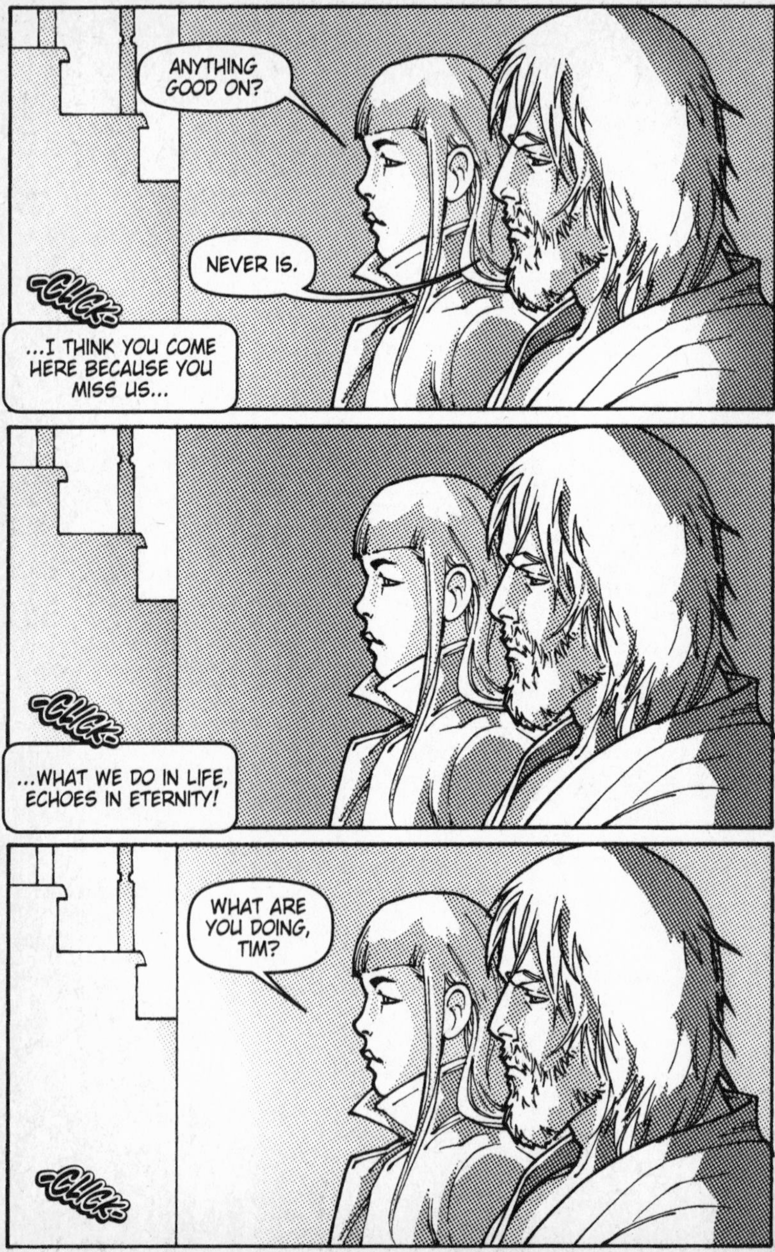
ANYTHING GOOD ON?
NEVER IS.
-CLICK-
...I THINK YOU COME HERE BECAUSE YOU MISS US...
-CLICK-
...WHAT WE DO IN LIFE, ECHOES IN ETERNITY!
WHAT ARE YOU DOING, TIM?
-CLICK-

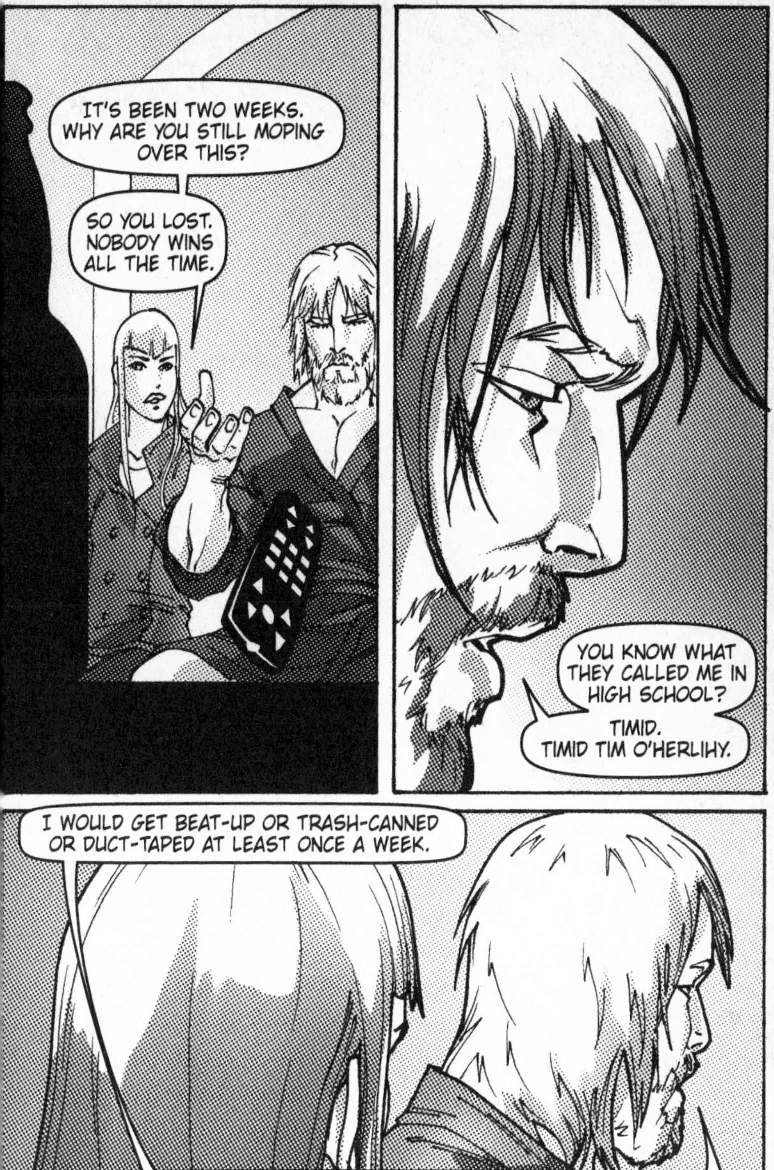
IT'S BEEN TWO WEEKS. WHY ARE YOU STILL MOPING OVER THIS?
SO YOU LOST. NOBODY WINS ALL THE TIME.
YOU KNOW WHAT THEY CALLED ME IN HIGH SCHOOL?
TIMID. TIMID TIM O'HERLIHY.
I WOULD GET BEAT-UP OR TRASH-CANNED OR DUCT-TAPED AT LEAST ONCE A WEEK.
AND I NEVER COULD STAND UP TO THEM ... THE POPULAR KIDS ... THE JOCKS ... I KNEW IF I DID, THEY'D JUST HURT ME MORE, AND IT WOULD NEVER STOP.

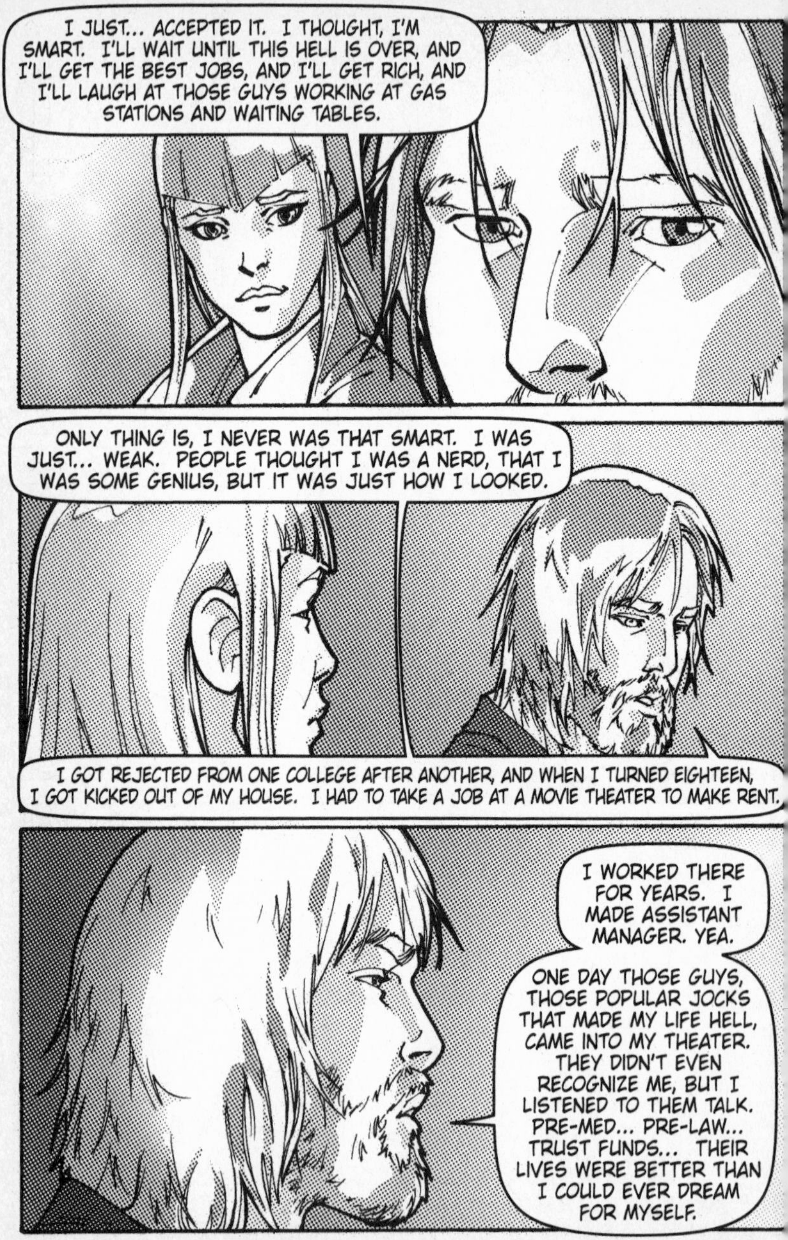
I JUST... ACCEPTED IT. I THOUGHT, I'M SMART. I'LL WAIT UNTIL THIS HELL IS OVER, AND I'LL GET THE BEST JOBS, AND I'LL GET RICH, AND I'LL LAUGH AT THOSE GUYS WORKING AT GAS STATIONS AND WAITING TABLES.
ONLY THING IS, I NEVER WAS THAT SMART. I WAS JUST... WEAK. PEOPLE THOUGHT I WAS A NERD, THAT I WAS SOME GENIUS, BUT IT WAS JUST HOW I LOOKED.
I GOT REJECTED FROM ONE COLLEGE AFTER ANOTHER, AND WHEN I TURNED EIGHTEEN, I GOT KICKED OUT OF MY HOUSE. I HAD TO TAKE A JOB AT A MOVIE THEATER TO MAKE RENT.
I WORKED THERE FOR YEARS. I MADE ASSISTANT MANAGER. YEA.
ONE DAY THOSE GUYS, THOSE POPULAR JOCKS THAT MADE MY LIFE HELL, CAME INTO MY THEATER. THEY DIDN'T EVEN RECOGNIZE ME, BUT I LISTENED TO THEM TALK. PRE-MED... PRE-LAW... TRUST FUNDS... THEIR LIVES WERE BETTER THAN I COULD EVER DREAM FOR MYSELF.

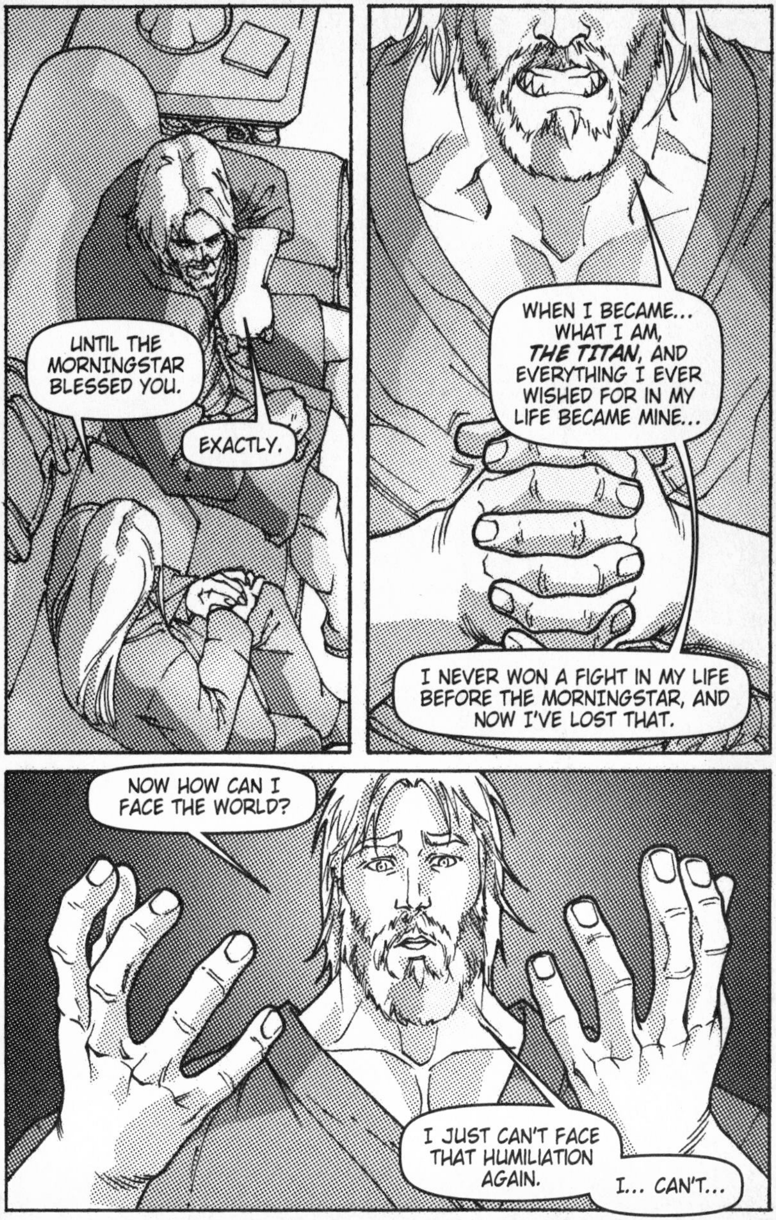
UNTIL THE MORNINGSTAR BLESSED YOU.
EXACTLY.
WHEN I BECAME... WHAT I AM, **THE TITAN**, AND EVERYTHING I EVER WISHED FOR IN MY LIFE BECAME MINE...
I NEVER WON A FIGHT IN MY LIFE BEFORE THE MORNINGSTAR, AND NOW I'VE LOST THAT.
NOW HOW CAN I FACE THE WORLD?
I JUST CAN'T FACE THAT HUMILIATION AGAIN.
I... CAN'T...

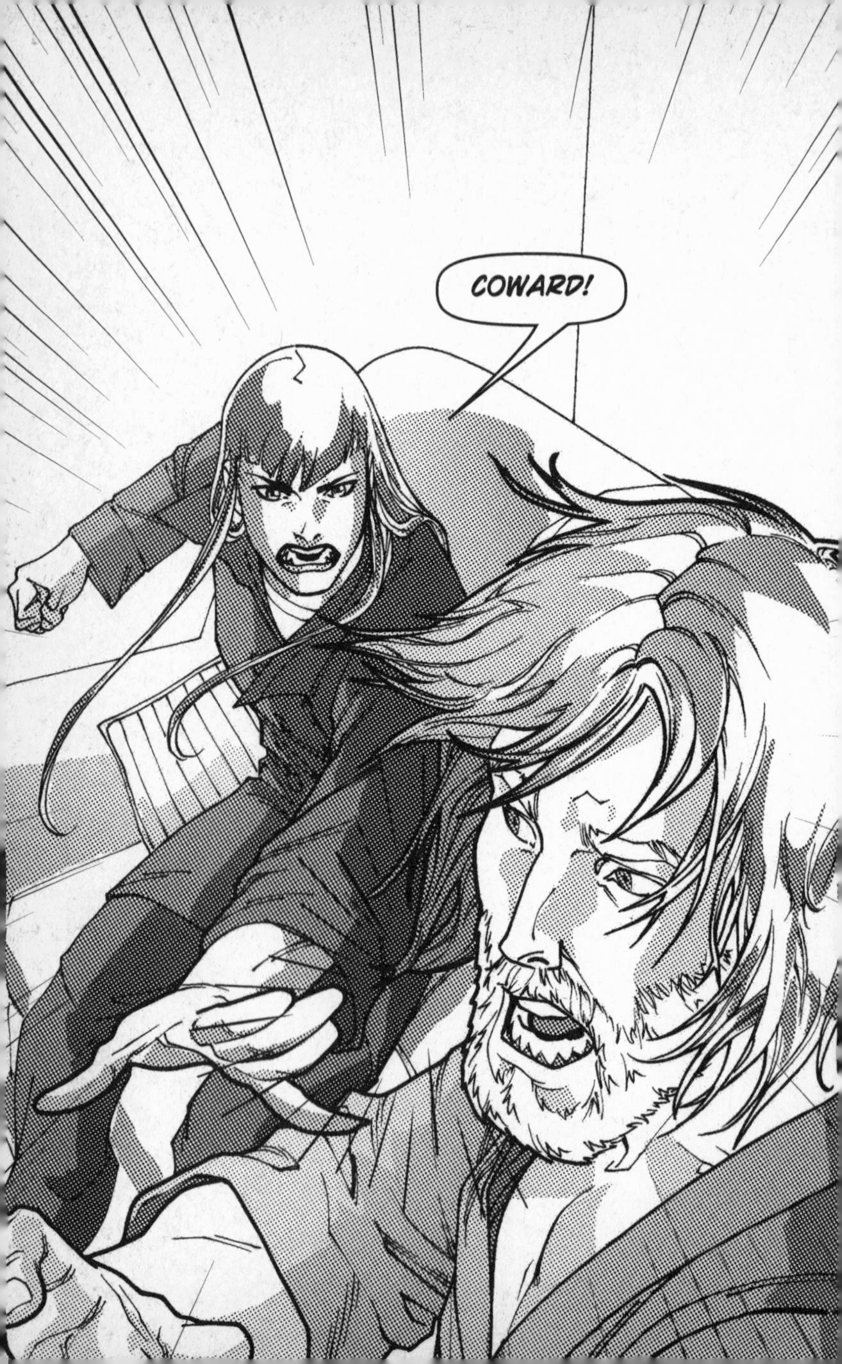
COWARD!

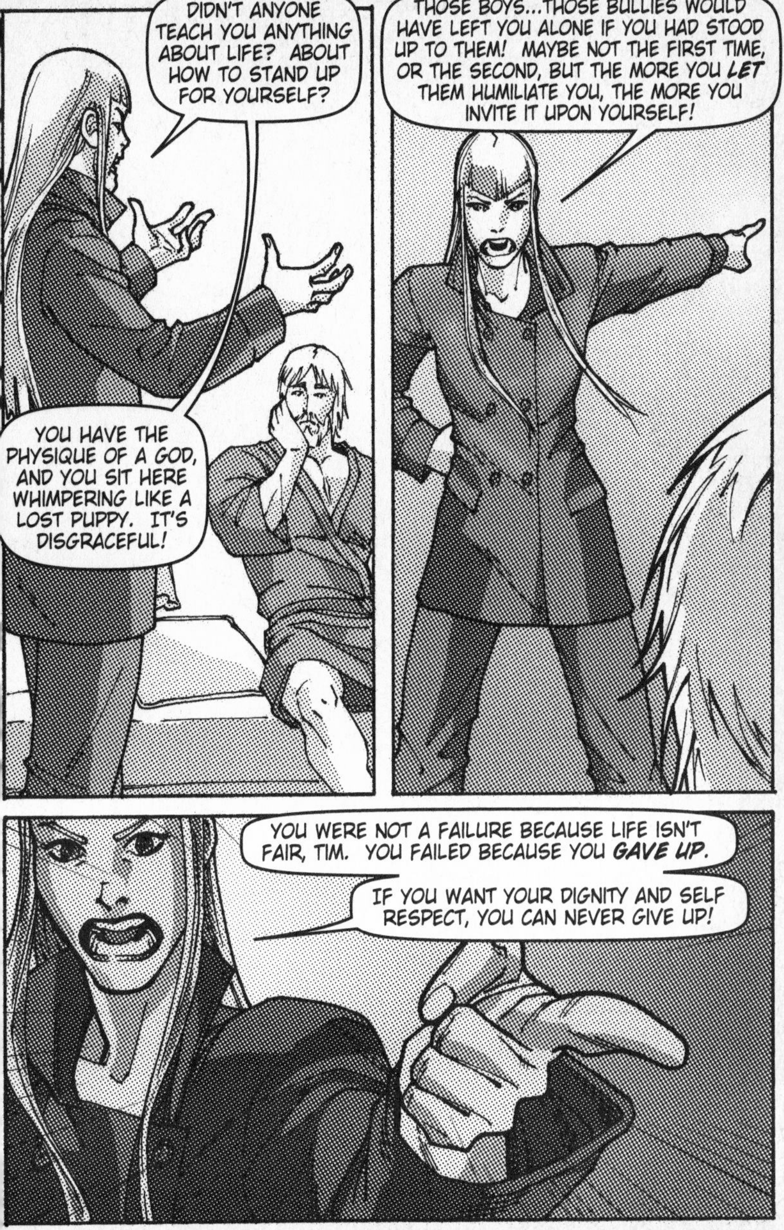
DIDN'T ANYONE TEACH YOU ANYTHING ABOUT LIFE? ABOUT HOW TO STAND UP FOR YOURSELF?
YOU HAVE THE PHYSIQUE OF A GOD, AND YOU SIT HERE WHIMPERING LIKE A LOST PUPPY. IT'S DISGRACEFUL!
THOSE BOYS...THOSE BULLIES WOULD HAVE LEFT YOU ALONE IF YOU HAD STOOD UP TO THEM! MAYBE NOT THE FIRST TIME, OR THE SECOND, BUT THE MORE YOU *LET* THEM HUMILIATE YOU, THE MORE YOU INVITE IT UPON YOURSELF!
YOU WERE NOT A FAILURE BECAUSE LIFE ISN'T FAIR, TIM. YOU FAILED BECAUSE YOU ***GAVE UP***.
IF YOU WANT YOUR DIGNITY AND SELF RESPECT, YOU CAN NEVER GIVE UP!

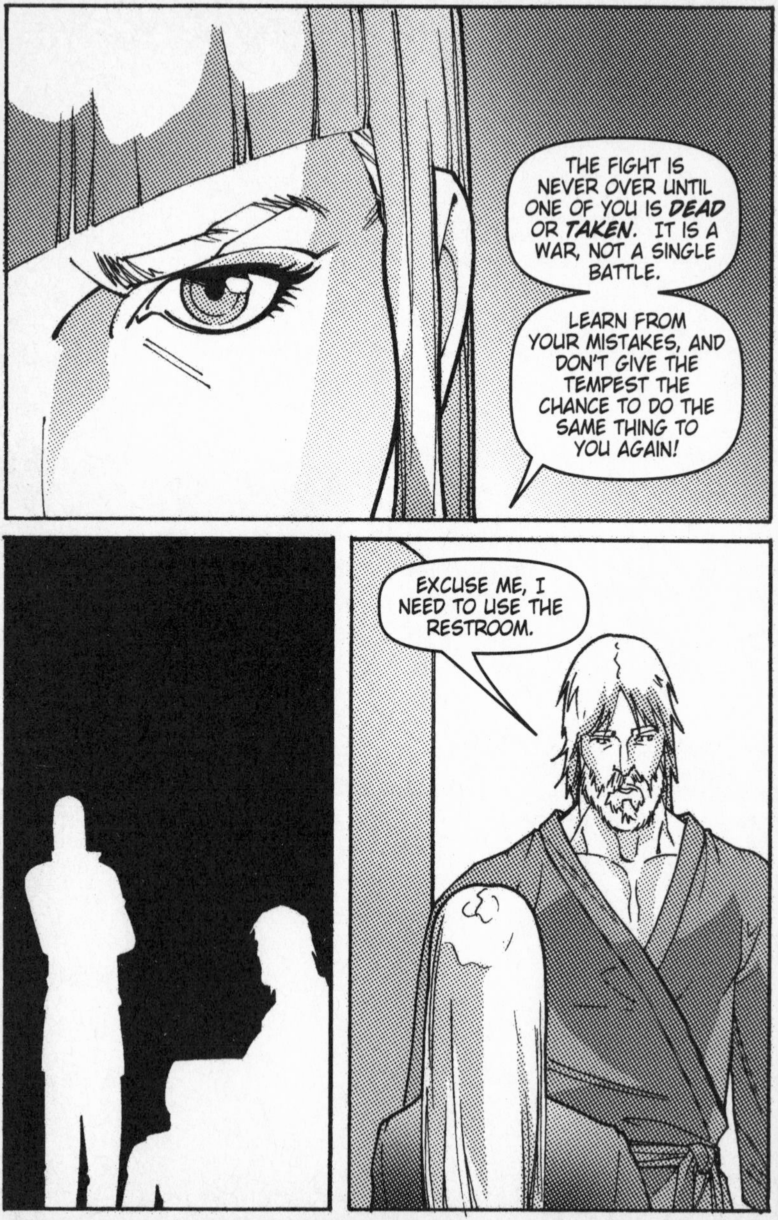
THE FIGHT IS NEVER OVER UNTIL ONE OF YOU IS *DEAD* OR *TAKEN*. IT IS A WAR, NOT A SINGLE BATTLE.
LEARN FROM YOUR MISTAKES, AND DON'T GIVE THE TEMPEST THE CHANCE TO DO THE SAME THING TO YOU AGAIN!
EXCUSE ME, I NEED TO USE THE RESTROOM.

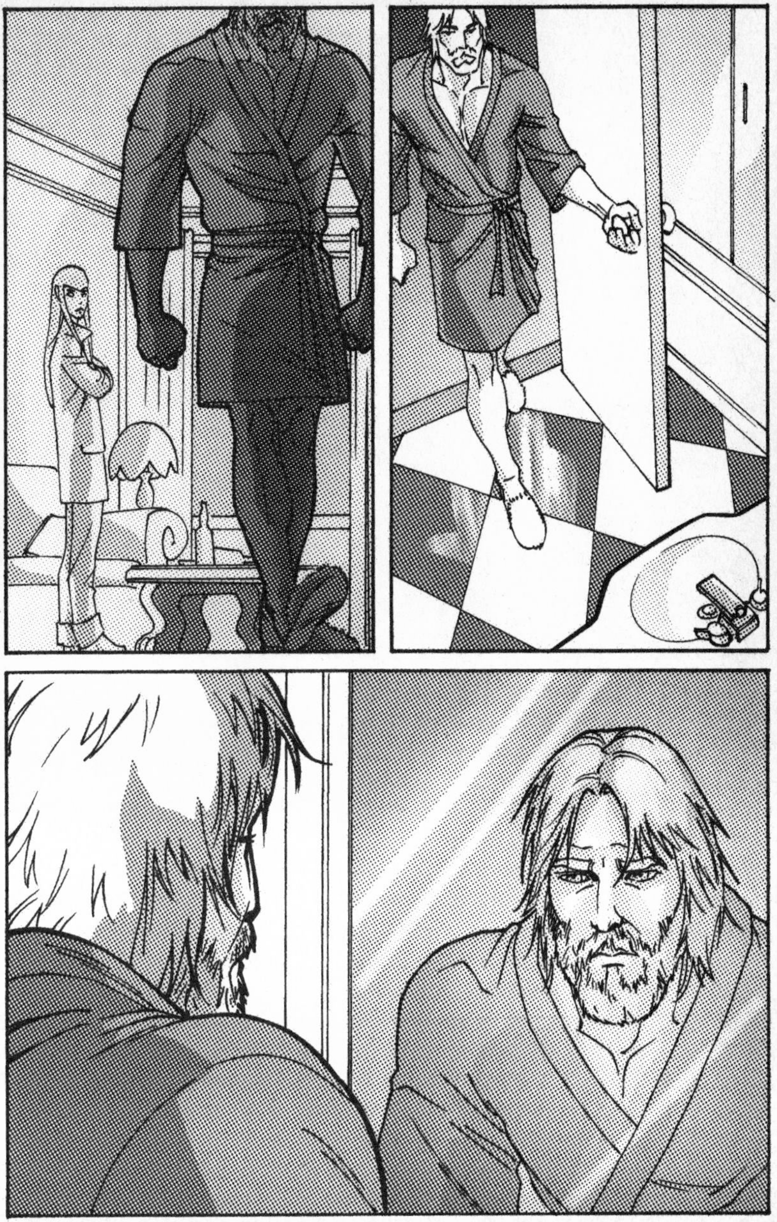

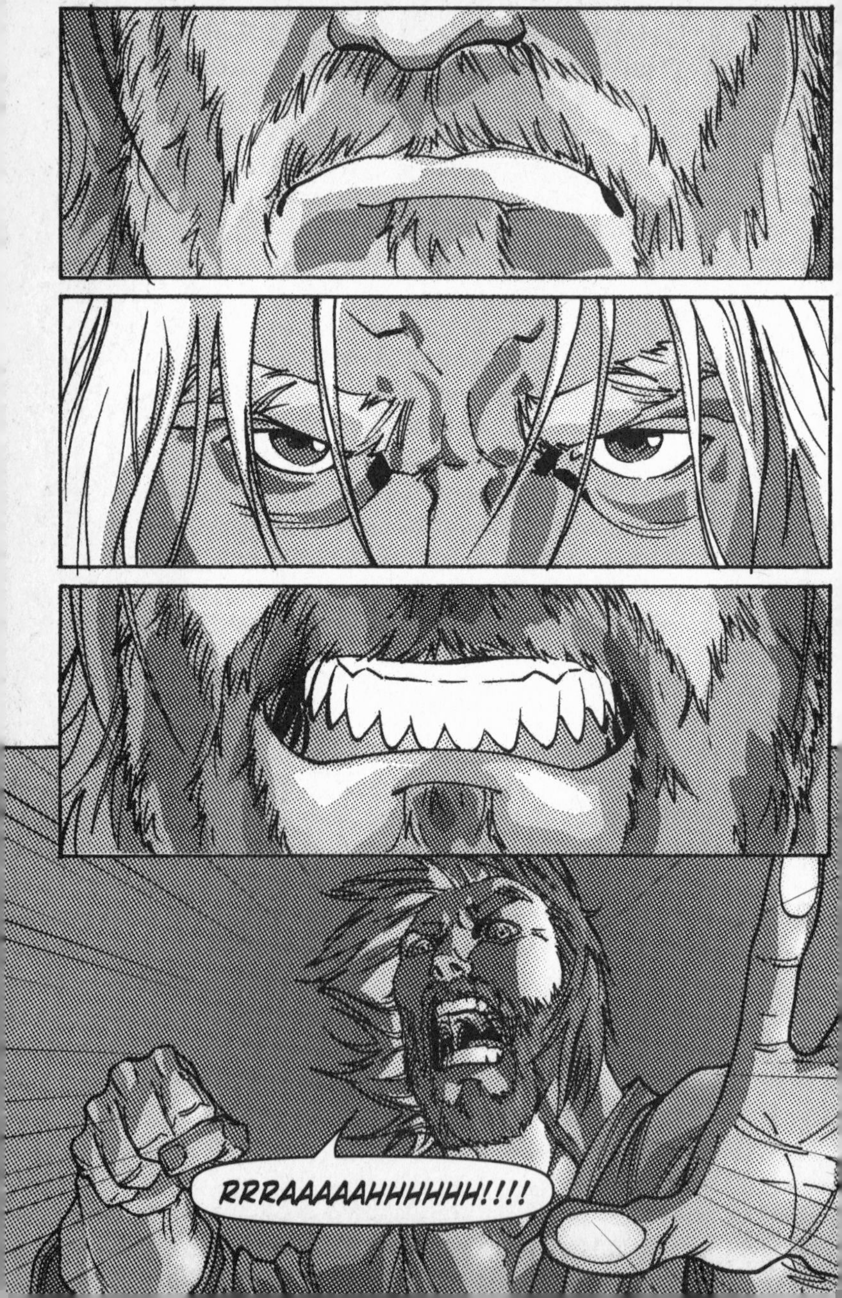
RRRAAAAAHHHHHH!!!!

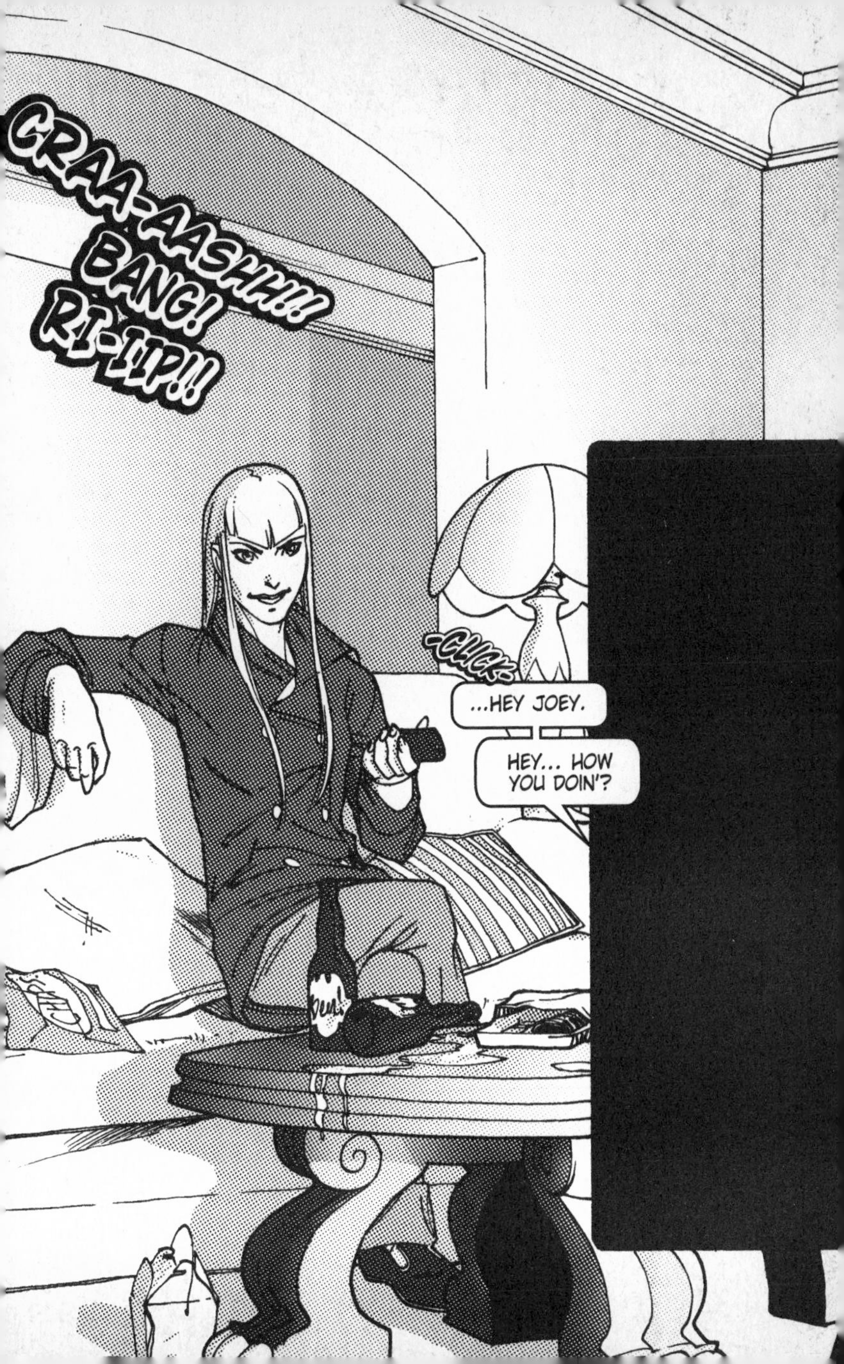
CRAA-AASHH!!!
BANG!
RI-IIP!!
-CLICK-
...HEY JOEY.
HEY... HOW YOU DOIN'?

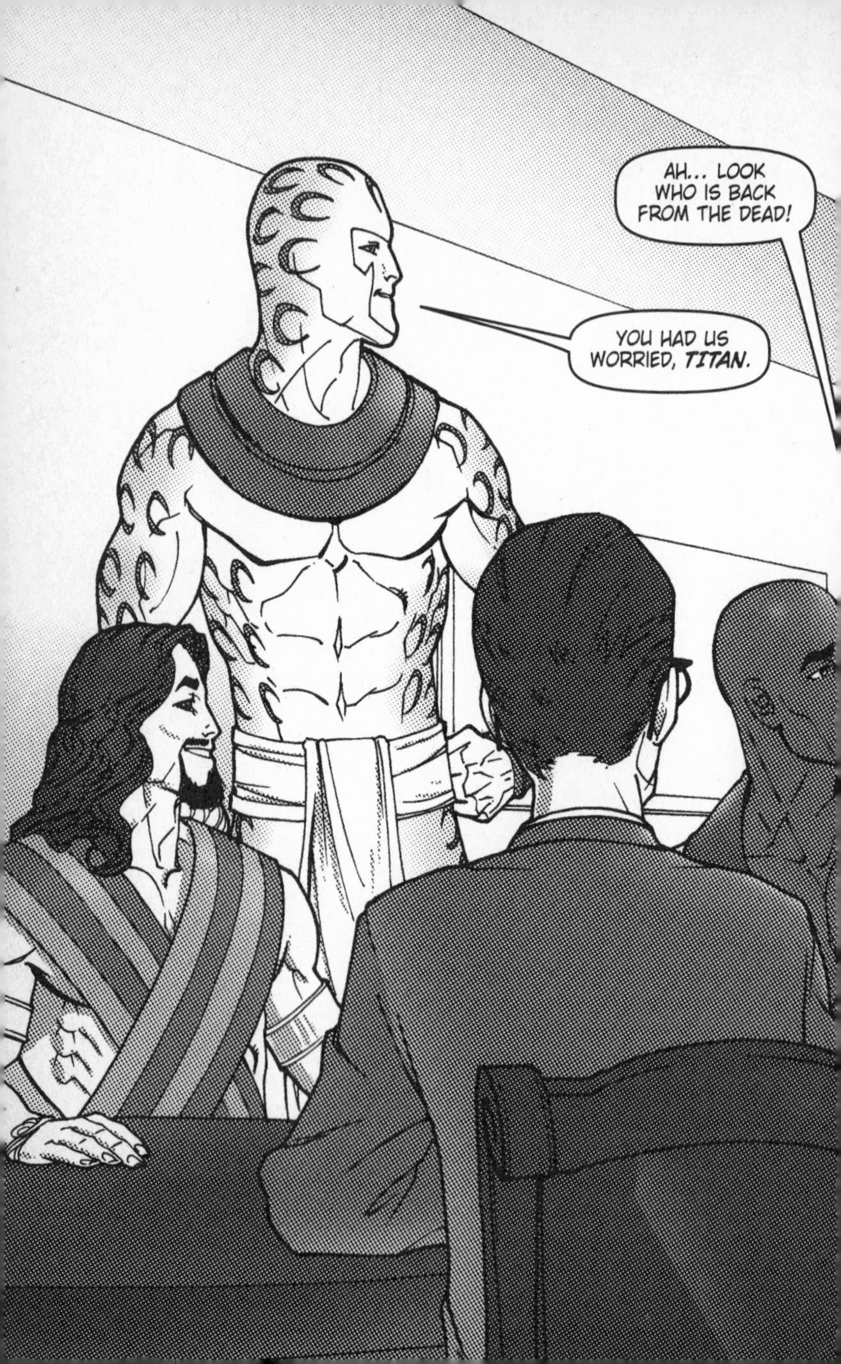
AH... LOOK WHO IS BACK FROM THE DEAD!
YOU HAD US WORRIED, *TITAN*.

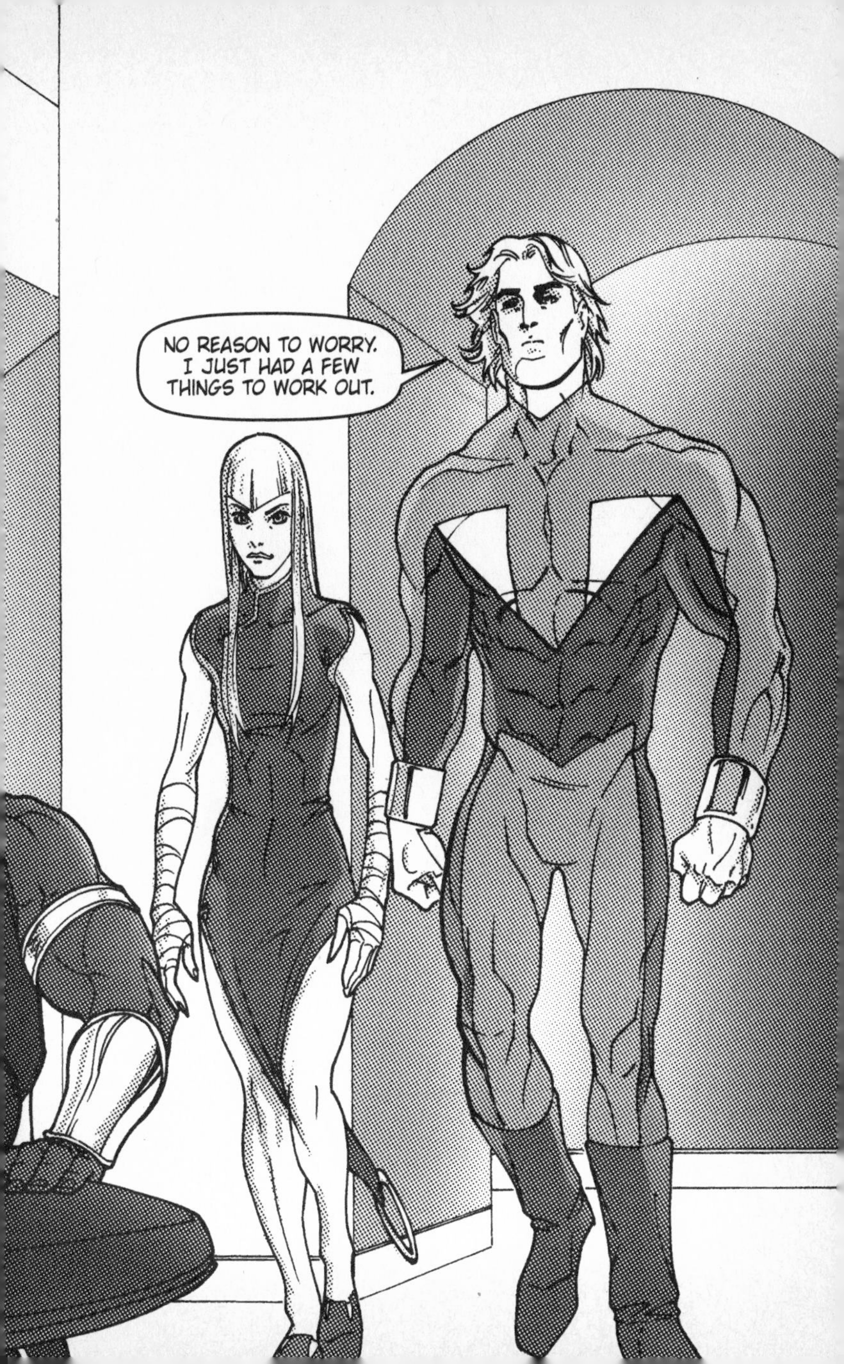
NO REASON TO WORRY. I JUST HAD A FEW THINGS TO WORK OUT.

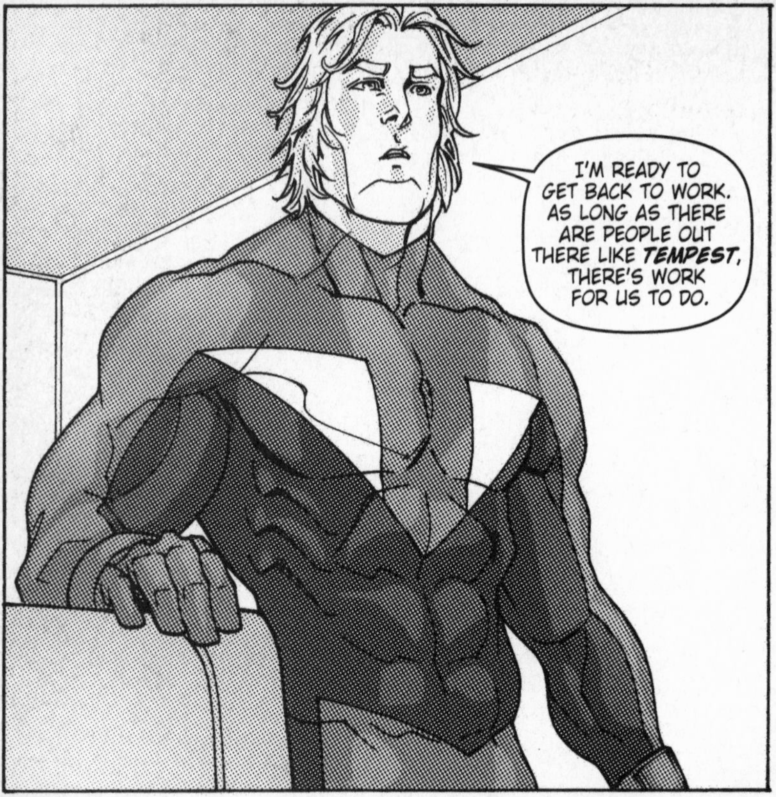
I'M READY TO GET BACK TO WORK. AS LONG AS THERE ARE PEOPLE OUT THERE LIKE TEMPEST, THERE'S WORK FOR US TO DO.

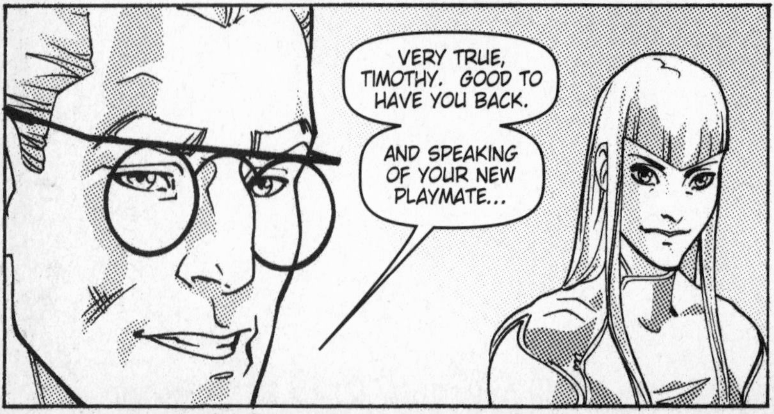
VERY TRUE, TIMOTHY. GOOD TO HAVE YOU BACK.
AND SPEAKING OF YOUR NEW PLAYMATE...

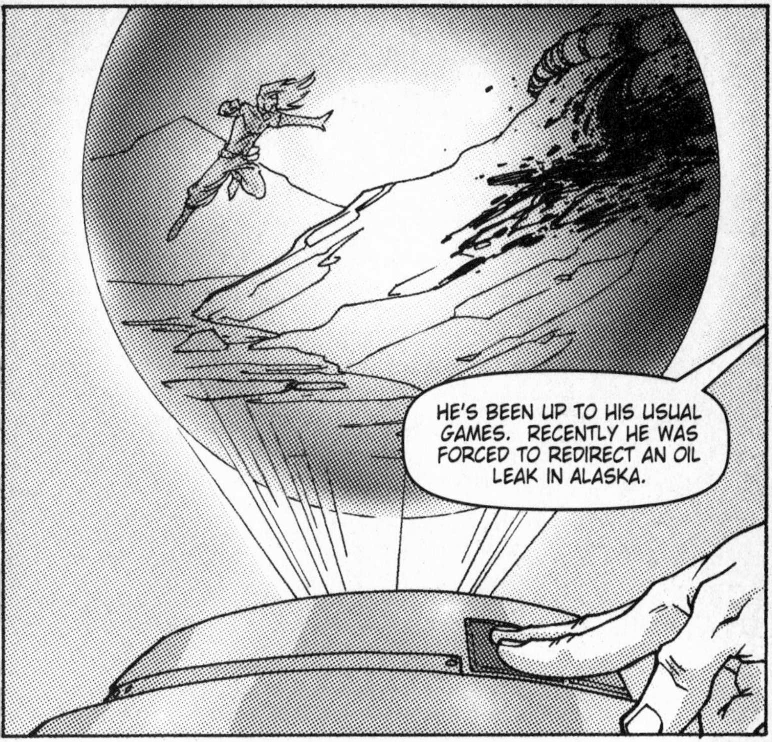
HE'S BEEN UP TO HIS USUAL GAMES. RECENTLY HE WAS FORCED TO REDIRECT AN OIL LEAK IN ALASKA.

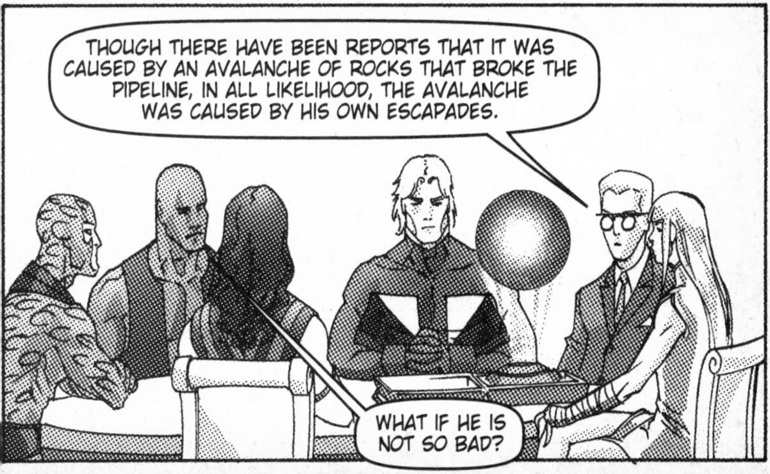
THOUGH THERE HAVE BEEN REPORTS THAT IT WAS CAUSED BY AN AVALANCHE OF ROCKS THAT BROKE THE PIPELINE, IN ALL LIKELIHOOD, THE AVALANCHE WAS CAUSED BY HIS OWN ESCAPADES.
WHAT IF HE IS NOT SO BAD?

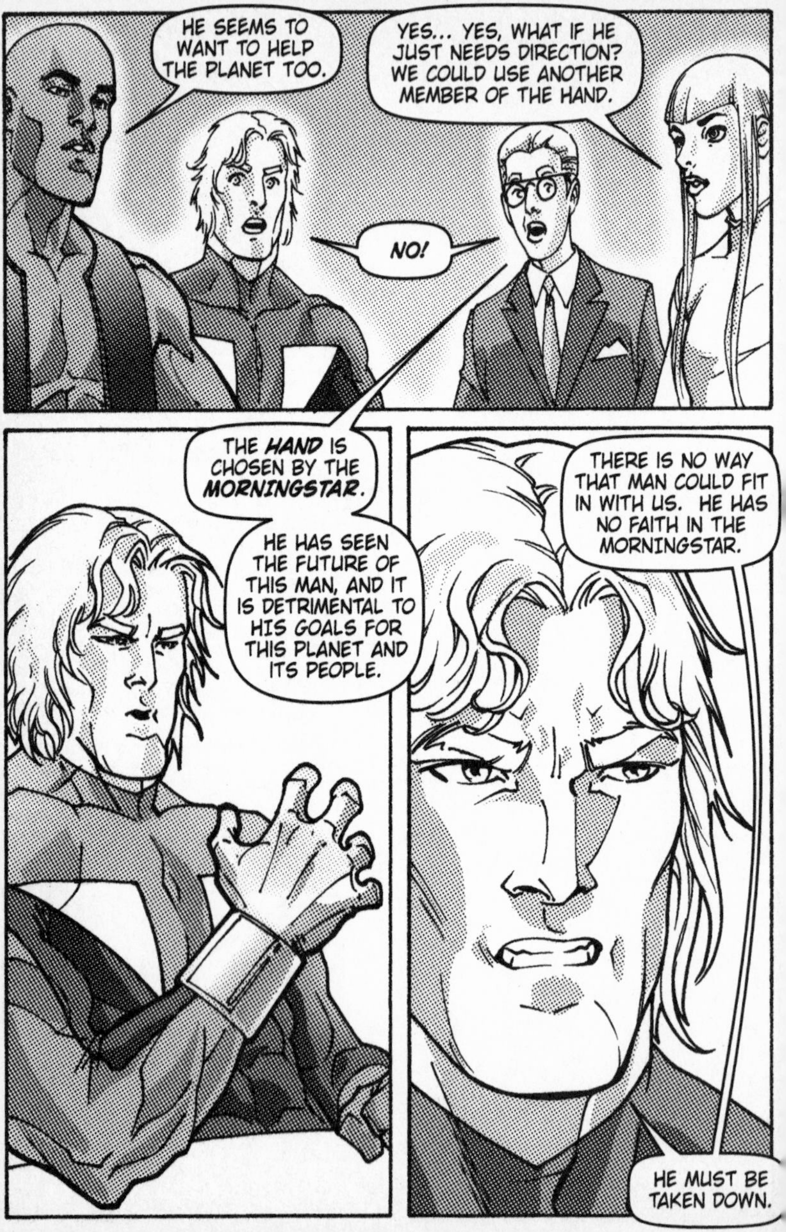
HE SEEMS TO WANT TO HELP THE PLANET TOO.
YES... YES, WHAT IF HE JUST NEEDS DIRECTION? WE COULD USE ANOTHER MEMBER OF THE HAND.
NO!
THE HAND IS CHOSEN BY THE MORNINGSTAR.
HE HAS SEEN THE FUTURE OF THIS MAN, AND IT IS DETRIMENTAL TO HIS GOALS FOR THIS PLANET AND ITS PEOPLE.
THERE IS NO WAY THAT MAN COULD FIT IN WITH US. HE HAS NO FAITH IN THE MORNINGSTAR.
HE MUST BE TAKEN DOWN.

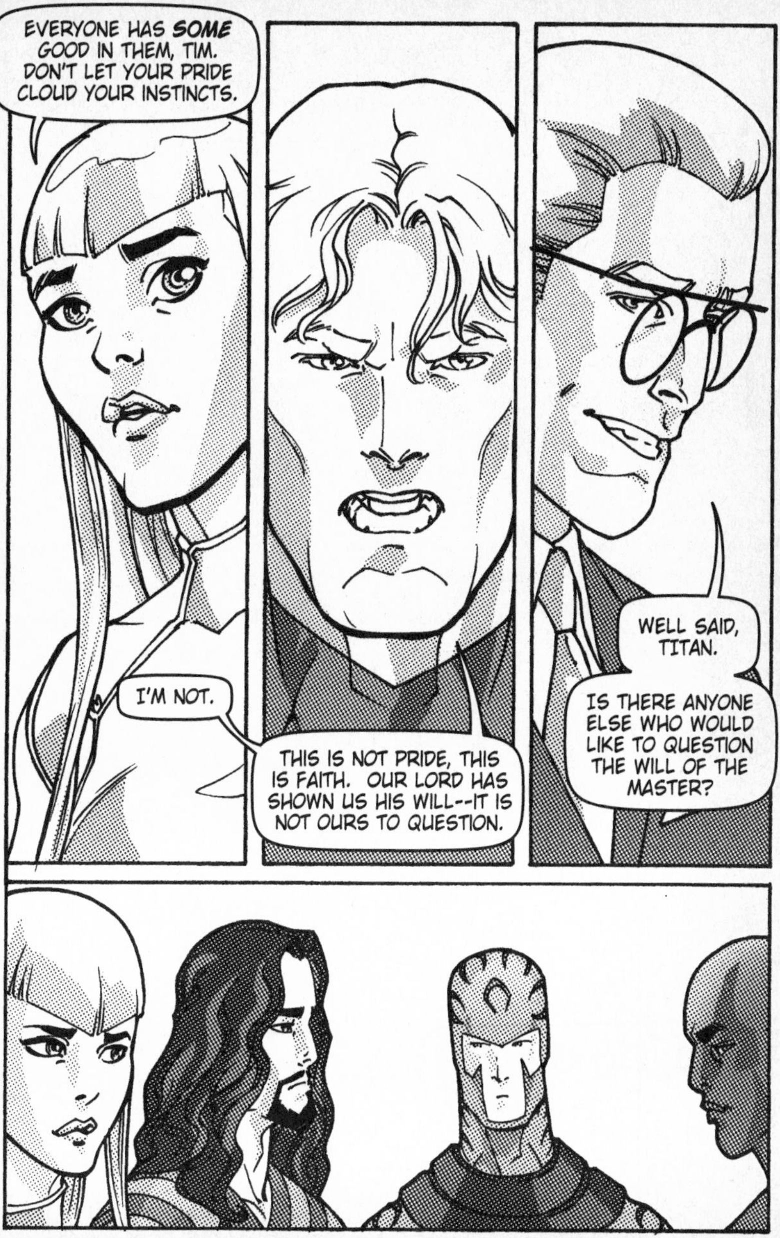
EVERYONE HAS **SOME** GOOD IN THEM, TIM. DON'T LET YOUR PRIDE CLOUD YOUR INSTINCTS.
I'M NOT.
THIS IS NOT PRIDE, THIS IS FAITH. OUR LORD HAS SHOWN US HIS WILL--IT IS NOT OURS TO QUESTION.
WELL SAID, TITAN.
IS THERE ANYONE ELSE WHO WOULD LIKE TO QUESTION THE WILL OF THE MASTER?

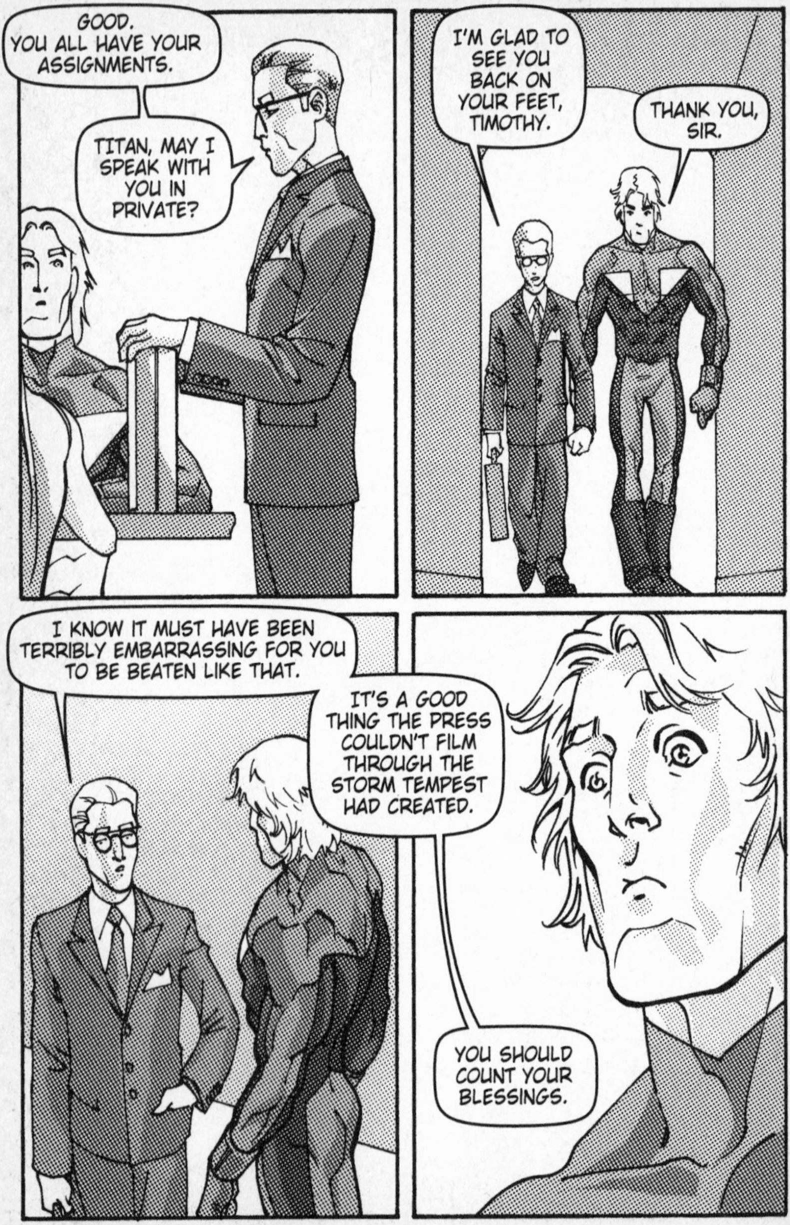
GOOD. YOU ALL HAVE YOUR ASSIGNMENTS.
TITAN, MAY I SPEAK WITH YOU IN PRIVATE?
I'M GLAD TO SEE YOU BACK ON YOUR FEET, TIMOTHY.
THANK YOU, SIR.
I KNOW IT MUST HAVE BEEN TERRIBLY EMBARRASSING FOR YOU TO BE BEATEN LIKE THAT.
IT'S A GOOD THING THE PRESS COULDN'T FILM THROUGH THE STORM TEMPEST HAD CREATED.
YOU SHOULD COUNT YOUR BLESSINGS.

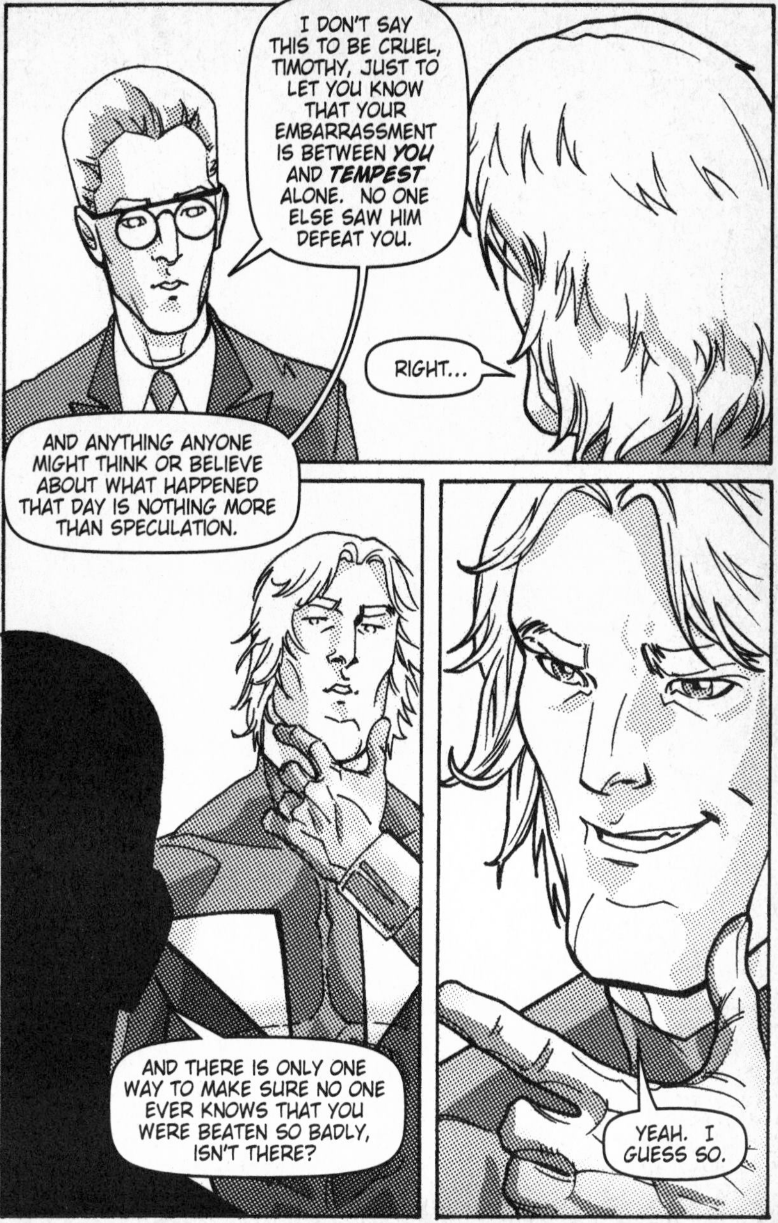
I DON'T SAY THIS TO BE CRUEL, TIMOTHY, JUST TO LET YOU KNOW THAT YOUR EMBARRASSMENT IS BETWEEN *YOU* AND *TEMPEST* ALONE. NO ONE ELSE SAW HIM DEFEAT YOU.
RIGHT...
AND ANYTHING ANYONE MIGHT THINK OR BELIEVE ABOUT WHAT HAPPENED THAT DAY IS NOTHING MORE THAN SPECULATION.
AND THERE IS ONLY ONE WAY TO MAKE SURE NO ONE EVER KNOWS THAT YOU WERE BEATEN SO BADLY, ISN'T THERE?
YEAH. I GUESS SO.

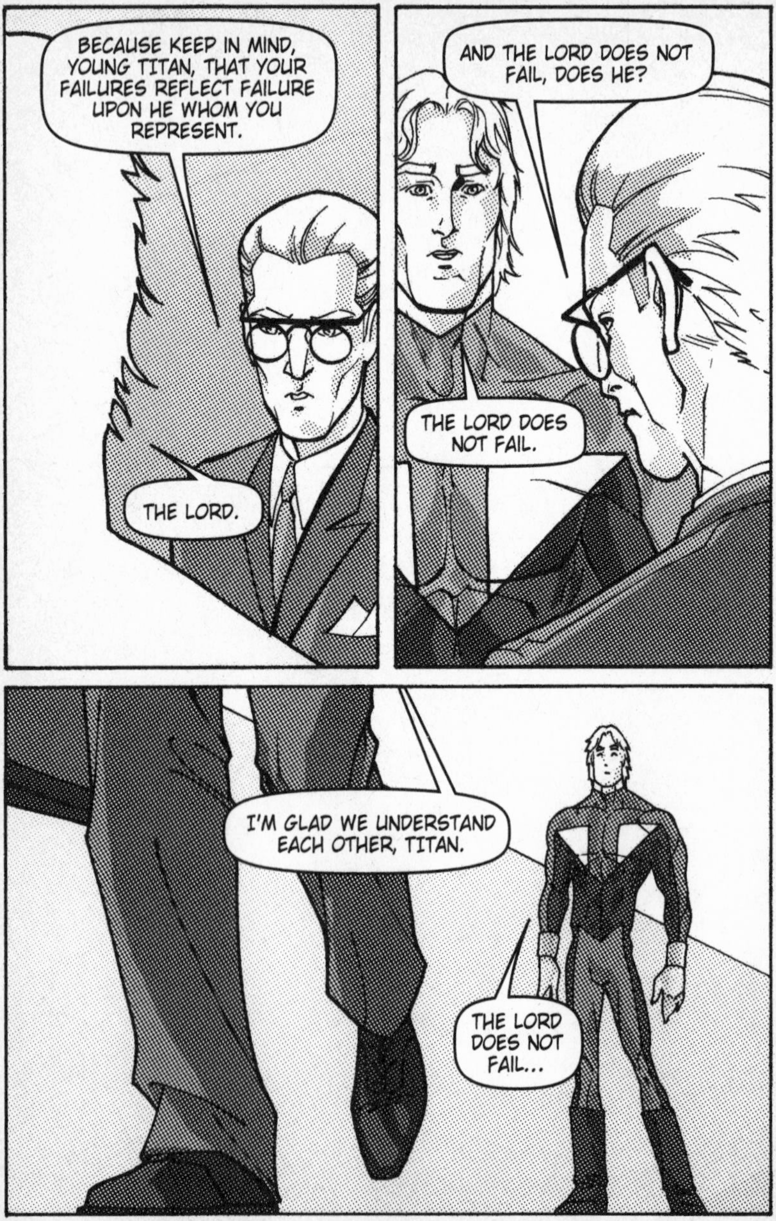
BECAUSE KEEP IN MIND, YOUNG TITAN, THAT YOUR FAILURES REFLECT FAILURE UPON HE WHOM YOU REPRESENT.
THE LORD.
AND THE LORD DOES NOT FAIL, DOES HE?
THE LORD DOES NOT FAIL.
I'M GLAD WE UNDERSTAND EACH OTHER, TITAN.
THE LORD DOES NOT FAIL...

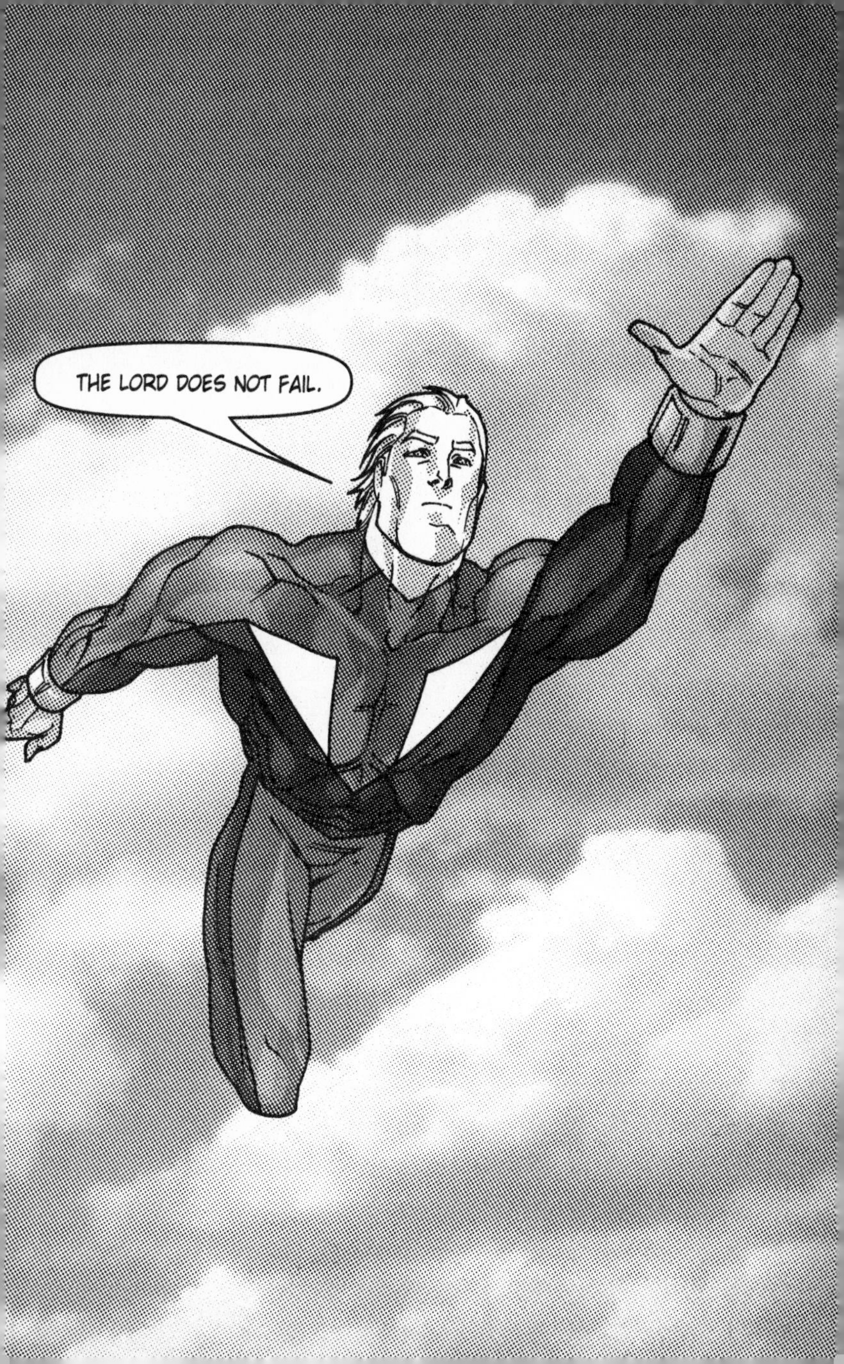
THE LORD DOES NOT FAIL.

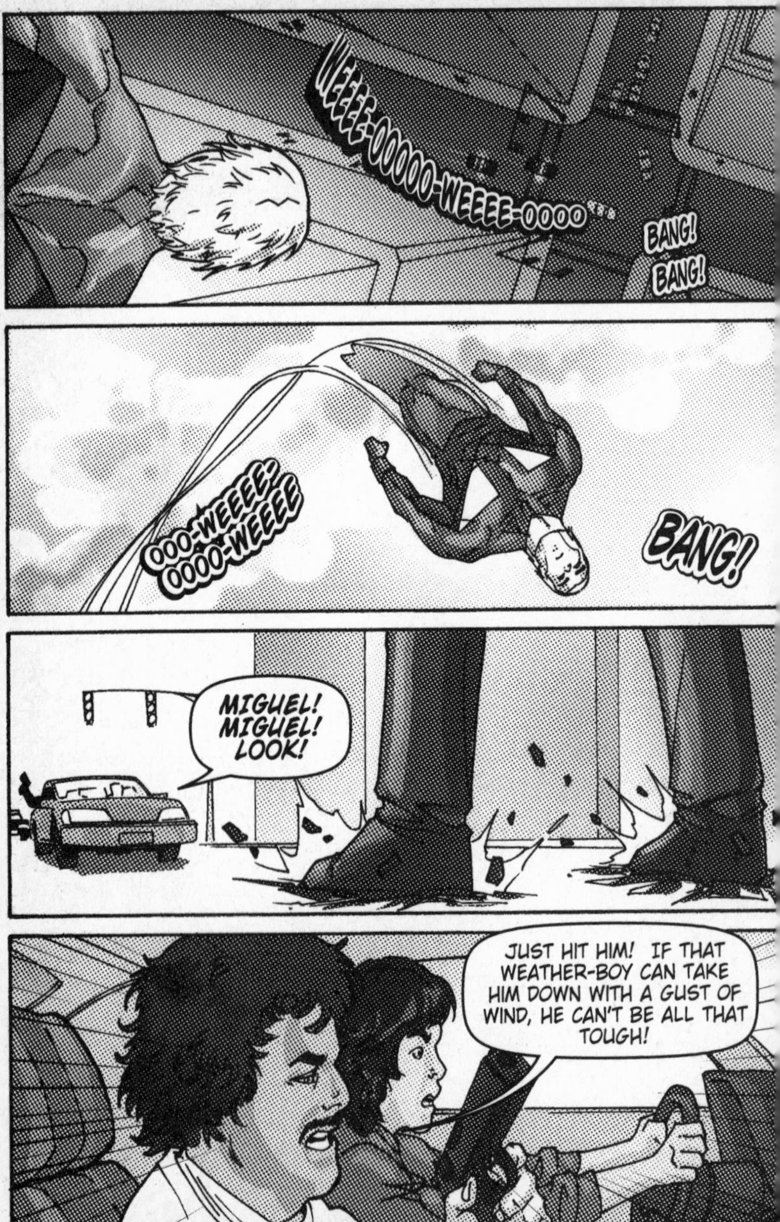
WEEEE-OOOOO-WEEEE-OOOO
BANG!
BANG!
OOO-WEEEE-
OOOO-WEEEE
BANG!
MIGUEL! MIGUEL! LOOK!
JUST HIT HIM! IF THAT WEATHER-BOY CAN TAKE HIM DOWN WITH A GUST OF WIND, HE CAN'T BE ALL THAT TOUGH!

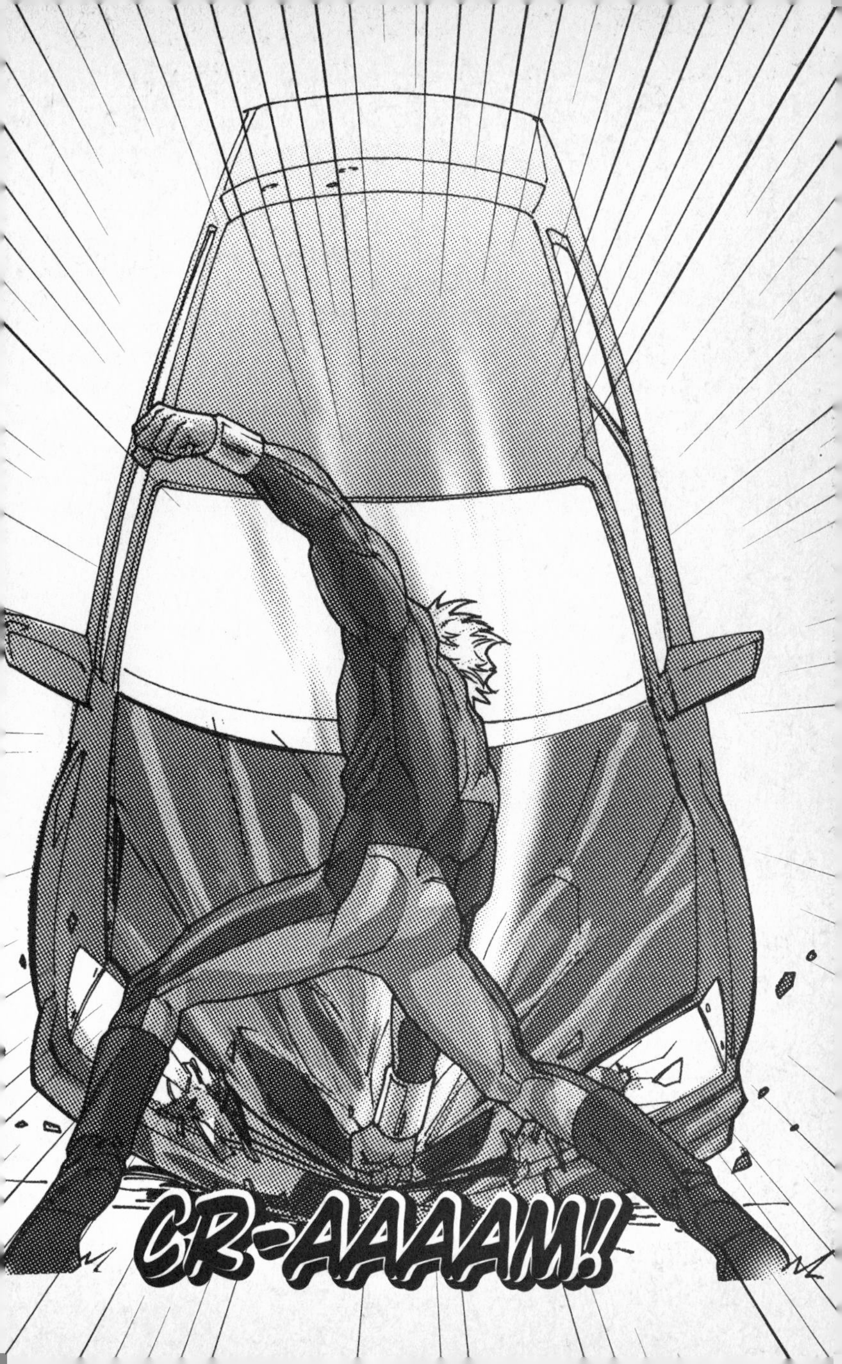
CR-AAAAAM!

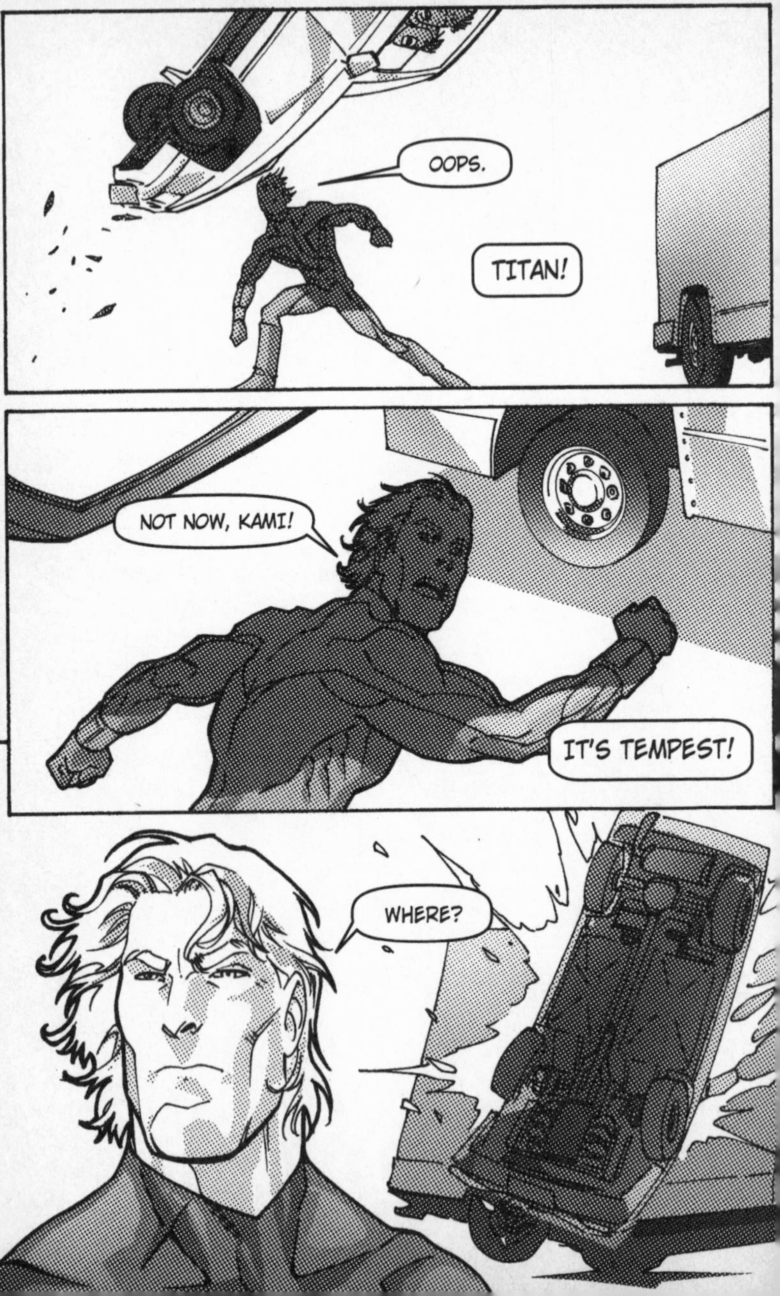
OOPS.
TITAN!
NOT NOW, KAMI!
IT'S TEMPEST!
WHERE?

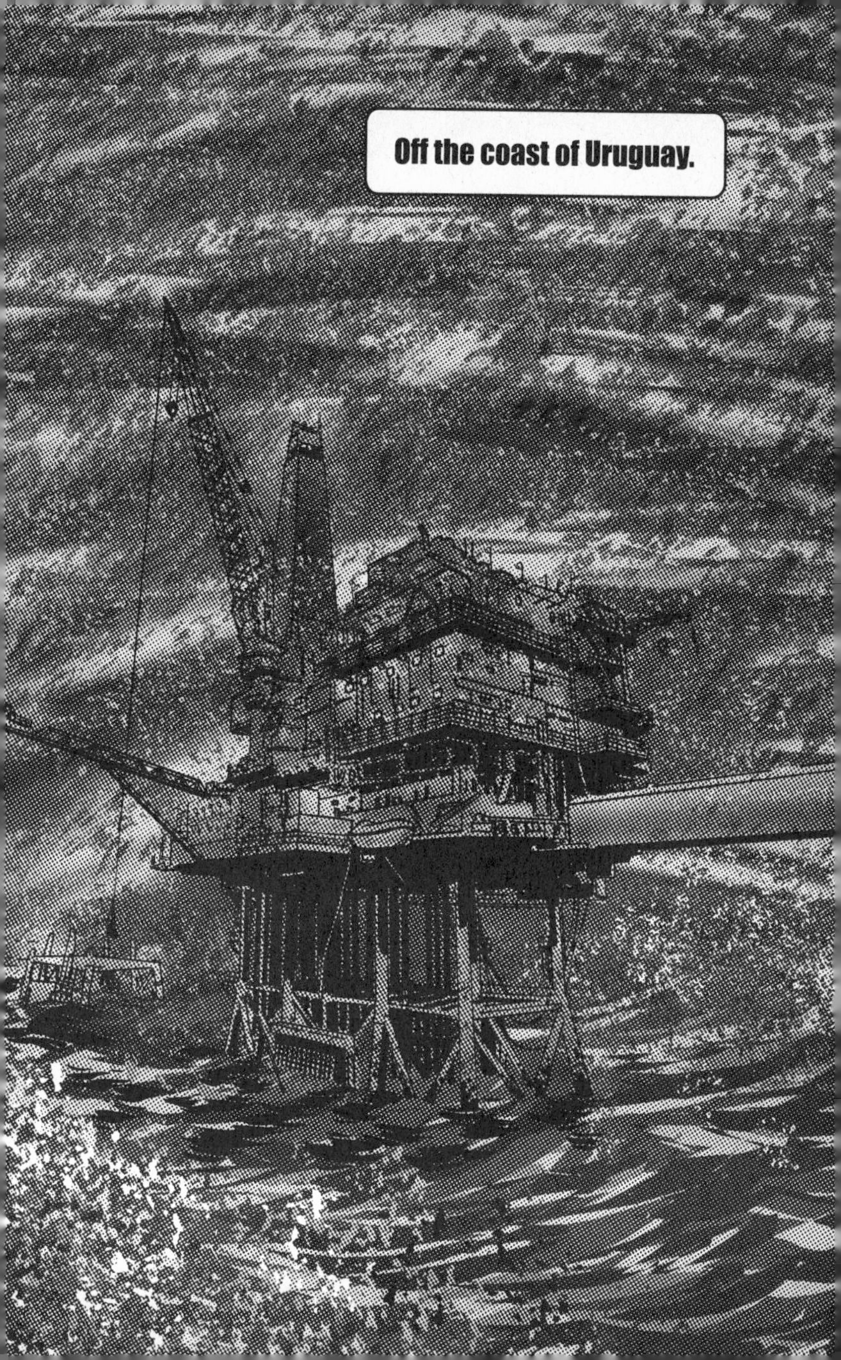
Off the coast of Uruguay.

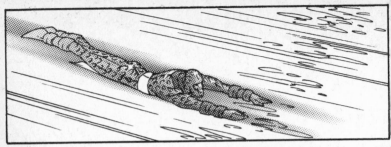

YOU WILL STOP RAPING THIS PLANET, OR I WILL MAKE YOU STOP! DO YOU HEAR ME?

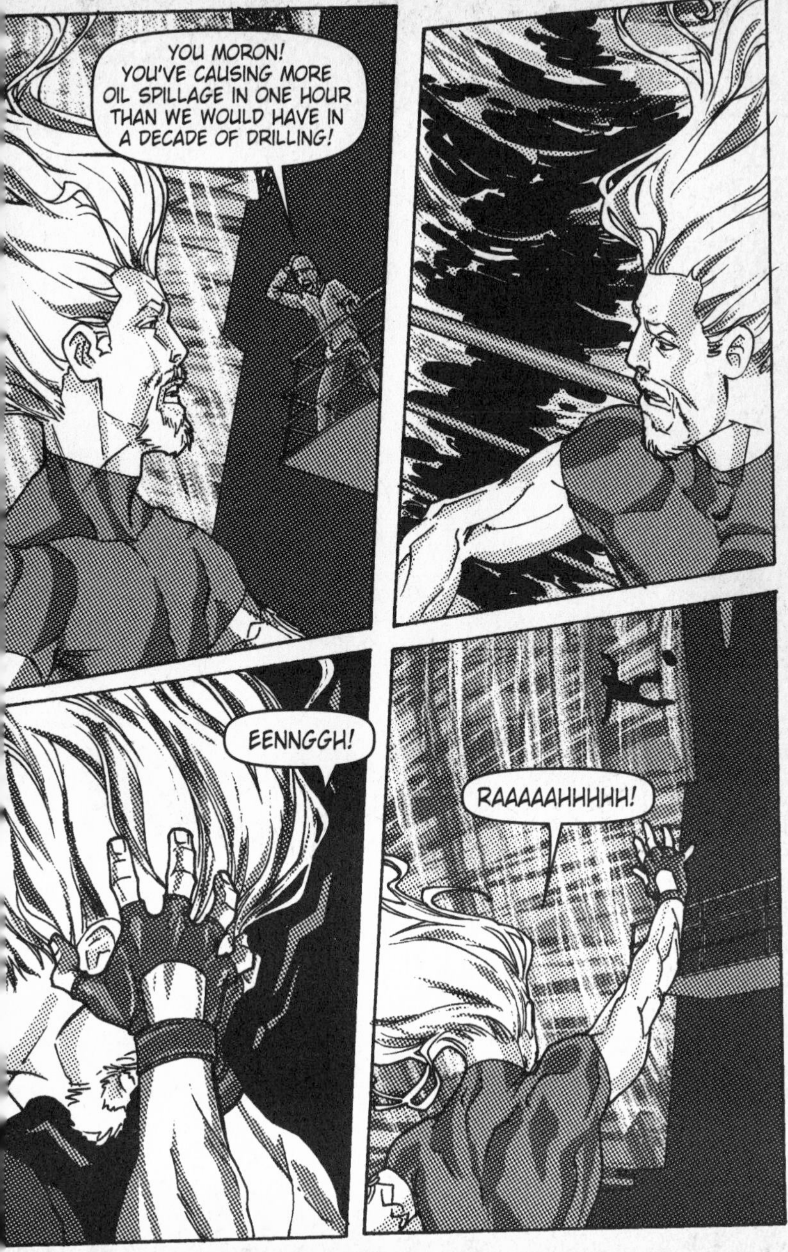
YOU MORON!
YOU'VE CAUSING MORE OIL SPILLAGE IN ONE HOUR THAN WE WOULD HAVE IN A DECADE OF DRILLING!
EENNGGH!
RAAAAAHHHHH!

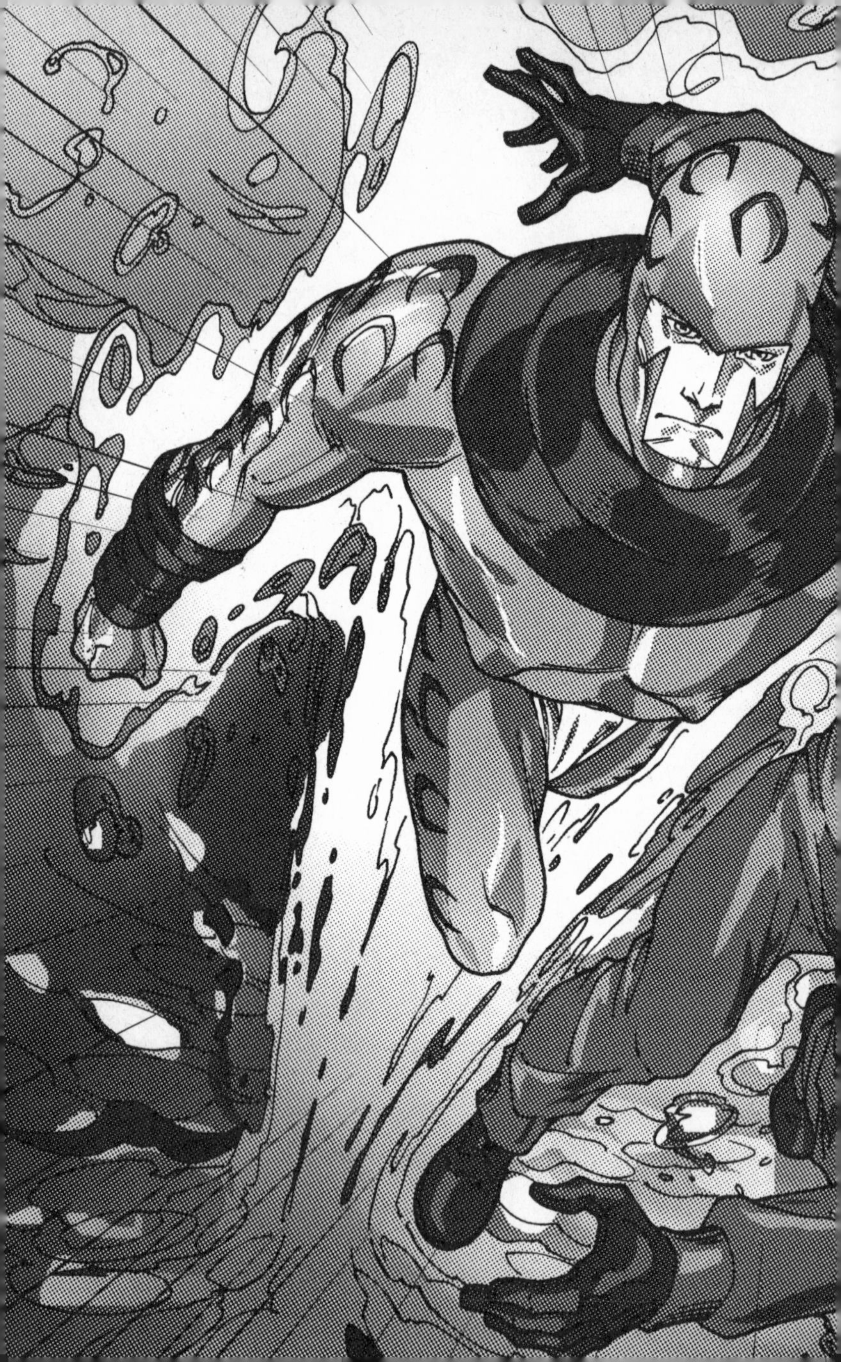

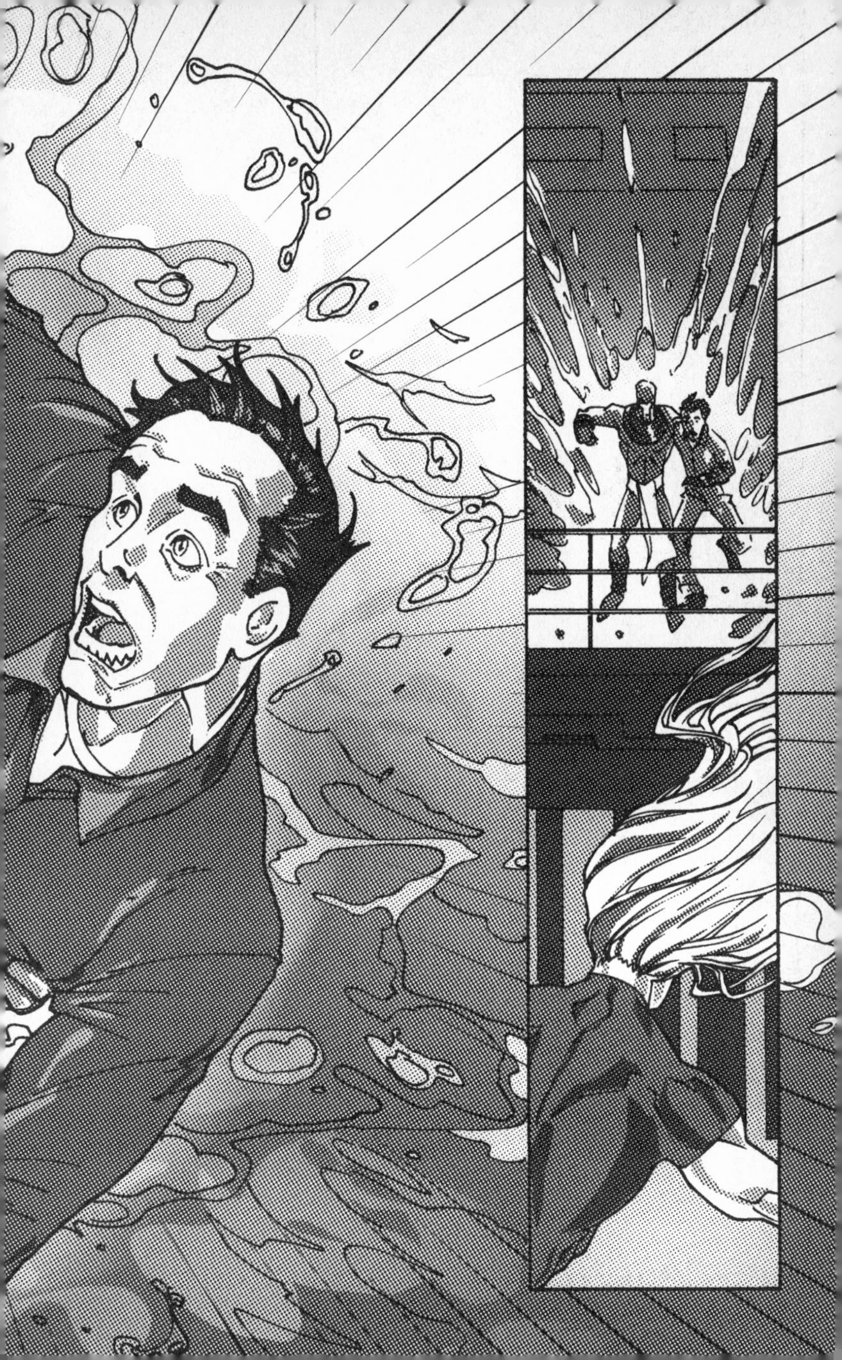

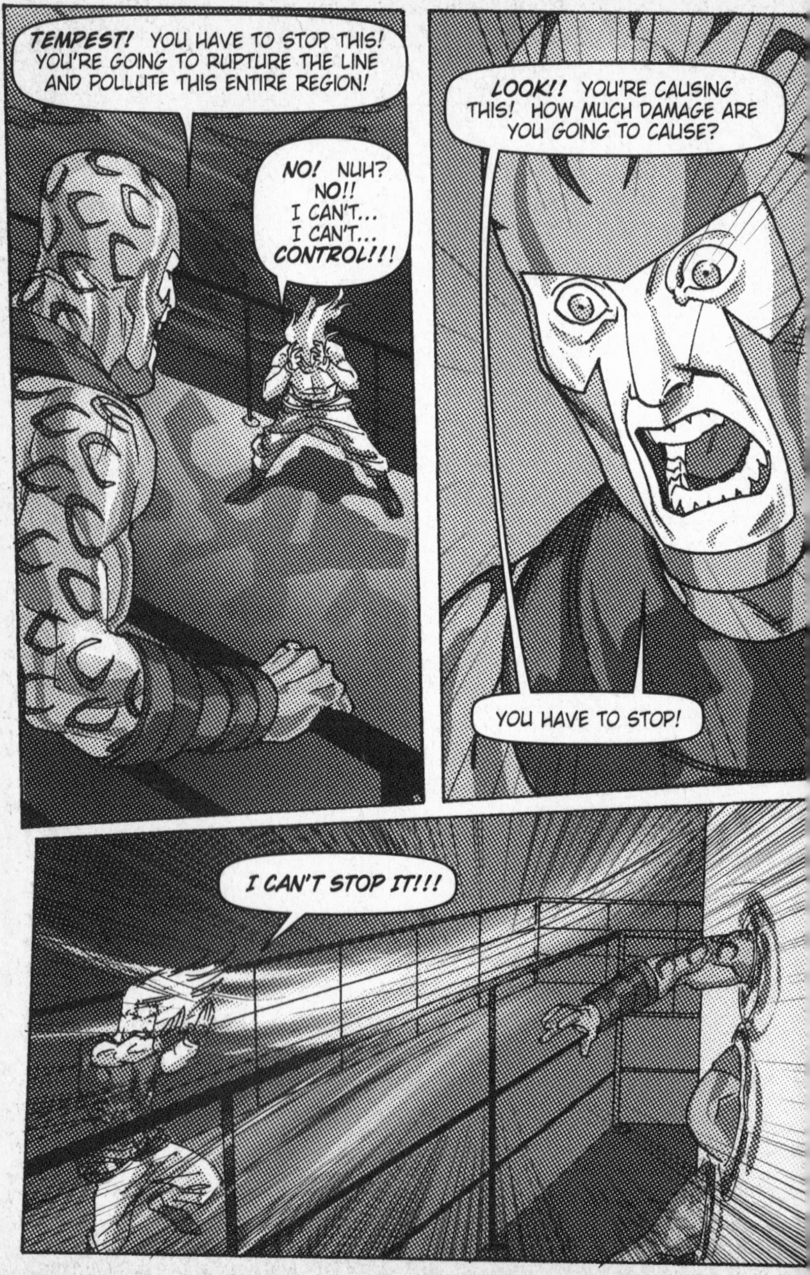
TEMPEST! YOU HAVE TO STOP THIS! YOU'RE GOING TO RUPTURE THE LINE AND POLLUTE THIS ENTIRE REGION!
NO! NUH? NO!! I CAN'T... I CAN'T... CONTROL!!!
LOOK!! YOU'RE CAUSING THIS! HOW MUCH DAMAGE ARE YOU GOING TO CAUSE?
YOU HAVE TO STOP!
I CAN'T STOP IT!!!

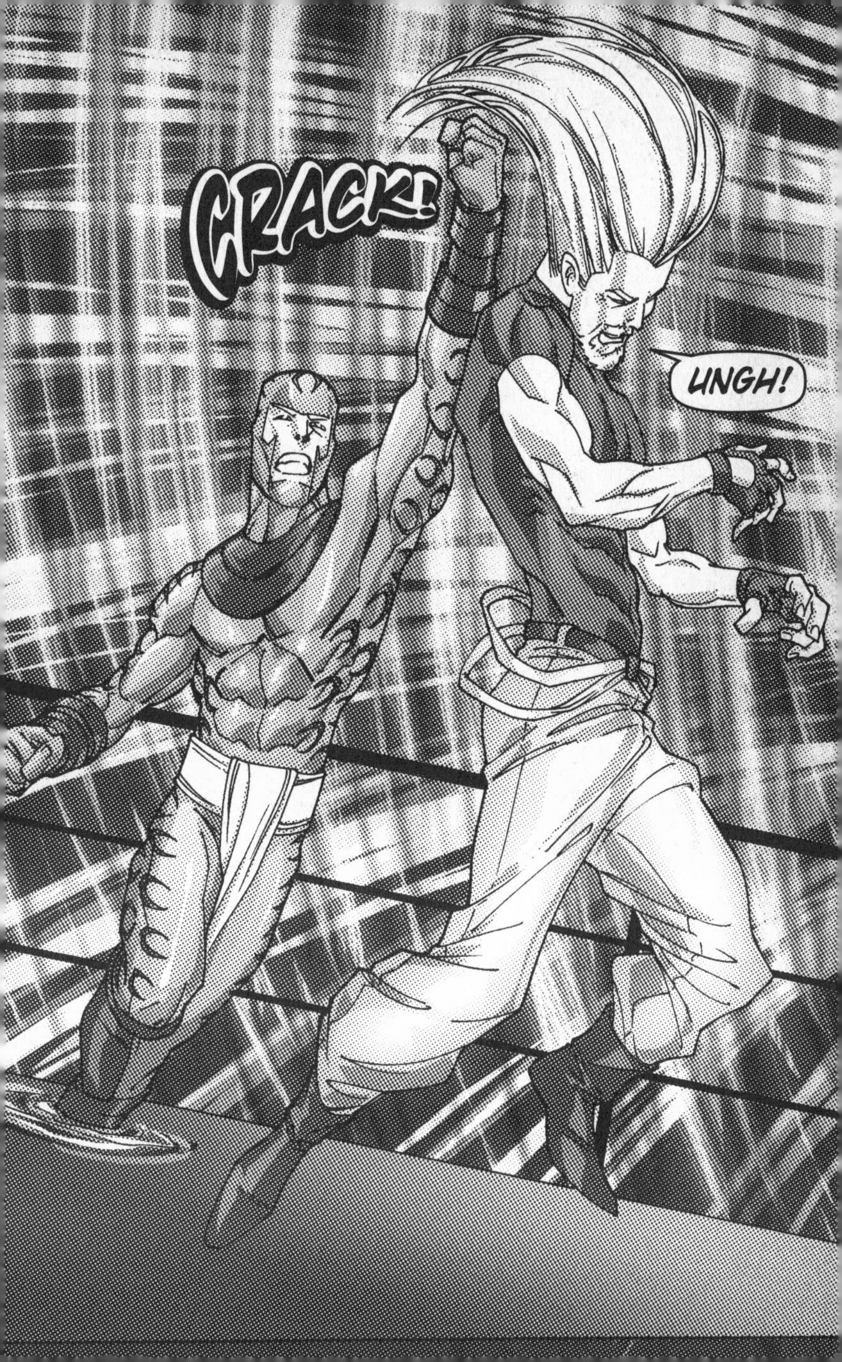
CRACK!
UNGH!

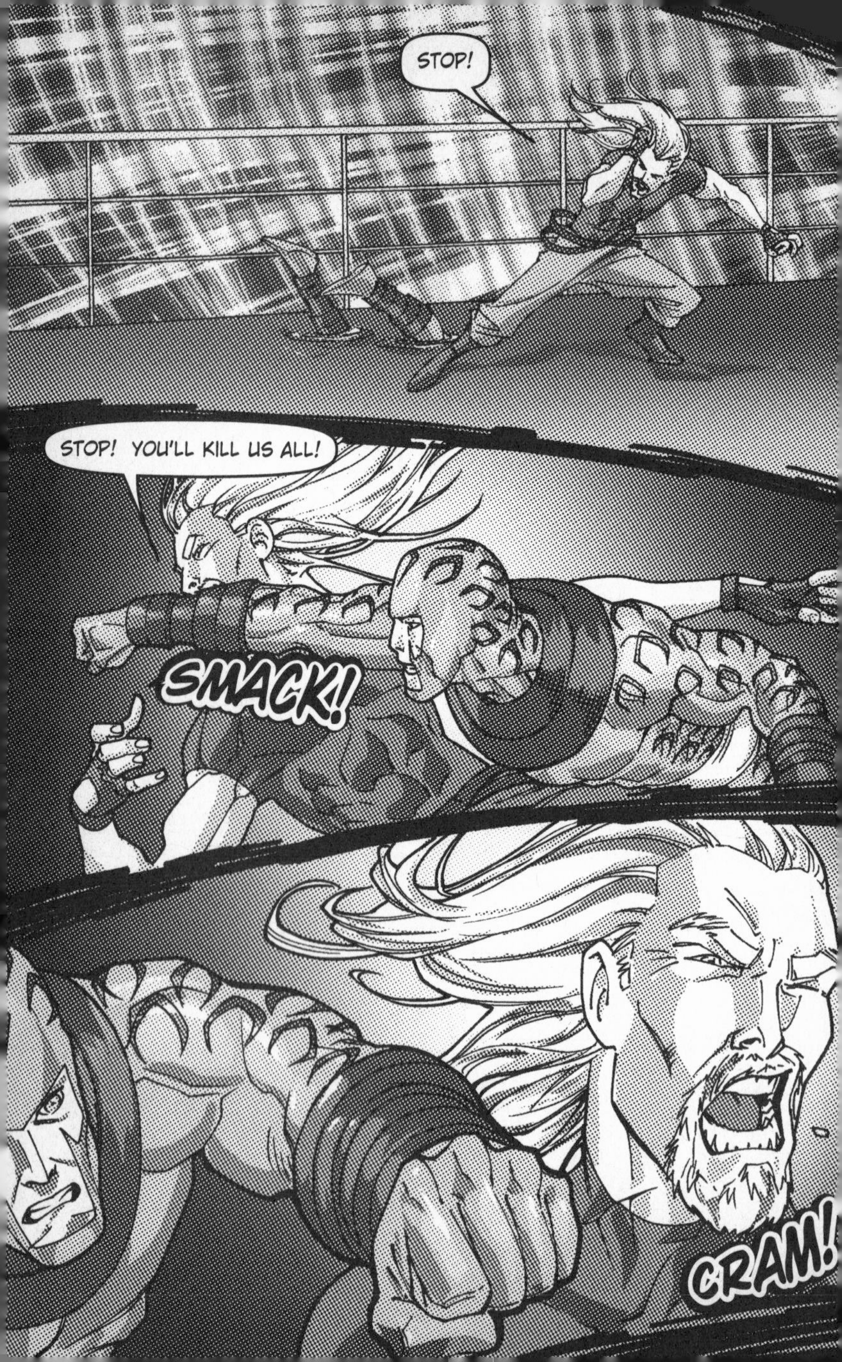
STOP!
STOP! YOU'LL KILL US ALL!
SMACK!
CRAM!

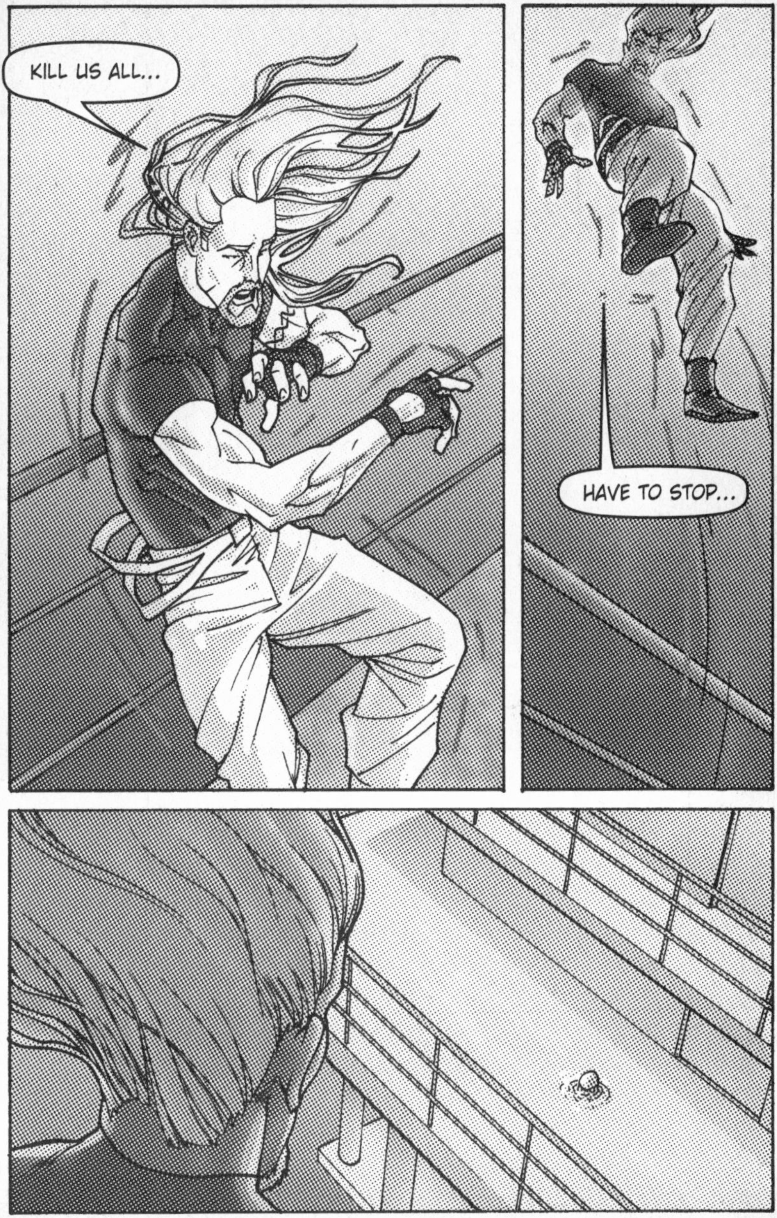
KILL US ALL...
HAVE TO STOP...

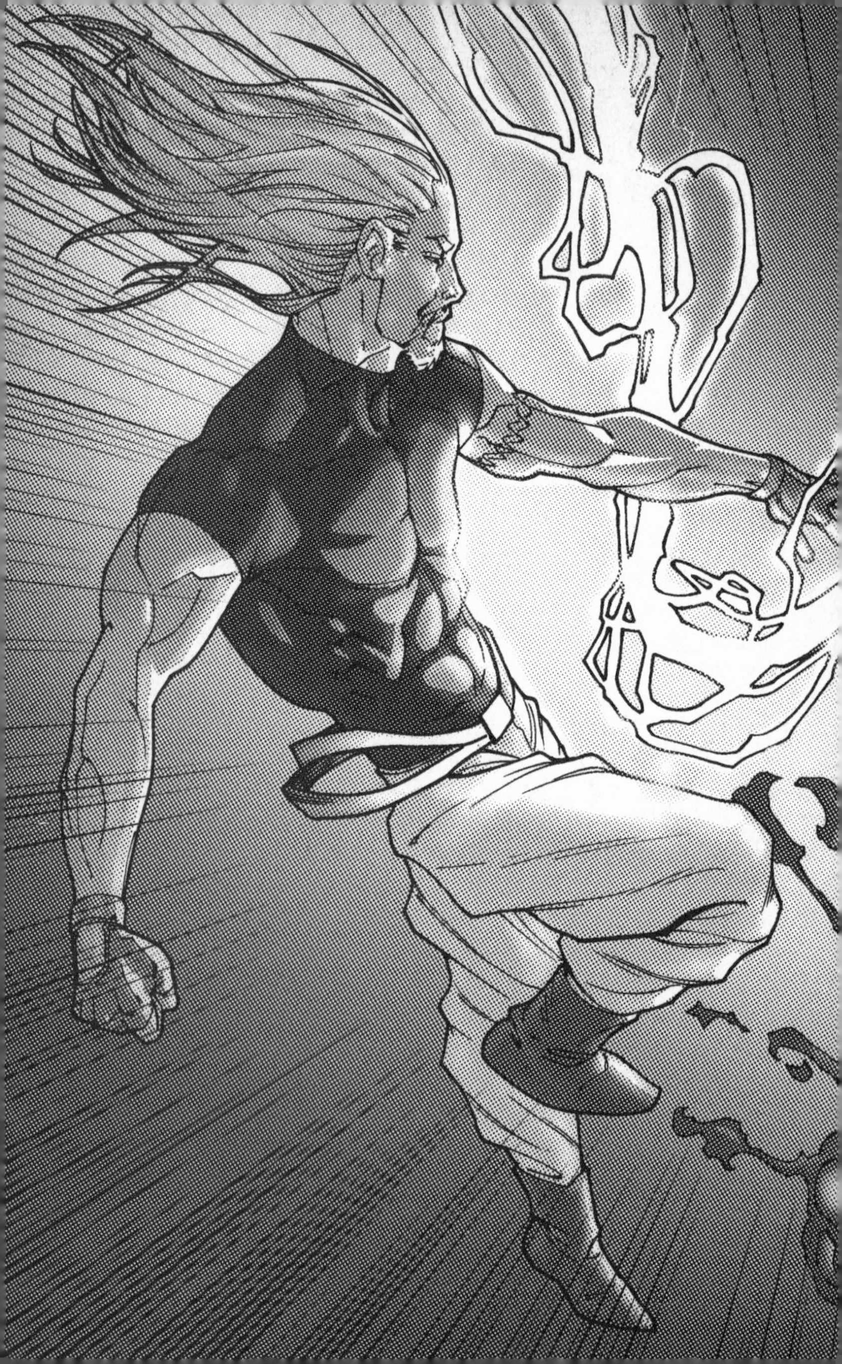

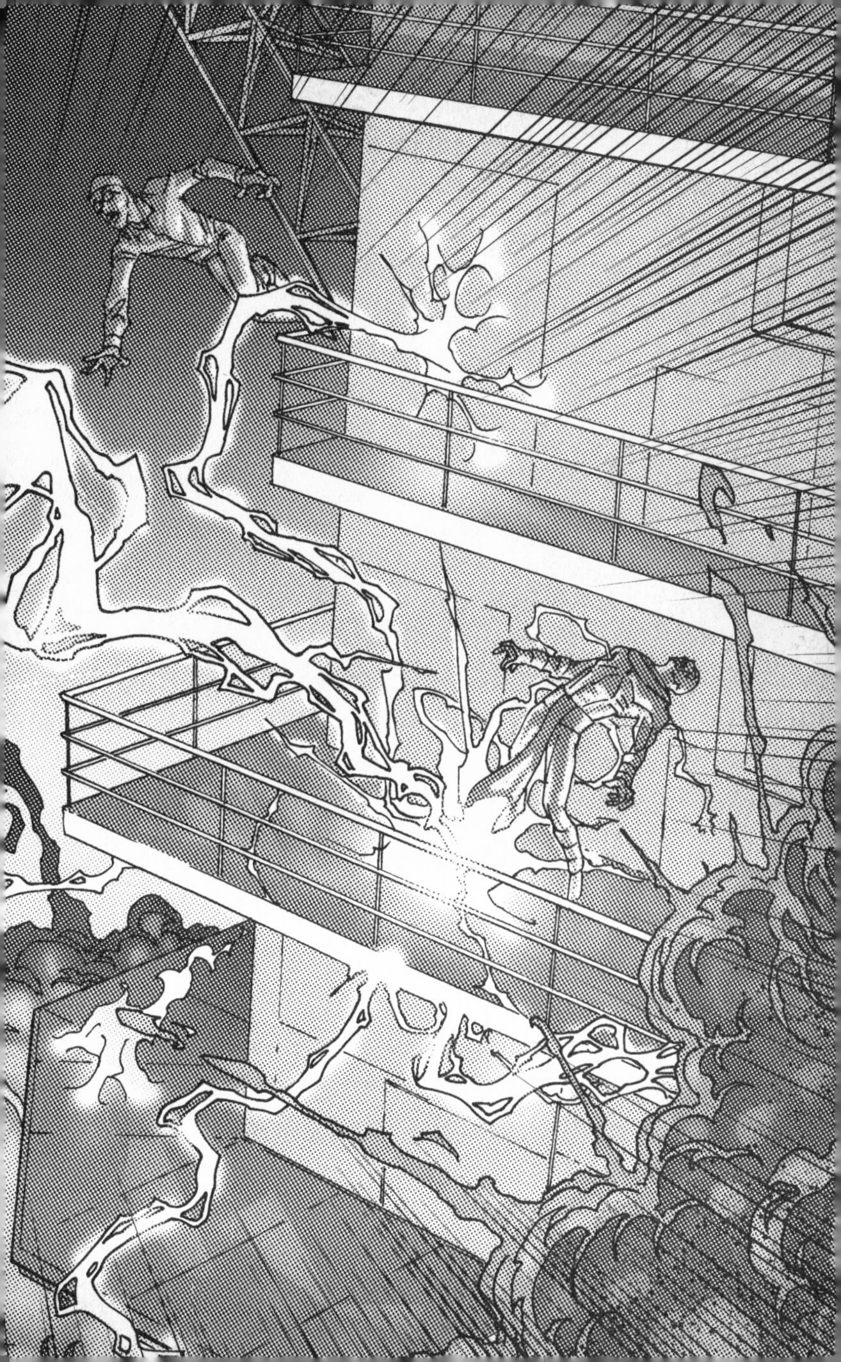

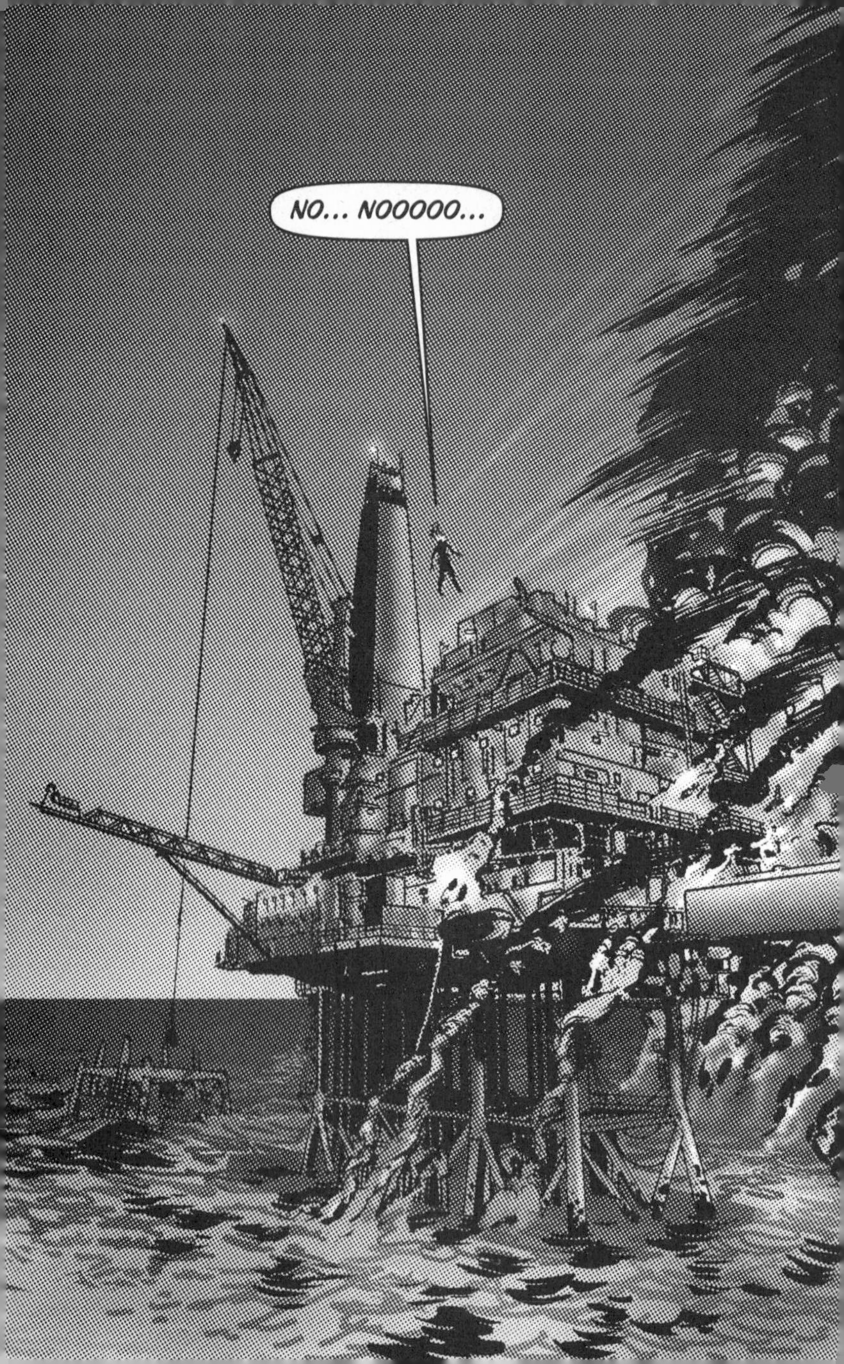
NO... NOOOOO...

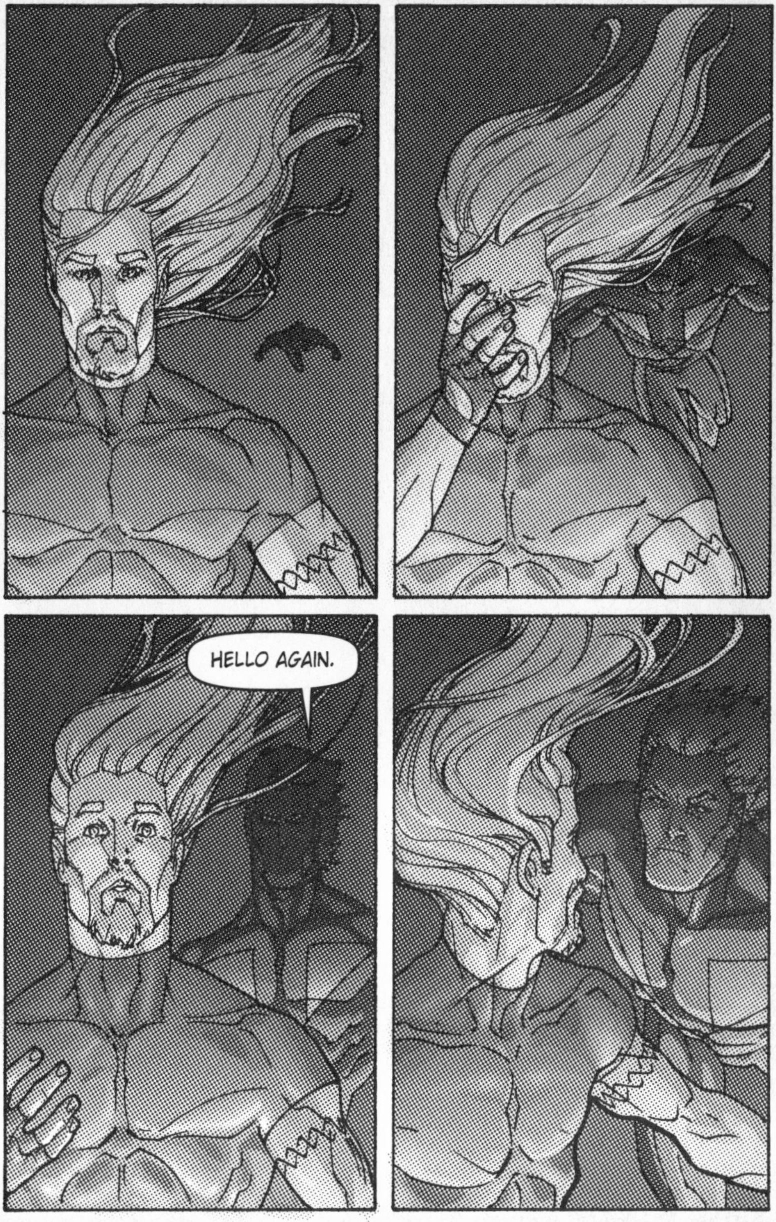
HELLO AGAIN.

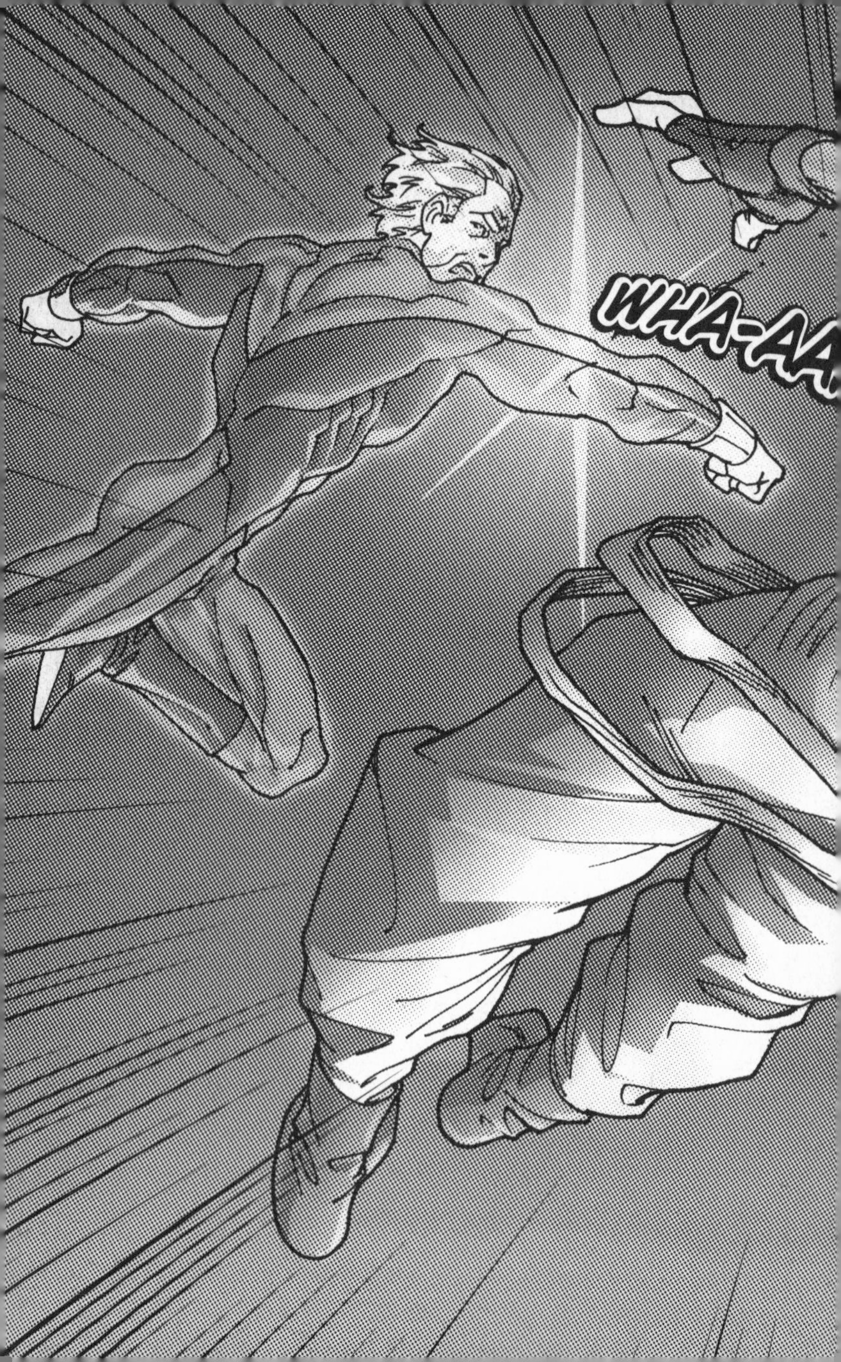
WHA-AA

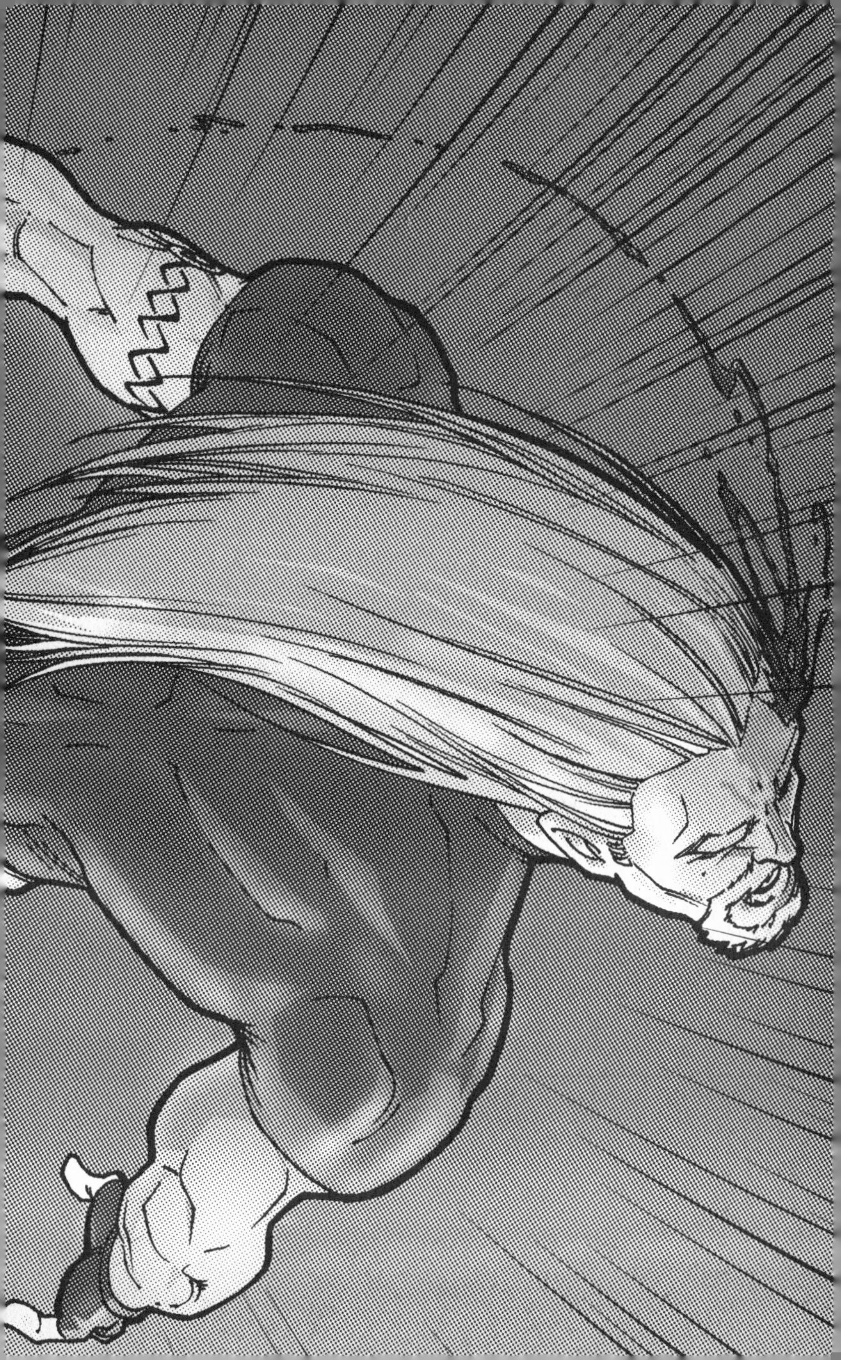

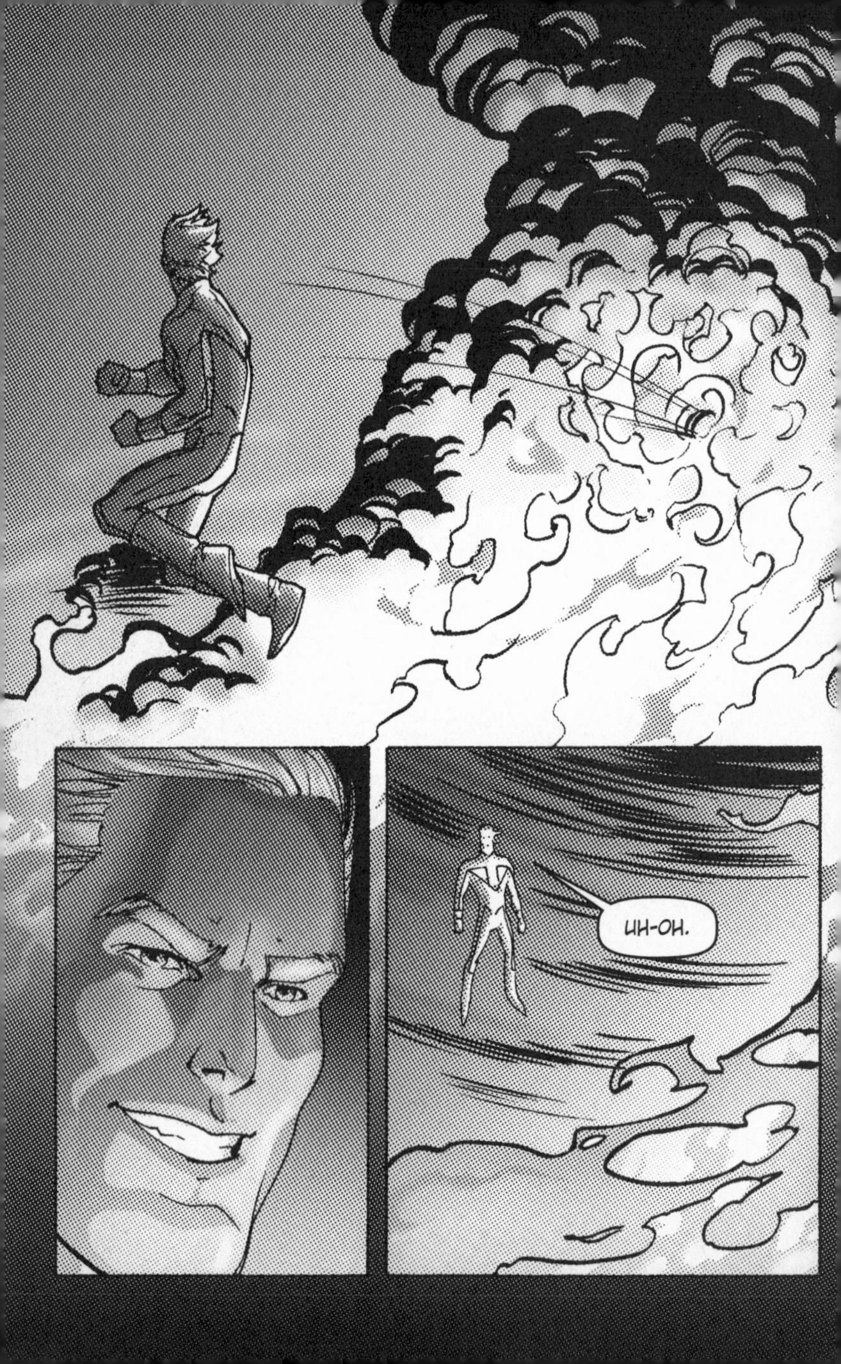
UH-OH.

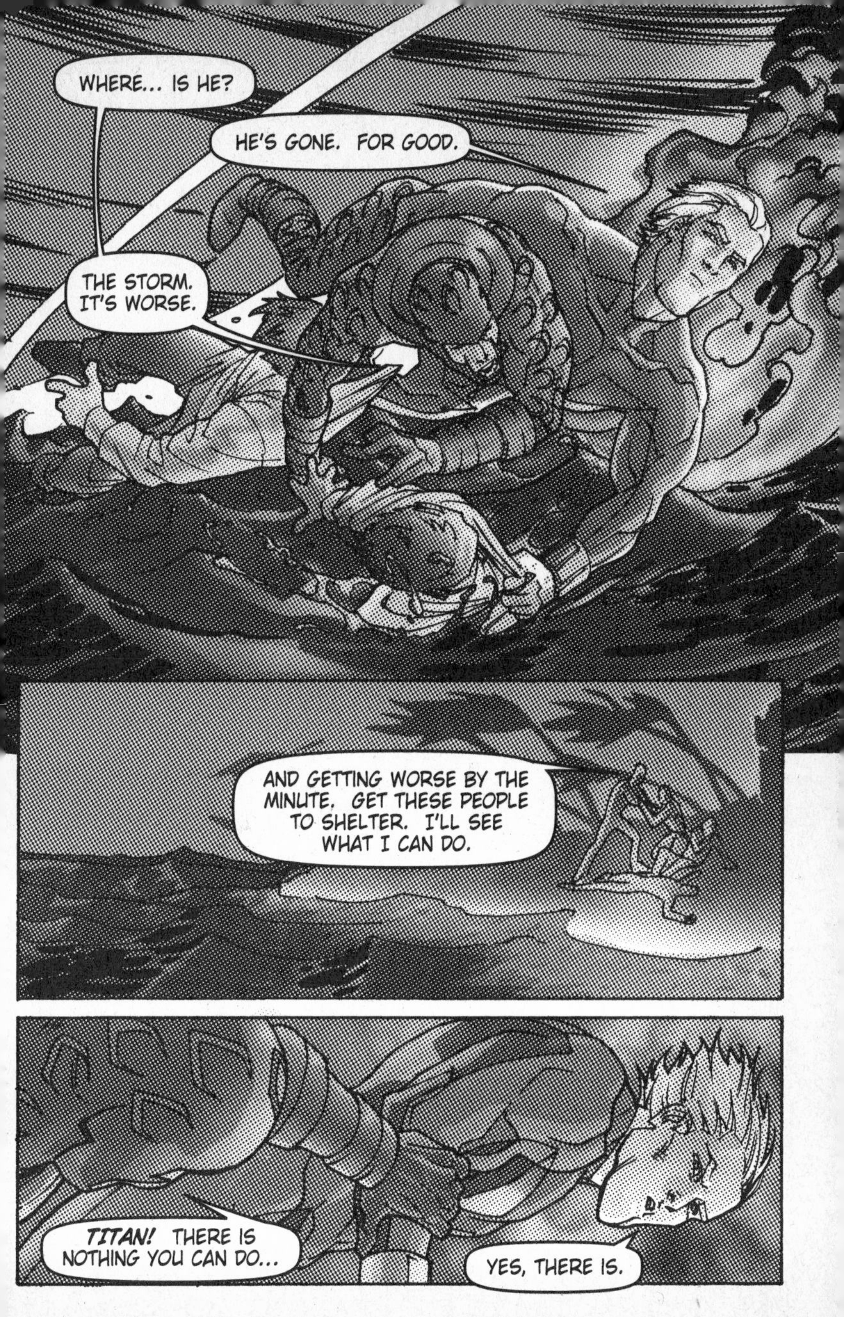
WHERE... IS HE?
HE'S GONE. FOR GOOD.
THE STORM. IT'S WORSE.
AND GETTING WORSE BY THE MINUTE. GET THESE PEOPLE TO SHELTER. I'LL SEE WHAT I CAN DO.
TITAN! THERE IS NOTHING YOU CAN DO...
YES, THERE IS.

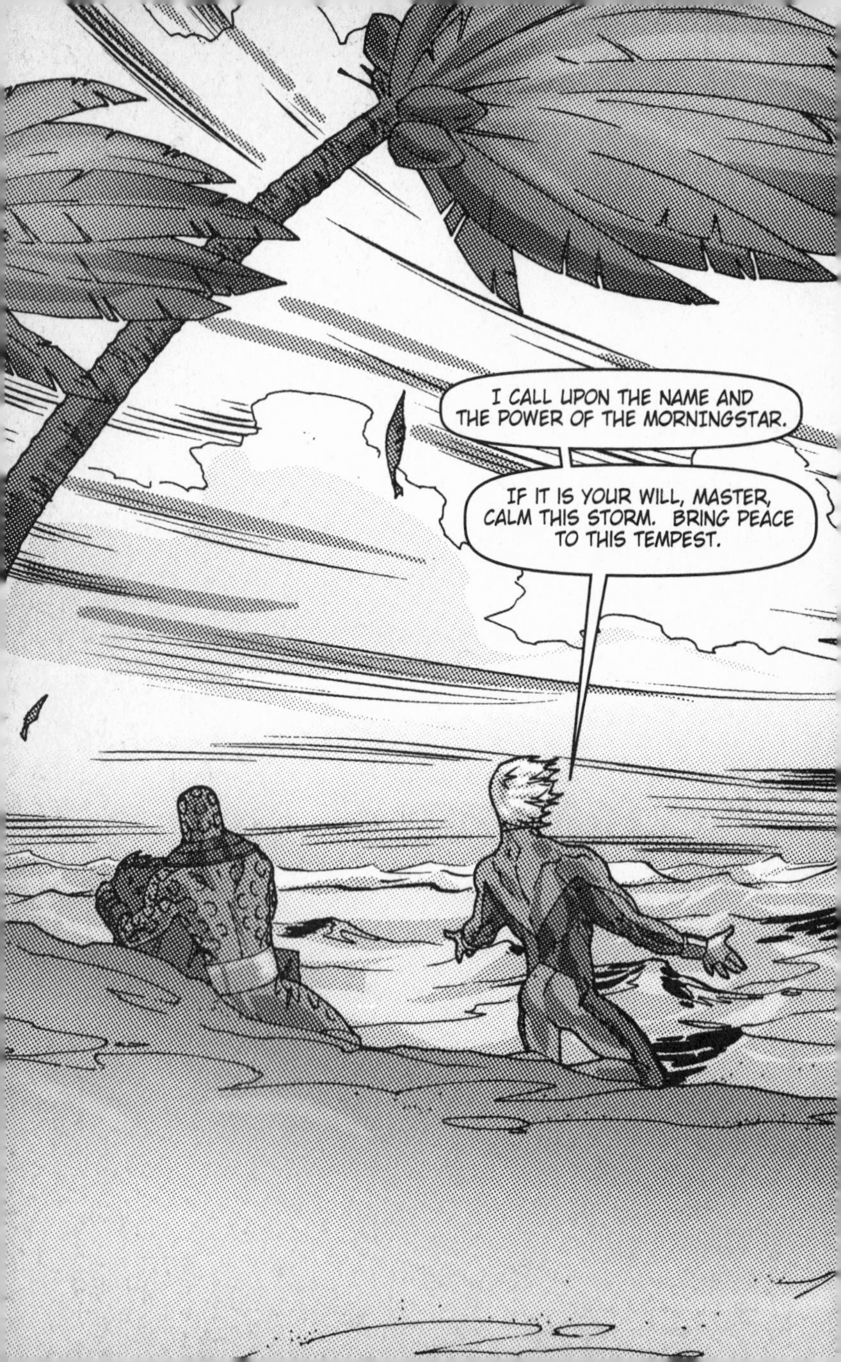
I CALL UPON THE NAME AND THE POWER OF THE MORNINGSTAR.
IF IT IS YOUR WILL, MASTER, CALM THIS STORM. BRING PEACE TO THIS TEMPEST.

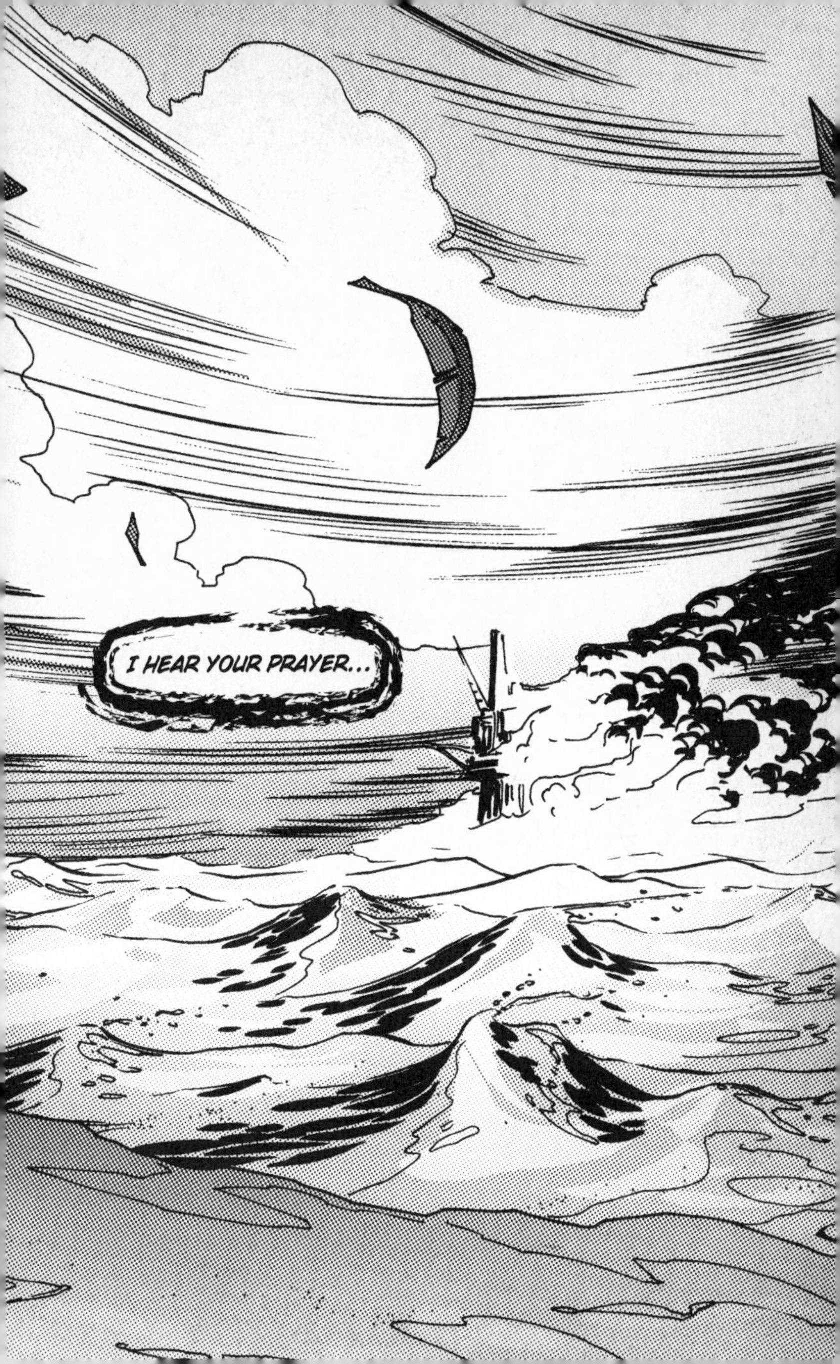
I HEAR YOUR PRAYER...

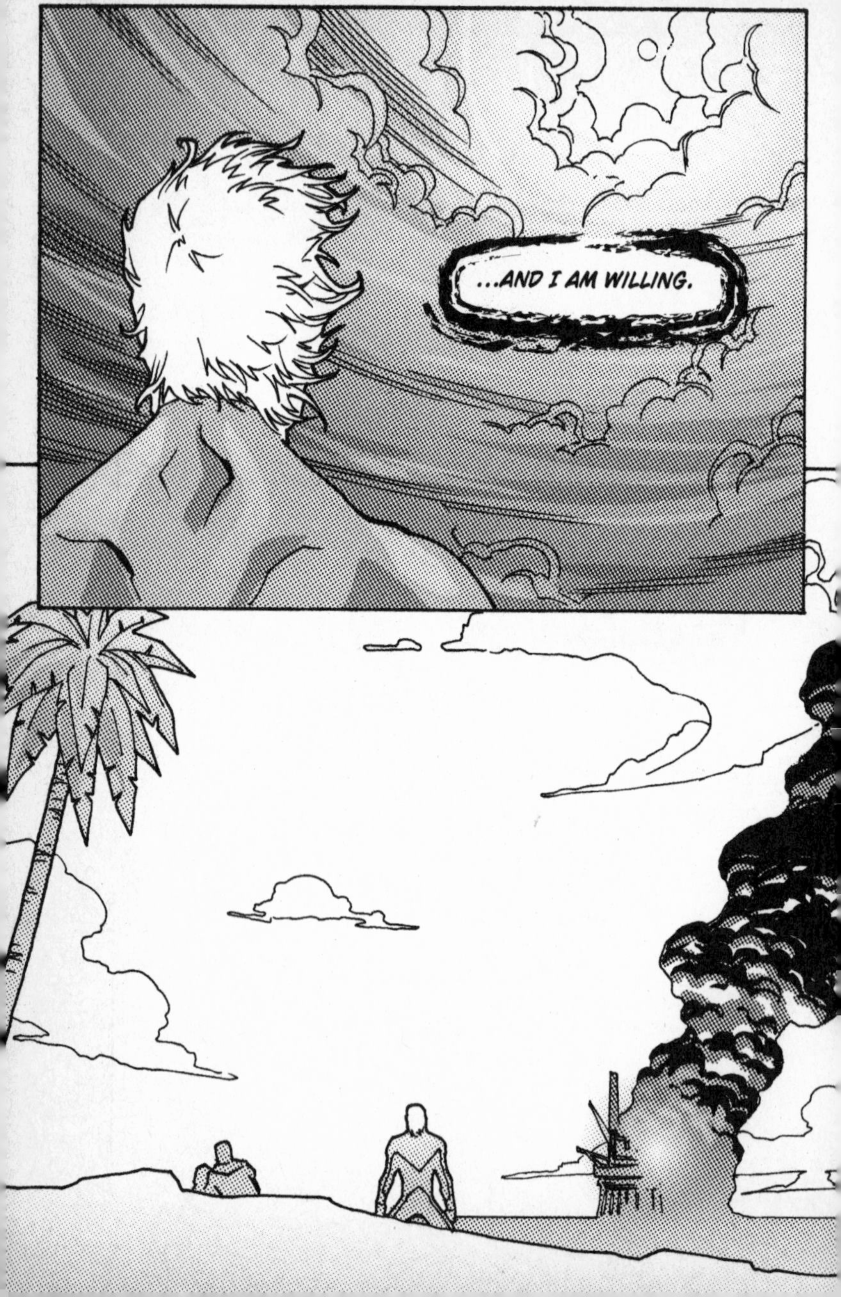
...AND I AM WILLING.

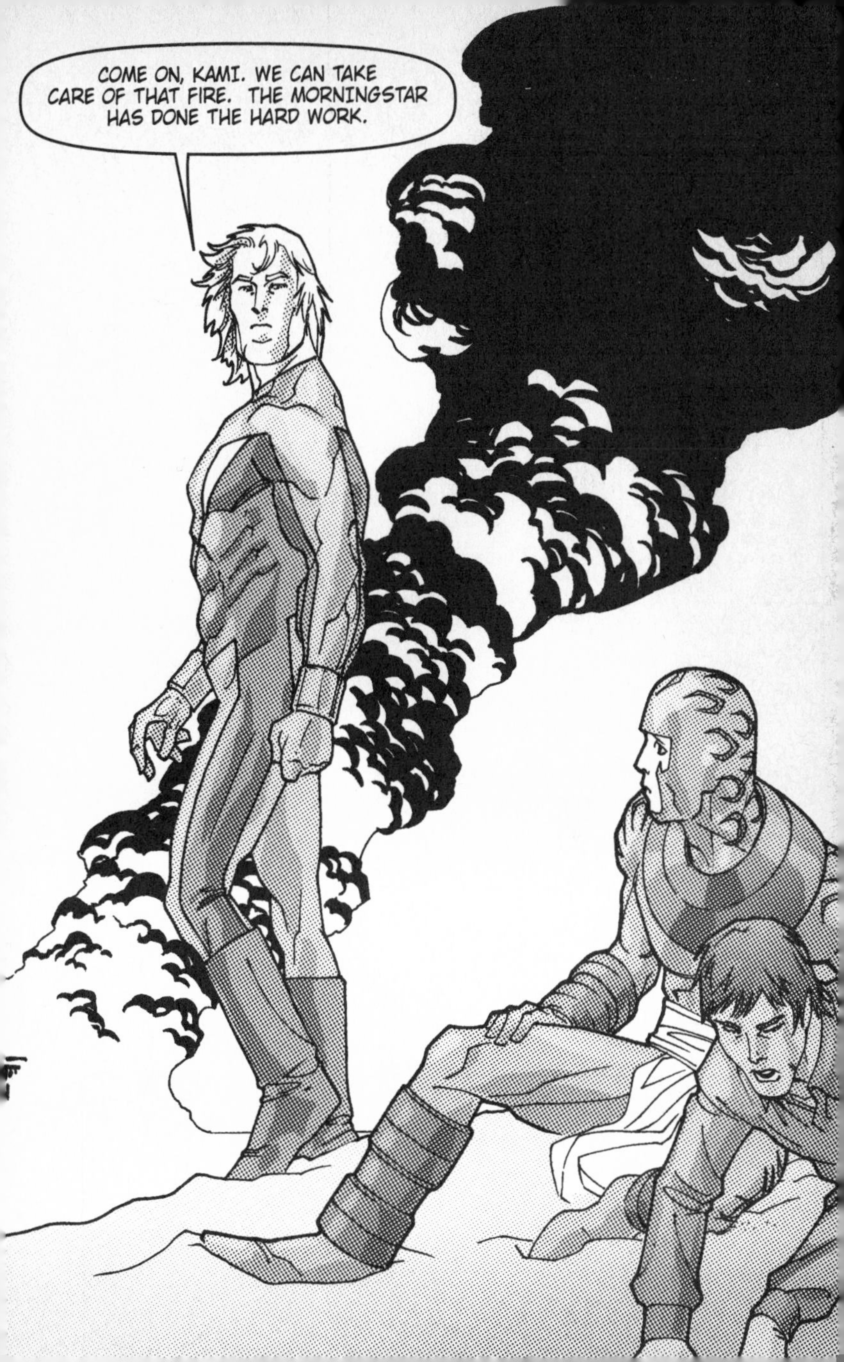
COME ON, KAMI. WE CAN TAKE CARE OF THAT FIRE. THE MORNINGSTAR HAS DONE THE HARD WORK.

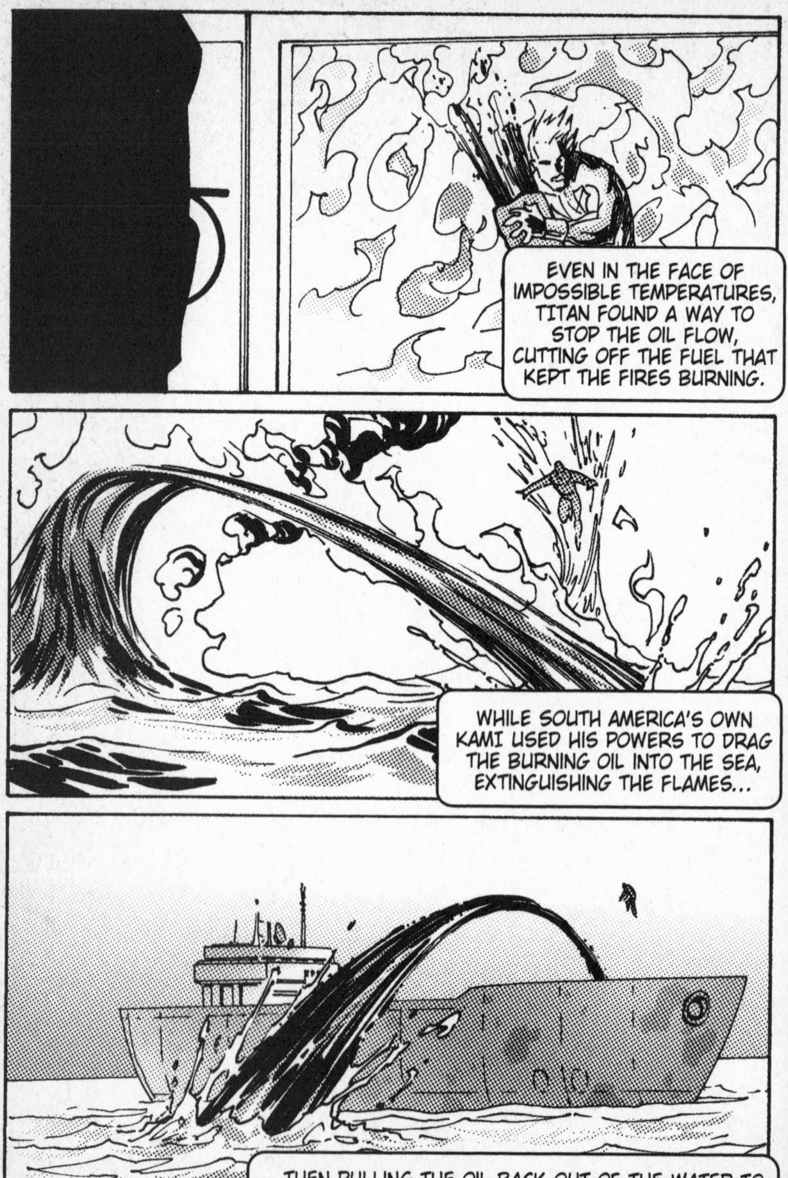
EVEN IN THE FACE OF IMPOSSIBLE TEMPERATURES, TITAN FOUND A WAY TO STOP THE OIL FLOW, CUTTING OFF THE FUEL THAT KEPT THE FIRES BURNING.
WHILE SOUTH AMERICA'S OWN KAMI USED HIS POWERS TO DRAG THE BURNING OIL INTO THE SEA, EXTINGUISHING THE FLAMES...
...THEN PULLING THE OIL BACK OUT OF THE WATER TO KEEP THE ENVIRONMENTAL DAMAGE TO A MINIMUM.

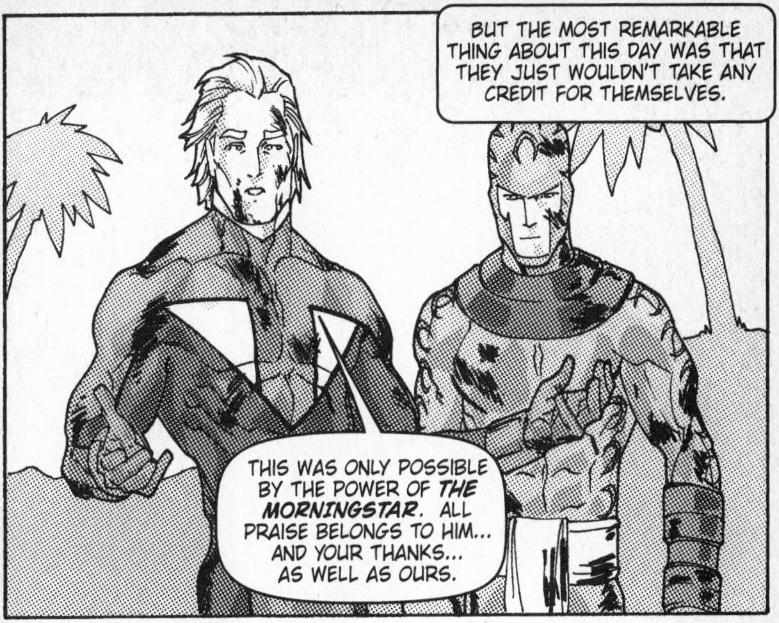
BUT THE MOST REMARKABLE THING ABOUT THIS DAY WAS THAT THEY JUST WOULDN'T TAKE ANY CREDIT FOR THEMSELVES.
THIS WAS ONLY POSSIBLE BY THE POWER OF ***THE MORNINGSTAR***. ALL PRAISE BELONGS TO HIM... AND YOUR THANKS... AS WELL AS OURS.

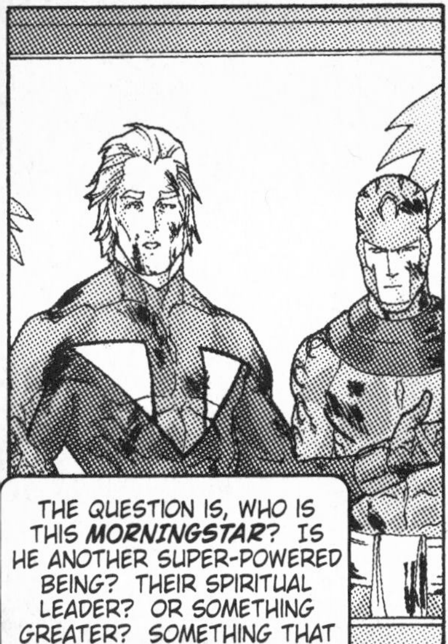
THE QUESTION IS, WHO IS THIS ***MORNINGSTAR***? IS HE ANOTHER SUPER-POWERED BEING? THEIR SPIRITUAL LEADER? OR SOMETHING GREATER? SOMETHING THAT DEFIES LOGIC AND SCIENCE?

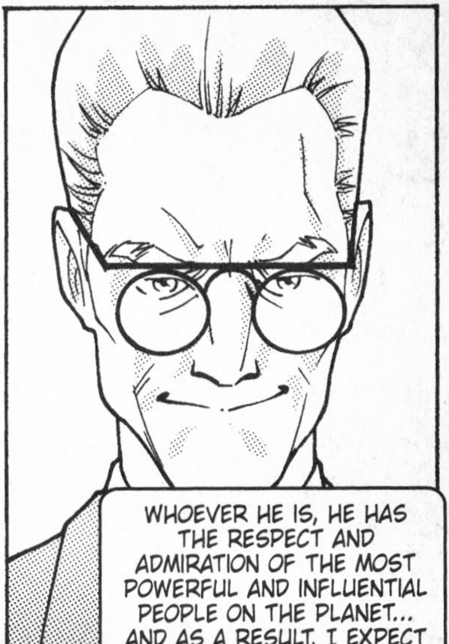
WHOEVER HE IS, HE HAS THE RESPECT AND ADMIRATION OF THE MOST POWERFUL AND INFLUENTIAL PEOPLE ON THE PLANET... AND AS A RESULT, I EXPECT THE REST OF US TOO.

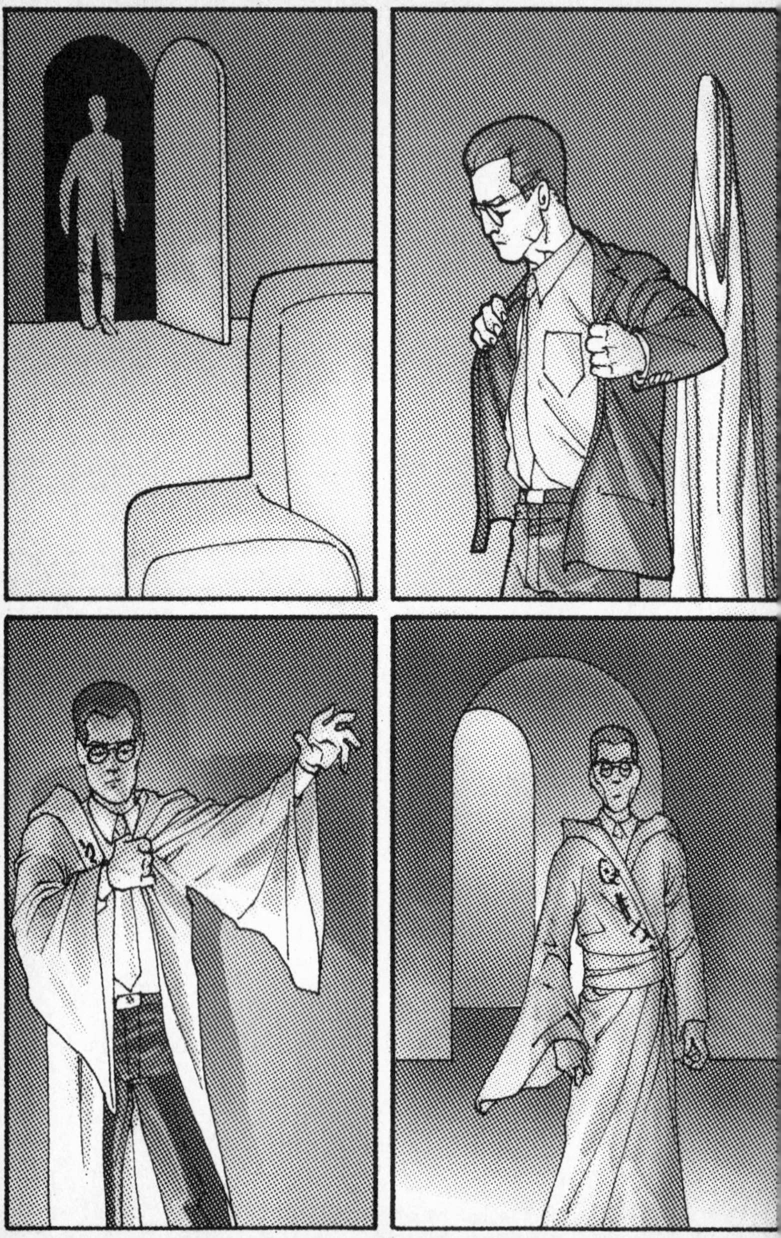

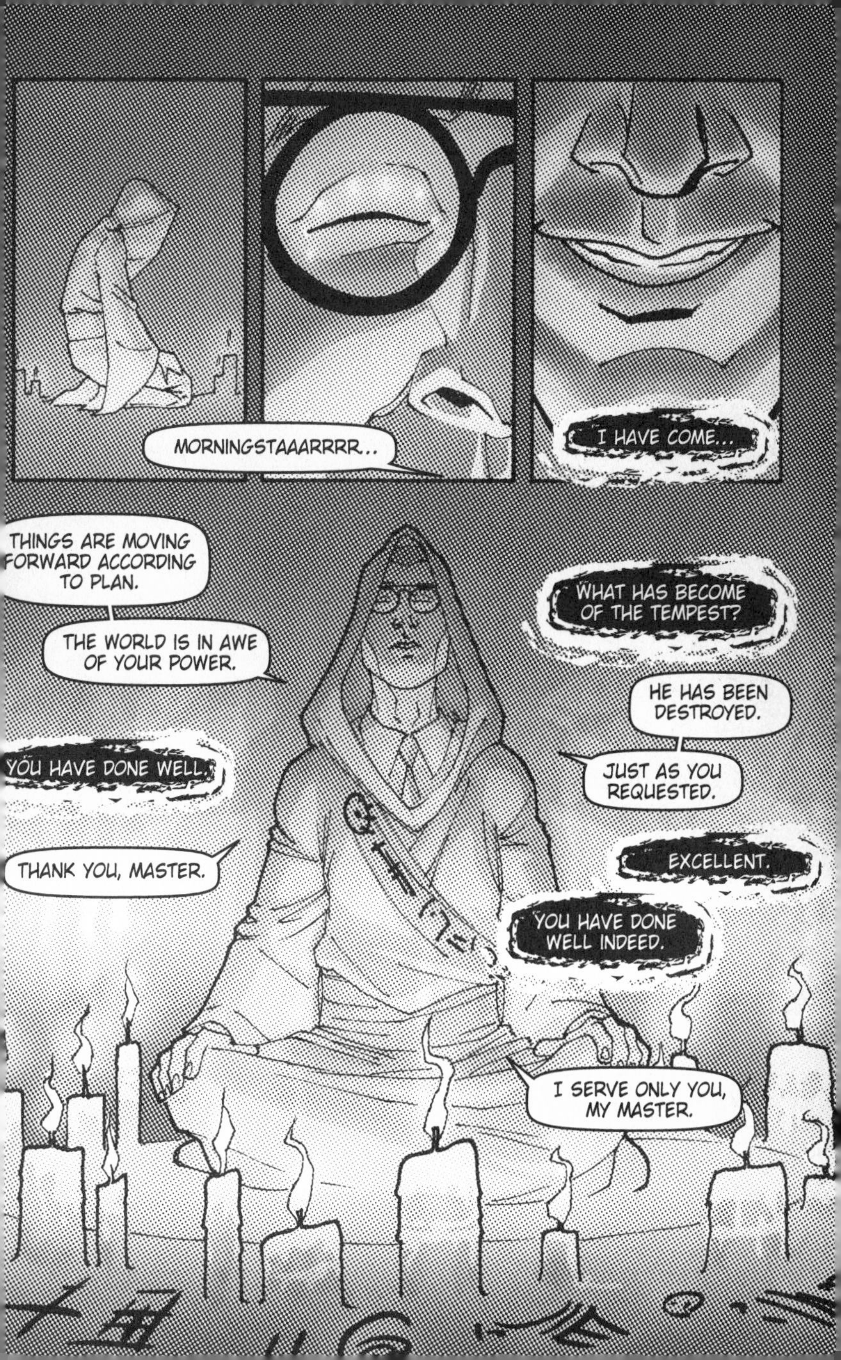
MORNINGSTAAARRRR...
I HAVE COME...
THINGS ARE MOVING FORWARD ACCORDING TO PLAN.
THE WORLD IS IN AWE OF YOUR POWER.
WHAT HAS BECOME OF THE TEMPEST?
HE HAS BEEN DESTROYED.
JUST AS YOU REQUESTED.
YOU HAVE DONE WELL.
THANK YOU, MASTER.
EXCELLENT.
YOU HAVE DONE WELL INDEED.
I SERVE ONLY YOU, MY MASTER.

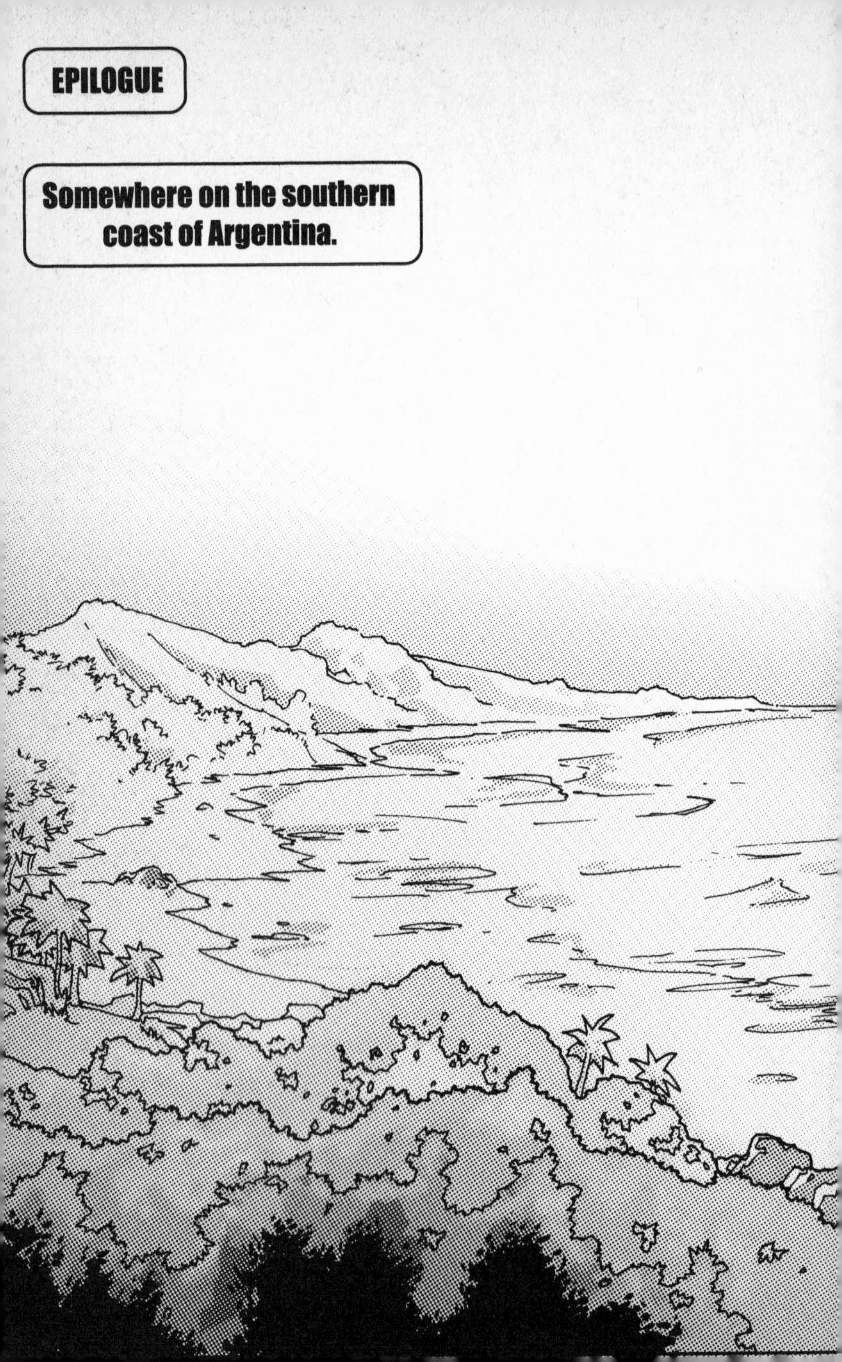
EPILOGUE
Somewhere on the southern coast of Argentina.

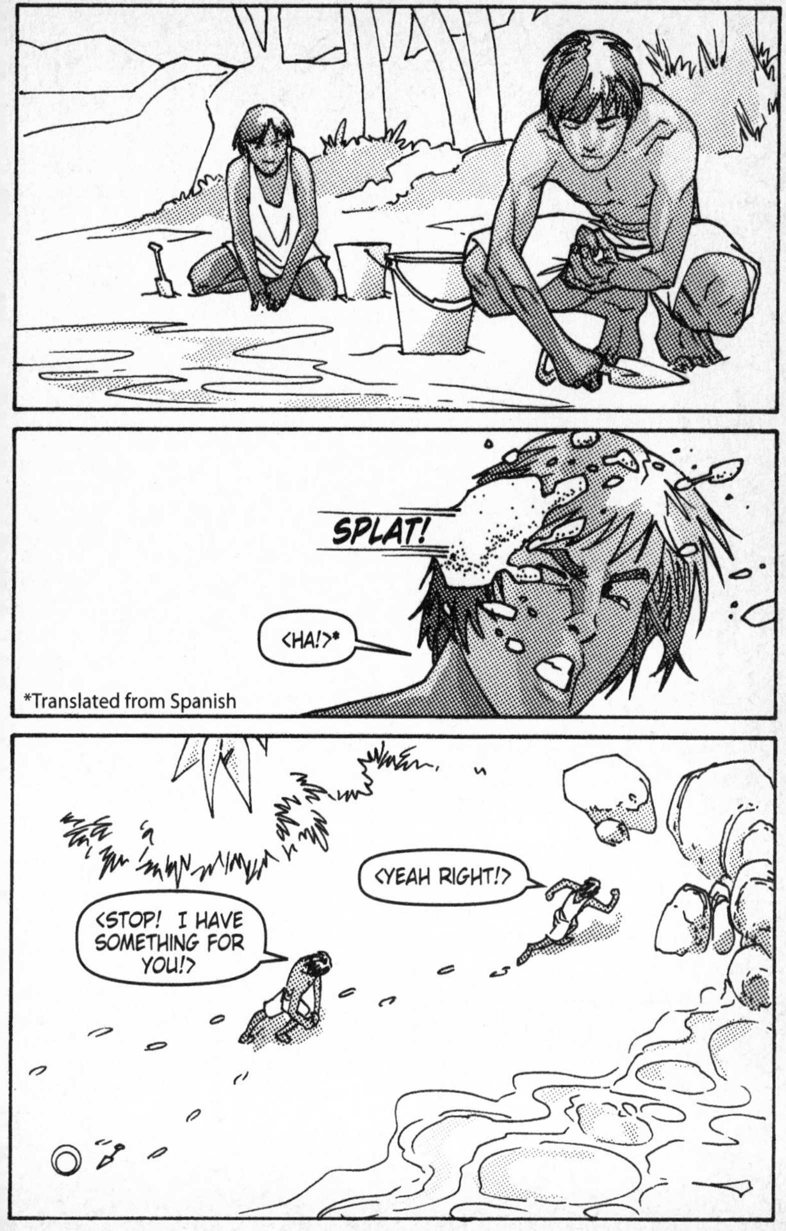
SPLAT!
<HA!>*
<YEAH RIGHT!>
<STOP! I HAVE SOMETHING FOR YOU!>

*Translated from Spanish

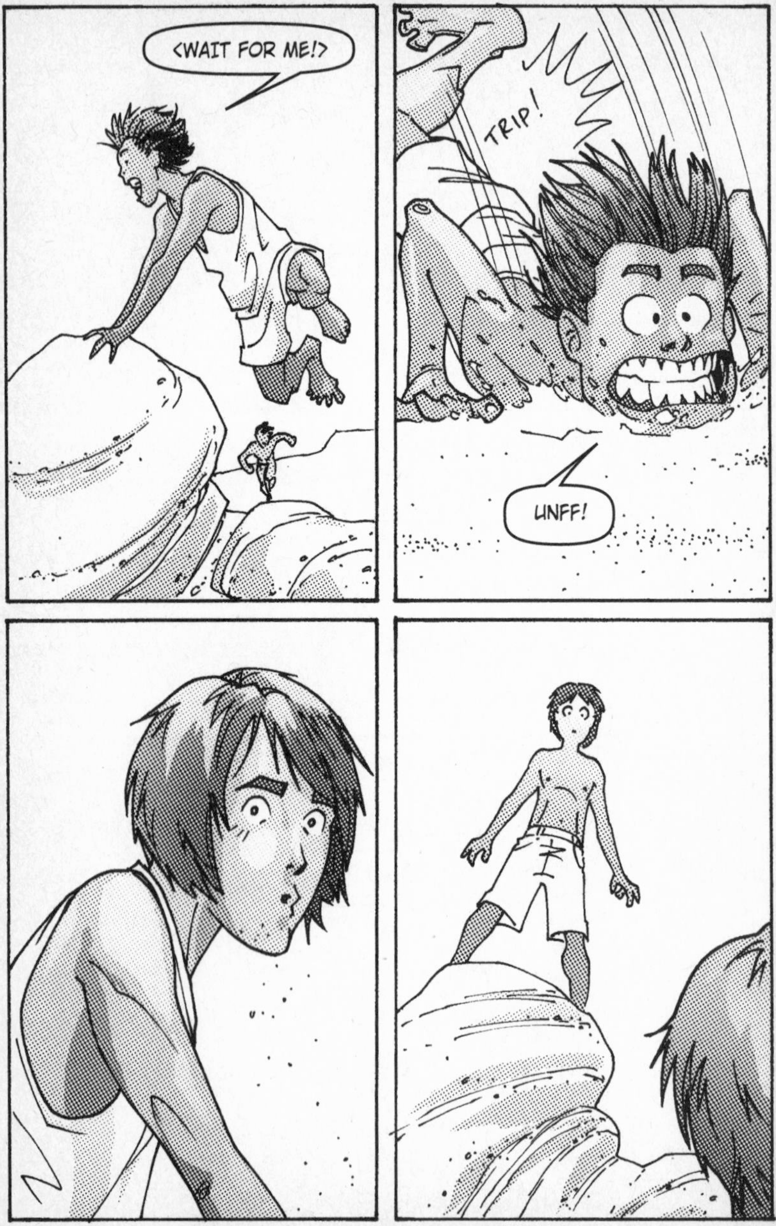
<WAIT FOR ME!>
TRIP!
UNFF!

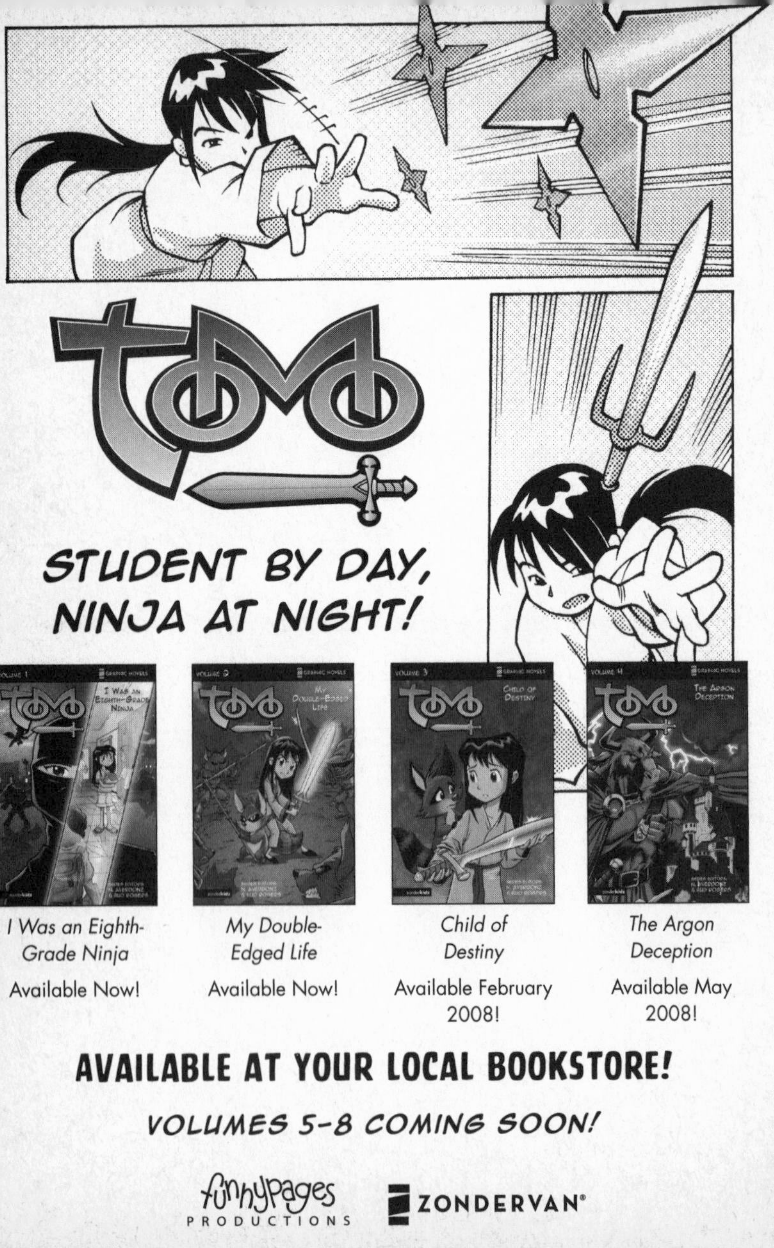
TOMO
STUDENT BY DAY, NINJA AT NIGHT!
I Was an Eighth-Grade Ninja
Available Now!
My Double-Edged Life
Available Now!
Child of Destiny
Available February 2008!
The Argon Deception
Available May 2008!
AVAILABLE AT YOUR LOCAL BOOKSTORE!
VOLUMES 5-8 COMING SOON!
funnypages PRODUCTIONS
ZONDERVAN®

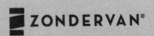